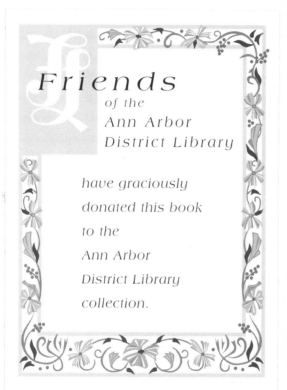

NEVER LOOK BACK

Recent Titles by Ted Allbeury from Severn House

BERLIN EXCHANGE
CODEWORD CROMWELL
THE GIRL FROM ADDIS
THE LANTERN NETWORK
THE LONELY MARGINS
NEVER LOOK BACK

NEVER LOOK BACK

Ted Allbeury

severn
House

This title first published in Great Britain 2000 by
SEVERN HOUSE PUBLISHERS LTD of
9–15 High Street, Sutton, Surrey SM1 1DF.
Originally published 1986 in Great Britain by
New English Library under the title *The Choice*.
This title first published in the USA 2000 by
SEVERN HOUSE PUBLISHERS INC., of
595 Madison Avenue, New York, NY 10022.

British Library Cataloguing in Publication Data

Allbeury, Ted, 1917-
  Never look back
  I. Title
  823.9'14 [F]

  ISBN 0-7278-5579-4

Printed and bound in Great Britain by
MPG Books Ltd, Bodmin, Cornwall.

Preface

I GUESS I HAD written four or five novels with the thought of this book always at the back of my mind. I was doing well; publicity trips all over the world and writing plays for BBC radio.

In both my civilian life and in my time as an Intelligence Corps Officer I was aware that many of us were faced from time to time with a decision that could decide the whole pattern of our lives from then on. We were usually not aware of the importance of the decision. It could concern our service lives or, more likely, our domestic lives.

I wanted to write a book that would show what happened to a man who was forced to make the choice between his wife and child and the girl who loved him so dearly.

It's not a book laying out high moral principles nor the portrait of a promiscuous man. All the people concerned have real and genuine feelings. I show what happens for the rest of his life if he chooses to stay with his family. And, as a separate story, what happens if he goes with the girl.

Two things have always been obvious. The first is how careless and illogical we are in who we fall for and marry. And secondly, when it all collapses, why does nobody just accept that both parties got the wrong part in the wrong film? And is it possible in the welter of spite and hatred to remember for a moment that you are two people who once loved each other dearly and genuinely?

Few people felt that it was a good idea for a reasonably established 'spy writer' to write a novel with no 'spies' and no Walther PPKs. So this book was published with no great fanfare, but it got smashing reviews and sold well, and I still get letters about it.

In its own separate way it's my favourite book and I hope that you enjoy it too.

'Thou'lt find thy manhood all too fast –
Soon come, soon gone, and age at last,
A sorry breaking-up!'

Thomas Hood
Ode: Clapham Academy

PART I

PART 1

Chapter 1

SHE REACHED up, one hand holding the taper and the other pulling the brass chain, its swivel stiff from verdigris. She could hear the hiss of the gas and then the mantle flared, turning from brown to orange to a soft white light that illuminated almost the whole of the large old-fashioned kitchen.

The small effort was too much for her and she sat down slowly on to the bentwood chair at the side of the bare kitchen table. She was twenty and very pretty and he had often said that she looked prettiest in gaslight.

The special box of Kunzle's chocolates for her birthday lay still unopened on the kitchen table as she sat with her chin in her hands, her elbows on the table. The torn buff envelope and the official telegram lay where she had thrown them beside the cup and saucer and the cold tea. She looked across to the old-fashioned wooden cradle that her father had made for them and the sleeping baby, then she looked back at the telegram, her eyes unseeing, her mind in turmoil. It was September 9th, 1918, and the papers all said that the war was nearly over. The Allies had taken Bruges and Zeebrugge. She had wondered how he would settle back into civilian life. She had never been able to visualise him as a civilian.

She remembered the first time she had seen him. A second lieutenant in the Gordon Highlanders. In his best uniform, his kilt and sporran swinging as he walked into the shop just as it was closing. He'd wanted twenty Gold Flake and a box of Swan Vestas and he'd grinned when

3

she made a mistake counting out his change and she'd had to start again. He'd asked her to have a coffee with him at the ABC and she'd refused. She had wondered at the time if he realised that she'd never drunk a coffee in her life. Working people drank tea. Coffee was for the toffs. But he'd come back the next day and the next, always just on closing time. And in the end she'd gone with him. Not to the ABC but to a small working-man's caff just off Dale End itself.

Her parents had taken to him immediately, impressed by his easy talk and the uniform. But when a few weeks later he'd asked her to marry him, they'd said no. They had said that he was too old for her. Nearly twelve years older than she was. There had been the old adage dragged out about Autumn marrying Spring. They were still impressed by him but now they were defensively in awe of him. Cautious and ready to find faults in him that they had not seen before. He had been cool and amused but she had felt humiliated and angry. They had married secretly two months later when he was on a week's leave. And they'd rented a house in Corstorphine when he had been posted to Edinburgh.

He was obviously fond of her but she found life with him strange. He treated her with an odd sort of tolerance. Somewhere between a daughter and a maid. As if she were something other than a wife. He wasn't condescending, but he was openly amused at her naivety and lack of experience of the world. She eventually realised that he had no money beyond his army pay and she frequently had sleepless nights wondering how they would pay the bills. He spent money rashly and generously, without seeming to count the cost. He had many friends and they were frequently at other people's houses for what they called 'dinner', and it was obvious that he enjoyed other people's company. She was aware that his friends' wives thought he had been foolish and impetuous to marry a girl who was so unsophisticated. But the men were obviously impressed by her good looks and were always amiable and

4

flirtatious although she despised them for flirting with another man's wife.

They had had to move house twice because they couldn't pay the rent and she was glad that her parents didn't know what she had come to. Her parents were humble enough but they had never owed a penny in their lives. And twice now they had come down to doing what her father had always disparagingly called 'a moonlight flit', their few possessions piled on to a barrow in the middle of the night. Sleeping on the floor of some friend's house until they could find a new place to rent in another part of the city.

The day she discovered that she was pregnant he had been promoted to full lieutenant, and the next week they had moved to the large Victorian semi-detached house with the garden and laurels and a privet hedge at the front. He had been given leave a few weeks after the baby was born and there had been a party. She had enjoyed being the centre of attention for once and had vaguely understood for the first time why he enjoyed the parties and dinners. She had thought then that maybe when he came back from the war she would get more used to him.

But now he wasn't coming back from the war, and her mind was a turmoil of doubt and fears. She had shed no tears at the telegram from the War Office signed by the Under Secretary of State for War. Not even tears of self-pity. It *had* been a mistake. They had had nothing in common except that they were both attractive to each other and it had all seemed so romantic. Her father had been right. She hadn't loved him. Not properly. And he hadn't loved her properly either. There had been a kind of hero-worship at first but for most of their time together he had been no more than a pleasant stranger with strange ways whom she was tied to until death did them part. And now his death had released her from all that.

She made the ten o'clock bottle for the baby and after feeding him she settled back at the kitchen table. For hours she went over what she should do. And she knew in the end that it was pointless; in reality she had no choice. She

5

had to throw herself on the mercy of her parents. Go back defeated to the grinding boredom of that old life. Its monotony, and, what was worse, the minute-by-minute control of everything she did, which was the price you had to pay for total dependence on other people.

She wouldn't have to plead. They weren't that sort of people. Widowed daughters had to be given shelter. But of course they ceased to be wives and became daughters again. Obedient daughters. And as she sat that night in the empty house she knew that she had learned a lesson. Men were irresponsible and feckless creatures, to be avoided in future at all costs. Profligate with money and fine words, and stupid enough to get themselves killed when the war was about to end; leaving a twenty-year-old girl with their child but no money, no home and no resources. Her thoughts about him were a mixture of despair and anger.

Before he came along she had had no responsibilities. She worked in her father's shop; she had a small room of her own at the back of the house where they had lived for years. She didn't have a wage but she had pocket-money and her clothes. And suddenly he had made it all seem boring and restricted. He never said it in so many words, just smiled at her ineptness and made her realise that there was another world outside that could be hers. What had seemed merely uneventful had come to seem drudgery. What had seemed like a freedom from the pressures of other girls' lives had been made to seem like a life of petty restrictions. A life of monotonous pettiness. She had defied her parents and robbed them of all those small pleasures that come from a wedding and a daughter's marriage. She had written to them when the baby was born, and the wooden cradle had arrived two weeks later, but those were her only contacts. As she knew her mother would have said, if she had bemoaned her lot: she had made her bed and she must lie on it.

And now what had she got? The humiliation of returning to that old life. A baby who would be a millstone round her neck. And in the worn leather purse in her handbag there was seventeen shillings. All the money she had in the world. A few clothes. A vase. A silver-backed hairbrush and a picture in a silver frame. It was true what they said about men. All those music-hall jokes and songs about not trusting them were really true. She clenched her small fists in resolve. She hated men and she would never let herself be at their mercy again.

The baby in the cradle was crying fretfully and she half-turned her head to look at it. That was one male who wouldn't get away with it. And although she didn't realise it, or perhaps intend it, that angry resentment was destined to affect the whole of that baby's life – until the day he died. Then, with her head cradled in her arms on the table, she cried. For herself, for the man who was dead, for the child, and for the whole ramshackle life that had come to an end.

Chapter 2

THE TWO women looked at each other, the calm one and the angry one.

Miss Marsh had been a primary school teacher for twenty years and she thought that she knew most of the vagaries of working-class mothers. But this one was different. There was none of the usual rough partisanship for her child, no feeling of warmth or protection. She seemed indifferent to the feelings of the small boy, as if she were his keeper rather than his mother. Miss Marsh wondered for a moment if perhaps the boy was not the woman's child. She looked down at the stained desk and then back at the thin woman standing a few feet away.

'I don't think there's anything to worry about, Mrs Collins. Six-year-olds do have their fantasies.'

'I don't know anything about fantasies, Miss Marsh, but I've never heard of a boy going round pretending he's a horse.'

'We all pretend to be something or other. And he's very good at drawing horses.'

'But all this tossing his head up and down.'

Miss Marsh smiled patiently. 'I expect he sees horses do that when they've got their nosebags on. It shakes up the oats, you know.'

'He'd take notice of you if you told him to stop doing it. He never listens to me.'

'I'll see what I can do.' And she walked with the woman to the classroom door.

She walked slowly back to where the object of their

discussion was seated at his desk and sat down on the desk in front of his.

She smiled. 'Why do you like horses so much, David?'

He shrugged. 'I don't know.'

'No reason at all?' she said softly.

'No. I just like them.'

She stood up, walked back to her desk and, opening the lid, picked out a postcard and looked at it. She closed the lid, walking back to the boy, handing him the postcard.

'That's for you. I wish it were a picture of a horse but I'll get you one of a horse another day.'

It was a sepia photograph of a large tree and along the bottom it said, 'The Boscobel Oak which gave shelter to King Charles'.

'Now you'd better run along, David.'

The small boy looked at the card then tucked it carefully into his pocket. As he was walking slowly to the door he stopped, and looked back. 'Thanks for the card, Miss Marsh.'

'That's all right, Davie.'

He liked it when people called him Davie instead of David.

He was spreading the strawberry jam generously on the large slice of bread and butter and his mother was talking from the scullery.

'If your father was alive you wouldn't behave like this.'

She came to the doorway wiping her hands on her pinafore, her face flushed with suppressed anger. He knew that she was always angry when she mentioned his father. He had sometimes asked her about him: what he was like and what had happened to him, but he had gradually learned that it only brought on her anger. His father was dead. Killed in the war. That was all she had to say.

'He's up there in heaven watching you. What do you think he would say?'

'I don't know, mother.'

'You can't go on like this.'

'Like what?'

'You know what I mean all right, so don't be cheeky.'

'They're too long, they hang down below my knees.'

'They keep you warm, my lad.'

'They're men's trousers. They're too big.'

'They were your grandfather's and they've been cut down to size specially for you. Mrs Carter did it herself.'

'I hate them. They hang down over my knees. Other boys laugh at me.'

'You should be glad you've got them, my lad.'

'Mr Pettigrew said that . . .'

'I don't want to hear what Mr Pettigrew said, he's a schoolmaster and earns good money.'

David drank his milk and went quietly up to his room. Sprawled on his bed he read an old copy of *Rainbow*.

At nine o'clock she brought him a glass of warm milk and a biscuit. As he sipped the milk she stood looking at him.

'You'll be going to your aunt's for the first two weeks of your holiday.'

'I don't like it there.'

'Why not?'

'They're horrible.'

'Don't say such things. They're good people. You should be grateful that they'll have you.'

When eventually he lay in bed, in the darkness, he wondered what his father had been like, and if he really was watching him. His father had died when he was four months old. He had no memory of him at all. But at eight all things can seem possible.

He carried the cardboard attaché case packed with its two shirts, two vests, two pairs of pants and a spare pair of socks, in one hand, and his raincoat in the other, his flat cap folded and stuffed into his jacket pocket.

It was about a mile from Windsor station, down seemingly endless roads of dreary houses. They were a cut above the houses in his street in Birmingham, with bay windows up and down and a small front garden. And they weren't terraced houses, they were built in pairs with a passage between them.

Aunt and Uncle Rodgers' house was modestly different from its neighbours: its plain brick had been covered with a thin layer of stucco painted cream. Uncle Leonard worked for a Friendly Society and was considered well-off by his neighbours. He earned £5 a week and was allowed an extra five shillings for the use of his own Raleigh bicycle. When collecting the weekly subscriptions he wore a bowler hat and leather leggings rather than the usual trouser clips. He was a sidesman at the local Baptist church and sang in the choir.

Aunt Ada showed David up to his room. They would be having tea when Uncle Len came home. And not before. Meantime he could go to the park and see the ducks on the pond.

Tea was a grim, silent meal and he was glad when they sent him to bed at nine o'clock. His room reeked of mothballs and lino polish. The only decoration was an aspidistra in a big china bowl and a large etching on the wall of a chair gazed at by a disconsolate-looking Irish wolfhound, entitled *The Master's Empty Chair*.

The next day he was given a list of addresses and was sent to collect those members' money. Some abused him, some refused to pay anyone but the proper agent, his uncle, but he came back with just over £15 from six hours' work. As a special reward the wireless had been switched on for him to listen to *Children's Hour*.

For three weeks he collected subscriptions or wandered alone in the park. He was strictly forbidden to talk to other children. It was the Monday of the last week when the trouble came.

He had been given a shilling by his mother for his two

11

weeks' stay and he had bought himself a boy's paper. The *Rover*.

As always he had gone into the kitchen after tea and started cleaning his uncle's brown boots, scraping the mud from the solid welts before he brushed on the polish. He jumped as the door from the hall passage was suddenly flung open.

His uncle stood there, his face pale with anger, the magazine in his hand.

'Where did you get this?'

'From the paper shop.'

'You paid for it?'

'Yes.'

'How much?'

'Tuppence.'

'Where did you get the money?'

'From my pocket-money.'

'What pocket-money?'

'My mother gave me a shilling.'

'Where's the money you collected today?'

'Where you told me to put it. In the front room on top of the piano.'

'My God, if you've taken any of that money I'll beat you within an inch of your life,' Uncle Len shouted, as he turned to hurry down the hall to the front room.

He came back a few minutes later looking no less angry for having found his takings in order.

'Show me the change from your shilling.'

The boy assembled the money from his trouser pockets. A sixpence and four pennies. When the man looked back at the boy's face and saw the hatred in his eyes it was too much. He lashed out with his open hand and sent the boy reeling so that he lost his balance and fell backwards against the kitchen sink. He was put on the train for Paddington early the next morning with a note for his mother. She read it but made no comment. She never mentioned the incident again.

*   *   *

Tom Makins collected the Latin papers and took them to Mr Lakey's desk. Mr Lakey picked them up.

'Right.' He looked over his glasses at the class. 'Get out your Gallic Wars and start reading at . . . let me see . . . yes – *Caesar jam adolescens* . . . read on from there. Quietly.'

Ten minutes later old Lakey looked up from his desk.

'Collins.'

'Sir.'

'Come here.'

Lakey pushed his glasses up on to his forehead and looked at the boy. He pointed at a paper on his desk.

'You don't try, do you, Collins?'

'Yes, sir.'

'What do you mean? Yes, you don't try, or yes, you do try?'

'I do try, sir.'

'What are the principal parts of *dare*?'

'*Do, dare* . . . er . . . *duxus sum.*'

'Decline *hic*.'

'*Hic, haec, hoc, horam, harum, horam* . . . I don't know any more, sir.'

'Isn't there anyone at home who can help you a bit?'

'No, sir.'

Lakey sighed. 'You'd better do a punishment. Write out the radio programmes from today's paper.'

'We don't have a paper, sir.'

'All right. A column from the *Radio Times*.'

'We don't have that, sir.'

Lakey sighed. 'How do you know what's on the radio?'

The boy stood silent, looking at the floor. Then he said, 'We don't have a radio.'

Lakey's tobacco-stained finger stroked the side of his face, and he placed the paper slowly back on the pile.

'All right, Collins. Try a bit harder in future.'

At the end of the lesson David Collins stuffed his text books in his satchel, and walked to the cloakroom. As he struggled into his raincoat he saw the handwritten list of the rugby teams for that Saturday afternoon. He was one of the six forwards in the third team playing away against Moseley High School.

As he stood at the tram-stop he wondered what excuse he could make. He had no idea how to get to Moseley and he had no money for extra tram fares even if he did know how to get there.

His lack of knowledge, his almost total ignorance of everything, and the lack of anyone who could help him, neither disturbed nor worried him. That was how it was, and outside his home he lived like a cautious wild animal. Alert to avoid trouble, scared when hunted, relieved when he escaped his just deserts. He knew that he could expect no help from his home. There was enough to eat. And there were boys in his form who didn't have enough to eat. But they were surrounded by people who knew how to get to Moseley. Who understood what went on in the outside world. Who knew the rules of Rugby Football and could explain what a 'knock-on' really was.

His mother stood watching as he ate his meal. Liver and bacon was one of his favourites.

'Mr Lakey asked if there was anyone who could help me with my Latin.'

'*He's* the one who's supposed to help you with that, isn't he?'

'He's the Latin master.'

'Well if he can't teach you who can?'

'I don't know.'

'You want to ask him, then. And while you're about it ask him what good Latin's ever going to do you. You just ask him that.'

He looked up at her flushed angry face. 'I'm playing football at Moseley on Saturday. D'you know how I get there?'

She leaned forward to gather up his plate. 'Why have you left the gravy?'

'I was full up.'

14

She was cutting a slice of pie, and he knew she wasn't going to answer his question. He'd have to put a stone in his shoe again, and say that he'd got a sore foot. They never questioned his stories. It was as if they knew, and no longer applied the normal rules to his behaviour. Bottom of the form in every subject and that seemingly impenetrable home background that was indifferent to the world outside.

Joseph Palmer MA (Cantab.) had been headmaster of the grammar school for twenty-five years. He was inured to the fact that in any school year not more than a dozen boys out of the school's 200 would gain any real benefit from the time they spent there. That had been his own assessment from the end of his second year of headmastership, and he had never had cause to change his mind. It was one of the facts of life in an industrial city like Birmingham where the school served a working-class area. There was an intake of thirty boys each year, and after a couple of terms he would know which two mattered. He was a social realist and not given to introspection. There were no complaints from the governors. He was producing the clerks and artisans their factories needed. Not that either he or they had ever considered it in that light, but if they had they would have seen no reason to change it. They were neither poets nor reformers.

So far as the parents were concerned they had no criteria to judge the headmaster by. They were merely thankful that their sons were grammar-school boys. It would stand them in good stead for the rest of their lives. They would be able to wear Old Edwardian ties, and that could make a difference when you were being interviewed for a job. As the headmaster boasted in his Founder's Day speech, there were four of his last year's boys with jobs in the Central Library, already earning as much as seventeen shillings a week and with a pension at the end of it.

Palmer always wore his full regalia when interviewing parents: his run-of-the-mill chalky black gown was enough

15

to impress the boys, but when there were harsh things to say, a little protective colouring did no harm. The electric-blue silk lining that indicated his MA undoubtedly gave him an air of superiority.

He sat now at his desk, his hands smoothing the mahogany moulding. The boy sat at the far end and the mother directly in front of him, her bulky handbag on her lap. He glanced again at the report and then moved it aside. He leaned forward, his hands clasped in front of him on the desk.

'We do sometimes make exceptions, Mrs Collins, but in this case I can see no grounds for that. There are long waiting lists for scholarships at the school. And public money is at stake. That was why I asked you to come and see me. To speak quite frankly . . . and I know you would wish me to do that . . . I think we should all be wasting valuable time.' He looked down for a moment to his blotter and then looked up again. 'Your son, Mrs Collins, is on the dust-heap of the school, and unless some miracle happens . . . ah . . . he will be on the dust-heap of life.'

'Does that mean you want me to take him away?'

He sighed. 'There's only another four weeks of term left. In the meantime you could use the time to look around for some kind of employment.'

He stood up slowly to mark the end of the interview. It was November 1931.

Chapter 3

Sam Thatcher was a big man. Just under six feet, he weighed over fifteen stone and his belly was a tribute to the staple food of the local iron-foundry moulders – Ansell's Beer. He nodded to the man holding the other handle of the ladle and they tilted it forward so that David Collins could move the slag rake across the molten iron. And when the slag and scum had splashed into the black sand the two men turned the handle so that the orange-coloured metal poured into the mould. They poured steadily as the dank-smelling steam rose from the black sand in the moulding box, and when the liquid metal flowed up to the top of the riser they moved on to the next moulding box.

David Collins had started in Number 1 Foundry just before Christmas, and as a moulder's labourer he earned ten shillings a week. The deputy foreman of the day shift lived at number 33 Alma Street, three doors away, and despite the depression and the massive unemployment the job had been arranged after an interview with the works manager.

David Collins was fourteen, and for the first time in his life he was vaguely happy. The rough, working men were ready to teach the boy how to do his job; amused by his politeness, they pulled his leg, but the jokes were friendly and fatherly. He suffered the normal practical jokes of being sent to the stores for glass hammers and sky-hooks but he took it all in good part. He belonged.

Like the others he brought sandwiches for his lunch. A sugar sandwich, or a sandwich of mashed banana, wrapped in a damp cloth. He sat with Sam Thatcher and five or six other moulders and their labourers on a pile of used cores. He sat silently as they talked of racing form, the local football teams, and women.

Home and his mother were no longer his dominating influence. He handed over his wage packet unopened each Friday evening and received a shilling for himself. Three nights a week he had to attend evening classes in town, walking the four miles each way to save the ha'penny fare on the tram. The evening classes covered mechanical drawing, mathematics and the theory of electricity. Just as it had been at school, he absorbed nothing of any of these subjects. But nobody minded, because nobody noticed or cared.

The following Easter he was sent for an interview with the chief draughtsman, a lean Scot with a leathery face and a pair of shrewd grey eyes. He was asked a few routine questions and the grey eyes watched him intently as he gave his stumbling answers. It took about ten minutes. There was no indication of what the interview was about.

On the Friday afternoon before the foundry closed for its annual August-week holiday he was called to the foundry foreman's office. It was a small wooden hut at the far end of the ladle gantry. There were rows of old box-files on two shelves, handwritten parts-orders on scraps of paper held in bulldog clips, and a picture of Shirley Temple torn from a magazine, tacked to the wall over the makeshift writing shelf.

Hector Monroe had been a foundryman all his life and his brick-red face came from cupolas being tapped rather than from beer. He was holding a buff pay packet in his hand and David Collins could see his own name and works number half hidden by a thumb. For the first time in months he felt a surge of fear. Workers lined up at the pay office for their wages on Friday nights as their shift ended, and in the 1930s as you were handed the brown envelope you automatically checked by reflex if it would bend. If it bent you were safe. If it was too stiff to bend it was because

18

your employment cards were inside and you'd got the sack.

'Well, young David. How have you been getting on?'

'All right, I think, Mr Monroe.'

'Well it looks like Sam Thatcher's had enough of you.'

He saw the boy's face go pale and he laughed. 'Don't worry, lad, I'm only pulling your leg. I've got some good news for you. They want you up in the drawing office when you come back from the holiday week.'

'I'd rather stay with Sam Thatcher, sir.'

'Oh. Why's that?'

'I like it in the foundry. I like Mr Thatcher.'

Monroe was silent for a moment then he reached for a packet of Woodbines. When he had lit one he shook out the match slowly and put it in a tin lid. Turning back to the boy he said, 'You went to the grammar, lad. You've had an education. You've got to make use of it. It's part of growing up and getting on.'

'I don't want to get on. I want to stay here.'

'That's no way to talk, lad. We've all got to try and get on. It's what life's all about.'

'What do I have to do in the drawing office?'

'You'll be working the blue-print machine. They'll show you how to do it. Anyway here's your pay. You'll get the same money in the new job.'

By the time David was seventeen he was a tracer earning twelve shillings a week. The drawing office and the clerical staff worked on Saturday mornings when the two foundries, the pattern shop and the machine-shop were empty. And once in a while he would walk down to the empty foundry as it echoed with the noise of the maintenance team. He still missed Sam Thatcher and the rest of them.

The evening classes were his alibi at home and he now had two shillings a week of his own, so at least one night of the week he spent a shilling at the Hippodrome variety shows, watching the big bands that came over from America to top the bill. And then there were all the home-grown

19

products: Roy Fox, Harry Roy, Jack Hylton, Lew Stone, Bert Ambrose and the others. Sitting high up in the dark gallery that reeked of carbolic and Lysol, this was the bright spot of his week.

Some need for company led him to go sometimes on Sunday evenings to the local church, and the vicar suggested that he should join the tennis club. His Daks trousers, a white shirt, tennis shoes and a Dunlop Maxply had cost him four pounds from his Post Office savings account. There were seven pounds four shillings left.

The young people at the tennis club were like him. More sure of themselves, but from much the same backgrounds. And when the light went on summer evenings they sat in the small shed alongside the tennis court and talked. A few bold ones smoked, and there was a kiss or two in the dark but nothing more. They talked of their parents and their jobs, and films they had seen or the dances at the Palais and the Masonic Hall. The others went to one another's houses without ceremony and were as welcome as the young people of the family. But there was no question of them going to David Collins' house. He had asked once if he could bring a boy home and his mother had ignored the question, which was her usual way of refusing.

There was a girl he rather liked but she was monopolised by Charlie Bailey who was already twenty-one and considered rather sophisticated. He wore a silk cravat after he had played tennis, carefully tucked into the V of his shirt. His mother and father ran a second-hand clothes shop near the tram terminus, and that made Charlie something of a catch. In fact a wallet had once been found by Georgie Miles on the gravel path that led to the hut. And in the course of checking to see who it belonged to, the contents had put Charlie Bailey into an even higher league. There had been three pound notes, four weeks' average wages; and those notes had been more talked about than even the creased postcard of a naked girl. In the inner pocket there had been a letter addressed to Charlie that had a London postmark: it was on pale mauve deckle-edged paper with brown ink and a strong smell of lavender. The letter had not been read but the conglomerate memories had lingered on, embroidered and envied in their imaginations.

The girl who David Collins rather liked was Joan Latham. She lived on the council estate off Slade Road. She was plump and pretty and he sometimes thought of her when he lay in bed at night. Eventually there was a Friday night when he knelt beside his bed on the cold linoleum when, after saying the Lord's prayer, slowly and carefully he put in three requests to God on his own account. The first request was that the rumour that Charlie Bailey was going to London for the weekend should prove to be true. The second was that there would be no rain on Saturday, and the third was that Joan Latham would be at the tennis club. He was going to ask her if he could walk her home.

By ten o'clock on the Saturday morning his prayers had been answered. Charlie Bailey was in bed with a sprained ankle, and Joan Latham was already at the club when he arrived. But only a strong wind kept the rain from falling.

The only other ones there were the girl and Mary Hawkins, Georgie Miles and Arthur West. They were playing a doubles and when they finished the set he played a singles with Joan Latham. When eventually the rain did come down they hurried to the small wooden shed. The others had gone, leaving them a note to remind them to lock the gate and put the key under the stone.

They sat together on the narrow seat and he watched her combing her hair. She had given him half her small bar of chocolate. As she tugged with the comb at the snags in her wet hair she said, 'Why don't you ever invite any of us to your house, Davie?'

'My mother isn't keen on visitors.'

'Why not?'

He shrugged. 'I don't know. It's just her way.'

'It can't be much fun for you.'

'I don't mind.'

21

As she reached up both her arms to arrange her hair he saw the shape of her breasts in her cotton blouse. For a fleeting moment he wondered what it would feel like to touch a girl's breasts.

'Why are you shaking your head?'

'Was I?'

'We shan't be able to play again even when it stops raining. The court will be wet and we'd ruin our racket strings.'

'It's stopped raining. It might dry out.'

'What d'you think of Charlie Bailey?'

'He's all right.'

'He wants me to marry him.'

He felt cold with a churning inside his stomach as he heard his own voice saying, 'That's nice.'

She stood up, brushing down her skirt, then she looked at him, smiling. 'You goin' to walk me home?'

He held his breath as they passed the end of his road, afraid that his mother or a neighbour might see him walking with a girl, and his heart was still beating fast when they got to her house. There was a narrow back alley and he walked with her between the battered wooden fences.

She held open the scullery door for him to follow her inside. It was neat and tidy like most houses in the district. He followed her through the kitchen to the small front parlour. There was an upright piano with brass candlesticks and the piece of music on the stand was 'Lover come back to me'. Along the side wall was a two-seater settee and the girl sat down and slipped off her shoes.

'Have you got a girl, Davie?'

'No.'

'Why not?'

He shrugged. 'I can't afford one, and the girls I know are fixed up.'

'They're not really. I'm not fixed up.'

'You're Charlie's girl.'

The bright blue eyes looked at his face.

'D'you want to kiss me?'

'Your parents might come in.'

She laughed. 'They're away for the day at Auntie Nellie's.'

She put up her mouth and he kissed her gently, and her tongue slid into his mouth to touch his. And then he felt her take his hand and put it over one of her breasts. It was warm and soft in his hand like when he held Bert Bagley's racing pigeons for ringing. Then he pulled away and looked at her face.

'It's not fair on Charlie,' he said.

'Jesus. You're chicken, Davie Collins.'

'I'm not.'

'D'you want to see me with me blouse off?'

'Yes,' he said, guilt smothered by lust, curiosity and bravado.

Slowly she unbuttoned her blouse and then reached round to unhook her bra. Then she was sitting there half-naked. Her breasts looked even bigger naked, their pink tips crinkled and hard. Half an hour later he was washing his flushed face in cold water in the enamel basin in the Lathams' scullery.

The girl stood watching as he dried his face and combed his hair. She was smiling when he turned round.

'What are you laughing at, Joanie?'

'I'm not laughing. I'm smiling. You're a nice boy, Davie, and I'll let you into a secret if you ask me nicely.'

'What secret's that?'

'D'you like Mary Hawkins?'

'I don't really know her.'

'There was a crowd of us talking about boys the other night. Who we fancy and all that. Who we'd like to marry. And Mary Hawkins said you're the only one worth marrying.'

'Why does she say that?'

'She says you're straight.' She laughed. 'Anyway, we all think you're good looking.'

'Me?'

'Yes, little boy, you.'

23

David Collins walked from Joan Latham's house to Brookvale Park and sat alone on one of the wooden benches that looked over the bowling green. There was probably another hour of light before the bell rang and the park was locked for the night. The old men had stopped playing, standing in groups talking, or walking slowly around the green checking its surface for signs of clover and daisies.

He was still wearing his grey flannels, and his tennis racket in its press was on the bench beside him. He wondered if Mary Hawkins really had said that he was the only one worth marrying. Not that until that moment there was any thought in his mind of ever being married. But it meant that a girl had noticed him and liked him. It had never entered his mind that someone could actually like him. He took it for granted that the boys and girls at the tennis club merely tolerated him. He was grateful for their tolerance. It was obvious that he didn't have the freedom that they had. There were strict rules laid down for him, and he obeyed them without thinking about them. Even on Saturday nights he had to be home by 9.30 and that meant that he could never join the others when they went in a group to the cinema at Erdington or Stockland Green. The others were openly amused but not unkind about the restrictions he lived under, and they no longer embarrassed him by asking him to join their expeditions to other tennis clubs or on their trips into the city.

At seventeen he still lived the life of a child with petty rules that brooked no argument. He was no longer caned in those mad flashes of anger that sometimes came over his mother at some infraction of the rules, but the rules were still there. His two shillings spending money could still be withheld. He could be forbidden to leave the house, and on occasions a note was sent to whoever was his immediate boss at the foundry, lodging some complaint about his behaviour and asking that he should be 'spoken to'. The requests were generally ignored but they always made him a laughing-stock for a day or two. None of the rules were particularly onerous, they merely left him, without realising it, totally without dignity and self-respect. He was not allowed to get up in the morning without being told to, and if he forgot he was sent back upstairs to undress and get back in his bed until he was told to get up. There were two or three boys who were mildly friendly towards him, but if they called at the house for him they were turned away coldly. So far as he could remember, Joan Latham was the first person who had ever kissed him. His mother was not given to kissing, or any other sign of affection.

Chapter 4

HE PULLED down the heavy lever on the switch-box and the bright arc-lights on the print machine died. In the main drawing office the draughtsmen were putting away their instruments and covering their boards and T-squares for the night. Two or three of them nodded to him as they headed past him for the door. Miss Carver, the lady tracer, was talking to Mr Bertram as she adjusted the lamp holder over her desk. It looked as if she might be doing overtime.

The teapot, the milk jug, the sugar bowl and the two pieces of toast were already laid out on Mr Harvey's tray. Mr Harvey, the works manager, was staying on in his office until 7.30 and that entitled him to the tea and toast at the company's expense. David thought it must feel marvellous to be so important that they gave you tea and toast just to tempt you to stay another hour and a half. That one solitary light in the empty office block, and the works closed down and silent. He wondered what Mr Harvey, with his bow-tie, did in that solitary office.

When he went into the works manager's office, Mr Harvey pursed his lips as he looked at the boy's face and pointed to the place on his desk where he wanted the tray.

As he walked back into the drawing office Miss Carver was bent over her desk. David Collins was madly in love with Miss Carver. She was always neatly dressed and she was very pretty, and from time to time she let him clean her tracing pen and compasses. And because their works numbers both started with a 9 they stood together in the wages queue on Friday nights and that gave him an excuse for walking with her up the hill to Aston Road where she caught the tram to Handsworth. It was fifteen minutes out of his way but well worth the extra journey.

He plucked up his courage and went down to the canteen and asked for an extra cup of tea for Mr Harvey. He took it back up the wooden stairs to the drawing office and put it beside Miss Carver's drawing board.

She looked up. 'Hello, Dave, you still here?' Then she noticed the tea. 'Oh, you are a love. You really are. What do I owe you?'

He shrugged and smiled. 'I told them it was for Mr Harvey.'

She laughed. 'You wicked boy. Whatever shall we do with you?'

'Miss Carver?'

'Yes?'

'Could I take you to the pictures some time?'

She looked at him, still smiling. 'How old are you, Davie?'

'Seventeen and two months.'

'You know I've got a steady boyfriend?'

'I didn't know. But it doesn't matter. He needn't know.'

'I'll think about it.'

'When will you decide? How long?'

She looked at his anxious face and said softly, 'Well, Johnny's playing snooker next Wednesday and there's Jack Buchanan on at the Cross in *Goodnight Vienna* – we could see that together. But it would be only the once. You understand?'

His face lit up. 'Oh yes. That would be marvellous. We could go straight from the office.'

'OK. We'll arrange it on Tuesday.'

'Thanks, Miss Carver, thanks a lot.'

He had bought her a small bottle of California Poppy perfume from Boots. Ninepence. And the seats had been a

27

shilling each. The best in the house. And she had obviously enjoyed the film.

It was raining when they came out of the cinema and they walked to the tram stop in Victoria Road, standing in the shop doorway to shelter from the rain.

She was wearing a green hat with a red feather swirled round it and a coat with a curly collar that swept up each side of her face, and she looked more beautiful than any filmstar.

As he leaned forward, looking out from the doorway, she said, 'The trams are always late when it rains, aren't they? And then there's usually two or three bunched up together.'

'Miss Carver.'

She turned to look at him. 'Yes, Davie?'

'Will you marry me, Miss Carver, when I'm nineteen?'

For a moment she said nothing then she touched his face with her gloved hand. 'I'm twenty-two, Davie. Far too old for you. And I'm engaged to Johnny. He'd be terribly unhappy if I changed my mind. We'll be getting married at Christmas. But I like you a lot. I really do.' She saw the disappointment on his face. 'There's lots of girls in the offices who think you're the nicest boy on the staff.'

He nodded, biting his lip, wondering if it would be terribly wrong to ask her which girls thought he was nice. He was deeply disappointed but a little relieved. He had actually taken her to the pictures and for ten minutes at the end he had held her hand in the darkness. He could think about her always. She could be his secret love.

They had walked from Salford Bridge to Erdington. It was just over two miles and they reckoned it was a waste of a ha'penny to take a tram. The poster outside the Palais announced: 'Gala Night with prizes. Ninepence', and as the two stood listening to the faint sound of the band inside Georgie Miles said, 'They've got another bloody think comin'. Ninepence. Let's go to the Masonic.'

The Masonic had none of the glamour of the Palais and it didn't have the selection of girls that the dance-hall produced. But it was never over sixpence and the girls were locals. If you were caught having to walk them home they didn't expect a tram ride and it wasn't too far to walk. Paying for a girl on a tram showed serious intentions and meeting her outside the hall and paying for her to go in was a virtual proposal of marriage.

As the two youths paid for their tickets they could hear the band playing 'Carolina Moon' and for a few moments they stood at the open inner door watching the dancers. They both had well-worn dancing shoes stuffed, toes down, one in each coat pocket; and with the expertise of experience their eyes sorted out the pretty ones and the good dancers. They were seldom the same. A pretty girl who could dance really well would be either at the Palais or the West End Ballroom in town. You got real bands in town like Jack Payne, a local lad who had made good and sometimes played in top London hotels. His father was a dentist somewhere in town.

Shod for dancing, the two stood watching the dancers. It was another slow foxtrot, one of Bing Crosby's called 'Please' and the band singer was giving it the full benefit of his deep voice in the Crosby style.

'Bugger thinks he looks like Bing with his hair brushed back.'

'Looks more like Nat Gonella,' Collins muttered, and Georgie Miles laughed. 'I'm going to try the tart with the green dress,' and he walked to where the girl sat with her friends on the wooden chairs around the walls. Calling a girl a tart was in no way an insult nor did it imply promiscuity. Any girl was a tart, and if you took a girl for a walk you were 'going tarting'. And the formalities of the dance-floor were strictly adhered to. You said 'May I have the pleasure?' or you got a frosty refusal. And you escorted your partner back to the bosom of her girlfriends when the three dances of a set were over.

David Collins was dancing with a tall girl who said she

had seen him playing football in the Park for Moor End Rovers. Her father had been the referee. And then there was a tap on his shoulder. It was a Ladies' Excuse-me and it was Mary Hawkins who had tapped his shoulder. She wasn't one of the good dancers but she danced well enough in her rather stiff way, and she was certainly one of the best-looking girls in the hall that night. Pretty enough for him to buy her an orangeade.

When they lowered the lights and the band played 'Who's taking you home tonight?' he danced the last waltz with her. Dancing the last waltz with any girl had a kind of significance. Nobody would have been able to define it precisely, but it was certainly a commitment of some sort. The least that it meant was that you were stuck with walking the girl home. But as Mary Hawkins lived only four doors from his house that was no great sacrifice. There would be boys stuck with walking to the top of Tyburn Road or the depths of Aston or Nechells. And there would be a week of frozen silence at home for staying out beyond the prescribed time.

Because Mary Hawkins had long black hair and green eyes she was often assumed to be Irish, but the families of both her parents had lived in the Midlands for generations. She was well liked locally and she had a quiet air of confidence that made her seem older than she actually was. Outwardly unemotional she had always seemed to hold strong views when they had chatted together, but she never expressed an opinion on anything until she was forced to by the conversation. She seemed capable of listening to all sorts of views on all sorts of subjects without finding it necessary to express any view of her own unless she had to. Some boys saw her self-contained assurance as hostility but most of her friends and the adults in her circle held judgment in abeyance and merely classified her as 'a deep one'.

Several boys from the tennis club had taken her to the cinema but it was obvious that there was going to be no fun and games. Not even hand-holding or a goodnight kiss on the doorstep. This was not seen as either virtuous or puritanical. Even the two girls at the club who had 'reputations' didn't go much beyond passionate kisses and a hand inside a sweater. Mary Hawkins' attitude to boys was typical and normal in their circle. Girls sometimes mistook her reticence for aloofness but her two or three close girlfriends found her easy to get on with and always ready to help.

At her house they stood talking at the garden gate. About their friends and the tennis club, and the possible closure of the foundry at Witton where her father was a moulder. David gave her a goodnight peck on her cheek and was turning to leave when she said, 'Would you like to come to tea tomorrow?'

He blushed in the dark and said, 'What about your mother? Will she mind?'

'Of course not. She likes you too. About four o'clock then.'

As he lay in bed he thought about what she had said. She wasn't the kind of girl who said such things lightly. And however you repeated it, the word 'too' was a kind of declaration. A glove thrown down, to be picked up if he wanted to.

Chapter 5

THE DOCTOR's dingy waiting room was crowded. All the seats occupied and half a dozen people standing. Two women spoke to each other in whispers but all the rest were silent apart from some racking coughs and an old man muttering quietly to himself.

Dr Lawson was in his early forties and he prescribed the standard pills and medicine bottles as he listened to the wandering descriptions of symptoms and pain. In his spare time he flew a small aircraft at Castle Bromwich aerodrome as a relief from his daily routine and he tried to forget the grim reality of his patients below as he circled the district where he worked.

Erdington was a typical Birmingham working-class suburb ranging from near slums to middle-class Victorian villas. It was the only practice available that he could afford when he took it over and he was quite wrong for it. He dispensed his medical skills as best he could against the prejudices of patients who wanted a bottle or a pill rather than change their diets, their habits or their lives. 'The same as last time, doctor' was what they wanted. Some coloured placebo that gave them comfort and miracle relief. And on his rounds it mattered too much what he said or did. He was much respected and for the wrong reasons. Not for his medicine but for the working-class symbols that his patients interpreted as signs of his approval. A chronically sick woman was consoled if he let her make him a cup of tea. To get him a kettle of hot water to wash his hands at the kitchen sink was an event that could be retold for weeks. They even cleaned their houses specially because he was calling. He cared for them and worried about them but he had long ago given up trying to change them. Even his brusque impatient manner at the end of a long day was seen as proof that he was a modern 'no nonsense' doctor rather than that he was just a tired man.

David Collins waited until he was the last patient in the waiting room. When the doctor opened his surgery door and beckoned him inside he sighed as he sat in the wooden chair, facing the doctor across his desk. The doctor's head was bent, his pen poised over his notepad.

'Name?'

'David Collins.'

'Age?'

'Seventeen.'

The doctor pushed his pad to one side and looked at the boy.

'So. What's the trouble?'

'My mother said I had to see you.'

'Your mother?' He frowned. 'Oh yes.' He smiled. 'I remember now.'

He reached to open the bottom drawer of his desk and pulled out a magazine, tossing it on to his desk. In large red letters it said *Snappy Stories* and the rest of the cover was taken up by the picture of a very beautiful blonde with long legs and a fantastic pair of breasts. She was wearing a swimming costume moulded to her perfect young body like a skin. The doctor looked at it for a moment, smiling, and then looked back at the boy.

'What did she say when she found it?'

The boy shrugged. 'She said I was depraved. I'd got a filthy mind.'

'And have you?'

'I suppose so.'

'What makes you think that?'

He shrugged. 'I bought the magazine. And I looked at it.'

33

'D'you like looking at pictures of pretty girls with big tits?'

The boy sighed and nodded. 'Yes, but I won't do it again.'

The doctor leaned back in his chair, tapping his pen against the edge of his desk.

'I gather your mother made you do some sort of penance. What was it?'

'I had to write out five hundred times that I'd got a filthy mind.'

Dr Lawson looked towards the grimy window and the faint outline of the ivy growing over it outside, then he turned back to the boy.

'Why do you think she sent you to me?'

'She says I'll end up in a lunatic asylum.'

'Have you got a girlfriend?'

'No.'

'A close mate. A boy?'

The boy shook his head. 'No.'

Dr Lawson sighed loudly and leaned forward with his arms on his desk.

'Well. Let me tell you first of all that you won't end up in an asylum because you like looking at pictures of pretty girls with big tits, or we'd all be in asylums long ago. The only harm such pictures and books can do is that they can build up expectations of what girls are like that are never going to be fulfilled in real life. The kind of girls you and I are likely to end up with may, or may not, be pretty but they won't be as pretty as the ones in the pictures because they're artists' creations not real girls. And the girls you and I end up with may or may not have big tits. If they do and they're as big as the ones on the girl on the cover they'll sag. The laws of dynamics will see to that. And our girls will probably have spots on their bums and snore in bed. So don't worry about asylums on that score. But – and this is just between you and me – I think it's time you got out in the world. How much do you earn?'

'Twenty-five shillings a week gross.'

'That's not bad for a seventeen-year-old. You could keep yourself on that, couldn't you?'

'I don't know. I could try.'

'You know what I'm saying, don't you?'

'That I should be more independent.'

'Not just that, boy. You need to get away from that atmosphere. It's too female. And it's not on your side, believe me.'

'You mean she doesn't like me?'

'Who knows? I don't know enough about her to say one way or the other. But I *can* say she ain't on your side and you'd best get away and make a normal life of your own.'

Dr Lawson stood up and walked to the door, opening it and checking that there were no more patients. He nodded to the boy. 'Slip the latch on the outside door for me, there's a good lad.'

'Yes, sir. Goodnight, doctor . . . and thanks.'

'Take care of yourself.'

Despite the mass unemployment, he'd got the first job he wrote after. It was at a foundry in Bedford. They had paid his fare to the interview and offered him the job at thirty shillings a week, to start in ten days' time.

He spent the rest of the day in Bedford looking for a room and finally ended up at a new boarding-house run by a father and his middle-aged daughter who were Plymouth Brethren from Manchester.

It was nearly ten o'clock when he arrived home and he was sent straight to bed. He said nothing about where he had been or the new job. As he lay in bed that night he felt neither elation at moving out nor regret at leaving. It was just something that he was doing.

He gave his notice in at the drawing office the next day. Nobody expressed any particular regret and nobody asked him why he was leaving or what he was going to do. He had decided not to tell his mother until the weekend, but as always, even that small flash of independence was short-lived.

As he put his pay packet on the table on the Friday evening she opened it carefully, handed him the half-crown and said calmly, 'I hear you're leaving your job.'

'Yes. I've got another job. In Bedford. I'll be going there to live next weekend.'

She smiled. A derisory smile. But he saw the anger in her eyes. 'Ashamed of your own home, is it?'

'It's got nothing to do with that,' he said indignantly. 'Why should I be ashamed? It's just that it's more money and new experience for me.'

'More messing about with girls more like. But none of them'll want you, my lad. You mark my words.'

His mother never mentioned his leaving again during the following week and on the Saturday morning as he packed his suitcase the house was empty. She had left his breakfast in the oven and she was not back at midday when he had to leave to catch the train.

He had to change trains at Rugby but the train journey on to Bedford was pleasant. Apart from the trips to his aunt and uncle he had never been outside Birmingham and the sight of the fields and rivers made it seem almost like a holiday trip rather than a major change in his life.

The foundry at Bedford was very different from the one in Birmingham. It was a couple of miles outside the pleasant town in an almost rural setting at the foot of a range of low hills. And the foundry itself was more modern, the people in the offices a little less friendly and more sophisticated.

The food at the boarding-house was plain but sufficient and the man and his daughter were amiable but kept themselves to themselves. He was the only permanent resident but there was a constant flow of theatricals, all-in wrestlers and commercial travellers who always seemed to be laughing and enjoying themselves, and elegant middle-aged actresses paid him compliments about his teeth, or his complexion, or some supposed physical attribute.

His response to Lawson's advice to strike out on his own had been largely instinctive. But he knew in his mind that his mother's shrewd comment about girls had not been far wide of the mark. He had little armour against the world but such as he had she could pierce unerringly. There was also the freedom to come and go as he wished and the relief from the compulsory night-school classes. In fact he went to bed at much the same time as he had been made to at home. He gave little but abstract thought to girls, and discovered in the local library that there were books to read that had nothing to do with mechanical drawing or mathematics. And soon reading became almost an obsession. His urge for information and knowledge was not part of some plan but his reading was mainly biographies and natural sciences and he began to read until the early hours of the morning. All electricity in his lodgings was switched off at 11 pm but he bought a torch and read in bed or with a candle in the rickety armchair in his room.

He was aware that the Chief Draughtsman tolerated him rather than liked him. Mr Mathews was a bluff local who had worked in the foundry drawing office for years. An odd mixture of false *bonhomie*, offset by sarcasm behind people's backs.

Collins' hero was the Chief Designer, a tall handsome man in his late thirties who played cricket for the county and who had a sharp imaginative mind. It was this man, Sid Hoskins, who taught David Collins his first real lesson about life. It was a salutary lesson, a mixture of harsh criticism and a vague hint of possibilities that he neither quite understood nor forgot.

On Friday afternoons Mr Mathews went from drawing board to drawing board, discussing the work being done, the next week's jobs, and handing out the individual pay packets. David Collins had worked there for a year when it happened.

37

Mr Mathews stood alongside him, glancing briefly at the wiring-diagram on his drawing board.

'The old man's got your pay packet, Collins. Wants to see you in his office right away.'

David Collins knocked at the door of the glass-partitioned office and Sid Hoskins said, 'Sit down, Collins,' over his shoulder as he added a couple of dimensions to the design on his board.

He drew a deep breath as he stood up straight and leaned with one arm on his board as he turned and looked at the young man.

'Would you say you're honest, Collins?'

'Yes, sir.'

'What's that mean? That you wouldn't steal money?'

'Yes, sir.'

'What about property? Would you steal other people's property?'

'No, sir. Of course not.'

'What about time?'

'I don't understand, sir.'

'Would you steal time?'

'I still don't understand, sir. How could I steal time?'

'There's an open book at the side of your drawingboard. Go and get it. Leave it open just as it is and bring it to me.'

'Yes, sir,' he said quietly, and he knew now what Sid Hoskins meant. He picked up the book and took it back to the small office, offering it to Hoskins who waved it away.

'Sit down there. Read me from the top of the left-hand page.'

Collins read to the bottom of the page and then Hoskins stopped him.

'OK. That's enough. Do you understand it, Collins?'

'Yes, sir.'

'Who wrote it?'

'Haldane, sir. Professor Haldane.'

'Tell me briefly what it is about.'

'It's about people's characters and behaviour, sir. And how they're affected in different ways by genes and environment. Genes are the characteristics that are born in us, inherited from our parents and their parents. We can't alter those, and some are good and others not so good. Environment is our surroundings. How we're brought up and educated and . . .'

He stopped as Sid Hoskins raised his hand.

'OK. That's enough.' He paused. 'That book interests you, does it?'

'Yes, sir.'

'More than doing your work?'

Collins sat silent, blushing and embarrassed.

'Answer me.'

'It does in a way.'

'You're paid to work here, Collins. Not read. What you're doing is stealing. Stealing the company's time. D'you understand that?'

'Yes, sir. I'm sorry.'

'There's no good saying you're sorry. It doesn't mean anything. It may just mean that you're sorry you've been caught.' Hoskins stood up straight, stretching his long arms and yawning as he looked at the young man. 'You don't want to end your days like Bert Mathews, do you? Surely you want better than that?' He paused then said, 'This is the only warning you'll get, my boy. The next time you get your cards. Understand?'

'Yes, sir. And I *am* sorry.'

Sid Hoskins raised his eyebrows as if he were not impressed. But he nodded and said, 'Come over here and look at this design with me. Tell me if you think it will work. I want to be able to save the cost of machining on cooker doors. Tell me what you think.'

As he walked back to his lodgings that evening he wondered what Sid Hoskins had really meant, about him not wanting to end up like Bert Mathews. To end up as a chief draughtsman like Mathews had been beyond his wildest dreams. Why did Sid Hoskins expect him to do better than that?

There was another shock waiting for him at his lodgings. As he walked through to the kitchen to ask for a cup of tea he saw his mother sitting there with his landlady. They stopped talking as he walked in.

'Hello, mother. What a surprise.'

'Not surprised to see your own mother I hope.'

'No. I didn't mean it that way.'

His mother turned to his landlady. 'From what you've been telling me he seems to be behaving himself.'

She smiled and shrugged. 'As far as I know, Mrs Collins. He's no trouble.'

His mother turned back to look at him. 'You just see you're not. Do as you're told and don't let me hear any bad reports of you.' She stood up. 'I'll be getting down to the station.'

His landlady said quickly, 'We can find you a bed for tonight I'm sure.'

'No. That won't be necessary. You and I have had our little chat. I'll be getting on my way.'

He walked with his mother to the station, puzzled by the unexpected and brief visit, and seething with suppressed anger. She had put him down to the landlady. He was paying for his room and his keep. He didn't need to do as he was told by people he was paying. Nor did he need their approval.

He waited until her train came in and found her a seat. She just nodded when he said that he hoped she had a good journey.

As he walked back to his room he decided to look for a new place. A place where he hadn't been made to appear a child. A place where they acknowledged his independence. Just somebody paying for a service, not someone to be reported on. He moved lodgings two weeks later.

*　　*　　*

Mary Hawkins and he wrote to each other regularly once or twice a week and on several Sundays he bought the special three-shilling day-excursion ticket to Birmingham and stayed at her house. Sometimes he called in to see his mother but it was more from pressure from the Hawkins family than his own wish. His reception was always cool.

He was in Birmingham on September 3rd, 1939 and he had been invited next door with the Hawkins family to hear the Prime Minister announce that the country was now at war with Germany. The Chamberlains were a Birmingham family, respected but not liked. David Collins went to the recruiting office in James Watt Street the next day. He passed his medical and was attested and sent away to await his call-up instructions.

In the waiting time he went back to Bedford, continued at work and spent his free weekends with Mary Hawkins.

The day after his call-up papers came he packed his few things into the cheap cardboard case. Mary Hawkins had taken time off from the office where she worked to see him off. She gave him a small packet as they said goodbye and stood waving on the platform until his carriage was out of sight. When he unwrapped the packet he found a pair of gold-plated cuff-links engraved with his initials, and there were tears in his eyes as he tried to read the green-covered Penguin he had bought to read on the train.

Chapter 6

PRIVATE COLLINS, D. 1905756, was posted to the Rifle Brigade barracks at Winchester for his three months' basic infantry training before his eventual posting to one of the county regiments. Or, if the Rifle Brigade found him a suitable recruit, he would stay at the barracks after his training and join one of their battalions being assembled for overseas service.

The army was strangely like it had been when he started at the foundry. Nobody knew or cared anything about his background and he was accepted by the other men in his barrack room as a fellow victim.

After the three months' basic training he joined the Brigade and was posted to a battalion, still quartered at the depot. In March 1940 the battalion was sent to France and at the end of May David Collins was one of thousands trying to find cover from the Luftwaffe in the dunes of Dunkirk.

The battalion was re-formed and re-armed and sent out again immediately to the Middle East, and by then Collins was a sergeant. He liked the army and his platoon liked him. He absorbed easily what he had been taught on various army courses on weapons, tactics and infantry training. His officers liked him because he was both enthusiastic and utterly reliable. His men liked him because he was efficient and fair-minded. A week before the Japanese bombed Pearl Harbor he was commissioned as a second lieutenant.

He wrote regularly to Mary Hawkins and infrequently

to his mother. But as with all the others serving in the Middle East the correspondence didn't draw people together. Passionate words were written by both sides but as the months slid by the relationships lost reality. It took three months each way for mail to arrive so that answers arrived to questions that had long been forgotten. And people and faces were forgotten too. You could look at the scuffed photograph of a pretty face but you no longer really saw it. It was a ritual that time had robbed of its meaning. And as time went on men got those personal time-bombs that announced that their wives or girlfriends had found new men. They were sorry but they were sure their husbands or boyfriends would understand.

Collins was wounded during the El Alamein attack. A modest but incapacitating wound in his thigh that kept him in hospital for a month. After a week's leave in Cairo he was given a staff appointment at Eighth Army HQ and assisted the Staff captain I(a) responsible for the flow of information on Rommel's Order of Battle. Like any good infantry soldier he had previously despised the staff at all levels above battalion, but he found his new colleagues to be bright, intelligent men. They found him pleasant, and intelligent, but naive. But Collins was a ready learner and he slowly absorbed a little of the more sophisticated thinking and attitudes of his fellows and superiors.

In September 1943 he was posted back to his battalion for the invasion of Italy. In Fifth Army's attack on Naples Collins had been wounded again. A bullet in his shoulder had torn muscles and ligaments as it glanced off the bone. After two months in hospital he was posted back to England for sick-leave and physiotherapy.

There had been no way to let anyone know that he was returning. He would arrive long before any message could get through.

It was mid-December when he landed at Hurn Airfield outside Bournemouth. Bronzed and in his best barathea, faintly proud of his Africa Star with its Eighth Army clasp. He had changed trains twice because of the effects of bombing and had got to Birmingham just after nine o'clock. The Africa Star had got him a taxi to his mother's house, and the driver had refused the fare.

Two neighbours waved to him as he walked up the short path to the front door. His mother showed neither surprise nor pleasure when she opened the door. He had a cup of tea and went exhausted to bed. Exhausted and depressed.

The next morning he shaved carefully and dressed in his uniform again. As he got to the foot of the narrow stairs his mother came out of the kitchen, her face flushed with anger. 'Who told you to get up?'

'I don't understand.'

'Get back to bed and wait till I call you.'

He walked slowly back up the stairs, packed his canvas hold-all and walked back down to the hall, closing the front door behind him. There were tears on his cheeks as he walked up the road to the Hawkins' house.

The fire had been lit under the boiler in the scullery and the week's wash bubbled and steamed in the soapy water as Mrs Hawkins stirred the tangled clothes and sheets with the wooden stick. Putting the lid back on she stepped back and looked at her daughter.

'Why the hurry, girl?' Her shrewd but kindly eyes looked at her daughter. 'You haven't got to marry him, have you?'

'Of course not, mum. Don't say such things.'

'That's all very well, my girl, but if it's that I'd want to know.'

'It isn't.'

'So why d'you want to marry him?'

'I like him. He's a decent chap.'

'Let's go in the kitchen and have a cup of tea.'

When they were sitting at the kitchen table Mrs Hawkins went back to the subject.

'Why d'you think he wants to marry you?'

'Same as me. He likes me. Wants to make a home.'

Mrs Hawkins looked at her daughter. She was a deter-

44

mined girl. Always had been. Knew what she wanted and worked hard to get it, whether it was a doll's pram or learning to type. She was pretty too and that helped, but she never used her looks to gain her ends. And she only asked for things that were attainable. There was no reaching for the stars with their Mary. She was down to earth and sensible.

'I'd have thought Georgie Miles was more your kind of boy.'

'I don't.' She smiled. 'Apart from that, he hasn't asked me. He's got other fish to fry.'

'Like who?'

'Like Kitty Macfarlane.'

'He's a fool if he marries her.'

'Why?'

'She's a sickly sort of girl. Always ailing with something.'

'So what about David Collins?'

'D'you want me to speak to your father?'

'Thanks, mum.'

'You'd better tell him your dad'll be speaking to him when he comes in for tea on Sunday.'

'OK.'

'And don't say OK, it's common.'

David had put on a clean collar to his Saturday shirt and after a slightly strained tea whose importance had been marked by shop cakes and butter instead of margarine, Mr Hawkins suggested the two of them went and had a look at his pigeons.

The pigeon loft was so low that David stayed stooped over as Mr Hawkins scratched around for the right words to start his little piece. He had gone over it with his wife and he had rehearsed it after lunch in front of the wardrobe mirror in their bedroom. He had always liked David Collins and he saw no point in going through this rigmarole if Mary wanted the fellow. His wife and Mary had already put their seal of approval on it so why not just say 'yes' and have done with it?

He looked up at the young man, taking a deep breath.

'You know why we've been sent out here, lad, don't you?'

Collins smiled. 'I think so, dad. I've got to ask you about Mary and me getting engaged.'

'That's it. It's what you want, is it?'

'Yes.'

'Well as long as you know *your* mind, that's it. She knows hers all right. Always has done. She's had a few after her but you was always the one. Take your time about it, both of you. It's a big responsibility. You don't know one another all that well. You ain't had the chance because of this bloody war. And you're both very young yet.'

'It'll be all right, dad. I'm sure it will.'

'Be tolerant, that's what I always say. Tolerance and patience is what counts between man and wife.'

David was momentarily disturbed by the words 'man and wife' being applied to himself and Mary. They had the smell of boiled cabbage and mothballs. It was just a fellow and a girl making a place to live in. The way they wanted, not how others wanted it. Why did adults always want to make everything so serious and forbidding and banal? Even a sunny day was only called 'a fine drying day' and laughter went hand in hand with being drunk. Man and wife sounded like the police-court reports in the *Birmingham Mail*.

They were married ten days later at the Register Office in town. When he went down the street and told his mother of the engagement she didn't reply and she didn't look up from the sheet she was ironing.

All the pre-wedding and wedding day superstitions had had to be ignored with the couple living in the same small house but Mrs Hawkins had made the two upstairs rooms into a forbidden zone. Calling down firm instructions to the men from behind the closed door of the bedroom.

The couple's insistence that the ceremony would be at

the Register Office had been a bitter blow to Mrs Hawkins who took it for granted that the neighbours would assume that her Mary was pregnant. But it was wartime and David was not only an officer but would be wearing his uniform. And it would save at least £10 by not having a formal reception.

David's mother had been invited but had refused. But when they climbed out of the two taxis in town she was already there in the waiting room of the Register Office.

Mr Hawkins had plundered his Oddfellows savings to take them for sandwiches and tea at the Grand Hotel. Warnings had been discreetly passed to all concerned about extravagances. Their wedding presents had been laid out on the sideboard at home. A green enamelled kettle, two sets of cotton sheets with pillow slips, a Bible from David's aunt and uncle, six ecru doilies, a set of shoe-cleaning things in an open wooden box with a carrying handle, a two-tiered cake stand and, in pride of place, a thirty-two piece set of crockery bought in the Bull Ring market. Mary's wooden chest already contained many other items of household linen, cutlery and cooking utensils. David's mother gave him a Post Office savings book with accumulated deposits of £31. Everybody was in various stages of good-will. Relieved that nothing had gone wrong and modestly aware that they had done the couple proud.

David and Mary Collins took the 78 tram to town to the Gaumont to see Laurence Olivier's *Henry V*. The *Pathé News* showed the first scenes of British troops entering Caen.

With only a day of his overseas leave remaining, he had to leave for London early the next morning.

They could both hear the long whine of the 'All-clear', and Fredericks opened the window and peered out. There was the confused clanging of ambulances and fire-engines heading towards Chelsea Bridge. He pulled back in and

47

said, 'Sounds like it was a V2 somewhere over in West-
minster.' He paused. 'What are you doing tonight?'

Collins smiled. 'I'm going to Hammersmith Palais.'

Fredericks stared at him. 'I can't understand you, Collins. You're an intelligent chap, how can you waste your
time with such rubbish?'

Collins laughed. 'It isn't rubbish. I like dancing and I
like the music. It's Joe Loss tonight.'

'Good grief. Do you call that music? And all those silly
little girls and the ridiculous clap-trap about "May I have
the pleasure of the next dance?" Surely that doesn't really
satisfy you?'

'It's not meant to satisfy me. It's just a pleasant way to
spend an evening.'

Fredericks shook his head. 'My God, what a waste of
time.'

'What do you think I should do then?'

'If you like music, then go to a concert. Hear some real
music. Open your mind a bit. Get away from that grim
puritanical background you come from. You're in London,
my boy. Use it. Enjoy it. Escape for God's sake.' He
reached for his Sam Browne. 'I'll take you to a concert
tomorrow night if you want. Nice *schmaltzy* stuff. Right
up your street. Rachmaninov or Tchaikowsky.'

'OK. What are *you* doing tonight?'

Fredericks smiled. 'I'll come with you to the Palais or
whatever you call it.'

Fredericks was his senior, a captain, and in civilian life
a don at one of the Oxford colleges teaching Eng. Lit.,
and Collins was mildly in awe of him.

To Collins' surprise Fredericks seemed to enjoy himself
at the Palais and seemed to get on well with the girls he
danced with. He only danced waltzes but he went round
in style. It seemed odd to see a man whose whole life-style
was based on the values of an intellectual, an ascetic, so
self-confident in the sweaty bustle of Hammersmith Palais.

They went to the concert the next night and there were
parts that he liked, but Fredericks' running commentary

on key changes and themes and movements was beyond him. As they sat drinking tea in Lyons' Corner House Fredericks talked music, trying to arouse his interest. Finally Fredericks laughed and said, 'You haven't absorbed a damn thing, have you?'

Collins grinned. 'Yes. Themes are the bits you can whistle. The tunes.'

Fredericks' eyebrows went up. 'Crude, but not bad for a start. At least you've taken in something.'

'Why bother, Freddie? Just let me stay in blissful ignorance.'

'There's no such thing. Ignorance is never blissful. And why bother? I suppose that's the teacher coming out. Trying to arouse a potential achiever.'

'Am I a potential achiever?'

'I don't know. I think you are, but sometimes I wonder. You've got a good brain. I'm sure of that. But it's an idle brain. Too easily coasting along in third gear instead of top.'

'In what way do I do that?'

'You're always doing it. Your body may be in Cairo or London but your wretched mind is still in the back-streets of Birmingham. If it's done in Birmingham it's OK, but if it isn't then you're suspicious. Your mind's always living in a world of cloth caps and black pudden.'

Collins laughed. 'What's wrong with cloth caps and black pudden?'

'They're fine if that's the best you can do. *You* could do better. Right now you're a rather pathetic Black Country prig with a closed parochial mind.'

'Thanks for the compliment.'

Fredericks shrugged. 'Forget it. Just bump along in your own sweet way. You'll survive. But it's a waste.'

Back at the Transit Camp house in Sloane Street Collins lay in the uncomfortable bunk bed and the things Fredericks had said went through his mind. They reminded him of what Sid Hoskins had said. Sid Hoskins was an intelligent man, so was 'Freddie' Fredericks. They both seemed

49

to think he could be something. But what? They talked as if they had some crystal ball and knew something that he didn't know, about himself. But they never said what they meant.

Collins was demobbed in Hull in September 1945 and he was taken back at the foundry in Birmingham as a senior draughtsman at £7.10s a week. Most of the old faces were still there. There was a slight, unspoken respect for his having been a captain in the army, and for the wound-stripes on his tunic sleeve when he went for his interview, but it faded quickly. The two years after the war were almost grimmer than the war itself, culminating in the dreadful winter of 1947.

Mary had found two rooms for them with shared bathroom and kitchen in an old house in Kingsbury Road, and she had kept on her job as a clerk at Dunlop's factory up Tyburn Road.

It took him several months to acclimatise himself to working regular hours and his work seemed grindingly humdrum compared with his responsibilities in the army. It was hard to feel vitally concerned about the minimum radius on a casting that would allow it to take vitreous enamel without cracking or crazing. But he recognised that this was now his life and he worked hard and conscientiously. There were times, though, when sheer lack of physical activity made him find an excuse to walk to the pattern shop or the foundry. There were still men in No. 1 Foundry who remembered him. They chatted if they too had been in the Services but there was no resurrecting the old days. And they saw him as changed and different. He had been an officer and now he was a brain-worker in the drawing office. For them he didn't belong in their world any longer. They didn't resent it, it was just a fact of life and they wondered why he didn't recognise it and not embarrass them by his visits.

He had mentioned it to Mary several times but she made

no comment. Things eventually came to a head when the foundry foreman took him on one side. It was his old friend Sam Thatcher, who had taken over during the war.

Collins had been watching the testing of a new cupola and Sam Thatcher had waved him into his office as he walked by.

'Are you terribly busy, Mr Collins?'

'No, Sam. What can I do for you?'

Sam Thatcher sighed. 'I always liked you when you first came here as a lad. You always tried hard but I've got to read you the Riot Act all the same.'

Collins laughed. 'What's that mean, Sam?'

'Things have moved on, lad, since those days. I'm foundry foreman and you're a senior draughtsman. You don't seem to realise that that makes a difference.'

'What kind of difference?'

Sam Thatcher waved in the general direction of the foundry floor. 'I don't belong in there any more. I belong in this little glass house. I'm not one of the boyos any more. I'm a foreman. They don't want me in there chatting about the old days. They'd think I was prying. They don't want you there, lad, neither.'

'But why, for God's sake? I'm still me.'

'You was an officer, Mr Collins. You don't belong on a foundry floor no more. Neither do I. It's nothing to do with not liking you, it's a question of . . . what's the word . . .'

'Proprieties?'

'Ah, I think that's the one. Anyway I'm asking you to stay upstairs. Don't hang around down here.'

Collins stood up and said quietly, 'I'll do as you say, Mr Thatcher. Don't worry.'

'Don't take it to heart, lad. If you'd had a father he'd have explained these things.' He paused. 'The family all right?'

'Yes thanks, Sam. And yours?'

'Jogging along. See you.'

Collins nodded. 'See you, Sam.'

He talked it over with Mary that night and it was the first time that he had seen her really angry.

'He's just a snob, David. Who is he to tell you how to behave and who you talk to? He may want to leave all his old mates behind but that doesn't mean you have to.'

'He's the boss of the foundry, kid. His word's law down there.'

'So see them outside the works in your own time.'

'They're not really that important, Mary. Just a few words in passing was all I intended. And he's right in a way. We don't have much in common any more. Those days have gone for good.'

'Oh, David. Half of them come from the street where you and I were brought up.'

He smiled. 'That doesn't mean we have to have them round to tea. Maybe the surprise of what Sam Thatcher said has made me exaggerate it. Let's forget it. What's for tea?'

She smiled. 'Don't forget it or I'll keep reminding you. There's too many people think they can throw off their past by moving out to Sutton or Edgbaston. What did you say? Oh, tea. It's haddock. And mother's made us a cake.'

The following week he was called to the General Manager's office. The same Mr Harvey who had once been the Works Manager.

Mr Harvey waved him to the chair in front of his desk.

'You know, Collins, I've often noticed you as I pass through the drawing office and I could swear I've seen you somewhere else. D'you play golf?'

'No, sir. But before the war I used to bring you your tea sometimes when you were works manager. I was the print kid in the drawing office in those days.'

'Of course. Of course. But that's by the way. I had an odd sort of report on you from the Chief Draughtsman. He does an annual one on all his staff for me. He said you were responsible, conscientious, bright, highly competent technically but he thought you didn't belong in a drawing office. What do you say to that, young man?'

Collins took a deep breath. 'I don't understand what he means by me not belonging in a drawing office.'

'He's a funny old stick, is Westray. Not as daft as he makes out. He thinks you feel cooped up after your time in the Services. He was in the first war himself so he probably recognises the signs. Anyway, the long and short of it is that I'm offering you a promotion that might suit you better. Your pay goes up to £650 a year and it's a new middle-management post in London. How about it?'

'What's the job, sir?'

'Technical support for our sales people. Half of 'em don't know a volt from a watt and those who do seem to manage to offend our customers. We want you to take charge and sort it out. Get it running efficiently.'

'When do I start, sir?'

'Does that mean you want it?'

'Yes, sir.'

'Good. Let's say you start the first of next month. That'll give you time to find a place to live.'

'Thanks for the opportunity, sir.'

'Make the most of it, do your stuff. Show those bloody Londoners what a Brummie can do.'

He hurried back to their rooms impatient to give the good news. Mary went suddenly quiet when he told her and there was no enthusiasm or congratulations.

'Maybe you could get a job in one of the other foundries. Maybe Witton or the one in Balsall Heath.'

'Why should I do that?'

She looked at him intently. 'They've really fixed you, haven't they? You want to go, don't you?'

'Of course. It's a much better job and a lot more money. It's our big chance, Mary.'

'Big chance for what? Getting away from the people we know. The streets and places we know. We belong here, not in London.'

'We have to go where the opportunities are. We can't just stand still.'

She shook her head slowly. 'They're tricking you, David. Dangling a carrot in front of you, hoping you won't notice that they're taking away the grass.'

'I'm not that important to them, Mary.'

She smiled. 'I sometimes wonder about you, David. You're like a terribly innocent attractive girl who doesn't realise how attractive she is. Innocent but not innocent. And highly dangerous.'

He laughed. 'What's all that mean?'

'It means you don't have to leave everything we know just because it suits them.'

'Does that mean you wouldn't go?'

She took a deep breath and then sighed. 'No. If that's what you want. We'll go. But remember if you don't like it that I warned you.'

'I'll remember. But we could have a house of our own with my new salary.'

She laughed sharply. 'There you go. You're already playing their game. It's salary now, is it? Not just wages.'

'Oh, come now. Let's celebrate. Let's go round and tell your parents and take them up to the pub at Chester Road.'

She smiled. 'The big sacrifice. David Collins going to a pub, like the rest of humanity.'

Chapter 7

THE INCREASE in what was now officially called his salary allowed them to take on a mortgage on a small semi-detached house in Streatham. Mary obviously resented the move that took her away from her roots, her parents and her friends, and had stayed on in Birmingham to the last possible moment. It was seven weeks before they were in the new house together. He had redecorated it in his spare time but he had been unhappy and lonely on his own. Although nothing had been said openly the move had become a battleground between them: Mary critical of everything in the new suburb, Collins driven to defend things he didn't particularly like himself. But the battle of wills gradually subsided as his new responsibilities took more of his time and the girl settled reluctantly into her new surroundings.

The Birmingham foundry had bought up and merged with a dozen other foundries in Scotland, Tyneside and Manchester and it was Collins' job to support the sales team with technical advice to potential customers and users of the group's products. Their customers were mainly in the building industry and local authorities and most of Collins' time was spent in travelling around the southern part of the country.

As the months went by the sales staff wanted him at their sales pitches to help them clinch an order rather than merely provide them with technical advice.

By the end of the first year he was spending more time initiating and clinching sales than providing technical back-up and there were requests for him to provide the same kind of service to northern England and Scotland. Most of them he had to refuse because he was too heavily committed in London. When a new sales record system was introduced one of the first pieces of information that it threw up was that David Collins' efforts had added fifteen per cent extra sales turnover to almost every sales representative's figures in the south.

Their son James was born in the autumn of their second year in London. Without either of them realising it, it was a decisive moment in both their lives. It was a beginning and an end that they couldn't possibly have recognised. Nothing seemed to alter, but in fact the baby was a catalyst. It wasn't that he was a problem for either of them. He was healthy, happy and much loved by both parents. But in different ways, and therein lay the problem.

Mary Collins was an ideal mother. Caring, hard-working and uncomplaining. Even Streatham seemed more tolerable now, although she frequently took her small son to see her parents in Birmingham when Collins was on his journeys around the country during the week. David Collins was a loving father but not an ideal one. Seeing his small son lying in his cot, helpless but happy, vulnerable but cared for, unleashed thoughts he had never had before. Or at least not consciously. Most fathers, most parents, will have looked at their babies and small children and wondered what fate had in store for them. But for David Collins it opened a Pandora's box of doubts, fears and introspection. For the first time in his life he actually analysed his own life and his own talents. The analysis was mostly inaccurate but his conclusions were much nearer the target. He felt that he had been wasting his life and that it was time that he changed his attitudes to almost everything. He had made progress but it had been a drifting, unplanned progress.

As could be expected of a man from his background he looked first at his work and his efforts became more precise and controlled, and his motive was no longer merely to

56

please, but to succeed. For the first time in his life he had a vague idea of what Sid Hoskins and 'Freddie' Fredericks had been trying to tell him. He had been content to coast along when he should have reached out with ambition.

His function gradually became more management than assistance and nobody seemed to resent it. Six months later his salary was increased substantially to £1,500 a year and his new designation was Technical Manager (Sales) South.

A year later there was another change to his career.

He reached for the internal phone as it rang, his eyes still on the table of figures that he was studying.

'Hello. Collins here.'

'Can you spare me a few minutes, David?'

'Yes, sir. I'll be right down.'

Jimmy Hansen was his immediate boss in London. Deputy Chairman of the group. Tough but amiable, and his current hero.

As he sat down facing Hansen he saw that he had the London office's accounts in front of him.

'How's the family?'

'Fine, thank you, sir.'

'I've been looking at last month's accounts, David. There's an item here I don't understand. It's cross-referenced to a petty-cash voucher signed by you. It says – "Nuns £1". What's that mean?'

'Two nuns called, asking for donations. They had a little book. Said we always gave them a pound. I gave it to them out of petty-cash.'

'Are you a Roman Catholic?'

'No, sir. I'm not anything in particular.'

'But you thought it was a good cause to support?'

'Yes.'

'So you gave them a pound of the shareholders' money?'

'Yes, sir.'

'How much did you give them yourself?'

Collins blushed and looked embarrassed. 'I didn't give them anything.'

'You didn't think it was *that* good a cause?'.

Collins shrugged. 'I suppose I just gave it to them because we always gave them something.'

Hansen raised his eyebrows. 'Just follow my leader. No views of your own.'

'I'll pay it myself, sir. I didn't think about it that way.'

Hansen shrugged. 'There's no need to do that but let it be a lesson. When you're in charge of something, *you* take the decisions not just go along with the old routine. And remember. It's always easier to give other people's money away than your own.'

'Yes, sir.'

Hansen leaned back in his chair looking across his desk at the younger man.

'That isn't why I asked you to come in, David. I've been talking with the board the last few weeks and we've decided that we need a Sales Manager in London. It's too important for us to continue operating out of Birmingham. This is where most of our business comes from. Your name was put up and I've been asked to offer you the job. There's a five hundred a year increase goes with it. How about it?'

'But I'm not really on the sales side, sir. I'm technical management.'

'Come off it, David. You've been selling more than any two reps we've got. Anyway, do you think you could do that job?'

'I'm sure I could, sir.'

'D'you want it?'

'Yes, please. And thanks for the chance.'

'That's OK. Don't let me down.'

'Was it you put my name up, sir?'

'It doesn't matter who put your name up. Just get on with it and do it well. You'll start on the first of next month. You've got two weeks' holiday in between, haven't you?'

'I'll give that a miss, sir. I'll need to hand over decently.'

'Good. Fowler will be moved from Birmingham to take over from you.'

He'd bought a bottle of red wine on the way home to celebrate, but when they were eating and he reached out to pour some for her she put her hand over the top of the glass.

'Not for me, David. I'm happy with our usual tea.'

'It's not just to drink, kid. It's to celebrate.'

'Celebrate what?'

'The new job. The promotion.'

Her green eyes looked at him coolly. 'I suppose you're satisfied now.'

'What's that mean?'

'You've made sure that we don't stand a chance of going back home.'

'Why should we want to do that for God's sake?'

'Because that's where my friends are, and my family.'

'I'm your family. Me and young Jimmy. And this is our home.'

'And the Thomas Arkwright Foundry Group Limited.'

'That's just not fair. I have to go where my job takes me and that applies to any husband, not just me.'

'Let's not argue, David. We shall all do as you want, as usual.' She stood up. 'I'd better clear away. We've got those people coming from your gramophone society, remember?'

He sighed and wondered how she managed to make a few people coming from the Streatham Music Society sound like a gang of intruders. He finished his meal alone and left the wine untouched.

They had listened to his new record of the Max Bruch and the last track of the Beecham Lollipops and then they talked music with their coffee and biscuits.

59

Arthur Partridge, the jovial Chairman of the Society, was holding forth about Delius.

'What always amazes me is you've got this chap with German parents, writes the most sublime English music that's ever been, the Germans love it and the English never heard of it until Tommy Beecham came along.'

Collins smiled. 'And Eric Fenby of course.'

'Of course. Delius is buried over here you know, in Limpsfield. They brought the body over from France. Those two old dears, bless 'em.'

The rather clenched-up Society Secretary said, 'What's your favourite music, Arthur?'

'Music or composer?'

'Either.'

'Piece of music I couldn't say. Drive me mad trying to decide. Composer? Well it ought to be Beethoven but in fact it would be Elgar. What about yours?'

'Both the same. Bach, and any one of the Brandenburgs.' He turned to look at Collins. 'What about you, David?'

Collins shrugged, smiling. 'Composer I think would be Brahms. Music? Well right at this moment that lollipop. The Massenet. "Last sleep of the virgin".'

Partridge laughed. 'You're a romantic, David. A through and through romantic. Isn't that so, Mary?' He turned to look at Mary Collins who was pouring coffee and seemed not to hear. Partridge leaned forward. 'I was saying I think your husband's a romantic. Am I right?'

She shrugged. 'Who knows? Maybe you're right,' she said without looking up from the coffee cups.

Ten minutes later Collins was seeing them out. Mary was busy in the kitchen. Car doors banged, engines turned over and then the road was quiet and still. He stood there for a moment, looking over the roofs of the houses opposite. They were nice people. Easy to get on with. It had been a nice evening.

He walked back into the kitchen where Mary was doing the washing-up.

60

'Thanks for doing the coffee and things, they obviously enjoyed the evening. I hope you didn't find it too boring.'

'It's rather amusing really. Listening to them all saying their party pieces. It makes me wonder why they don't play some instrument if they like music so much. Instead of just making silly speeches about it.'

'Most of them know what they're talking about, you know.'

'Oh come off it, David. You have to listen to them saying their little party pieces and then they have to hear yours. What do you know about that kind of music? You've just read it somewhere and repeat it.'

He laughed. 'It's not quite as bad as that. I don't know much I'll admit, but what I say is my own views.'

'Oh for heaven's sake. Two years ago you didn't know the difference between a symphony and a concerto. Your real musical taste is somewhere between Lew Stone and Harry Roy. It always amazes me that they actually listen to you giving your views on classical music.'

'But I'm genuinely interested. I really am.'

She laughed. 'You were playing Glenn Miller on your gramophone just before they came.'

'That doesn't mean that I don't like classical music as well.'

'No. But you wouldn't let on to them that you liked Glenn Miller.'

'You're just being a grouch. It's time we were in bed.'

Chapter 8

COLLINS HAD taken over responsibility for the group's advertising as part of his new assignment. The budget was small and allowed little more than price-lists and instruction manuals. His standing was high enough at their headquarters in Birmingham for them to agree to a meeting to cover the whole subject of advertising and publicity. The fact that five of the group's foundries were working only part-time both inhibited their thinking where spending money was concerned, but equally made them willing to listen to any proposal that could bring in more orders.

The full board of six plus the Chairman had assembled at nine o'clock. They were all Scots except one Tynesider and they had all actually worked in iron-founding most of their lives. Collins' reputation made them agree to listen but not one of them had an open mind. Young men like Collins were useful employees, but they were only sales people. You never knew where they were at any time. Glib and amiable, they sat in cinemas on wet afternoons and were full of dirty jokes. And it wasn't their money that was wrapped up in the business.

The Chairman looked round the table at his colleagues. 'Mr Collins from London is asking for a word with us about advertising. As you know, he's done a fine job for us down there with his slick London ways of selling.' He nodded to Collins. 'Go ahead, mister, we're listening.'

'Mr Chairman, gentlemen. Our rivals selling to the building industry spend roughly one per cent of their turnover on advertising of one kind or another. Their turnover is rather less than ours in most cases. The retailers who sell our cookers, baths and kitchen appliances spend eight per cent of their turnover on advertising. Does anybody know what we spend on advertising?' He looked around but nobody responded. 'We spend one-tenth of one per cent on advertising and publicity. And almost all of that is not really advertising but cheap leaflets and instructions on how to use our products.'

Old man Campion from Glasgow said, 'Sounds like we're doing pretty good, my friend. Spending less but more turnover.' He acknowledged the smiles of one or two of his fellow directors.

'That's not from planning or intention, sir. Just a question of luck, and turnover's not everything.'

'Tell me something better,' the Chairman said, smiling.

'Profits, sir. And control of the market. We're in the hands of the merchants, the retailers. They decide whether our goods get sold to the public. They've got us in their hands. They demand bigger and bigger discounts and they could bring our appliance business to a halt if they chose to. We've got to get out of their grip.'

'It's the way the trade's always been, Mr Collins.' Tawney's watery eyes looked at Collins aggressively.

'That's why we're going to be stuck at our present turnover, Mr Tawney. I've increased southern sales as far as they'll go. Just taking up the slack and giving our salespeople proper training and control. There's little more to come from that source.'

Hansen chipped in on cue. 'So what are you suggesting, Mr Collins?'

'I'm suggesting we mount a trial campaign on one of our appliances. A campaign aimed at the public, not at the merchants. We sell our own appliances hard, we coupon the ads so that we can refer enquiries to those merchants who will really cooperate with us. We prepare top quality leaflets and we contact all the women's magazines. Invite their feature writers to come and see the care and technical skill we put into making our appliances.'

63

There was a long silence and then Hansen said, 'And how much would all this cost?'

'We'd have to spend between £30,000 and £40,000.'

'How many years would that cover, Mr Collins?'

'Three months only. But the effect would last for a year.'

There was a shaking of heads and a muttering of dissent as Collins sat there and Hansen again came to his rescue. 'Say we gave you a reasonable annual advertising budget and you spend it over all our goods for a year?'

'We'd be throwing money down the drain, sir. Nobody would notice the difference. It wouldn't be effective.'

'If it were that or nothing what would you say?'

'I'd say let's save the money. And plan for all the foundries to be on short-time two years from now.'

Hansen shrugged and leaned back in his chair looking at his colleagues' glum faces. He looked across at the Chairman. 'I think we should release Mr Collins and talk together about what he's told us.'

The Chairman nodded. 'Fine, Mr Hansen.' He turned to look at Collins. 'Thank you for your time, Mr Collins. You can get my driver to take you to the station. Have a good journey.'

As Collins sat in the train, his eyes closed, he wondered how Hansen was faring. He had put the idea up to Hansen, he'd accepted it, and they'd worked out the strategy together. There was a fifty-fifty chance he could persuade them because they were all having sleepless nights from foundries on half-time and grossly uneconomical production costs. Even the threat of foundry closures. There were drain-pipes and gutters going out that barely made a tenth of a penny a foot on full-time costs.

He smiled as he told Mary of the meeting as she sat sewing name tabs on Jimmy's clothes for his first day at the nursery school.

'Aren't you taking an awful risk saying all that?'

'Why?'

'It might not work and then you could lose your job.'

'I'll make it work, Mary. And I can always get another job.'

She looked up from her sewing. 'You've changed, David. You used to be glad to have a job, but these days you seem to be always taking risks. Pushing all the time.'

'It's paid off. I earn a lot more money now.'

She bent her head back to her sewing. 'Have you ever thought of going back to Birmingham? Getting out of this rat-race?'

'I couldn't get this kind of money in Birmingham. And it's not a rat-race. I'm just making a bit of progress. The rat-race is a lot tougher than anything I have.'

'Does the money matter all that much to you?'

'It's what keeps us, my dear. I'd rather be here than in those two rooms in Erdington.'

'We were happy enough there.'

'I wasn't. And I don't see the attraction of Birmingham. Except for your parents, of course.'

'They're real people there, David.'

'And what are they here?'

'Most of them are terrible phoneys. Living beyond their incomes. Buying everything on the never-never. Always wanting something more. They're just never satisfied. People at home are more content.'

He smiled. 'You ought to write ads for holidays in Birmingham. You make it sound wonderful.'

'Now you're being sarcastic.'

Shaking his head, he said, 'I'll make you a cup of tea. Or would you rather have coffee?'

She half-smiled and put down her work. 'I can take a hint.'

He was suddenly aware that they seldom talked with one another. In fact they seldom talked unless she was pushing for them to go back to Birmingham. She wasn't interested in any of his new ideas.

*   *   *

65

Hansen strolled into Collins' office mid-morning on the Monday after the Birmingham meeting. He sat himself down on the far side of Collins' desk waiting for him to finish talking on his phone. As Collins hung up he looked for a clue on Hansen's face. There was no clue.

'What did they decide?'

'I'm afraid you won't like it. They dithered, of course, and I came out with a compromise. You get your budget of £30,000 but it has to cover everything and it has to cover twelve months. And if it doesn't show a marked difference in sales it's the last advertising appropriation you'll get.'

Collins looked unabashed. 'Could we ask for one condition from my side?'

'What condition?'

'If I increase sales enough to make the appropriation better than self-liquidating will they agree to a proper appropriation across the board?'

'Maybe you could convince them to do that after you've showed that it works. They wouldn't agree now.'

'Can I tackle this present budget my own way?'

Hansen looked at him. 'Does that mean what I think it means?'

'Yes.'

'You'd be putting your job on the line, David. If it didn't work they would reckon that you had deliberately disobeyed their conditions, and maybe they'd be right to think that. They didn't come even to this decision easily. You may not think so but what they've agreed to is virtually a vote of confidence in you personally. If you cut corners and it goes wrong you'd have thrown away your reputation. I'm not sure it's worth the risk, are you?'

'I'm sure that what I'm suggesting is right. Even at £30,000 and even dodging the conditions I'll be working on a shoestring. And one thing I am sure of, and that is that there's no alternative. It's this or we just die slowly and peacefully. In five years or maybe a bit longer.'

Hansen stood up to leave. 'I won't interfere. I'll leave you to get on with it, but bear in mind what I've said.

You'd be throwing away all your hard work and reputation if it doesn't work.'

For the three summer months Collins worked even longer hours, cutting down his normal work to a minimum, spending every moment he could find with the advertising agency he had appointed to handle the account.

He had decided to spend the whole of the appropriation on advertising a re-styled version of a pre-war solid fuel fire. It was the least expensive appliance they manufactured, every one of their foundries was capable of producing it, it burned inferior fuel and because of machining improvements on the air control it could stay alight all night. An attempt had been made to market the original model before the war and it was a failure. But with its new styling and design Collins was convinced that the timing was right. The £2,000 he spent on market research supported his thinking and the advertising agency team were equally enthusiastic.

Every aspect of the work – photography, copy-writing, printing and media selection – was closely supervised by Collins, and the slogan that was finally chosen to link every facet of the campaign had been his suggestion. The usual technicalities or references to the long experience of the foundries were ignored. What Collins wanted was a simple phrase that would make ordinary people want the product. He had written out variations again and again until he was finally satisfied and 'Come down to a warm room every morning' was the final copy.

The bulk of the media appropriation was being spent in the first two weeks and after the space was booked there was no more that could be done except wait.

The first advertisement appeared in the national press on a Thursday and there was a disappointing trickle of coupons the following day. He drove up to the office on the Saturday morning, apprehensive and, for the first time, doubting his judgment. As he arrived, a Post Office van was unloading ten bags of mail and it came flooding in for the next ten weeks. Every foundry was working round the clock trying to satisfy the demand and Collins was the only one who was not delighted with the outcome. Not even his appointment as Group Sales Manager brought back the enthusiasm he had felt while he was planning the campaign. For the first time in his life he realised that he was bored. He had proved his point and the excitement was over. As he looked back over the post-war years he realised that his work had always been boring. But he hadn't recognised it then. It was just what you had to do to earn a living if you had no qualifications. Most people would have said he was lucky to have made such progress and to have a good job, but he knew that as far as he was concerned he was neither lucky nor happy.

Chapter 9

As THEY walked down the wide stairs to the restaurant in the Mayfair, Stringer said, 'You want to wash or anything, David?'

'No, I'm OK.'

'I've booked us a nice quiet corner table. I've known old Kunz, the *maître d'*, for years.' He laughed. 'You have to have influence even to spend money these days.'

They were having coffee when Stringer gave him a small package. 'That's from the agency team, to celebrate your promotion.'

Collins smiled. 'Can I open it?'

'Of course.'

It was a blue Parker 51. They were still hard to get. He looked up at Stringer. 'Will you thank them for me? I'll drop them a note of course. You couldn't have chosen better. I've wanted one since I first saw the ads in *Life* magazine.'

'It's nothing. Just a token. I brought it back from New York.'

'And thanks for the congratulations. I've got the agency to thank in many ways.'

'It was your campaign, David. We just did what we were told. But it certainly worked. *Ad Weekly* are doing a piece on it in a couple of weeks' time. They'll be calling you this afternoon or tomorrow.'

Collins smiled. 'I'll see that the agency gets its due.'

'I'm sure you will. Actually, in one way we were a bit disappointed at your promotion.'

'Why, for heaven's sake? We shall have a much larger appropriation now for the whole group.'

Stringer looked at Collins intently. 'We'd rather have you.'

'You've got me, Peter.'

'I mean we were about to offer you a directorship of the agency when your good news came through. We were pipped at the post by a couple of days.'

'But I'm a marketing man, Peter. I've had no agency experience except with you chaps.'

'It's marketing skills we need. No agency's complete these days without a marketing man at director level.'

'Are you sure about this, Peter? That it should be me?'

'Oh, it isn't just me, and it isn't just a whim. It was a board decision and we were even prepared to lose your account if you came to us and your people resented it. We should expect to pay you another thousand a year on top of whatever you're getting now, and a company car of course. A Rover, something in that bracket.'

'Can I think about it over the weekend?'

'Of course. You'll want to discuss it with your wife. If you've got any queries, contact me at home, I'll be there all the weekend.'

'I'm very flattered, Peter. And definitely interested.'

'I'll look forward to hearing from you.'

He took a week's holiday between leaving the foundry group and joining the agency and they motored up to Birmingham with Jimmy.

They stayed at a small commercial hotel in Erdington which pleased nobody except him, but her parents accepted that it would be cramped with the extra three of them in the small terraced house.

Mary had taken the boy to see Collins' mother the day after they arrived but Collins had avoided seeing his mother by using the excuse of going to say his goodbyes at the foundry. He found it irksome to have to spend time with his mother, and listen to her pathetic attempts to criticise what he said as if she still controlled his life as she had done in the old days. She was always amiable towards Mary and her grandson, but when Collins was there she did her best to make Mary seem like a fellow conspirator who shared the same critical attitude towards him. His independence, his soldiering and his business success were part of a man's world that couldn't see him for what he really was. A nonentity. A phoney.

He left it until the Thursday before he made his routine visit to his mother. He'd gone on his own with his son, and his mother had seemed strangely relaxed. They had had tea together and his mother had praised Mary's upbringing of the boy. He had told her briefly about his new job but she'd busied herself with Jimmy and had made no comment.

When she stood on the doorstep to see them off he thought he was imagining it when she seemed to look at him as if she knew something that he didn't know. Something that he wouldn't like.

When he got back to their hotel Mary was agitated. A man had called to see him. He had said he was an old friend from army days. A Lieutenant Colonel Fredericks, but he was wearing civilian clothes. He was calling back later, after dinner, about 9.30.

Fredericks arrived at 9.45 and Collins took him into the gloomy residents' lounge.

'What are you doing in Birmingham, Freddie?'

'I contacted your old firm because I was going to be in Birmingham. I thought you still lived here and it would be nice to see how you've turned out. They gave me your old home address and I called there and your mother told me you were here.'

'I was there this afternoon but she didn't mention that you'd called.'

Fredericks smiled. 'And how are you doing now you've shaken off the dust of Birmingham?'

'Not bad. I'm just changing jobs. Joining an advertising

agency. How about you? I gather you're a Colonel now.'

'Half-Colonel anyway. Oh, still jogging along. The army suited me and I seemed to suit them. So I stayed on.'

'How's the music?'

Fredericks laughed. 'What a memory. I go to the odd concert. Even started taking lessons on the flute. And you?'

Collins laughed. 'I'm on the committee of our local gramophone society. Even gave a talk in the winter programme on my favourite composer.'

'My, my. Progress indeed. And your favourite was Elgar, no doubt.'

'Delius, actually.'

Fredericks smiled. 'Same thing, almost. Good for you. I gather from your mother that you've got a son.'

'Yes. He's in bed now or you could see him.'

'I hope I didn't scare your wife. She seemed highly suspicious of strange men appearing from your past.'

'Our circle of friends doesn't rise to colonels.'

'I had an interesting chat with your mother about you.'

'She's not usually very talkative with strangers.'

Fredericks smiled. 'Lieutenant Colonels get the same respect that ladies like your mother have for doctors and dentists and chiropodists. Messengers from on high who don't really count as mortals and are not going to gossip to the neighbours.'

'What did she talk about?'

'Well the words were about you, and life, but she was talking about herself although she didn't know it.'

'What's that mean?'

'Hearing her talk about you explained so much of why you are what you are.' He paused and looked at Collins. 'You must have realised by now that she made you that way. She couldn't help it. And it took a lot of guts on her part.'

'How?'

'She's a Stoic, that woman. Resigned to her fate, but hating her resignation. And you were her fate. You were a man – and she obviously hates men, despises them. But you'd be wrong not to acknowledge her guts. Even if you are the victim.'

'She's just a working-class woman who got left in the lurch and blamed it on me. I've survived, Freddie. None of it matters any more. I escaped all that a long long time ago.'

Fredericks smiled. 'I doubt if you have escaped. I doubt if you ever will. You think you survived, because you've never tested yourself. You never reached out beyond what you knew you could do. You've always played safe.'

'Why should I take risks? I'm responsible for a wife and a child.'

'You're missing the point, David. Your mother made your son sound like an infant prodigy and your wife like a saint who'd come down on earth and been led astray by the devil himself. She never said one single word of praise about you. You don't exist so far as she is concerned. I wouldn't have mentioned it but I realise that you must be used to it. It won't be either a surprise or a disappointment. Like I said, it's what she is. What life has made her. I asked about your father and it was the same. A diatribe of criticism that added up to one thing: he was a man and men are God's curse on women. Unless they are doctors of course, or half-Colonels.'

Fredericks leaned forward and looked intently at Collins, his hand briefly touching his knee. 'It's sad, but it's a fact of life. But you've survived, my friend. And if you keep your courage you'll do much better than mere survival. You've got something. I'm not sure what it is. But it's there all right. Don't let that background get you down.'

'It doesn't matter to me, Freddie. It never did and it doesn't now.'

'Don't kid yourself, David. No man would escape unscathed from that influence. It's there, waiting to take over. Don't let it work.'

Collins shrugged. 'When I saw her this afternoon she

gave me an odd look. As if she were pleased about something. I'd assumed she'd just been putting down the poison with my wife.' He sighed. 'But it was with you. A fresh audience.'

Fredericks sighed and smiled. 'Let's forget it. Can we get a drink in this dump?'

For several days the things Fredericks had said drifted across Collins' thoughts, and then he dismissed them as the overheated, over-intellectual analysis of a humble woman by a man who had never done a day's work with his hands in all his life. Amateur psychology, instant diagnosis, and over-dramatic. Fredericks just didn't understand how working-class people lived.

It had been embarrassing giving his notice to Jimmy Hansen. Hansen had obviously been surprised and disappointed, but he had made no effort to persuade him to stay. And as he worked out his month's service Hansen had never spoken to him again apart from a brief 'Good luck' and a handshake on the Friday when he actually left.

For once, Mary had been neutral about the move, saying it was his decision. He was the bread-winner and it was up to him.

The challenge of the new job was enough in itself to decide him, but subconsciously he knew that he needed to get away from foundries to wider fields. He no longer belonged with the slow, cautious, traditional management routines of iron-foundries.

The transition to an advertising agency had more problems than he had expected. It was obvious that not everybody at the agency found him a welcome addition. Two senior men made it all too clear that they felt they had better claims to a seat on the board than any newcomer. Especially one whose only advertising experience was on the other side of the fence.

He was introduced to the more important clients but wasn't called on to give advice on any marketing problems they might have. He had an office and a secretary but nothing to do.

At the end of the first month Peter Stringer took him to lunch at a local restaurant in Victoria. He didn't keep to the normal ritual of waiting until the coffee before he discussed business.

'How are you getting on, David?'

'I'm not, I'm afraid. All I've done is read a lot of books on advertising and the trade magazines.' He grinned. 'None of our clients seem to have marketing problems.'

Stringer frowned. 'They do, by God, but there's a problem, David. Not you. It's the account executives and account directors. They don't want to let you near their clients in case you grab them.'

'How could I? And they're agency clients not personal clients surely?'

'That's how it's supposed to be but in agency life it isn't like that. Despite what everybody says, an account executive is judged by the number of accounts he handles successfully. If he loses one he goes down the ladder. Even if he loses it to someone inside the agency. We pretend that it isn't so, but in fact that's how it works.'

'But I don't come in on the advertising, I'm only concerned with marketing. I assist them. I couldn't handle an account if I got one.'

Stringer smiled. 'That's not true. You could handle an account more efficiently than most of them. You know more about the other side of the fence. Sometimes even the most experienced advertising men seem to think that clients advertise just for the hell of it. If the results are satisfactory they think they've done their stuff. The fact that it could be better doesn't concern them. They care more about the ads than the pay-off in sales and distribution. You've had to actually cope with those problems and you've got a good eye and a good mind in advertising terms. You've got a good instinct for what will work and what won't.'

'So what do I do?'

'I've got three small accounts for you to take over. One of them will never grow any bigger but it's a prestige name that gets us other accounts. One might grow a little, and the third could be very big if the right things were done.'

'What about the marketing?'

Stringer sighed and pulled a face. 'I guess we'll forget it. For the moment anyway. Bow to the storm, bend with the wind or whatever the appropriate phrase is. Time, and you being around and successful, can change things.'

'How?'

Stringer laughed. 'Thrusting account directors will look at your expanding accounts and lust after them and wonder if you shouldn't be spending your time on marketing and be ready to let you loose in their group of accounts. With your accounts becoming theirs of course.'

'A rather haphazard way to build up an agency.'

'To build up a business, yes. To build up an agency, no. It's the norm. You've got to remember that agencies are nearly always owned by three or four of the people who work in them. It's too risky a business for outsiders to put money in. And it means that agencies don't make book profits. Just that the chaps who own them live off the hog's back. Or fall off in some cases.'

'When can I take over the accounts?'

'When do you want to?'

'As soon as we get back to the office.'

'Good man. That's the spirit. I'll talk to the clients this afternoon and take you to see them myself as soon as I can arrange it.'

Chapter 10

ARTHUR BRYANT sat at the head of the table in the board-room, Harry Parsons on his right and the company's accountant, Vincent Hayles, on his left. Collins, Treadgold, Stringer and van Gelder were the only other directors.

Bryant pursed his lips and said, 'Right, Vincent, let's have your report.'

Hayles was a small, brisk man with glasses. He had only one sheet of paper in front of him.

'Right, Mr Chairman. It's not very different from last year. Turnover is up by ten per cent and you've made a trading loss of £7,431.'

And with that brief statement Vincent Hayles pushed his glasses back up his nose and sat back in his chair. For a moment his eyes caught Collins' eyes and he noted the surprise and horror on the new man's face.

Arthur Bryant seemed unperturbed. 'Any comments, gentlemen?'

Collins waited for someone else to speak but when no comment was forthcoming he said, 'Does that mean that we're insolvent?'

Bryant smiled. 'Under pressure, David, but not insolvent. Vincent and I will be making arrangements after this meeting to ease the situation.'

'But does this mean that our budget forecast hasn't been met or what?'

'It's not possible to budget in this kind of business. Too many unknowns. Too many intangibles.' He smiled. 'But we've been jogging along quite happily for twenty-three

77

years and I'm sure if you young men keep doing your stuff we shall be here for many years more.' He turned to look at Vincent Hayles. 'Right then, Vincent. Let's adjourn to the club.'

'I shall not be able to sign your accounts, Arthur, until the matter's been rectified.'

'Of course not.' He smiled his charming smile. 'Let's go and rectify it right now.'

David Collins sat for over an hour in his office after the meeting. Deeply disturbed and apprehensive. He had increased the billing of his three accounts by £50,000 in the last three months, so what would have been the agency's position without that increase, which they couldn't have expected?

When somebody knocked and the door opened it was Harry Parsons, group account director of the agency's largest group. He sat himself down at Collins' desk.

'What did you think of that little scenario down-stairs?'

'I find it hard to believe. It sounds crazy.'

'It may be crazy, but it's a fact. Mind you, it's not quite as bad as it looks.'

'Why not?'

'If you look down your sheet you'll see an item "Director's Loan £7,000". Sounds like one of the directors has lent the company seven thousand quid. But what it really means is that it's a loan *to* a director and the director owes the company that money.' Parsons laughed softly. 'And which director do you think it's likely to be?'

'I've no idea.'

'Our venerable chairman, Arthur Bryant. We usually have this little ritual at this time of the year. Bryant puts in the seven thousand quid four days before Vincent produces the accounts, and after the meeting and the accounts are signed, he draws it out again.'

'But that's virtually fiddling the books.'

'It's perfectly legal, my boy. They call it bed and break-fasting in the City. He's been doing it for years.' He paused. 'Maybe you didn't notice one other small thing. The accounts weren't signed when Vincent presented them and they weren't signed at the meeting.'

'So?'

Parsons laughed. 'Our Arthur was trying to pull a fast one this year. Not even going through the ritual of paying the money in then taking it out. And Vincent Hayles was letting him know that he won't sign the accounts until he coughs up.'

'Why did Bryant try to avoid it? It's only for a matter of days.'

'I'd guess his bank won't let him sign a cheque for that amount. Not even for a few days. They've probably threatened to bounce the cheque. He could snuff it in those four days and they'd never see a penny.'

'My God, what a set-up.'

Parsons smiled. 'Most small agencies are much the same. Even the fairly efficient ones barely make one per cent on their turnover. But they live in style all the same. The ones who own the shares do, anyway.'

'Is there anything we can do?'

'Not at the moment.' He stood up, smiling. 'We'll talk about it again some time. Not here.'

It was over nine months before Harry Parsons talked again about Bryant and the agency set-up. He and Collins had pitched for a new account together and were sharing a taxi back to the agency.

It was seven o'clock and the building was empty, and as they went up the stairs Parsons said, 'Are you in a hurry, David?'

'Not particularly.'

'Let's go in my office.'

In Parsons' office was all the evidence of an efficient administrator. Files laid out neatly on a side table, charts and lists pinned up on a cork panel along the length of one wall, and a clear desk-top.

As Collins sat down Parsons said, 'What I'm going to say is completely confidential. Is that understood?'

'Yes. If that's what you want.'

'You don't mention any of it to anybody. Agreed?'

'Yes.'

Parsons sat down behind his desk. 'You've been here for over a year now. What do you think of the outfit?'

'Creatively not too bad. A bit unimaginative but so are our clients. Administratively terrible. Atmosphere reasonable. I guess that's about it.'

'How much business are you handling now?'

'Just short of £250,000 gross.'

'And how much are you making now?'

'Four thousand and the car, and my pension.'

'Are you satisfied with that?'

'It's not bad for my age.'

'I asked you if you were satisfied with it.'

'More or less.'

'And the job? Are you satisfied with that?'

'For the moment I am.'

'You're wasting your time doing account work.'

'Why do you say that? I'm getting the business. More than the others.'

'Account executives are ten a penny. You're an ideas man and they're harder to find. Good ones, anyway. You should stick to creative work.'

'I wouldn't make as much.'

'Not at first, but you'd make a hell of a lot more after a year or two when you'd built up a name.'

'What's this all about, Harry?'

Parsons settled back in his chair and looked at Collins. 'I'm going to set up my own agency. I'd like you to come with me.'

'Tell me more.'

'Are you interested?'

'Interested enough to want to know more.'

'I've got capital available. Some mine, most of it from a merchant bank. You're the first person I've asked, but I've got others in mind for other functions. If you join me right at the start, you put in a thousand quid and get ten per cent of the equity which will be worth six times what you've paid on day one.' Parsons smiled. 'We'd be the founding fathers.'

'What would my work be?'

'You'd be a director on the main board and you'd be the creative director, picking your own team.'

'Do I have to bring my accounts with me?'

'No. You don't *have* to. But it would help if you did.'

'Who are the others?'

'There's only one you already know. I'll tell you who I've got in mind if you say you'll join me.'

'How long do I have to think about it?'

'I want to know in principle right now. If you say no I rely on you to forget our whole conversation.'

'OK. In principle I'll join you.'

Parsons smiled. 'Good man. It's going to be nothing like this dump. We're going to be small, creative, and bloody good. And we'll make a pile, David. We really will. Is there anything else you want to know?'

'When are you going to do this?'

'I'll be leaving in two months' time. If you join me I'll want you to hang on here for two more months to keep an eye on things for me.'

'Have you got premises?'

'I've got an option on a place just off Chester Square. A nice small house. It'll be too small in three years if all goes to plan.'

'What would my salary be if I joined you?'

'No more than you're getting now. But you'd get ten per cent of the profits as a bonus, and ten per cent of distributed profits as a shareholder. It would be the same for all of us. It's going to be run on a shoe-string, David. Even when we're making big profits we're going to have minimum staff, but all top-flight guys. No passengers. And no fancy premises. We'll have to put some profits back in the business but what we make we take home, not put into ankle-deep carpets and fancy furniture. And those who come in at the start will be the ones who get the big rewards as we grow.'

'You seem very sure of it all, Harry.'

'I am. I was planning it long before you came here. Learning here how not to do it. I've got it all worked out to the last drawing pin.'

Collins smiled. 'I'll tell you tomorrow, Harry, what I think.'

'OK. But either way, don't talk.'

'Goodnight.'

'Cheers.'

For several moments Collins stood on the landing out-side Parsons' office, then he turned and walked back in again. Parsons was dialling a number and hung up as Collins walked in.

'What is it, David?'

'I don't need to wait, Harry. I'll join you.'

Parsons sighed, smiling. 'Fantastic. I'm delighted. Let's go and have a drink on it.'

As Collins drove up the hill from Putney Bridge he won-dered if it was the single whisky or the new horizons that made him feel so elated.

At the roundabout he drove on to the Common and stopped the car. Parsons was in his late forties and he'd been in advertising since he left university. A two-year stint at Proctor and Gamble and then two or three top agencies. It was Stringer who had lured him to the small agency in the hope of making it more successful, but nobody was going to alter the easy-going agency routine while Arthur Bryant was chairman.

There was a lot to learn from Arthur Bryant. He was completely phoney, pseudo upper-class, elegant, member of three good clubs, MCC tie, hand-made shirts and shoes, and he hadn't got two ha'pennies to rub together. But he was one of the best front-men in the business. He had a solemn, strong face, the kind they cast for tycoons on TV, his black hair greying at the temples, his big eyes expressive; and his manner spoke of old money and current wisdom. Clients rose to him like starving fishes, taking the bait and counting themselves lucky to have such a man's agency actually willing to advise them. His only other virtue was that he was a good picker of men to do the actual work for him.

Stringer was roughly the same age as Bryant but he was a first-class advertising man. Originally a copywriter, he had made his way through several good agencies until Arthur Bryant had lured him across with the managing directorship ten years ago. It was Stringer who had kept the agency together while Bryant plundered it. They were both too old to change and both too old to move elsewhere.

Carter, the copy chief, was the only really creative man on the staff. The two studio men were competent, plodding graphics men bored by years of four-inch adapts.

It was certainly going to be exciting and Collins had an instinct that any agency controlled by Parsons would be a winner. Parsons seemed to know exactly what he wanted and who he wanted, and he'd mortgaged his house to make sure he kept control of the shares. That had apparently tipped the scales so far as the merchant bank was concerned. The bank were putting up far more money for only twenty-nine per cent of the equity. And the advertising account of one of the bank's principal clients was coming with them.

There were countless meetings after hours with Parsons, planning, budgeting and philosophising on the new agency's image and intentions. They got on well together but Collins recognised that Parsons was more ambitious for money and prestige than he was. He counted it as an advantage. They made a good combination.

The two months went quickly but the two or three days before Parsons was to put in his resignation seemed interminable.

Parsons broke his news just before lunch-time and the raised voices from the boardroom alerted the staff. Long before the official note was pinned on the notice board everybody knew what had happened. Bryant went up with Parsons to his office and watched as Parsons emptied his desk of personal things and handed over the keys of the offices and his company car. There was to be no working-out of his notice.

Parsons had already arranged to meet Collins that evening. Despite his self-confidence he was strangely subdued.

'What was their reaction?'

Parsons shrugged. 'Bryant went berserk, called me a traitor, an ingrate and prophesied that I'd come to a bad end. Stringer was upset but polite and civilised. Asked me what accounts I'd be taking. That was about it.'

'Did you tell him?'

'Not all of them, but most of them. Those I've already got written agreements with.'

'What's made you so down?'

Parsons smiled ruefully. 'I don't really know. I guess it was an anti-climax. And Bryant standing there making sure I didn't pinch a pencil seemed a poor way to end a relationship. As if I'd committed a crime, not just decided to leave. It made it all seem rather tatty and undignified.'

'At least I'll know what to expect.'

'I doubt if they'll be as rough with you. I've been at the agency for nearly nine years and losing most of my accounts is going to hit them hard.'

'What are you doing this weekend?'

'A bit of work on our cash-flow with the guy from the merchant bank. He'll be on our board. A real go-getter and he'll bring in accounts too.'

'Call me if you want to talk. I'll be in most of the weekend.'

'What does Mary think about your move?'

'I haven't told her yet.'

'You haven't got cold feet, have you?'

'No. She leaves those sort of things to me.'

'My good lady thinks I'm crazy. Especially mortgaging the house after we'd struggled so hard to pay it off.'

'When do you want my cash?'

'As soon as it's convenient.'

'Let's meet on Tuesday night at the Grosvenor. I'll give it you then with the latest news from the agency.'

'OK. Let's do that.'

As Collins drove home he kept thinking of what he had said so glibly to Parsons – 'She leaves those sort of things to me.' It wasn't a lie but it wasn't the truth either. He and Mary seldom argued any more because they seldom spoke to each other. Not because of anger or conflict. Not even for the sake of peace. If he talked about his work she listened but never responded, looking at him sometimes as if he were a child prattling of childish things. They had settled down to a routine of two different lives. The house, the garden, their son were part of her domain. How he earned a living and his life at work were his concern alone. She neither encouraged nor discouraged, unless her indifference could be considered discouragement. They were polite to each other and most outsiders would have seen them as a conventional married couple: the man the bread-winner and the woman the home-maker. And the outsiders would not have been totally wrong. People from Alma Street were not given to analysing their marriages. You married and then you got on with it.

He felt guilty when five people were sacked from the agency because of the loss of Parsons' accounts but his guilt was assuaged by Arthur Bryant's behaviour. Ruthless with others he made no sacrifices himself. When he had suggested at the board meeting that all directors took a fifteen per cent cut in their salaries Stringer had asked if the Chairman too was taking a cut, and Bryant had walked out angrily from the meeting, pointing out on the way that he was the major shareholder. Staff morale was desperately low and he felt frustrated that no effort was made to boost it. Collins could have done it easily himself but it seemed hypocritical in view of what he intended to do.

Bryant offered him an additional shareholding if he would sign a three-year contract and he had said evasively that he would think about it. A piece had already appeared in *Ad Weekly* that Parsons was forming his own agency and some of its accounts were named.

Bryant was away the day he resigned and he went into Stringer's office dreading a scene. But Stringer just sat there behind his desk. Reaching for his pipe then putting it down again.

'I suppose we ought to have expected it, David. Are you joining Harry Parsons' lot?'

'Yes.'

'What accounts are you taking with you, may I ask?'

'All, except the three you originally gave me.'

Stringer smiled wryly as he looked towards the window. 'You know this will finish this agency?'

'I hope it won't, Peter. If there's anything I could do to help . . .'

Stringer looked back at him. 'Forget this place, David. Just think of it kindly sometimes in the future as the place that gave you a start. I suggest you clear out your desk and go. That seems to be company policy these days. Leave your keys with my girl.' Stringer stood up and held out his hand. 'Best of luck, my boy. I'm sure you'll do well.'

'Thanks for being so decent about it.'

'It's just one of those things. Part of agency life. We should have altered our ways, and we ought to have looked after you better. Both of you. But you know how it is here. Remember that in your new outfit. Keep showing you love them and they'll stay.'

Chapter 11

THEY OFTEN worked through the night for the first six months and at the end they had a billing that would be over two million at an annual rate. But despite the grindingly long hours Collins loved every minute of it. All studio work went outside and he wrote the copy himself. Parsons looked after all their client contact and administration and they seldom saw each other until after closing time. They had one secretary between them and they didn't discuss taking on extra people until they were becoming inefficient despite their long hours.

Carter was their first hiring and he came to them from their old agency where he had been senior copywriter. He now worked under Collins and looked after print and production as well as writing copy.

At the end of the first year their turnover was over three million and they had made a clear net profit after tax of £57,000. Collins' salary had been increased to £7,000 and he'd had a bonus of £4,000. But what pleased him most was winning an award from the Creative Circle for one of his major campaigns.

His home life seemed more settled. Mary spent a lot of time with Jimmy at her parents' in Birmingham. And she seemed less critical of him, more relaxed, more happy-go-lucky. Most weekends they were away. She had her own car now and seemed to enjoy the independence it gave her. When she was away he worked on Saturdays at the office and Harry Parsons was there too, more often than not. He had no children and his wife generally came with him, shopping in the morning and the three of them lunching together at midday. Collins had spent one week-end with Mary and the boy at the Parsons' house in St Albans.

It was much bigger than their house. Five bedrooms, a three-car garage and an acre of garden. They had really bothered with Mary and Jimmy and he had never felt so pleased with life as he did at that moment.

As he drove them back home on the Sunday evening he said quietly, 'We'll have a house like that before long, Mary. Maybe next year if it all goes well.'

'I'm quite happy where we are.'

'But you liked that house. There's room and space and . . .'

'They're snobs, David. You don't need me to tell you that.'

'For Christ's sake. I thought you enjoyed yourself. How do you make out they're snobs?'

'Don't lose your temper. And don't shout.'

'So how are they snobs?'

'The velvet smoking jacket. All that twaddle about wine. The gardener and the daily-help. The swimming pool. All of it.'

'What's wrong with any of that for God's sake?'

'Why have a home so big you need other people to do the work for you?'

There was no point in arguing about it. She wouldn't ever understand that other people wanted different things out of life. And at least she hadn't said anything offensive to them while she was there.

By the third year they were a well-established agency with a turnover of fifteen million and a creative reputation that was reflected in the framed awards in the foyer. The average agency was making one per cent on its turnover and they were well over three per cent, with all the perks accounted for.

David Collins' talent as creative director had played a major part in getting them household-name accounts. He gave talks at Institute meetings and was constantly featured in the trade press.

They heard that the old agency had been bought up by a more successful but equally ageing one and then the two of them had been taken over by a large agency looking for the few plum accounts and their tax losses.

Harry Parsons, despite his new wealth, still worked as hard and effectively as when they were first starting up. He had created a stir in advertising circles when he actually resigned two major accounts on the grounds that although they were big they were still unprofitable. There was a staff of forty, every one of them hand-picked and top of their respective leagues. There were still no passengers. Just a little waste, but it was eliminated as soon as it was recognised. Their staff were constantly approached by other agencies but the existing financial rewards and working atmosphere ensured that there were few recruits elsewhere. When anyone left they were treated like good friends and sent happily on their way with a strong feeling that they might be doing the wrong thing. Company policy laid down that nobody ever came back once they'd left.

After three years with Parsons and Collins any of their staff could walk into any other agency and get almost whatever they asked. Few did and some of them regretted it; others made it to the top in their new agencies.

The relationship between Parsons and Collins was as friendly as it had always been but Parsons was indisputably the agency boss. Not solely because of his shareholding but because he was a natural leader. They argued as equals about the advertising itself but on other matters Parsons would listen but seldom change his mind.

David Collins was perfectly content with their relationship. He was a leader of creative people because his talent was obvious and undeniable, and the general running of the business and its finances he was happy to leave to Parsons. They had discussed it once over lunch.

'Let's talk about us for a few minutes, David.'

Collins smiled. 'I think we're great. Why talk about it?'

'Are you happy with things as they are?'

'You mean the creative team?'

'No. I mean the running of the agency.'

'Why? Is anything wrong?'

'Of course not. I'd have told you if there was. I mean the way we function. You and me. Do you mind that I control everything except the creative team?'

'No. Of course I don't. That's how we always planned it. It works well. Are you fed up with doing it?'

Parsons smiled. 'No. But I wouldn't want you to feel left out of things.'

'I like being left out of those sort of things, Harry. They bore me stiff.'

'Maybe they shouldn't. For your own good.'

'What the hell are you trying to tell me?'

'You may want to have your own outfit some day and you won't have had the management experience here that you'll need. Or you may want to change agencies and you'd be limited to only the creative side.'

'My God, you do look a long way ahead. Is this a sort of veiled criticism? Not pulling my weight and all that.'

Parsons laughed. 'You know me better than that. No, I just wanted to make sure you didn't mind the set-up and you were aware that in some ways it limits your experience. I just wanted to be fair, that's all.'

Collins reached out and touched Parsons' hand as it lay on the table holding the bill. 'You're a good man, Harry Parsons, and if you're taking advantage of me it suits me fine.'

'How's the family?'

'Mary's fine and Jimmy's doing well at school.'

'Let's go. I've got old Pringle coming in. Thinks he should run a Beauty Queen Competition.'

Collins smiled. 'He's just a dirty old man.'

Chapter 12

THERE WERE motes of dust in the slanting summer sunshine from the tall windows, and a streak of gold across the surface of the boardroom table. One tall window stood open, its net curtain lifting slightly from the gentle breeze. And the noise of the traffic from the street below came faintly into the room.

Harry Parsons was sitting at the head of the table. Tanned, with his smooth black hair and alert blue eyes, he had an air of authority despite his apparent inattention to what was going on. Harry Parsons always looked what the advertising magazines said he was – the successful agency chairman and majority stock-holder. Collins, on Parsons' left, sat with his arms on the table with the sleeves of his blue shirt rolled up to the elbows. His tie was pulled down from his collar and his cord slacks and desert boots were almost a uniform. He rolled a pencil back and forth across a clipboard as he listened to the younger man who was talking.

The young man was dressed in the dark formal suit that account executives wore as armour against the top executives and management of the clients who employed the agency. Ground between the agency's creative people, its financial controller and their clients' demands, accounts men were well-paid but insecure. Seen as no more than expensive messengers by their creative colleagues and as plausible con-men with large expense accounts by their client contacts. With his blue three-piece suit Peter Lloyd wore an MCC tie and neat black brogues, and in his late twenties he had one of those ruddy, well-scrubbed faces that belong to hearty beer drinkers.

Lloyd stopped speaking and turned his head as the door opened and a pretty girl came in with a wide tray set out with china tea things. As she put down the tray on the boardroom table Lloyd turned back to the others.

'But I have to deal with him and he's raising hell about the creative charges on the new campaign. We have to face the facts of life. It's a big account but he goes through every invoice himself. I haven't got a leg to stand on. They're fifteen per cent up on last time.'

Collins shook his head. 'Not true, Peter. I've checked them all through myself and the only item that's up is typesetting and that's his own doing. I've warned him, and you, a dozen times, that if he keeps making extensive alterations after typesetting it's going to mount up. He's altered every ad at least three times, and the brochures . . . well, I give up.'

'For God's sake, David. You don't imagine that clients are just going to follow some arbitrary rules laid down by the agency?'

Collins looked across at the young man. 'Let me tell you the facts of life just one more time, Peter. Clients can make all the copy changes they like at typescript stage. No charge at all. But if they sign copy as OK and then when it's been set they make alterations, they've got to pay for them. It costs three bloody shillings to take out or put in a comma. They're not our charges. We make nothing out of them. And they are costed at standard federation rates. We just pass on the charges.

'It's up to the account executive – you – to stop him wasting his money. Warn him at the time.'

Peter Lloyd jabbed a stubby finger at Collins. 'D'you know why we're not making a profit on this account, David?'

Collins nodded. 'Yes . . . I'll . . .'

The girl's voice cut across what he was saying as she

stood there, her face flushed with anger as she looked at Lloyd.

'It's because you haven't got the guts ever to say no to a client. That's why.'

As the three men looked at her she looked at Collins and said, 'I'm sorry,' and turned and swept out of the room.

'Well, really,' spluttered Lloyd. 'Even the damned secretaries join in. This is more like . . .'

'Be quiet, Lloyd.' And Parsons' voice from the head of the table barely concealed his anger. 'You're letting your client waste his money. You tell Hopkins that alterations at typescript cost nothing and that's the time to make them. If he wants to alter after setting that's his privilege. But he has to pay for it. OK?'

Lloyd sighed extravagantly and leaned back. 'Yes, sir,' he said, with an air of martyrdom.

Parsons looked at Collins. 'You'd better check that Hopkins had the usual copy of our conditions of business when we started, David.'

'I've already checked. He did and he signed them.' Collins turned to look at Lloyd. 'I know he's a bastard, Peter, but he's either got to pay or stick to the rules. Everybody else does.'

'His secretary told me in strict confidence that he's been having talks with two other agencies about his new-product advertising.'

Collins smiled, looked at Parsons and then back at the young man. 'For God's sake, Peter. That's the oldest dodge in the book. He'll have told her to tell you. D'you want *me* to talk to him about the charges?'

Lloyd looked relieved. 'That would help a lot.'

The meeting ended ten minutes later. Parsons was obviously thinking of other things. When the two men stood up to leave Parsons said, 'Hang on, David. I want a word with you.'

As Collins sat back again Parsons pushed the papers in front of him to one side.

'We'll have to get rid of Lloyd, you know. He's just weak.'

'He's very young, Harry.'

'OK. So he's weak and young. He's no good to us. You'd better keep an eye on him until I've found a replacement.'

'OK. I'll do that.'

Parsons smiled. 'I had a call from Sellars just before lunch. We've got the account from January one. There's a confirmation coming by hand this afternoon. Well done.'

'Thanks. That gives us four months to get it on the road. I'm going to need extra studio staff.'

'That's up to you. Or you can put work out.'

As Collins gathered up his papers Parsons said, 'When are you going to do something about your girl?'

'I'm sorry about that.' Collins smiled. 'Must be the heat. Anyway I'll tick her off.'

'That wasn't what I meant.'

'I'm sorry, I don't understand.'

'You don't have to pretend with me, you know. We're mates.'

Collins gave a puzzled smile. 'What else has she been up to?'

'You really don't know?'

'No. I assure you I don't. What's she done?'

'How long has she been working for you?'

'Three months, maybe four. I don't remember exactly.'

Parsons' pale blue eyes watched Collins' face intently.

'She's in love with you, David. I'd say she has been from the day she started.'

'With me? For God's sake I'm almost old enough to be her father. She's got dozens of boyfriends.'

'Maybe. She's very attractive. But she's in love with you all the same. You must be the only one in the agency who doesn't know it.'

'You mean that she's told people that she's in love with me?'

'Not so far as I know. She doesn't need to. Why do you think we had that little explosion at tea-time?'

94

'Because she heard Lloyd talking nonsense and it got her worked up.'

Parsons smiled. 'How old are you now, David?'

'Thirty-seven.'

'Well, you know a lot about advertising, but you don't know much about pretty girls. Pretty girls don't give a damn about office politics. That little outburst was the tigress defending her young. You.'

'You're kidding.'

'Maybe. Anyway, bear in mind that I might be right.'

Collins nodded. 'OK, Harry.'

There was a note on top of the two files on his desk. Neatly typed, and held in place by a Mars Bar.

Dear David,

   I waited on until half past six but have to leave now as I'm going to the Albert Hall. My apologies for the vapours, but he *is* a moral coward.

   You need the two files I've put on your desk for your first meeting tomorrow morning with the film people. I've told Powell to be available and I've briefed him.

   You didn't have any lunch, so eat the Mars Bar before you go home.

   Sally

He sat for a few moments at his desk, and then walked into the girl's small office and opened the bottom drawer of the white filing cabinet. He looked through the buff file-covers until he came to M. He checked the card and did some mental arithmetic. Sally Major was eighteen. And she had been working for him for six months.

He walked round to Chester Square for his car, and as he drove towards Chelsea Bridge he thought about the girl. He had always been aware that she was very pretty and that she had long legs and nice breasts but he couldn't, even now, remember any details of her features. He had always seen her as a whole. A pretty girl who happened to be his secretary. He knew that she had a number of boyfriends and several times he had given her the double-tickets for film premières that were sent to him. If what Parsons had said was true, he'd have to find some tactful way to get her transferred. In the meantime, was it better to be particularly nice or particularly aloof? There would be no more dictating letters after the others had gone, and he would leave her out of the creative sessions from now on. By the time he was crossing Clapham Common his mind was on Lloyd, wondering how a man like that had ever got into advertising.

The film director niggled his way through the story-board, frame by frame, obviously hoping that Collins would settle for one of the production company's standard jobs with new copy and a different voice-over. It had taken two hours and a lot of restraint to convince him that the agency actually intended to have exactly what they wanted.

A meeting with the agency print-buyer was followed by half a dozen phone calls, and then he had used the boardroom for a routine creative meeting. They were sitting around the coffee table in the leather armchairs when Sally Major came in with her notebook. Collins said, 'We shan't be needing you, Sally. There's no need for notes.' And he turned back to the layouts on the table. He heard the door close quietly and then looked up as he sensed the silence in the room. It was Trevor Amis, a senior copywriter who looked back at him, eyebrows raised.

'A bit rough wasn't it, David?'

'What was?'

'Sending Sally off with a flea in her ear.'

'She made a scene in a meeting yesterday. I wanted her to get the message that I didn't approve.'

'What happened?'

'She was offensive to Lloyd.'

'For Christ's sake, we're all offensive to Lloyd. He asks for it.'

'Maybe, but secretaries can't join in, especially in front of Parsons.'

'She likes being in on these sessions, you know.'

'Too bad.'

'OK.' He shrugged. 'You're the boss.'

Collins broke up the meeting after half an hour. His mind wouldn't latch on to the discussion and he knew that he had behaved like a bully.

When he went back to his office there was a typed list of his afternoon appointments on his desk. He phoned his home but there was no answer and he went out for a sandwich and a coffee. He took a taxi to the photographic studio that was doing the shampoo pictures.

It took nearly an hour to check the set and the lighting, sketching out for the hairdresser what he wanted and arranging to be back at five o'clock for the shooting session.

Back at his office he checked the colour proofs of a brochure and dialled the numbers on his pad to return calls. When he buzzed the intercom for Sally to get him a cup of tea, there was no reply.

She came into his office half an hour later when he was talking on the phone and he waved her to the seat in front of his desk. When he hung up he said, 'Are you punishing me?'

She looked surprised. 'I don't understand.'

'No tea.'

She smiled. 'I had to go and see Mr Parsons.'

'Nasty?'

She shrugged. 'No. Not really. More a fatherly talk.'

'I see. I'm going to Jason Studios at five, you'd better come along and make notes. It's the shampoo ads.'

'OK. It's twenty to now.'

'Right, get your things and we'll go in my car.'

There was pandemonium at the studio. The model hadn't turned up and her agent wasn't answering the phone.

Collins was annoyed, and turned sharply to the photo-

97

grapher. 'Does she know where you are? Has she been to this studio before?'

'Yes, a couple of times.'

'Let's give her another half-hour. We can deal with the pack-shots while we're waiting.'

'I'd like to take a precaution.'

'What's that?'

'How about the hairdresser washes and sets your girl's hair?'

He was looking at Sally Major and David Collins turned to look too. She had long, blonde hair, and it would do for the test shots.

'Would you mind, Sally?'

'No. It would be fun.'

The model's agent phoned ten minutes later, full of apologies that the girl had not turned up. He had only just heard from her. Her flat had been burgled and she was still with the police, and she was fully booked for the next ten days.

The black silk dress was too large for Sally, but they pulled it in with clothes pegs and clips at the back, and Collins stood watching as the photographer adjusted the silver umbrellas for the flash units. He used a couple of rolls in the Hasselblad and then abandoned it for the Nikon which seemed to put the girl more at ease. With a long flash cable and a motor-drive he walked around her, giving her instructions and making flattering comments as the flashes winked in unison. Eventually he had taken enough shots.

As the girl was escorted off the set by the assistant, Collins said, 'How was it?'

'Hard to say, David. She's very pretty but she ain't a model. But there's a couple of hundred shots and we might be lucky. We'll process them tonight and I'll send them round mid-morning.'

Collins waited for the girl to change and when she had signed the model releases he drove her to Victoria Station to catch her train.

He saw the folder of processed transparencies on his desk when he arrived the next morning but it was midday before he had time to look them over, lifting them to the light as he held them carefully by their edges.

The Hasselblad shots were hopeless. The big blue eyes looked out from a tense face. But the last four sheets of 35 mm Ektachromes were fine. She was better in some ways than the model would have been: she was the girl next door, natural, smiling, alive and pretty. The light from the umbrellas had left her shampooed blonde hair soft and loose. There were almost a couple of dozen they could choose from.

In the afternoon Collins called the first creative meeting on the airline campaign. Carter was the agency's top copy-writer and Wainwright was the art-director Collins had chosen for the account's creative team. They had only just begun when Parsons came into the room, keeping silent as he pulled up a chair. An account executive had not yet been assigned.

'Don't stop, please, gentlemen. I'm just an interested listener.' Parsons half-smiled at the looks of mild disbelief but he knew that the agency's creative people had a soft spot for him. They knew that he had been a copywriter himself in his early agency days, and he never stuck his oar in unless it was to help.

Collins looked at his two men. 'You've both seen the agency's own research. Any comments?'

Carter shrugged. 'It's no use to us, David. It's what you would expect from the questions they asked. They were all about check-in and cabin service. That's just a me-too approach and the check-in's not in their hands anyway.'

'I agree.' Collins looked at Wainwright. 'Any views, Tom?'

'I agree too, and the research company's suggestion about running another survey is crazy. Anybody who asks twenty thousand quid to find out if businessmen prefer pretty girls to plain ones must think the airline management are suckers.'

'Have either of you got any positive suggestions?'

Carter sighed. 'I suggest we use this meeting to kick it around a bit.'

Collins shook his head. 'Not necessary. I've worked out what we should do. What every passenger cares about is safety. Even the experienced ones. We can cover it indirectly. Big blow-ups of captains and navigators. Emphasising their experience and training. Give their backgrounds. Men with wives and kids, with a strong sense of responsibility, and just as safety conscious as the passengers. And some hard stuff about the aircraft they use.'

'It's a possible,' Carter said.

'It's more than possible. It's absolutely right.'

They all turned to look at Parsons as he spoke, and he went on, looking at Collins. 'Give it to them next week, David. They'll go for it. I'll come to the presentation myself.'

There was a rep from Artists' Partners waiting to see him in his office with the portfolio of a new photographer and a new, reasonably priced scraperboard artist.

Parsons walked back into Collins' office as the rep was leaving. He settled himself in the only armchair and waited until the man had left. Then he turned to look at Collins.

'Olby of Marshall's Foods has just phoned me. They're going to launch a salad dressing and they want our recommendations on TV. Olby said quite frankly he wondered if we have enough TV experience to handle it.'

'Do they mean media-buying experience or creative experience?'

'Both.'

'You'd better hire Jerry di Maggio for the media department, and I'd say we can convince him on the creative side.'

'You know how much di Maggio is asking? More than you get.'

Collins smiled. 'So we pay me more. TV's going to be

100

big, Harry. We've got to be in it seriously or all the big stuff will go to the American-owned agencies with TV experience in the States.'

'We've only got four clients at the moment who could seriously consider TV.'

'We'll get more. They'll all be in it in the end. They won't have any choice.'

'How do you get on with di Maggio?'

'I guess we'll fight but that's good for the client.'

'I'll think about it. How's Mary and the boy?'

'Fine. She's off to her mother's tomorrow.'

'You going too?'

'I may go at the weekend. But I'm very behind with my admin.'

Parsons stood up, looking at his watch. 'My God. It's seven already. We're off to see that new thing tonight. *Look Up in Anger* or whatever it's called. Don't hang about too long.'

'OK.'

Collins picked up the transparencies and walked down to the studio in the basement. There were no windows and he put on the main light, walked over to the long table and switched on the light-box. He held the cellophane sheets up to the ceiling light for a quick check and picked out the four good strips.

One by one he laid them on the light-box and swung over the magnifying glass. He marked eight shots with a chinagraph pencil and then moved back to the second sheet. She was more than just pretty: the big blue eyes, the full, soft mouth, and the neat pert nose, went together to make a whole that was maybe not beauty but . . . perhaps lovely was the word. And the photographer had smoothed Vaseline on her lips to give her a sexy look. He moved the magnifying glass along a couple of frames and the new camera angle emphasised the wide cleavage of the black dress, and her full breasts were half naked as she leaned forward. He had seen Sally every working day for months and had been aware that she was pretty, and aware too of the long slim legs and the full mounds that filled her sweaters, but he had looked at her without seeing. He wondered fleetingly, as he looked at the shot, if she slept with any of her boyfriends. And for a moment he thought of her naked. At eighteen, and so pretty; with those long legs and the large firm breasts she must drive them crazy.

He switched off the light-box, gathered up the sheets and went back to his office.

Chapter 13

THE NEXT week was one of those strange, magic weeks that
sometimes happen, when everything goes right. Clients
accepted new schemes, and the creative team burnished
basic ideas until they shone. And even the dullest market
research seemed to yield some creative approach. On the
Wednesday Collins led the team that pitched for a leading domestic-appliance account. There were two other
agencies in competition and by the Friday morning
Parsons had been told unofficially that the account was
theirs. It was worth nearly half a million.

On the Friday afternoon he took Sally to the studio
for the final shooting of the shampoo ads. And this
time neither the lights nor the big 10 x 8 camera
scared her. They sat around afterwards, waiting for
nearly an hour before the colour film was processed.
There were four perfect shots from the two dozen
takes. Collins finally decided on the one to be used and
phoned the blockmaker to send a messenger for the
transparency so that it could be worked on over the weekend.

As they stood in the cobbled mews outside the studio
he looked up at the summer sky, almost as if he were
saying a prayer, and then he turned and looked at the
girl.

'How about I treat you to dinner?' He saw her hesitate
and said quickly, 'How stupid of me. You've probably got
a date.'

'That doesn't matter.'

'What is it, then?'

She shook her head. 'Nothing.' She smiled up at him. 'Take me to eat.'

And there was some magic in the words that pleased him without knowing what it was.

'Do you need to go back to the office?'

'My weekend case is there.'

'We can get it after we've eaten.'

'Fine.'

He drove to the Hilton and they ate in the first-floor restaurant, and he noticed the men who turned their heads for another look at the girl. They talked shop for most of the time, and they were drinking their last cups of coffee when he remembered.

'By the way, you never told me what Parsons said to you.'

'No. I didn't.'

'What did he say?'

'He asked me not to tell you.'

'I see.'

She reached out and put her hand quickly on his as he reached for the bill.

'I'll tell you if you want to know.'

He shrugged, smiling. 'It's up to you.'

'He told me that he thought I was in love with you and that I could ruin your career. And he said your wife was a very good woman.'

'And what did you say?'

'I said I wasn't in love with you.'

He laughed. 'Good for you.'

There was a pause and then she said, 'I told him that I love you and that's a very different thing from being "in love".'

He looked across at the glowing face and sat silent for long moments. Then he said softly, 'What on earth makes you think that you love me? You don't know anything about me.'

It was a long time before she answered him, and her

heavily lidded eyes were looking at her coffee cup as she spoke.

'I don't really know. I just love you.' She looked up at his face. 'I admire you. The way you think. Your self-confidence.' Her lips trembled. 'Everything.'

'Why did Parsons feel you would ruin my career?'

She sighed and looked across the room. 'He said that I was young and sexually attractive, and that those were powerful weapons if I chose to use them on a man.' The blue eyes looked at him intently, and she said softly, '*Is* your wife a good woman?'

He frowned, shifting uneasily in his chair. Then he shrugged, not dismissively but in doubt. 'I don't really know what that means. She doesn't play around if that's what you mean.' He shrugged again. 'She's very straight-forward. Yes, I guess she's a good woman all right.'

The girl looked at his face, unsmiling. 'What do you talk about with her?'

'She's not a talkative sort of person. We talk about my son.' He leaned back in his chair. 'The usual family things.'

'Do you love her?'

'Of course. I've no reason not to.'

She looked across to the darkness of the restaurant windows, her teeth slowly moving on the softness of her full lower lip. When she looked back at him she smiled. 'Will you take me back to the office to pick up my case?'

'Sure.'

He looked at the bill and made out a cheque.

He pulled up his car just before the blue-painted office door and switched off the ignition. He turned to look at her: her face looked pale but beautiful in the light from the street. And it seemed a long time before his mouth was on hers. Her soft lips parted so that her teeth touched his for a moment and her arms went round him as his hand slid inside her light coat and closed over her breast. He moved his head back so that he could look at her face and her eyes were closed as his fingers explored the firm young flesh. When his hand slid under her sweater to cover the

105

warm mound she said softly, 'Let's go inside, David.'

They stopped at the first turn of the winding stairs and he pulled her to him. And there was no longer any doubt about what they were going to do.

On the top floor there was a small room that was sometimes used for private meetings and by directors or staff who needed to stay at the agency overnight. A divan, three armchairs and a coffee table. A few books on a shelf, and a small bathroom next door. There was a standard lamp with an old-fashioned pink shade and when she was naked it cast a soft pink glow over her. She stood there letting him look at her and a few moments later she lay beside him on the divan. He sat in silence looking at her body. The elegant neck, the full breasts, the flat belly, the long shapely legs and the golden fleece between her thighs. She lay with her eyes closed as his hand explored her, and her arms went round him lovingly as he lay between her legs.

It was almost one o'clock when he drove her to Victoria Station and she wouldn't let him check her trains or see her to the platform. She kissed him gently and then he watched her as she walked across the concourse to the indicator board.

He stopped his car half-way over Battersea Bridge and then turned on the deserted carriageway and headed northwards across the city. He was on the outskirts of Birmingham by three o'clock. He turned down the hill from the main road to Castle Bromwich, past the Dunlop factory and on to Salford Bridge. He stopped there at the traffic lights.

There was the short parade of tatty shops, looking even more neglected in the darkness, and the island in the middle of the road where he had stood as a boy to catch the Number 5 tram to school, and later, the tram that stopped outside the foundry when he first started work. In his memory it had always been raining and there had always been a cold wind blowing up from Slade Road.

He was startled by a tap on the car window beside him.

It was a policeman, bending down to look at him as he lowered the window.

'Anything the matter, sir?'

'No. Thank you.'

'You let the lights change twice without moving off.'

He laughed. 'I'm sorry. I was daydreaming about the days when the trams stopped here.'

'I think I know you don't I, sir? Isn't it David Collins?'

He peered up to look at the policeman's face. But he didn't recognise him. He saw the arm with the sergeant's stripes come up and the helmet come off.

'My God. It's Georgie Miles, isn't it?'

'It certainly is. What are you doing down in these parts?'

'Mary's been down here with my boy for a few days with her parents.'

'How is she?'

'She's fine. And your family?'

'So so. Kitty's still got her asthma. If you've got time perhaps you could come round and have a cuppa. She'd love to see you both again. She likes talking about the old days before the war.'

'Where are you now?'

'Still the same old place at Stockland Green.'

'I'd like to do that. I'd better get moving.'

'OK. But don't daydream down Slade Road. The road's up as usual by the railway bridge.'

He laughed. 'Thanks, George. See you.'

There were no houses with garages in Alma Street. They had been built before cars had been invented and there were still no more than half a dozen car owners in the couple of hundred households in the street. He glanced at number 27 as he cruised past and pulled up quietly at number 35. Number 27 had once been his home.

The low privet hedge was grey with dust from the factory chimneys and in the faint light of dawn he stood looking at the house. It was exactly the same as the house he had been brought up in. The solid front door with its two glass panels patterned with faded pink diamonds. The white

107

stone sill under the front window, and the window frames grained with a painter's comb to give them an appearance of solidity. Net curtains flanked by heavier curtains in plum, and in the centre of the window the china figure of a boy dangling a fishing rod into an empty glass bowl. It was always that or a plaster Alsatian. He could have walked into any house in the street blindfolded, and walked around without any trouble; their only variation was which side of the hall the stairs were on. Two up, two down, a scullery at the back and a toilet in the back garden.

He rapped softly twice on the glass door-panel and waited.

It was the old man who came to the door, breathing heavily. He was wearing an old woollen shirt and his gardening trousers.

'Ah, it's you, Dave. Come on in,' he whispered.

They sat drinking tea in the small back parlour, the old man full of his grandson's virtues. The watery eyes looked at him.

'There's a lot of you in him you know. I was telling our Mary. He ain't goin' ter be like us, just hanging about. He's goin' ter do something with his life, same as you have.'

It was five o'clock when he walked as quietly as he could up the steep, narrow stairs and slid into the old-fashioned, brass-knobbed bed alongside his sleeping wife.

Chapter 14

ALTHOUGH COLLINS and Sally made no elaborate attempts to conceal their association they saw no point in flaunting it. At work they maintained a businesslike relationship but they were seen by members of the staff in local restaurants and they frequently left the offices together in the evening. Attempts to probe for gossip by the other girls in the agency were ignored by her, and nobody made any comment on the situation to Collins.

Parsons was his usual mixture of boss and friend but he asked no questions of Collins and was polite to the girl.

For David Collins it was a period of happiness that seemed too good to be true. It wasn't just the lovely face and the exciting young body but the warmth and affection she so obviously had for him. She didn't want to change him, she didn't criticise him, and when their views on something were different it wasn't a challenge, or a confrontation.

When they had made love they talked and she plied him with questions about his childhood and his life before they met. She never mentioned his wife but he frequently talked about his son.

Sally Major came from a middle-class family. An only child and obviously much loved. Her father was a writer, a columnist for one of the serious Sundays and book-reviewer for a group of provincial newspapers. She went back to them at weekends when Collins was at home.

The agency still went on gaining more and more business, and his work load increased, but because of his new life his energies seemed renewed and his thinking even more positive and creative. One of the agency's strong points was the creative effort it put into even its smallest accounts. In most agencies they were left to the studio hacks with a few lines of copy pushed in at the last moment. But Collins made his team give them the same analysis and care that they gave to the household names. Several big accounts had come to them because of the work that had been done for the small accounts. Their typography, layout, photography and copy had frequently been featured in the trade press.

It was part of Parsons' skills that he was not only aware of the skill of the creative team but praised it and gave it his support. And the support was always practical. He was quite prepared to give up his own time to join the discussion of a small client's marketing and advertising problems and the clients appreciated it. It was after one of these minor creative meetings with a comparatively small account that Parsons asked Collins to stay on as the others left. When the door was finally closed he turned in his chair to face Collins.

'You know what you should do for that guy, David?'

'Tell me.'

'When you're doing the photography for that campaign, take duplicate shots in colour at our expense. Get colour prints done and do finished layouts for him. He can't afford it yet. But let him see what it could be like if he upped his appropriation a bit.'

Collins smiled. 'You're a wicked man, Harry. He won't rest until he's having four-colour ads once he's seen them.'

'Of course. He's got a nice little business. He'll take the layouts home to show his wife and she'll sell him.' For a moment he looked towards the open window and then he looked back at Collins.

'Don't jump down my throat, Dave. Just let me say my piece.' He paused. 'It's fairly obvious about you and Sally Major. I've no intention of commenting or interfering. It's not my business or the agency's business. All I want to say is – don't let her come to any harm. And don't come to any harm yourself.'

Collins looked back at him and said quietly, 'I won't, Harry.'

Parsons sighed. 'The trouble is that you're not cut out for that sort of caper, Davie.'

'It's not a caper, Harry. It's not a game.'

'Are you going to marry her?'

'We'll have to see. Was there anything else?'

'Don't be offended, you're both nice people. I just don't want you to get hurt. I mean that.'

'Thanks.' Collins stood up. 'Will you be at the airline meeting tomorrow? They're always impressed if you're there. Even if it's only ten minutes.'

'I'll come down just before lunch. Are you giving them lunch?'

Collins smiled. 'I still stick to the old rules, Harry. I've never given a client lunch. We're having sandwiches and beer in the boardroom.'

Parsons laughed. '*You* don't have to stick to the old rules. I don't. I couldn't get away with it these days.'

He told her about Parsons' comments that evening and she was amused. When he had finished he said, 'Why are you smiling?'

'He's a very shrewd man is Harry Parsons.'

'In what way?'

'He tells you to see that I don't come to any harm so that it looks as if he's a nice guy.'

'You're cynical, my love.'

She laughed softly. 'And you're romantic.' She looked at his face. 'Can I ask you something? Something very personal?'

'Of course.'

'Were you happily married before you had me?'

He smiled. 'You must be a mind-reader. I was thinking about that after Parsons spoke to me.'

111

'And what did you think?'

'It's hard to explain because it doesn't make sense.'

'Try.'

'You'll find it hard to believe, but until the last few months I had never, and I mean never, thought about whether I was happily married or not. Working-class people in those days got married and that was the end of it. The man earned the money and the woman looked after the house and the children. They just went on. You didn't ever sit down and think about whether you were happy or not. That would have been like digging up a tree to see if the roots were OK. You just plodded on and on.'

'And now you've thought about it what do you feel?'

He looked at her face. 'It's terribly unfair on Mary but it's been like coming out of a long dark tunnel into the sunshine, being with you.'

'Are you happy, David?'

'Unbelievably happy. But guilty as well.'

'She could have tried to make you happy.'

He smiled. 'Nobody ever told her how to do it. Or even that it was necessary. And I don't think I made her very happy either.'

'If she was loving she wouldn't have needed telling how to show it.'

'Let's forget it and enjoy being us.'

She smiled. 'I love you, Davie, but like your friend Parsons said – I don't want you to come to any harm.'

They had gone down to Marlow for a long weekend and were staying at the Compleat Angler. On the Sunday Collins hired a launch and they went up-river, through the lock at Temple and then tied up alongside the jetty in the pool above the weir.

It was late September and there were few boats on the Thames. Sally poured coffee for them both from the hotel's Thermos and as she leaned forward to hand it to him she put up her mouth, smiling, to be kissed. And after they had kissed, for a moment he rested his head against her shoulder and she touched his cheek with her hand, stroking it gently.

'What are you thinking about, David?'

'Just vague thoughts. Nothing special.' He leaned back to look at her face. 'Tell me again that you love me,' he said softly, and the girl was moved by the pleading in his eyes.

'Are you worrying about me again?'

He sighed. 'I love every minute I'm with you, Sally. But it's strange. When I'm happy I worry that maybe I ought not to be, because it's at your expense. When I'm unhappy I just worry about you anyway.'

'Don't let it spoil things for you, love. It just isn't necessary. We are both happy with one another. Just let it stay that way. You worry too much.'

'I dread anything going wrong that stops what we've got.'

'David. Look at me.' He put his head up to look at her face. 'You're supposed to be older than I am. But in some ways you're not. You're a child. You're terribly good at your job. But there are whole parts of being alive that you don't seem to know anything about.'

'Like what?'

She smiled. 'You don't understand about somebody loving you. I'm nearly nineteen. I love you and that's all there is to it. You seem to feel you have to deserve it or that there should be some sort of pay-off for me for loving you. Or a guarantee that I won't get hurt. Love isn't like that. Not real love.'

'Tell me what it's like.'

'Being "in-love" with someone is terribly intense, but it isn't loving. When you love someone you love them more than you love yourself. If one of you is going to get hurt you pray that it's you. I love you that way. Nothing will change it. If you decided that it had to end for some reason it wouldn't change it for me. I'd have to go on with my life but I wouldn't stop loving you.

113

'And you don't have to deserve it, my love. There was a time when I loved you and you didn't even know it. Just relax and be happy with me. Don't feel guilty that you sleep with me and like it. Just do it. Gather ye rosebuds while ye may.'

'What are you telling me?'

She smiled and shook her head slowly. 'You're incorrigible. God knows how they did it to you. I'm telling you that I love you. That I like loving you. That you deserve it. That the Good Lord will look after us.'

'Has Harry Parsons ever said any more to you about us?'

'No. Why should he? It's not his business.'

'He virtually owns the outfit we work for.'

She laughed softly. 'David Collins, you're an idiot. He wouldn't have taken you on at the start if he wasn't getting far more than his money's worth. He needs you just as much as you need him.

'He may seem terribly important to you. The tycoon and all that. But to me he's just one more man, who stares at my sweater just as other men do. Road-sweepers and brickies. If he said anything to me now I'd tell him to get stuffed. And he wouldn't do a thing. Believe me.'

He smiled. 'It must be wonderful to have everything sorted out like you have.'

She shrugged. 'Whoever made you the way you are never gave you a chance. Between one and another they've made you jump one bloody hurdle after another. And when you did it they didn't give you a prize or a round of applause, so you're never quite sure that you should have even been allowed into the gymkhana. Answer me something, little boy. How many people have told you that they love you?'

He sat in silence, looking across towards the island in the river and after a few minutes she said, softly, 'Tell me. How many?'

He looked back at her face. 'Just you, Sally. Nobody else. But I think a few people said they liked me.'

114

'Big deal. My God. Didn't it ever dawn on you that you were being short-changed by those bastards?'

'Which particular bastards have you got in mind?'

'All of them. Your mother and your wife for a start.'

'They're not like you, sweetie. They never had a chance. They're working-class people from harsh backgrounds.'

'What absolute bullshit. You don't have to be rich to be loving. I know dozens of working-class people who are just as loving as I am. You just picked duds. And I doubt if it was even that. It was they who picked you.' She sighed. 'Let's go back to the hotel and make love.'

'When can I see you next week?'

'Whenever you want.'

'If I found a room would you live there with me?'

'Yes. But you don't need to. If you pay Julie's half we can have my place. She wants a place of her own.'

'If I found an excuse to stay in town during the week and went home at weekends would that be OK with you?'

She nodded, smiling. 'I'd love it.'

Chapter 15

As HE closed the garage doors he looked up at the sky. There was a full moon and when the doors were closed he stood there, still gazing upwards. It was October and it was the Hunter's Moon, deep gold and low in the sky, and for a moment everything seemed to stop, and he felt that if only his mind could hold on to what he was thinking he could solve all the world's problems. Somebody called out 'Goodnight, David,' and he turned and saw that it was Hargreaves who lived just up the hill, walking his dog. He called back 'Goodnight,' and turned to walk down to the house.

As he put his key in the lock he saw a light from the sitting room and when he had closed the door behind him he walked through to switch off the light. Mary must have forgotten the reading lamp by the piano. As he reached out to turn off the switch a voice said, 'Don't switch it off.' He turned, and Mary was sitting there in her brown woollen dressing-gown.

'Why aren't you in bed?'

'I suppose like you that I've got other things to occupy my mind.'

'What does that mean?'

Her green eyes looked at his face intently as if she were looking at him for the first time ever. He stood there in his coat, cold despite the heating, because he had a premonition of what she was going to say.

'Don't you think you'd better sit down, David?'

'What is it, Mary? What's wrong?'

'You know what's wrong as well as I do. Why pretend?'
'So say what it is.'

She raised her eyebrows, smiling her contempt. 'You didn't finish the sentence, my dear. It goes, "So say what it is and get it over with."'

He reached out for the carved cigarette box, took a cigarette and felt in his pocket for his lighter. She sat waiting until he had lit his cigarette. When he had inhaled she said, 'I know about the girl.'

As he heard the words he tried not to shiver. He had sometimes vaguely imagined a confrontation, but he had only imagined the words. There had been no setting, no scenario. But now he was aware of the things in the room. The grand piano he had bought with a Christmas bonus and the gate-leg table that they had bought for £5 two years after the war. A framed print that he had once admired of trees and sunshine on snow, that he now found too trite for words, alongside a good reproduction of a Mondrian as if to make a point. There seemed nothing to say. Words formed and re-formed in his mind but none would come out.

'I said that I know about the girl.'

The aggression in her voice seemed to trigger a release, and for a moment it felt no more dangerous than a tricky meeting with a client.

He nodded. 'Yes, I heard you. Maybe you'd better expand your comment.'

'Don't be more childish than you can help. I'm talking about Sally Major. The girl you've been having an affair with. Or to be more precise, the girl you've been sleeping with.'

It was like in a dream where you jumped in slow motion across the chasm to escape your pursuers and you hung in mid-air, their hands reaching up to grab you in the moment before you woke. And you never knew whether they caught you or not. There was a chasm now between him and her. There was nothing to say. Nothing he could say. He had wanted time. Months not weeks, before he would know what he should do. Why, after all the months, should it be this day she chose? He heard his own voice, seemingly far away.

'I think this is something we should discuss some other time, Mary. It's very late, and we're both tired.'

She shook her head slowly. 'No. We'll talk about it now.'

He shrugged. 'OK. You talk.'

'You don't apologise, David? You don't feel a need to explain? To find some excuses?'

'Of course.' He paused and looked at her. 'How long have you known about this?'

'Two months.'

'I'm sorry that you had to . . . that I didn't . . .' He shrugged again, helplessly. 'You know what I mean. I should have told you.'

'Very few men tell their wives that they have found themselves a mistress.'

'She's not a mistress, Mary. She's just a young girl. We work together and we got to like each other. It grew out of that.'

'So now you have to decide.'

'What does that mean?'

'You and your kind of people know all about mistresses. I don't. So you have to choose.'

'I don't understand.'

'Oh, but you do, my dear. I'm telling you that you've got to decide between her and me.'

'You mean you want a divorce?'

'I'm asking you what you want.'

'Can I explain? Can I tell you about Sally?'

'I'm not interested in her or your stupid office romances. I want to know what you're going to do about me, and Jimmy.'

'Let's talk about us, then.'

'No. Let's talk about you. There is no us. There hasn't been for years. You were too busy making your so-called reputation. Like that piece about you in *Ad Weekly*.

"David Collins, the creative genius who put Parsons, Metcalf, Collins on the map. Who made TV commercials look like Fellini and Godard. The man who put the romance in tomato soup."'

'That was five years ago, Mary, when they printed that.'

'So?'

'You've remembered every word. You must really hate me.'

'What makes you say that?'

'You remember it word for word but you hate it because it praises me. You're angry that people think I'm good at my work.'

'Maybe I'm angry about your work. Or maybe I'm angry for what it has made you.'

'Go on. What has it made me?'

'A phoney. A man who wants to forget where he comes from. The place and the people. The creative genius who is only interested in the arts. Who has views on music, theatre, films. But not on the back streets of Birmingham. Who the hell do you think you are?'

'There's nothing to stop you being interested in those things.'

'Why should I be? I'm not running away from anything.'

'For God's sake! Neither am I. Those things interest me.'

She shrugged and said nothing. He leaned forward to look at her.

'Do you love me, Mary?'

'Love's a phoney word, David. And people who use it are phoney. Who knows what it means? But I've brought up our son. I've looked after our home. I've provided a background. I've not messed about with other men. I've kept my side of the bargain. I don't have to justify what I've done. It's you who have to do that.'

'Why do you think that I care about Sally?'

'Blonde hair, long legs and a big bust.'

'That's the best you can do?'

119

'I don't have to provide reasons for why you sleep with a teenage girl, surely.'

'What do you want? Tell me what *you* want to happen.'

'I didn't change anything, David. It's you who changed it all. I'm asking you. Do you want her or me?'

'You won't discuss how I feel?'

'How you feel is up to you. Like I said, it's for you to decide. It's your life.'

Collins sighed. 'I'm sorry about all this. It's my fault. I'll try and think it through in the next few days and then we can talk again. I'm sorry, Mary, I really am.'

'I want to know now, David,' she said quietly.

'But that's crazy. This is important for both of us. We can't decide this just off the cuff.'

'It isn't *me*, David. It's just you. I've had to live with this for two months. I want to know now.'

He looked at his watch. 'D'you know what time it is?'

'No.'

'It's half-past one in the morning.'

'You always told interviewers that you did your best thinking at night.'

'You'd better tell me what my choice is as you seem to have it all worked out.'

'If you want to continue your . . . relationship . . . with the girl then you won't expect our lives to go on as if nothing were happening.'

'You mean you want a divorce?'

She laughed sharply, with a quick intake of breath. 'No. I imagine that *you'll* want a divorce.'

For a few moments he sat in silence and almost without realising what he was saying he said, 'You mean either I finish with Sally or it's a divorce?'

'There isn't any alternative, David.'

'And you don't mind either way?'

'I married you. I've done nothing to disrupt our marriage. It's you who has opted out. You've had several months having your cake and eating it. Surely that's long enough.'

120

'But she cares about me. She loves me.'

Her eyebrows went up but she made no comment. He sighed deeply and stood up.

'Where's the dog?'

'In the kitchen.'

'I'll walk him round the block and try to clear my mind.'

'And you'll tell me your decision when you get back?'

Slowly he buttoned his coat. 'Yes,' he said grimly, 'if that's how it has to be.'

He walked through to the kitchen, and lifted the lead from the hook by the sink; the dog wagged its tail as he unlocked the kitchen door. He turned up his collar as he walked across the patio to the garden gate. There was the scent of lavender in the air and from the woods he heard the soft call of an owl. He latched the garden gate quietly behind him and as he walked up the hill the street lights went out and there was only the moonlight.

PART II

Chapter 16

AS HE turned the corner he looked at his watch. It was twenty past two. He had walked for only half an hour or so but it had seemed like a lifetime. Some instinct made him go to the front door. For a moment he stood there with his eyes closed. Then he opened them and pressed the bell. The hall lights came on and he saw her shadow on the leaded lights in the door. Then it opened and she was standing there. He looked at her face and said softly, 'I've decided to stay with you, Mary.'

As she stood there he realised for the first time for a long while that she was still very pretty. The green eyes, the black hair and the soft sensual mouth, but there was no smile, no pleasure at his decision.

He smiled wryly. 'Hadn't you better let me in?'

She stood to one side and as she closed the door she said, 'I'm surprised. I really am.'

'I'm sorry I've made such a mess of things. I was irresponsible.'

'D'you want a sandwich or something before you go to bed?'

He sighed. A deep sigh. 'Thanks. No, I don't think so. I'll be OK.'

'My parents are coming tomorrow for a couple of days, do you want me to put them off?'

'No. They'd be disappointed. Jimmy OK?'

'Yes.'

'Are you coming up?'

'I've got to do some things in the kitchen for tomorrow. I'll be up later.'

He feigned sleep as she switched out the light, and two hours later he slid out of bed, put on his dressing-gown and made his way downstairs.

Opening the curtains in the sitting room he poured himself a drink. It was already beginning to get light and he shivered as he looked around the room. He felt like a stranger. His mind hadn't been in this house for months. He hadn't belonged here. He put his glass on the low table and put his hands to his face. Sweat was pouring from his forehead and his body shook as if he had an ague. Never in his life had he felt so desperately unhappy and so confused.

He had tried so hard to think as he walked the streets with the dog, but it had been like some dream. Visions of a young girl naked, a small boy playing with his trains, trees waving and bowing in a wind, the orange glow of a tilting cupola and he had found himself crazily trying to decline *mensa*.

There was an oak bench under the trees on the hill, that had been donated by the Residents' Society and he had sat there in the darkness, his eyes closed, the dog lying patiently beside him. She had said he had to choose between them but there wasn't really a choice. If there were he would be on his way to the girl. He had no doubt about that. But he was married and he had a son and the responsibility was his because the fault was his. As Mary had said, she had done nothing to disrupt the marriage. It was he who had walked away, physically and mentally. And for what? Lust for a young girl's body and the self-indulgence of loving words and loving arms and eyes? It was inexcusable. And irresponsible. And the tears had been burning hot on his cheeks as he stood up and walked back to the house. At least she and Jimmy would be pleased.

He was asleep in the chair when she came down in the morning and she stood looking at his pale face as he slept, the sunken cheeks and the blue vein pulsing at his temple, the muscle quivering at the corner of his mouth. And she despised him. He was a fool. Blundering through people's lives, looking for praise for his talents, and those big brown eyes searching for a pat on the back, just like the dog's. He was pathetic, but she would make her own life now, and he could get on with his. He would throw himself into his work and she had no intention of joining him in his penance.

Half an hour later she shook him awake and pointed to the cup of coffee on the table. He had smiled as he woke and then she had seen his face grow old again as he realised where he was and what had happened.

Mary's father didn't like eating in the dining room so they ate in the kitchen and when Mary and her mother had taken Jimmy into the garden the old man sat stirring the sugar in his china mug. He looked at Collins.

'You done well for our Mary and the lad. It can't have been easy makin' your way in the world like you've done. But she won't ever let you down. You know that, son. She's a good solid lass, our Mary.'

'I'm sure she won't, dad.'

'And that boy of yours. He's gonna surprise us all. A lawyer or a doctor I shouldn't be surprised.'

Collins smiled. 'As long as he's happy, that's all that matters.'

'Are you happy, lad?'

'What made you ask that?'

'You seem kinda quiet. But we ain't seen you for a long time. Maybe it's just your way.' He grinned. 'You was quiet enough in the old days when you came courting our Mary. Couldn't get a word out of you.'

'How're the Villa going to do this season?' he said desperately to change the subject.

'I stopped going to see 'em. There's no characters in the game any more. Billie Walker would die laughing at these chaps tapping the ball about. Right Jessies the lot of 'em, if you ask me.'

'More tea?'

'Ah. I wouldn't mind a fill up if there's any in the pot. I saw your ma the other day. A lively woman that. Keeps herself to herself. Don't neighbour at all. But she's all there.' He paused, watching as Collins filled his mug. 'Ta, that's enough, lad.'

'I've got an early start at the office tomorrow morning so I'll be going up to London tonight. Stay as long as you want. Mary likes having you both here.'

'I hope they pay you overtime, boy. Here's mother and Mary.'

He had sent her a cryptic telegram and as he drove into London in the slow stream of cars returning from a day at the coast he tried to think again of how he could start and how he could go on. But he found no inspiration. He said to himself that the truth was enough and then realised that he didn't even know what the truth was. How could you explain a decision that wasn't what you wanted? How could you excuse a decision that wounded them both for no apparent prize beyond conformity and avoiding upheaval? Was it just cowardice? Using responsibility as an excuse to avoid disrupting his life. A mere acknowledgment that for him that dreadful cliché was true – you can't have your cake and eat it.

She was already in their room, putting flowers that she'd brought from home, in the vases they had bought in Portobello Market. But it wasn't a sign of confidence. She knew. He could see that in her face. It was pale, and her eyes were red from weeping.

As she looked at his face she said softly, 'She's found out, hasn't she?'

He nodded and her arms went round him, her face lifted to look at him. 'Don't be upset, my love. Don't be upset.'

'Oh, Sally. You don't understand.'

'I do, Davie. I do. She made you choose. Me or divorce.'

'How did you know?'

128

'I didn't know. But that's what that kind of woman always does.'

They sat down together on the edge of the bed and she took his hand in hers. 'It's best to stay with her, Davie.'

'Why?'

'If you leave it's irrevocable. There would be no going back. She wouldn't let you go back because she doesn't really want you. There'd be the divorce and all the usual shambles that goes with divorces. If you stay it doesn't have to be for ever. If it doesn't work out I'll still be around.'

'She made it a condition that I didn't see you.'

'Of course. I took that for granted. She enjoys being able to control your life and make it as dreary as her own.'

'If it was the other way around and you were my wife, what would you have done?'

'I'm sure that I'd have wondered how I'd failed. What I'd done to make it happen. And I'd wonder how to work it out so that you could be happy. Hopefully with me. If not . . .' she shrugged, '. . . then the other way.'

'I can't believe it, Sal. It's like a terrible dream. A nightmare.'

'We won't let it be like that, Davie.'

'We can't do anything about it.'

'We can. Let me tell you what we do. I've written out my notice for the office saying that I shan't be coming back because of family problems. I'm going back home for a few weeks before I look for another job. Wherever I am Julie will be able to contact me. You'll get on with your job. I meant what I said so many times. I'll always love you no matter what happens to both of us. You'll know that, and I'll know that. That can be our saving grace, our talisman.' She turned to open her handbag and took out a small box, handing it to him. 'I bought you a ring some weeks back. It was for your birthday but have it now.'

He opened the box and saw his initials – DC – on the boss of the ring and he turned to her clumsily, like a child, his head on her shoulder, sobbing as her hand gently stroked his head.

They made love that night, not sleeping, drinking coffee as she tried to help him fight off his depression. She made him go to the office early and tried not to linger as they kissed goodbye, aware of his haggard face and his trembling body as they clung to each other before he turned and went down the rickety stairs without looking back.

As he sat in his office in the empty building it was as if he'd never been there before. He hadn't been aware of it for months. The Monet print in its white frame, the outdated printers' calendar, the layouts tacked to the cork display board. Half a dozen postcards of foreign towns from holidaying staff and a neatly typed schedule of that week's meetings. Her initials – SM – at the foot of the page.

He put her letter of resignation on Harry Parsons' desk. They had both been at meetings all morning but Parsons' secretary had phoned him. Parsons suggested they had lunch together at the Mayfair.

He remembered the day he had gone there with Peter Stringer and he'd been offered his first agency job. It seemed a long time ago. It was six or seven years at least.

Parsons was already there and he'd been shown to his table.

'What'll you have, David?'

'A whisky. No water or ice.'

Parsons waited until the drinks had come and then lifting his glass he said, 'Cheers.'

'Cheers, Harry.'

As Parsons put down his glass he said, 'Does that note on my desk mean what I think it means?'

'Yes.'

'Your doing or hers?'

'Mine I suppose. But not my choice. It was that or a divorce.'

'I'm sorry. Very sorry. But I think you've made a wise decision.' He sighed. 'She was very pretty and it must have done your ego a lot of good, but divorces have a way of messing up careers and it would be a pity to throw up all that you've worked for.'

'Does that mean you'd have wanted me to leave if I'd gone for the divorce?'

'Of course not. But it puts a black mark on the sheet whichever way you look at it.'

'How does it do that?'

'It's a sign of instability. You get new pressures. Pressures from trying to support two families. Hassling with lawyers. I've seen it too many times not to know that it has an effect on a chap's capabilities.'

'What if he's actually happier from the change?'

Parsons shrugged. 'They never are, old scout. Especially if there's kids involved. Always the old guilt complex hanging over them. You can see them at weekends at the Science Museum and the Zoo. Guys on their own with a kid, trying to look like they're enjoying it, and both of them wishing it was over. Sunday fathers. Anyway, that doesn't apply. I'm just glad you played it down the middle.'

'Let's change the subject, Harry.'

'Right. Have you ever heard of Crombie, Swenson and Schultz?'

'The name rings a bell, what have they got?'

'They're not in London, they're a New York agency. I'm thinking of buying them or merging with them. I'd like you to look over the reports I've had and tell me what you think.'

'Are they in trouble?'

'No. Well, not financial trouble. But read the stuff and form your own opinion.'

He read the long reports on the New York agency all afternoon and took them home with him in the evening. As he put the car away in the garage and walked back to

131

the house he wondered what sort of reception he would get.

As he turned the key in the lock the house seemed strangely quiet. There was a note for him on the kitchen table. She had gone back to Birmingham with her parents for a few days. It could have been an office memo it was so formal and cold.

He poured himself a drink, switched on the standard lamp and finished reading the report. He looked at his watch as he closed the file and tossed it to the floor beside his chair. It was ten o'clock.

He walked round the house, standing in the doorway of every room, looking at it, its furnishings and its decorations, and then walked slowly back downstairs to the hall. As he pulled the front door to behind him he took a deep breath and walked slowly back to the garage.

He drove through the darkness oblivious of where he was going, his mind a blank, his driving automatic. He only stopped when he came to the promenade in front of the beaches at the coast. There were no other cars and he parked near a white wooden building with a sign that he couldn't read in the darkness. He had no idea where he was. He got out of the car, walked round the ornamental flowerbed and across to the railings. The tide was ebbing and he could hear the hiss of the receding waves on the shingle. Far out to sea he could just see the lights of a merchant ship, and as his eyes became accustomed to the darkness he could read the notice on the white building. It was the yacht club and he was in Bexhill-on-Sea. He'd brought Jimmy down here one weekend when Mary had gone to Birmingham. They'd played football on the beach and eaten at the restaurant in Battle on the way back. He turned impulsively and walked back to the car. All he could think of now was Sally Major.

Two hours later he drove into the garage and closing his eyes, he sat in the car and slept.

*   *   *

Parsons hung up the phone and looked at him. 'Why don't you take a few days off, David? You look done in.'

'I've read the report on the agency.'

'What do you think?'

'I was trying to work out why they were willing to sell. I don't understand the US tax system but they look financially sound. Too big a bank loan but that's probably to fund the new business. They've got more staff than we have to handle roughly the same amount of business but they supply research and we don't. If I had a criticism it would be that they're weak creatively. Their stuff is competent but uninspired. Always the easy way out. And that's why they lack a creative image. And the lack of image means that they only attract routine middle-of-the-road accounts.'

'Anything else?'

'Yes. Why do you want to buy them? They're not in our league.'

Parsons smiled. 'That's exactly why I want to take them over. They're financially sound and we could double their turnover very quickly. And their profitability is better than our own.'

'Why do they want to sell?'

'They don't. But one of the owners, Schultz, wants to because he wants to get out and start his own shop. The others are dithering. Would like a foot in Europe.' He laughed. 'But not half as much as I'd like a foot in New York.'

'What's your next move?'

'Oh, I'll let them simmer for a bit. If they come back for more I'd like you to go and look them over for me from a practical point of view. The nuts and bolts. You'll like New York. It's your kind of place. And it's people like you, the creative boys, who earn the real big money over there.'

'Sounds interesting.'

'How about that break? Just for a few days.'

'I'd rather plod on.'

133

'How were things at home? It can't be easy.'

'The house was empty when I got back. She'd gone to her mother's for a few days.'

'Come and stay with us until the weekend. Sarah would love it. Let me ring her now.'

Parsons reached for the phone and it was all fixed in a couple of minutes.

Sarah and Harry Parsons sat talking after Collins had gone to bed.

'What do you think, Sarah?'

'I think he's going to have a breakdown if he doesn't see a doctor. He looks at the end of his tether.'

'Let him sleep on in the morning and ring Fowler and ask him to pop in on his rounds.'

'Fancy just leaving him to go back to an empty house.'

'I doubt if it was done intentionally to hurt. She just lacks imagination. Remember what she was like when they stayed here that weekend. A frightful bore. But . . .' he shrugged '. . . the salt of the earth by some people's reckoning.'

'God knows how they picked each other.'

'I'd say she did the picking, in that quiet way of hers. And you can't blame her. He probably looked like all the other local kids. A little bit brighter than some maybe, but nothing more. She must feel that fate played her a dirty trick when she chose David Collins.'

'What do you think he saw in her?'

'If I was being brutally frank I'd say that he's pathologically insecure and she was the nearest lifeboat to hand. He never talks about his childhood. It's as if it never happened. His father died when he was a baby and he never mentions his mother.' He paused. 'But there's no denying that out of all that comes a real talent. He knows he's talented but somehow it doesn't give him security. He needs to be praised. And that's a weakness.'

'Will it affect his work?'

'I don't know. We'll have to wait and see. I hope not. I've got a lot of things planned for him in the next couple of years.'

She smiled. 'How long ahead do you work things out?'

'Four years. Five if I can. Anybody can plan for the next six months or a year and it doesn't mean a thing. Old Whiting our accountant was congratulating us the other day on being spot-on with our budget. I told him. It just means we were too unambitious when we made it. Budgets should be exceeded, not achieved. Let's go to bed. I've got a terrible day tomorrow.'

The doctor prescribed mild tranquillisers and Collins slept almost continuously for two days. Harry Parsons persuaded him to stay over the weekend and by the Saturday he seemed well under control. Ready to talk business with Parsons or music with Sarah. By the Monday as Parsons drove them back to London Collins seemed his old active self again.

Not even the cool reception that he got at home seemed to affect his new self-confidence. He merely wondered how he had found it tolerable all those years. There were no quarrels and they slept in separate beds. It seemed much like what he could remember of the boarding-house in Bedford when he was a youth. They no longer invited people to the house and most weekends he took Jimmy away. Staying at small country inns. Fishing inexpertly, walking over the countryside and reading in their room at night. Slowly his tenuous relationship with the boy improved, but at home the tension diluted their affection to a kind of arm's-length politeness when the boy's mother was around. There were few days when he didn't wonder how Sally was managing. And there were days when she was never out of his mind. Days when he could barely recall in the evening what he had done or said at the agency. Days when he was sorely tempted to ring her friend Julie, find where she was and go to her. But as time went by he wondered if she would feel the same. Perhaps she would reject him because he hadn't had the courage to leave Mary when given the choice. And gradually the little confidence that he had preserved in their relationship seeped away. He didn't deserve her love.

People at the office were obviously aware of what had happened but nobody referred to Sally's leaving. Parsons had given him his secretary and taken on a new girl. But as time went by Collins sensed a slight difference in the attitude of some of his creative people. Especially in Cooper, who was now his deputy. It showed in a tendency to argue with his instructions beyond mere creative differences. A slightly aggressive attitude in meetings, bordering on a rather childish belligerence. Thinking it was probably his imagination, he ignored it for several weeks until finally a particularly flagrant display of petulance made him send for Cooper after the meeting was over.

He felt a flash of anger as Cooper sat down facing him, eyebrows raised as he draped one arm over the back of the chair.

'Is something worrying you, Len?'

'Not that I know of.'

'You seem a bit belligerent in meetings these days. I thought something might be bugging you. If it is you'd better get it out.'

'Are you complaining about my work?'

'No. Your attitude.'

'Just your imagination, gaffer.'

'Don't call me gaffer. Especially when you don't mean it.'

Cooper grinned. 'Are you finished?'

'I don't like your attitude, Cooper. You'd better watch it.'

'You forget something, my friend. I'm an executive director of this company now. But maybe you've been too occupied to notice these last few months.'

'You'd better go, Cooper,' Collins said quietly.

Cooper stood up, grinning, and strolled slowly to the

136

door, where he turned and looked at Collins. 'You're losing your grip, sweetheart. It's you who should watch it.'

He phoned down to Parsons who said that he would be free in ten minutes.

He retailed what had happened to Parsons who sat silently until he had finished.

'He's been building up to this for some time, David.'

'You knew already?'

'I didn't know about his behaviour but he came to see me a couple of months back suggesting that he should take over the creative side completely.'

'On what grounds?'

'That most of the ideas were his and your mind was occupied elsewhere.'

'What did you say to that?'

'I told him that he was getting ideas above his station and that if you ever left I should bring in an outsider. And I told him that I'd never promote disloyal seconds-in-command. They wasted too much company time grinding axes.'

'Thanks.'

'Nothing to thank me for. He's a second-rater.'

'What do I do about him?'

'What do you want to do?'

'Put him in his place and keep him there.'

Parsons shook his head. 'A waste of time. You should sack him.'

'But he's a director.'

'So what? Directors aren't immune to reality. And he's not on the main board. It's just a courtesy title. Leave it to me. I'll sack him.'

Parsons reached for the phone and told his secretary that he wanted to see Cooper at six o'clock.

Chapter 17

As THE months went by he tried to discipline his mind not to think about her. What she was doing. How she was surviving. But there were times when he saw a girl in the street with long blonde hair, and was sure it was her, hurrying to catch up with her, until a strange face looked at him accusingly. When he was entirely alone he was tempted deliberately to think of her, to wallow in thoughts of the things that they had done and the gentle things she had said to him. And twice, when he had worked late at the office and he was mentally exhausted, he had suddenly found himself standing outside the building where their room had been.

Aware of how close he had been to a breakdown in those first few days he tried to keep all thoughts of the past out of his mind. If he thought about her too much he knew he would be finished.

The week he had spent in New York had charged his batteries as Parsons had intended it should, and when he met Collins in at Gatwick they had gone to the restaurant at the airport for a drink and a snack.

There had been greetings and messages from Parsons' contacts and friends in New York but Parsons was impatient to have Collins' views on the New York agency.

'Tell me what you thought of them, David.'

Collins smiled. 'Let me say that they're brighter and better than I had expected. It's a different market over there. Totally different. Easier in some ways because clients believe in advertising. They don't begrudge the money as our people do, they actually want to scrape up a few more dollars for their budget.

'You were right about being able to double their turn-over. I got them a new account while I was there. But there's one thing that's wrong. Do you know what it is?'

'Tell me.'

'Schultz. The guy who wants out. He's the best of the bunch. Without him they'd be in trouble inside a year.'

'He's the only one who actually wants to sell.'

'Too bad. If you want that outfit we've got to put together a package that keeps Schultz on the board full-time.'

'Why is he so important?'

Collins laughed. 'To use a terrible New York jargon word, he's multi-talented. He isn't creative but he's got an eye for recognising what will work. He's got contacts all over the city. And he's the best accounts director I've ever seen. I saw him in action half a dozen times.' Collins laughed. 'I could have stroked him he's so good.'

'Any thoughts on a package that would keep him?'

'Enough ideas to discuss.'

'I've promised to come up with a proposal during the next two months.'

Collins smiled. 'We don't need that long, Harry. I reckon we can thrash this out in a couple of days.'

'Come back to my place for the weekend.'

'I'm taking Jimmy to the Oval tomorrow.'

'Bring him back in the evening and stay with us overnight.'

'OK. He'd like that.'

They had all taken Jimmy to the early evening show of *633 Squadron* at the local cinema and treated him to eggs and chips on the way home. Sarah Parsons had tucked him into bed and left the two men alone in the study.

'Tell me what you've got in mind, David.'

'I think you've got to re-jig this whole deal. They know Schultz is restive but they don't do the right things to persuade him to stay. Offering him more money won't work. He wants to be independent with his own shop.'

'Surely he either goes and does his own thing or he stays. You can't have it both ways.'

'I think you can, Harry. They know they're on the skids right now. I think they'd all be happy to sell at a reasonable price. You could probably get control for less than we'd have had to pay Schultz.'

'And what do we do about Schultz?'

'You offer to fund him for his own agency. Take substantial equity in it and Schultz works for both outfits. With a stake in each that means both have to pay off if he wants to get rich. I think the offer would be enough. He wouldn't take it . . . but he'd feel satisfied because of the gesture. And I've told Schultz that it isn't as easy starting up on your own as it sounds. I think he's beginning to realise that. The banks aren't rushing to lend money to virtually unknown advertising men.'

'How much do you think we'd have to pay?'

Collins smiled. 'How much were you reckoning on paying Schultz?'

'Between ninety and a hundred grand for his third. Pounds.'

'In a lump sum?'

'He wouldn't do it any other way.'

'So we take half his shares, fifteen per cent. We pay him cash. We take eighteen per cent of the other two guys' shares which gives us control and they're paid over three or four years and given five-year service contracts at more than they get now.'

Parsons didn't look impressed. 'Any alternatives?'

'Sure. Let Schultz pull out and you buy up the other guys' shares for peanuts in a year's time. They won't make it without him.'

'I'll think about it. Maybe I should forget the whole idea.'

'I'd guess that with accounts of theirs who want to sell in Europe you could recoup the money in less than two years.'

Parsons shrugged. 'Maybe, but you have to find the money first.'

Chapter 18

HE WAS showing Jimmy how to hold a cricket bat and they were at the far end of the garden. It was the boy who heard her calling. She was standing by the open French windows pointing to the telephone on the small desk by the piano.

As he walked inside the room she put her hand over the mouthpiece. 'It's my father. Something's happened. Your mother had a heart attack. They took her to the hospital, but she didn't recover. He's in a callbox. He wants to know what to do.'

'Tell him I'm on my way. I'll get the car out. I'll contact you when I get there.'

'I'm sorry, David. She was a good woman.'

'I'd better get on my way. I'll call you later or tomorrow morning.'

It seemed strange in that house on his own. Smaller, even, than he remembered. His old room had long ago been cleared of furniture. Now there was just the worn linoleum and a bentwood chair.

It seemed unfair for him to be going through her belongings; it was as if he were taking advantage of her death. Her body was at the funeral parlour, the funeral arranged for the following morning. Mary's mother was going to gather up the cooking utensils, the carpet sweeper and the few vases and the kitchen clock.

He was going through the drawers of the big chest-of-drawers when he found it. Pushed to a back corner under a pair of corsets. The frame was silver, decorated with embossed roses and ribbons with a small hinged back to use for standing it or hanging on a wall. She had never shown it to him. It was a beautifully painted miniature portrait of a girl. Extraordinarily pretty, with her head to one side, her blue eyes smiling and her red lips curved in a smile. A mass of blonde hair down to her shoulders. The expression on her face was gentle, one elegant eyebrow slightly raised as if she was amused at being painted. As he held it in his hand he found it hard to believe that she had once looked like that. Young and pretty, and innocently aware of her attraction. He walked over to the bed and put it in his case.

Her sister and her husband were at the funeral. The Hawkinses and Mary and Jimmy. Both neighbours and three women whom he didn't recognise. The service had been short and simple and then they'd gone back to the Hawkinses' house for sandwiches and tea. Fish-paste, cucumber, tongue, and two plates of fancy cakes. Mary and Jimmy had stayed behind and he had driven back to London.

He stayed at the Dorchester for the night and dined alone in the restaurant. The orchestra was playing a selection from *West Side Story* and as he looked at the dancers it seemed a long way from the Masonic Hall and orangeade. He wondered what his mother had been like when the portrait was painted, and he wondered who had paid for it. She couldn't have afforded it and if she could she would never have dreamed of using money so profligately. Did she go to dances? Was that where she had met his father? He wondered who had loved whom and why.

He remembered a Christmas Day when her sister, Aunt Ada, had been visiting them. They had been sitting in the kitchen with port-wine and biscuits and he had heard Aunt Ada say, 'So why did you marry him?' and she'd said, 'He'd got such a beautiful voice.' Then they'd seen him at the door and he'd been bundled off to bed. It was a crazy answer and an even crazier reason, but it was romantic in its stupidity. There could be worse reasons for marrying

142

or falling for a man. He half-smiled to himself as he wished he could have known her in those days, before whatever it was that created such havoc in her personality. What was sad was that nothing would change his negative feelings, or lack of feeling, for her. It was there, immovably printed, having nothing to do with weighing her in the balance or passing judgment on her. They were simply part of his life.

He rang Parsons at his home to let him know he was back. Parsons went through the formalities of condolences and then said, 'Can I talk work just for a moment?'

'Yes, of course.'

'I've done the New York deal. Signed, sealed and paid.'

'Which way did you do it?'

'More or less your way. Schultz stays.'

'Congratulations, Harry. You must have grafted hard.'

'Congratulations to you too.'

'Good grief. What I saw anybody would have seen.'

'I didn't mean that.'

'What did you mean?'

'It's part of the deal that there is no president. Four vice-presidents. The three existing guys plus my nominee. I want you to take it.'

'You mean work in New York permanently?'

'I guess we'd allow you back here now and again, but, yes. Full-time vice-president.'

'How long have I got to think about it?'

'A couple of months at the outside.'

'It appeals to me, but as you can guess it's got a lot of problems attached to it.'

'You mean moving the family to the States?'

'Yes.'

'Well, think about it. Maybe there's some sweetener that we can conjure up to keep her happy.'

'Sure. Like taking Alma Street, Birmingham, lock, stock and barrel, and putting it on Madison Avenue.'

Parsons laughed. 'We'll talk about it tomorrow. Don't forget we're pitching for the paint account next week.'

'I won't. Goodnight.'

143

Chapter 19

PARSONS HAD bulldozed them into letting him choose where they came in the batting list for the presentation. There were three agencies pitching for the account and the presentations were to be made in the major suite at the Hilton. Parsons had opted to be last despite the fact that the panel would be tired from having had two agency presentations before them. He had warned the top brass of Imperial Paints Limited that their presentation would be a long one.

There were eleven top men from Imperial including their Chairman and their Chief Executive. They were ranged around the long table, jackets on the backs of their chairs and with the flushed-faced look of men who had been cooped up too long in one room.

Parsons was sedately dressed and he stood up slowly, brushing an imaginary speck from his jacket.

'Gentlemen. You've had a hard day today. We don't want to make it harder than it has to be. But we are – you are – deciding today the future of a long-established family firm in the paint business. Not just deciding who does your advertising. Because to move from your present share of the market to being one of the giants your choice of advertising consultants is vital. And that means that you are not looking for fancy layouts and a glib slogan but marketing thinking. Original thinking.

'You make first-class paints. So, at the last count, do at least one hundred and twenty other paint manufacturers. But your fine reputation is with architects, not with the general public. And as you know, gentlemen, you are

144

making less than one penny a gallon on your big contract sales. So we have seen it as our task to show you that you have a wonderful opportunity. You can either be the largest manufacturers of paints, in gallonage, in the United Kingdom. Or you could be one of the most profitable.

'So let me introduce my colleague, David Collins, who most of you already know personally or by reputation – David.'

Collins stood up slowly, looking at each man in turn around the table.

'Good afternoon, gentlemen. It is usual at this stage to show prospective clients a film illustrating agency staff, policy and achievements. And a list of impressive account names. What I am going to show you is a film about yourselves and your products – Joe.'

As Collins raised his hand the lights dimmed and the screen lit with the opening shot of the film. The camera moved from a shot of the factory, to rows of tins of paint, lingering on the names of the colours and their different finishes. Then a lorry, fully loaded as it drove out of the works' gates. Then the room lights came up. Collins was already standing in front of the microphone.

'Gentlemen. That lorry carried one thousand five hundred gallons of paint for a contract for one of the London boroughs. Your sales people fought hard for weeks to get it, and it took one production line in your works fourteen hours to produce it.' He paused. 'Your profit from that transaction was exactly six pounds five shillings net before tax.'

There was a stir around the table but Collins pressed on. 'In addition to the cash, you enhanced your company image by being specified for that contract by one of the finest architectural practices in the UK. The two companies who also competed for that contract because it specified "Imperial Paints Hi-Led or equivalent" would have made roughly the same profit. Perhaps a little less.

'So how do we cash in on your well-earned reputation with the professionals? – Joe.' The lights dimmed again and Collins went on. 'These are the ads that can do that for you. We have thought about them carefully – they will be displayed for only ten seconds each. Go ahead, Joe.'

A dozen advertisements appeared one after the other on the screen. Some in full colour, some black and white, some full pages and some quarter pages. Then Collins pressed the clicker. 'And this, gentlemen, is what every ad has as its basis. Watch the words carefully – "The home decorator uses Hi-Led because he doesn't know any better – architects specify it because they don't know any better either."'

The lights went up and Collins was aware of some smiles and nodding but he pressed on with the rest of his presentation and finally handed over to Parsons who stood up smiling.

'Gentlemen, I've taken the liberty, and it is a liberty, of taking the next fifteen minutes of our allotted time and handing it back to you. You need a stretch. I've arranged for a cold buffet in the adjoining suite. Please be our guests, but . . .' and he wagged his finger, smiling, 'strictly fifteen minutes, gentlemen, because we have a surprise for you. Thank you.'

It was obvious in the interval that they had done well and for a moment or so Collins wondered whether his final pitch might not be counter-productive. But Parsons brushed his doubts aside.

When they had re-assembled Collins started again and he had two long lines of empty tins of paint on the table in front of him. He looked up, smiling.

'I hope that I am not being presumptuous when I say that my impression is that some of you went along with the basic thinking behind our proposals. So I also hope I shall not be giving offence if I say that what I showed you is not what we advise you to do. You came to see the advertising approaches of three agencies. We showed you what we feel is a strong and creative platform for your advertising campaign . . . but we don't recommend you to use it.'

There were murmurs around the table and Collins waited for them to subside. 'I have representative examples of your product tins in front of me. You have nine different sizes of tin from five-gallon drums to pints. You have twenty-seven different colours on your colour-cards and every one of them can be supplied in three different finishes, gloss, matt and egg-shell.' He looked around the table. 'That's an awful lot of tins, gentlemen. Far too many. Too many colours in too many finishes. It means that you are borrowing money at high rates from the bank to maintain unnecessary stocks. Fourteen per cent of your total costs are for tins. Another ten per cent for financing stocks.' He opened an envelope and pulled out what looked like a string of rectangular plastic sausage cases. He held it up. 'Not sausages, gentlemen. But small plastic sachets of pigment. You manufacture white paint, the domestic user buys and mixes the colouring he wants, with infinite variation, and your cash-flow improves at a rate of roughly sixty per cent. Maybe a little more. You will appreciate . . .'

Curtis, Imperial's Chairman, held up his hand. 'You've made your point, Mr Collins.' He turned to Parsons. 'Mr Parsons, if you were told at the end of this presentation that your agency had our account, what would be the first thing that you would do?'

Parsons smiled. 'Sir, I should go downstairs to Trader Vic's and get smashed.'

There was a roar of laughter and Collins knew that Parsons' cheeky response had done its work. It was spontaneous, frank, flattering and unexpected. The Imperial account was worth at least £3,000,000 a year.

Two or three of Imperial's top men, including Curtis, had taken Parsons to one side and the others said their smiling goodbyes to Collins and his agency team.

He had booked himself a suite and took five or six of his team up to his rooms for a drink. An hour later Parsons joined them. They'd got the account with an increased expenditure.

147

It was eleven o'clock when he and Parsons were alone.

'You really impressed the bastards, Davie. Great work. Great thinking.' He looked at his watch. 'By God I must ring Sarah.'

Parsons spoke with bubbling enthusiasm to his wife for several minutes and when he hung up he turned grinning to Collins.

'She says congratulations to you and says I sound pissed.' He took a deep breath, still smiling. Then he stood up, slightly unsteadily, looking at Collins.

'How's your thinking going on New York?'

'I'm still thinking, Harry. I haven't made up my mind.'

'Don't take too long.' He looked at his watch. 'God. I'd better push off.'

Left alone at last Collins felt no euphoria about getting the account. The whole scenario seemed suddenly pathetic and tawdry. Those pompous idiots sitting in judgment at the table. His own words, carefully chosen and rehearsed to sound spontaneous. And Parsons' witty but spurious reply that had impressed them with its 'all boys together' frankness. No doubt that it was spontaneous but it was phoney as well. Parsons would no more get drunk because of landing an account than he would himself. Parsons was far more likely to sit working out how he could skin them for an even bigger appropriation.

So why was he doing all this? What did he get out of it? Parsons had phoned his Sarah, but if he phoned his own home Mary probably wouldn't be there. And if she was, she wouldn't give a damn how many accounts they'd got. It was time he sorted his bloody life out. Decided what the hell he did want. And, inevitably, he thought of Sally. He looked at his watch. It was nearly midnight. But despite that he took his diary from his pocket and reached for the phone. Twice he picked up the receiver and heard the dialling tone, and twice he let it slide back on to its plastic cradle. Maybe he was going crazy, and for the first time for years he thought of the time when his mother said he

148

would end up in an asylum. Despite the air-conditioning he was sweating as if he was in a Turkish bath.

He ran a bath and then slept. A deep, troubled sleep that left him lethargic and exhausted when he woke. As he got back into the routine of washing and shaving he began to feel calmer. As he dried his face he looked in the mirror. He hadn't noticed his face for months but it was different; thinner, with deep furrows from his nose to his mouth and his eyes looked hard and aggressive. Yet it was a mature man's face and despite the lines it was not a bad one. At least it looked lived-in.

He phoned Parsons at the office and told him that he would accept the New York job if the conditions were mutually satisfactory.

'They will be, David. Come in and we'll work it out together.'

'Let's make it tomorrow. I'm going home to break the good news to Mary.'

'She isn't going to like it, pal. That's for sure.'

'She can stay here, then. It's up to her.'

'Are you OK? You sound kind of worked-up or something.'

'I'm OK, Harry. See you tomorrow.'

Chapter 20

JIMMY WAS with his grandfather looking at the pigeons while Mary and her mother sat in state in the front room. The dust covers had been removed from the three-piece suite for the occasion.

'But a wife has to go where her husband goes. It even says that in the Bible, girl. If a man's job takes him somewhere then she has to follow him. It's the law, and anyway that's how it is.'

'Let me come and stay with you and dad.'

'Oh, we couldn't do that, love. It wouldn't be right. Defying him and all that. But you can come back for the holidays. Summer and Christmas.'

'He doesn't really care whether we go or not. It's just a formality. Just so that everything looks all right to the rest of the world.'

'And what's wrong with that, may I ask?'

'He's a hypocrite. Why should me and Jimmy have to do that just because it suits David?'

'That wasn't how you spoke, my girl, when you wanted to marry him. Are you tellin' me you don't care about him no more?'

Mary Collins looked at her mother, opened her mouth to speak, then turned away saying nothing. Between the two women the silence was enough. And the older woman appreciated that if that was how things were it was better not to say it aloud or even acknowledge it openly.

Mrs Hawkins said quietly, 'I'm sorry, girl, I really am.' She took a deep breath. 'But you should go with him.

150

Make a life for yourself with the boy. Don't throw everything away for the sake of showing your feelings. Better you put a good face on it. These things have a way of working out one way or another if you give 'em time.'

It angered her all the more that it was good advice and that she knew she had little choice. She had consulted a solicitor who had said there were no grounds for divorce. The adultery had been wiped out when he came back and she accepted him. She could refuse to go to America but a court could see her as being unreasonable if it ever became evidence.

When David had told her about the move she had given vent to her anger, using the excuse that she didn't want their son brought up in such a grasping, violent society. But her real reason was her impotence in the face of what other people saw as a wonderful opportunity. Their married life was a sham but her carefully contrived compromise had suited her and for it to be used to make her leave her roots and background had turned her neutrality into positive dislike. A dislike that bordered on hatred and a seething desire to wound in return.

At Heathrow he paid for his excess baggage and walked over to the Duty-Free shop with just his briefcase. As he handed his airline ticket to the girl on the check-out desk it came home to him what he was doing. It was a single ticket, London–New York. It wasn't a holiday trip or a business visit, it was a one-way ticket; he was going there to live.

Mary had said that she would come over when he had found them a place to live. She had insisted that it had to be outside New York and that seemed sensible enough. But it was going to take time. The pressures of his new job would take all his time and energy for the first few weeks.

151

Chapter 21

Jack Schultz called him at the Waldorf a few minutes after he had booked in.

'Welcome to New York, David. D'you have a good flight?'

'Thanks, Jack. Not bad. How about we have breakfast together tomorrow before we go to the office? We could have it in my room here.'

'OK. What time?'

'To suit you.'

'Seven o'clock OK? We open at eight usually.'

'See you at seven then.'

'Take care. Sleep well.'

As Collins hung up he looked around the hotel room. His cases were piled up on a slatted table and the maid had turned down the sheets on the bed. He didn't feel lonely but he suddenly felt unsure. Unsure because of the lack of real thought that he had given to his move to New York. He hadn't discussed the decision with Mary because it would have been pointless. Her attitude after he had told her had made that obvious. And alone, with no one to go over the pros and cons, he hadn't made a sensible analysis, he had just decided impulsively that he would do it. He had taken for granted that the talents he had would work just as well in New York but now he was actually there he felt less certain. There was a lot he would have to learn, and the others would be watching to see if he stumbled.

He took the elevator down to the lobby and walked through to the street. It was Sunday night but Park Avenue was crowded. He hesitated and then walked down to the Pan Am building and bought a paper, a couple of Ed McBain paperbacks and a street map. Back in his room the red light was on on the telephone and the operator gave him a number to call. It was Steve Crombie's number but there was only an answering machine responding.

Steve Crombie, one of the New York agency's directors, introduced Collins to the assembled staff. An embarrassing ten minutes as Crombie read out the advertising awards he had received and gave the names of the important international accounts that he had worked on. It was overdone, and Collins was aware of the resentment that would inevitably follow such a fulsome introduction.

There was an informal meeting in the conference room afterwards and Collins was at pains to establish that although it had been agreed that he would be in charge of all creative services, he would nevertheless be ready to accept comment and criticism from anybody who felt that he was not meeting local conditions.

Schultz had sat on with him after the meeting.

'Maybe you should have a quiet word with the appropriate people, Jack, and tone down any hard feelings there might be because of the intro.'

Schultz smiled. 'I'm glad you noticed. I should keep an eye on friend Crombie. That little speech was typical. Quietly digging a hole but not saying anything you could reasonably object to. Marvin Swenson hates his guts and I'm not exactly a fan myself.'

'Why doesn't he get on with Marvin?'

Schultz smiled. 'Marvin's got him marked down as the all-comers' asshole . . . thinks he's too ambitious for his talents and ready to stab anyone in the back just for the pleasure of doing it.'

'And is he all that?'

'You judge for yourself, David. Let's say that I invited him home once. And he's never been invited again.'

'What happened?'

'Nothing you could object to. Full of praise for my advertising talent and then went on to imply that I had a way with the girls that he really envied. Pauline didn't really go for that as you can imagine.' Schultz shrugged. 'Keep your eyes skinned and your powder dry. You must have met guys like that in England . . . they're not all that rare.'

'I'd like you to warn me if I produce anything that's too English . . . not American.'

'I told you at breakfast, David. Except for a few differences in words, a good ad is a good ad anywhere. Don't try to be American – just human, that's all. Despite the tough talk we're all just suckers and dads and husbands underneath. You'll do fine. Don't worry.'

Schultz and Delgado, the man who looked after the account, were facing Collins across his desk.

'What do they do that their rivals don't do?'

Delgado shrugged. 'Nothing. The top four moving companies are all first-class. Our clients are number two in the league.'

'You mean for turnover?'

'Turnover and number of jobs they do.'

'Anything in the research that could be used?'

'Not that I can see.' Delgado pointed at a plastic file. 'It's there, Mr Collins.'

Collins leafed through the sheets of the analysis and report. He turned back to the second page and then looked at Delgado.

'It's interesting that every client seems to be highly delighted with what they do. Very few breakages, willing staff, dates and times kept to . . . but in the column asking them if they enjoyed the move . . . sixty per cent said no. And if you carry on across the column . . . of that sixty per cent eighty per cent were women. And in the "yes" figures ninety-four per cent of the respondents were men.'

154

Delgado smiled. 'Maybe men are easier to please than women.'

'I'd say it was something more fundamental than that.'

'Like what?'

'Like two things. First of all most of the men won't be involved. They'll be at work. And secondly moving is a more emotional thing for women. They're not just moving house, they're moving home. They may like the new place better but it's not yet home. They go in when it's empty and wait for the furniture to arrive. They're strangers in a new environment. And they're on their own.'

Delgado shrugged. 'There's not much we can do about that.'

'How about . . .' Collins hesitated then smiled, '. . . how about when the lady gets to the empty house there's a red rose in a nice glass vase waiting for her with a note . . . a nice Swedish single-flower glass vase . . . and the note's handwritten. A piece of poetry maybe . . . something romantic?'

Schultz grinned. 'They could have a red rose as their company logo and we could feature the rose in their women's magazine advertising. They'd go for it, David, I'm sure they would.' He turned to Delgado. 'What do you think, Joe?'

Delgado smiled. 'Sounds like it doesn't much matter what I think.'

Collins said quietly, 'What *do* you think?'

Delgado shrugged. 'I think it's a great idea but the copy would have to match . . . no hard sell.'

Collins nodded. 'Can you sell it to them, Joe?'

'I'd like you two with me. It would show them that the top brass had been thinking about their problems.'

'OK. I'll get my team to prepare the copy and layouts. And how about we design a rose motif for their vehicles?'

Schultz leaned forward. 'We could extend the whole concept. I was wondering how they'd get the rose in the new house at the right time and I reckoned the company could pay a small fee to some local lady to fix it. So why not take it a step further and she prepares a list of shops and facilities in the district for the newcomers.'

Collins smiled. 'How about . . .' he paused, thinking, '. . . how about a new category of service – super service. The research shows that everybody, men and women, hates the hassle of the move. The company gets a lady who not only puts in the rose but supervises the furniture going in . . . the family moving are put up for the night at a good local hotel and in the morning their new house is ready to move into. They haven't had to lift a finger and they've had a night out as well.'

Delgado stood up. 'You know what's wrong with you two . . . you don't just do the client's advertising, you start running their company for them.'

But all three of them laughed and Delgado turned and headed for the door.

Collins had moved from his single room at the Waldorf to a small suite, and had talked with a number of people about a suitable place for him and his family to live. It was obvious that for a director of a busy and successful agency commuting was out of the question. A cottage in the country or on Long Island, for the summer and weekends, was fine, but during the week he would need to be in New York after office hours as well as the normal working day.

Schultz introduced him to Art Mankowitz, a friend of his and one of the agency's small clients who was dealt with by a special team. Art Mankowitz had confirmed that living in New York was essential for his work and when Mary Collins' antipathy to the whole of Manhattan had been explained and discussed he offered to look for an apartment that would be really tempting to any woman. Art Mankowitz had warned that it would be expensive but Collins had given him the go-ahead to start looking.

During the three months he had been in New York he had phoned Mary several times in the first few weeks but she had never been there or if she was she hadn't picked

156

up the phone. He wrote every week but there was little to write about. She wasn't interested in his work so his letters were mainly concerned with young Jimmy. He had received only two letters in return. They were brief and cool, mainly concerned with household details. There was nothing personal and no answer to his questions about his son. And no questions about whether he had found them somewhere to live or when they would be able to join him in New York. He accepted that she had never been a communicator but the indifference made him feel more isolated than ever. But he already felt at home in New York and he had fitted in well at the agency.

Most days he worked late into the evening and so did the other directors. They had no choice. The competition was fierce and the fight to get new accounts was far tougher than in London. But his advertising instincts seemed to work just as well in the new market as in the old, and the agency's account executives, seeing his success with clients, clamoured for him to visit their own clients. His doubts about surviving in New York had gone within the first few weeks. The talents were working and he enjoyed the pressure of the new environment.

Collins was careful not to show preference for any one of the three American directors but he found it easier to get on with Jack Schultz and Marvin Swenson than with Crombie. Steve Crombie was good at his work which was mainly the general administration of the agency, and he had a smoothness and urbanity that impressed a lot of people. But he had a meanness of spirit and judgment that was obvious to those who worked closely with him. It had been demonstrated during their first formal board meeting.

They had gone through a review of the major accounts, the previous month's financial figures and a handful of items concerning personnel. It was when they had got to the end of the items on the agenda that Crombie had turned to look at Collins.

'Don't see this as personal, David, but the agency are

picking up the tab for you at the hotel. How much longer do you expect to be there?'

Before Collins could answer Marvin Swenson said, 'For Christ's sake what's it matter, and what the hell's it got to do with you?'

Crombie smiled. 'Because I'm in charge of our finances, that's why.'

'You're not, pal. You're in charge of the book-keeping not how the money gets spent.' Swenson was red in the face with anger. It was Schultz who interposed.

'We picked up your tab for seven months when you came down from Boston, Steve. And that was at the Algonquin which was a damn sight dearer than the Waldorf.'

Crombie shook his head. 'No way. We were paying around a hundred bucks a week all in. David's costs are three or four times that.'

And Swenson came in fast. 'You bloody creep, Crombie. Don't try to con us. Your hundred bucks was eight years ago. It would be more like five hundred bucks in today's money.' He glared at Crombie. 'Don't think you're the only one who can multiply and divide.'

Collins smiled. 'Maybe I can answer Steve Crombie's query myself. I'll take some time out and look for a place. Say another month.'

Schultz laughed harshly. 'You see how it goes, Crombie? This guy's been working his ass off. Early starts and late finishes. That's worth a hell of a lot more to the agency than the hotel costs us.'

Crombie shrugged. 'You take it all so personally. David hasn't.'

Collins said quietly. 'I did, Steve. Because it *was* personal. Personal and embarrassing. Maybe you see it as your role to raise these things but it makes me doubt your judgment.'

Crombie flushed, picked up his papers and left, crashing the door to as he went.

Swenson looked at Schultz. 'It's time we taught that

sonofabitch a lesson. He came in my office the other day with my expense return for last month. Wanted to know how I justified a trip to Hartford when we didn't have a client there.' Swenson turned to Schultz. 'I had to meet Bauman there . . . the boss of Ultronics . . . he was in hospital there . . . anyway I told friend Crombie that I'd justify it after he'd shown me his own expense sheets for the last twelve months.' Swenson grinned. 'Needless to say . . . he never brought them in.' Swenson looked at both the others. 'He goes over all our expenses but I've never seen one of his. Maybe we should put it on the agenda for our next board meeting. Or slip it in under "any other business" and catch him on the hop.'

Collins smiled. 'Let's forget it.'

Swenson said angrily, 'Why should we, David? We always let him get away with this sort of thing.'

'Maybe it's a kind of conscience money on our part.'

'What's that mean?'

'We let him off the hook because we're guilty about not liking him.'

'I'm not goddam guilty believe me. And I detest him. You mark my words, that little sod's a troublemaker.'

Collins said, 'Let's get one of the girls to get us some sandwiches. I'd like to talk about a new colour print process we could use. It's half the price, far better colour values and it's non-fugitive. The colours are guaranteed stable for five years minimum.'

Swenson grinned. 'Collins the peacemaker . . . let's just eat.'

Art Mankowitz phoned him five days later. He had found them the ideal apartment.

He saw it with Art Mankowitz late the same afternoon and he knew it would make a perfect home. He phoned Mary and for once she was there. Their house had been sold and the completion date was only two weeks ahead. He said nothing of the New York flat and she didn't ask where she would be living. But she would be coming in two weeks' time. He was telling her how much he hoped she would enjoy New York when she hung up.

Chapter 22

THEY STOOD looking up at the front of the well-preserved brownstone behind Bryant Park. He had taken an option on the fourth-floor apartment that had been created when the house was converted five years earlier. There were four years left of a five-year lease and the lease was for sale with all fixtures, fittings, carpets and furniture included. A couple of thousand dollars above his ceiling but within ten minutes' walk of his office. And no need to spend money on furniture. It would stretch his budget but it would make them an ideal home.

He turned and smiled. 'Let's go up and look it over. You'll like it, Mary.'

It had been the home of a successful actress for two years and the decor and furnishings had been chosen with discrimination and taste. Only the kitchen was modern. Being on the top floor it had more light than was usual in converted houses and the late afternoon sun gave a welcoming warmth as it lit the clean white walls and washed over the well-polished furniture.

The living room and dining annexe was large. A major bedroom and bathroom *en suite*, two smaller bedrooms, another bathroom and separate shower. A study and a spare room alongside the kitchen.

When they walked back into the living room he switched on the hi-fi. The radio was playing a lush version of 'Smoke gets in your eyes'. He turned, smiling, to look at her.

'Nearly as big as the Masonic Hall, and the same old music too.'

161

She shrugged and walked over to the window. Standing there without comment, looking out over the park. She saw a man haranguing a group of onlookers, waving his arms, his long hair streaming in the breeze. She had hated the city even before she saw it. Its reputation had been enough. What she had seen confirmed her fears and prejudices. There were other negative factors too but she pushed them from her mind.

She turned and said harshly, 'Switch it off, David, please.'

He pressed the switch and the music faded from the four speakers around the room.

'I don't want to live in New York, David. It scares me and it's quite the wrong place to bring up a child. I'm sorry if it's inconvenient but that's how I feel.'

He hesitated, trying to work out what to say. But she said quietly, 'Don't try and convince me that I'm wrong. Wrong or right I don't want to live in New York.'

'We could keep on the suite at the Waldorf for a few weeks until you've settled.'

'I don't want to get settled. If you want me to stay I want to live somewhere outside. People do, you know.'

He saw the open anger in her eyes and he nodded his head slowly. 'OK. I'll start looking around. I'll talk to the real estate people. We've got a client in real estate. He got me the option on this place.'

'Let me talk to him. I can tell him what I want and go and look. It'll save you having to give up the time.'

'Are you sure?'

'Of course I am.' She frowned. 'I'm not entirely helpless.'

'No. Of course not. I just thought . . . ah well . . . it will save me breaking appointments. Let's go back to the hotel and get a bite to eat.'

It was four days later when Art Mankowitz phoned him.

'That's some gal you've got, Dave. A real tough cookie.

162

Knows exactly what she wants. I just want to check it's OK with you.'

'Tell me more. What is it? Where is it? And how much?'

'It's less than half what you'd have been paying for the brownstone. It's a good soundly built house on a small estate. And it's just on the edge of Southampton.'

'Southampton? Where the hell's that?'

'Long Island. Right the east end. First-class area. Most of it upper-class. Millionaires' and film stars' summer cottages at a million bucks a throw and round the edges plenty of normal human beings. You've got a good price and let me say that it was she who beat them down, not me. I was almost ashamed of her but I'd be glad to give her a job as a negotiator, believe me. It will appreciate in value year by year.'

'So what's the snag?'

'Not a snag exactly but it's not really commuting distance. About ninety miles by road.'

There was a long silence and Mankowitz waited. Then he chipped in, 'Mind you, I can fix you up with a small place in town and the two together would still cost you quite a lot less than the place you had in mind.' He paused. 'She seemed to be pretty set on it, Dave.'

Collins sighed, 'OK, Art. Go ahead. And find me a place as near the office as you can.'

'Will do.'

As Collins hung up he looked towards the window. The lights were going on in the offices across the street but he was barely aware of them. He was relieved that she had found what she wanted so quickly but it seemed a deliberate snub to pick somewhere where he could only be at weekends. Maybe it wasn't a snub but a punishment. One more reminder that things had changed. Ah well, it was something he'd have to get used to. He closed his eyes and for one fleeting moment wondered what the hell he was doing in New York and what the hell he was doing with his life.

*   *   *

163

She had left a note for him at their suite at the Waldorf. She and Jimmy had already left for Long Island to be near the house. They could move in in ten days' time. She was going to buy furniture and carpets locally and the kitchen was already equipped. There was no point in him coming down until they had settled in. She gave the telephone number of the motel where they would be staying.

As he sat there with the note in his hand he was consumed with anger and resentment. It wasn't just her usual coldness or indifference, the note was meant to anger him. A sheer, deliberate affront. No discussion, no hint that morning that she was leaving the hotel. It wasn't for this that he had given up Sally Major. He had accepted the coolness and was long ago used to the lack of affection but it was becoming impossible. To harbour the grudge for so long. To let it become not just coolness but a callous open indifference to his feelings was not what he had bargained for. Marriages had survived far greater strains than he had put upon theirs, with at least the common courtesies maintained. Couples made at least some attempt at a relationship. But not Mary. And he realised that it was unlikely to change. She didn't want it to work. She didn't want anything except revenge.

He stood up and walked to the phone. The number he wanted was on the back of his American Express card and he gave it to the long distance operator. Three minutes later the number was ringing. It rang a long time before it was answered. The voice that answered sounded sleepy and he realised that it must be about four in the morning in London.

'Yes.'

'Who is that speaking?'

'Who are you?'

'My name's Collins. David Collins. I'd like to speak to Sally Major please.'

There was a long pause.

'She doesn't live here any more, David. This is Julie – I've moved back in.'

164

'Where can I contact her, Julie?'

'She's in Italy.'

'When will she be back?'

'She lives there, David. She works there.'

'Do you know where I can contact her?' There was a long silence and he said, 'Are you still there, Julie?'

'Yes, I'm still here. Look . . . I don't want to be interfering but I think you should leave it.'

'Why?'

'Are you still married?'

'Yes, but . . .'

'Don't do it, David. It's been a long time . . . too long. She was very unhappy but she's survived. Just about. She's made a life for herself out there. Don't rock her boat again.'

'Why should it do that?'

'Oh David . . . be reasonable . . . where are you calling from?'

'New York.'

'My God, this must be costing a fortune. Look. Oh God. Why do you want to contact her?'

'I want to talk to her.'

'About what?'

'About changing things. Maybe getting back together. I may get a divorce.'

'Then let me tell you straight. When you've got your divorce phone me again. Meantime leave her in peace.'

'You think me contacting her would upset her?'

'Maybe . . . who knows . . . but more of what she had before would finish her off.'

'Are you quite sure of that?'

'Absolutely. Just get your divorce and then maybe . . . just phone me again. But right now I'm not telling you where she is.'

'There's other ways to trace her.'

'Maybe. But that will be on your head . . . not mine. Look . . . it's four in the bloody morning here.'

'I'm sorry, Julie. Bye.'

He hung up and almost without thinking he dialled Schultz's number. It was Schultz himself who answered and he could hear music in the background.

'Schultz.'

'Is that you, Jack?'

'Is that my favourite Brit?'

'Yes.'

'What can I do for you?'

Collins didn't know what to say. He couldn't think why he had phoned Schultz. He had nothing to say to him.

'I must have dialled you by mistake, Jack. I'm sorry.'

'What's going on – are you OK?'

'Yeah, I'm OK.'

'Why don't you come over? We've finished eating but Pauline can fix you something. You sound down. Are you?'

'I guess I'm tired.'

'Are you at the hotel?'

'Yes – I'm OK – I just wanted to hear a friendly voice.'

'Well, well . . . I tell you what. You just ring room service for some real good coffee and I'll be right over. OK?'

'You don't need to do that, Jack. I'll be OK.'

'Sure you will – and I just want some coffee. What's that thing you always say? Get weaving. I'm on my way.'

Schultz had listened, his cigar unlit, his body hunched forward, arms on his thighs, his craggy face intent on Collins' words. When Collins finally stopped Schultz leaned back in his chair.

'So what you got in mind, Dave?'

'Nothing.'

'You know I'd say that wasn't a bad thing.'

'How do you make that out?'

'How long since you saw Sally?'

'Seven . . . eight years I suppose.'

166

'So she's coming up to twenty-six, or twenty-seven maybe. That's a long time, fella. It really is. And if she's made some sort of life . . . well . . .' Schultz shrugged, 'I reckon you've got to tough it out. What the hell does it matter what your wife does – or says? It only hurts if it matters. And it shouldn't. She's a bitch. Just accept that. It's a fact of life.' He paused. 'How do you like it in New York?'

'Suits me fine, Jack. I like it.'

'And the job?'

'I like that too. Everything's fine except for the private bit.'

'So switch that off. Just ignore it. Don't expect anything from it. She won't change. I only saw her the once when you came round for drinks that night. She's all coiled up like a spring . . . you could see it . . . Pauline said afterwards that she'd got some fantastic chip on her shoulder . . . I guess you're the chip, old pal.'

'It's not much of a life, Jack.'

'Look, pal. It's what you make it. If you keep putting your hand in the fire it'll hurt. Just wipe it out. You felt you had an obligation to her, and the boy . . . so you carried on. But what she's been doing to you isn't normal. She had grounds to be hurt or resentful. But the way she behaves with you is kinda sick. She doesn't want you. You're just the whipping boy. She knows you inside out. She's got you all worked out . . . and you play into her hands like a sucker. Just take a deep, deep breath. Go to the place in Southampton just to keep the flag flying with the boy . . . and ignore everything else. When she sees it's not working maybe she'll come down to earth. If not . . . too bad . . . for her, not you.'

Collins smiled. 'Thanks for listening. And thanks for the comment. I know you're right. I'll try it . . . but it's not my style.'

'Just play it cool, man . . . that's all you've gotta do.'

167

Chapter 23

MARY PHONED him a week later. They were already installed in the house on a rough-and-ready basis and if he came the next weekend she would be putting on a small house-warming party for the neighbours who had all been so helpful. He had told her that he would be there and she had given him directions.

As he made his way out of Southampton, following the instructions she had given him, he wondered for the first time what kind of place she would have chosen. After about six miles he saw the sign – The Willow Garden Estate. They were all ranch-style houses laid out in a wide semi-circle and they looked well-established and cared for. Mary had said it was almost the centre house and as he turned into the drive he saw a house with several cars parked outside.

As he pulled up he sat looking for a few moments. It was nothing like the house he would have expected her to choose. It looked pleasant and welcoming with a magnolia on the front lawn and what looked like at least half an acre of planted-out garden. The lawns were close-cut and the place looked as if it had been lived in for years.

Collins got out of the car, reached in for his jacket and walked up the drive to the door. The front door was open and he could hear voices and laughter from one of the rooms. As he followed the noise he came to a long wide room with a dozen or more people chattering with drinks in their hands. And then Mary saw him, and was walking

168

towards him, smiling, a large middle-aged man with grey hair and a crew-cut in tow.

'David, this is Lew Harris – he arranged this welcome party for you. We thought you'd never get here.'

Lew Harris was tanned and big and his massive hand shook Collins' hand vigorously.

'Welcome, friend. Welcome to Southampton and the best little community in the US of A.'

'Thank you.'

Mary took his arm. 'Let me introduce you to everybody.'

It was nearly two hours before the last of the welcoming party left and Collins sank gratefully into one of the deep chintzy armchairs.

'You've made a lot of friends in ten days, Mary.'

'They've been wonderful. Showing me around. Helping straighten the house and the garden. I don't know how I would have managed without them.'

He smiled. 'I'm glad you've settled in so well.'

'Lew cut the lawns this morning and he trimmed the hedge yesterday. He took Jimmy to see the fishing boats every day. He loves Lew. Listens to his stories about cattlemen and cowboys and pesters him for more.'

'Where is Jimmy?'

'He's with the Marston children three houses away. They've got two girls and a boy and a pool.'

Collins was amazed to see her so enthusiastic. All his resolve to be indifferent melted away. He had never seen her so expansive before. Maybe middle-class America was going to thaw her out. He almost enjoyed the weekend and drove back to Manhattan late on the Sunday evening despite the crowded roads.

The summer months passed as if there was some unspoken truce. Mary seemed to have settled easily into the new surroundings and the new community, and to know a lot of people. Couples who stopped for a chat when they were shopping or at the beach, women who seemed to know

169

her well and liked her. She played tennis and swam most days and at the weekends there were generally half a dozen people she invited round for barbecues on the patio.

He wondered as the weeks went by if he had been unreasonable in his assessment of her attitude. There was no affection from her but there was no overt attempt to wound him, and by contrast with their previous relationship it was at least tolerable.

In early September he took ten days off and they explored the neighbouring towns and villages. There were few phone calls from the agency and he was aware that the rest and change had done him good.

The first day back in New York there was a board meeting and it seemed that for once there were going to be no points of friction. But when they got to the fifth item on the agenda – 'Personnel' – Schultz interrupted Crombie's usual report on overtime and time-keeping.

'Let's skip that, Steve . . . there's more important things to discuss.'

'Can't they wait until we've dealt with Personnel?'

'It's Personnel I want to talk about.'

Crombie shrugged. 'OK. Go ahead.'

Schultz leaned forward, looking intently at Crombie. 'Last Monday I had two new people start. A senior account executive and a girl-clerk. They followed the usual instructions and reported to you for registering . . . the paperwork. At noon I couldn't figure why I hadn't seen them. I asked my secretary to find out what had happened. She came back and told me they'd both left the building. I contacted them by phone at their homes that afternoon.' Schultz turned to look at Collins. 'You'll hardly believe this, David, but it's a fact. They were told that Mr Crombie was busy . . . would they wait in reception.' Schultz turned back to Crombie. 'By ten-thirty the receptionist had phoned your office, Crombie, four times, to remind you that they were kicking their heels in reception. The fourth time you, personally, told her not to ring again. You'd see them when you were ready. At eleven-forty they both left and they told the receptionist that they were disgusted and wouldn't be coming back. She phoned you, Crombie, and told you what had happened. According to her you said "Too bad" and hung up. You didn't tell me. And now, a week later you still haven't told me. What's your excuse – and I warn you – it had better be good.'

Crombie shrugged. 'It's not a question of excuses, Jack . . . reason, maybe, but not excuse. The simple fact is that I was terribly busy.'

'Doing what?'

'Finalising the monthly accounts for August.'

'You've got book-keepers to do that, for Christ's sake.'

'I do the fine-tuning myself . . . it's very important.'

'So why didn't you let me know, so that I could take them over?'

Crombie shrugged. 'It's our standard practice . . . new staff are processed before they go to their departments.'

'Don't give me that bullshit, Crombie. We're not the State Department or the Prudential, we're an advertising agency – or hadn't you noticed?'

'Do we really need people who walk off in a huff just because they're kept waiting a bit? They must be extremely arrogant to do that.'

'You sonofabitch . . . I've worked for a year persuading that guy to leave Doyle Dane and join us. Slow, careful approaches . . . detailed discussions . . . emphasising how creative, informal and friendly we all are . . . you make me sick, Crombie. You really do.'

'Maybe you didn't really convince him, Jack. Maybe . . .'

Schultz stood up and stormed from the room and Crombie shrugged and looked at Collins.

'Sometimes I think I'm the only sane guy on the board. What does it matter if . . .'

Collins interrupted. 'When you're starting a new job – the first morning – half of you thinks you've probably made a terrible mistake leaving your old familiar background

. . . it doesn't go down well if you're shown that you're just an employee . . .'

Swenson leaned forward towards Crombie. 'You realise that that guy will tell everyone he knows how he was treated . . . You're so . . . so self-important and so stupid I can't think how we put up with you – maybe it's time you got the hell out of this place. I'd chip in for a severance payment . . .'

'Hold on, Marvin,' said Collins. 'We've all got some responsibility in this. What we need is a proper inauguration programme for new people . . . planned to make them feel at home and wanted.'

Swenson shrugged. 'You're the creative boss, David. Why don't you do it?'

Collins was just about to speak when the internal phone buzzed. He leaned over and lifted the receiver.

'Collins . . . we're still in our meeting, Jean. What is it?'

'Your wife rang, Mr Collins. I told her you were still in the meeting. She says could you get back home. There's a problem.'

'See if you can get her on the phone.'

'OK.'

Collins looked at Swenson. 'I'll rough something out for our next meeting . . . could you tell Jack that I've got to go back to Long Island? I'll phone when I get there.'

The phone buzzed and he answered quickly. The girl said, 'There's no reply, Mr Collins. It's rung for three minutes. Maybe there's no one there.'

'Thanks.'

As he walked to the underground car-park he wondered what could have happened since he left. Maybe Jimmy was ill or had been hurt. Whatever it was it must have happened overnight.

As he parked the car in the drive the sun was beginning to go down and everywhere seemed unusually quiet as he walked to the front door and took out his key.

172

The house seemed strangely still and almost empty of furniture as he walked through to the kitchen and then back to the living room.

Mary was hanging up the telephone as he walked in, turning to look at him, a strange look on her face.

'You got my message, David?'

'Yes. They just said there was a problem and you wanted me to come straight here. What's up? Is it Jimmy?'

She shook her head, half-smiling. 'No. It's not Jimmy. It's you and me.' She pointed to a large buff envelope on the marble-topped coffee table. 'That's for you. It's my petition for divorce.'

Collins stood looking at her, disbelieving and bewildered.

'You're joking, surely.'

'I'm not, David. You'd better read it if you think I'm joking.'

'But I don't understand.'

'Of course you do. Why are you so surprised? Did you think it was only men who could opt out of a marriage?'

'But I had no idea. You've never said that you wanted a divorce. You've never discussed such a thing with me.'

She stood with her arms folded across her chest, her head to one side as she looked at him.

'It's what they call a no-fault divorce by mutual consent. Easy, economical and painless. If you want to play it tough we can fight it out some other way in court. But that wouldn't do your career any good.'

'Who prepared this petition?'

'My attorney.'

'Who's he for God's sake?'

She smiled. 'You seem amazed that I should have an attorney. Out of character for the little woman, is it? Anyway his name's Goldberg and Lew says he's real good.'

'What's it got to do with Lew?'

'Quite a lot, actually. We're getting married when the divorce is final.'

173

'Lew? *Lew?* You hardly know him – and he's almost old enough to be your father.'

'So what? Better a loving father than an absent snob.'

'What on earth made you want to do this? We've got a nice house, money in the bank. Why the sudden change? Things seemed to have settled down.'

'It wasn't sudden, David. You probably never bent that much-praised creative mind of yours to wondering about what I got out of being married to you. Let me tell you that apart from food, clothes and a roof over my head I got nothing. And never have had anything. You probably think I'm an awful bore compared with your slick friends in London and Manhattan. But if I am a bore then it's you who made me so. You used me, you know. You didn't do *me* any favour when you decided to stay. You didn't stay because you loved me. You stayed because it was convenient to you to stay. It saved you a lot of trouble. A lot of talk. You didn't love that girl, either, or you'd have left me for her.' She paused. 'You may be a genius in advertising but as a man you're a washout. So. I've had enough. And I'm off.'

For long moments Collins looked at his wife's face in silence. The hatred for him was so open and obvious. Her cold assessment of him so wounding because it was not exaggerated and had elements of the sad truth in it.

'What are you going to do when it's through?'

She smiled triumphantly. 'I'm not waiting till it's through. That's why I asked you to come and see me today. I'm leaving tonight. Moving to Texas. I've left you your half of the furniture. My attorney will let you have my new address.'

'What about Jimmy?'

'He's already there.'

'Have you talked to him about us?'

'I didn't need to. Lew has told him about the new arrangements and he's delighted to have a real father at last.'

Collins stood up slowly. Cold with shock and anger.

'You don't think you're just going to take him thousands of miles away and get away with it?'

'I've got notarised reports from three psychiatrists that Jimmy is suffering from the lack of a father's attention and that it would be better for him to have a minimum of contact with you in the future.'

She couldn't hide the triumph in her eyes as she stood there looking at him. For a fleeting moment he thought he would strike her. He was trembling as he said, 'Let me know how you want to share out the house and money.'

'I don't want, or need, a cent from you, David. You're going to need it. All of it.'

'And Jimmy?'

'He doesn't need it either. Lew will provide for him. I don't want to be obligated to you for anything.'

She stood up, and for what seemed long long moments they stood facing each other. Adversaries. Undisguised loathing on her face. Resentment and unease on his.

Then he turned and walked back up the hall, let himself out, and walked back to the bright red Mustang.

Chapter 24

COLLINS HAD gone to the attorney who had acted for him on the lease of his small apartment in Manhattan and the house on Long Island. Bernstein agreed to act for him and phoned a week later to arrange a second consultation.

Bernstein was a large, heavily-built man, almost bald, with gold-plated half-glasses which he peered over as he looked at his client.

'I've looked through their papers . . . First question: do you want to stop the divorce?'

'You mean contest it?'

'No. I mean stop it. Tell her to go to hell.'

'How can I do that?'

'Her attorney has drawn up this petition assuming that you're as willing to be divorced as she is to divorce you. They've cut corners that a court wouldn't like.'

'I don't understand.'

'You don't need to, but for instance . . . she established Texas residence a month after she moved into the house at Southampton and even with that they fiddled the dates . . . she wasn't even in the US at the date she gives . . . we could expose that and the court would throw it out.'

Collins shook his head slowly. 'I don't see any point in stopping it. I assume she'll get the divorce if I do nothing and go along with it.'

'Almost certainly.'

'So let's go along with it.'

'She claims total control of your child . . . your son. Access to be limited and at her disposal. Is that agreeable to you?'

'Can I contest just that point?'

'You could, but because of what she has said in her statement I think the court would go along with her wishes unless you were contesting the truth of her statement. It looks like she's kept a record every day for years of everything you've ever done that a court could construe as a minor marital offence. Read together it's quite a formidable list.'

'So I'd have to rely on her goodwill?'

'You'd be unwise to do that, Mr Collins.' Bernstein pointed at the file of papers in front of him. 'There's no goodwill in all this. The woman – forgive me – obviously hates you. It's meant to hurt. Maybe the new marriage will cool her down, but I doubt it. I'd almost go so far as to say that this new marriage is being entered into more to strike at you than because of any affection for the other party.'

'What do you advise?'

'Surprisingly, she's making no financial claims. If you contest this she could still win eventually on other grounds and I suspect that the next move would be a claim on your resources and income. I think you should let her go through with it.'

'How long will it take to be finalised?'

'Five or six months roughly.'

'And you'll deal with it? I don't have to be involved?'

'I shall need your signature on several documents but that's the only involvement you need to have.'

'OK, Mr Bernstein, I'd be grateful if you'd do that.'

Bernstein leaned back in his leather chair.

'Can I give you some advice from an old man, Mr Collins?'

'I'd be grateful.'

Bernstein smiled. 'I doubt that. Anyway . . . the advice. I don't usually handle divorce cases, but I have to from

177

time to time because the person concerned is already a client – as you are. But I've done it all for enough years to have, what shall I say, collected some data, some experience.

'You must have wondered when you came to see me a few days ago why I asked you so many questions that didn't seem relevant to this divorce business. Your answers were very revealing . . . shall I go on?'

'Please do.'

'You must be feeling pretty low after the last few years of your marriage. Most people would see your wife as a first-class bitch . . . a shrew. But all that was wrong, for both of you, was that you were in the wrong film with the wrong script. Do you understand what I mean?'

'I'm afraid not.'

'I see it all the time. Not only in divorce cases but in private life. Miscast people like your wife. When she was growing up she was learning a script. From her background, her parents and associates. A script about being married and being a wife. She learnt all the words, and the lines, and then she married you. She took it for granted that you'd learnt the other half of the same script. But you hadn't. Maybe you'd read it but you didn't like the part. So you got another part. Your part never had a script, you were ad-libbing, making it up as you went along because you weren't sure what part you were playing. She said her lines from her script and you came back with words from some other play.' He paused and smiled. 'So all I want to say to you, Mr Collins, is this. You're young enough, attractive enough, successful enough, to get married again. But for God's sake . . . next time . . . see that both you and the girl are in the same film. If she's been rehearsing her part in *Rebecca of Sunnybrook Farm* don't, please don't, be surprised if she can't understand the script of *Butterfield 8*.'

Collins smiled. 'I'll try not to . . . and thanks for the advice.'

'Don't worry, it'll go on your bill . . . under sundry disbursements.'

He intended to tell nobody at the agency about his divorce but Schultz saw him in New York one weekend and asked why he wasn't in Southampton and Collins told him. Schultz made no comment but Collins was invited to Schultz's house for dinner several times during the next few months. He had written a note to Parsons in London but there had been no reply. When Parsons had been in New York for the year-end meeting he had never raised the subject but he had been no less amiable than before.

The apartment near Bryant Park was still vacant and he had taken the rest of the lease and moved in over the Christmas holidays. In his new circumstances it was well within his resources and the Long Island house had sold in a matter of weeks at a small profit.

After the first few days of shock, Collins deliberately pushed all thoughts of the divorce from his mind. He behaved as if it was not happening. He was just on his own. But that was nothing new. The new apartment was perhaps over-large for one person but he enjoyed its luxury and its calmness. The divorce decree came in the post in February with a bill and a covering letter from Bernstein. The note explained that he no longer had any financial responsibility for either his wife or son. Bernstein had run a check and informed him that his former wife had married Louis Ronald Harris the same day that the decree was finalised.

Crombie was in full spate about cash-flow, profitability, and the slow payment of fees by the larger clients. It was Marvin Swenson who finally raised a limp hand and waved him to a standstill.

'Just tell us what you've got in mind, Steve. We don't need the build-up. We see the weekly print-out.' He shrugged and shook his head. Not in disbelief but as a sign that he knew what was coming because he'd heard it all before and didn't like it.

Crombie pushed aside his pile of papers as if it were a symbolic clearing of the decks.

'We've got to hike our fees up to everybody by five per cent and we've got to charge interest on overdue accounts. Two per cent above bank rate.'

Schultz said, 'How do you justify the two per cent?'

'It's what we have to pay and we ain't in the money-lending business.'

'How much do we still have to pay off from our bank loan?'

'We cleared it last month.'

Collins said quietly, 'You should be congratulated on that, Steve. It's your careful budgeting that's made that possible.'

All three Americans looked at Collins as he spoke. They were surprised at the praise because they were well aware of the antagonism between the two men. They shared the antagonism.

Crombie smiled. 'Praise indeed, coming from you, David.'

'Well deserved, but why the concern now about finances? Our gross profits are way up and with the bank loan finished it means our net profits are even better.'

'It's just a question of good housekeeping. Setting a standard.'

'What's the standard?' Schultz asked.

'I go by what we could get on our capital if it was creatively invested in Wall Street stocks.'

Swenson laughed amiably. 'I thought you said we weren't in the money-lending business, Steve.'

'That's just a smart-ass comment, Marvin. Somebody has to set the bench-mark.'

Collins said softly, 'What exactly are you after, Steve? More profits or what?'

'Exactly that. More profits.'

'And for what purpose?'

Crombie looked pained. 'For Chrissake. What are profits usually for? To plough back in the business or distribute to the shareholders.'

Swenson rolled up his shirt-sleeves and Collins noted the gesture and intervened before Swenson could speak.

'Can I suggest a compromise?'

He looked at the three in turn and when nobody answered he started.

'I think we should look at our organisation afresh. We've got an exceptional creative reputation. That's where our strength lies and that's what brings us new business. It's our only real asset. The rest is just what most agencies can provide. We still have creative capacity to take on more accounts without upping our costs.

'Hiking our fees could be a real can of worms with a number of clients. Our rates are a bit above average already but nobody minds because at least we cut the mustard. Put them up and it gives them grounds for thinking again and testing the market. We're in advertising, and Wall Street thinking can lead us right down the dull end of town. Our shareholders have all had their capital back and are getting a good return on their money right now.

'But there are things we could do that would save us money and not be detrimental. We shouldn't, as an agency, run our own research section. It's part of the marketing mix but, despite all the hogwash, we're not marketing people. We're creative advertising people. And that's why people use us. The clients have their own marketing men and research is their responsibility. Let them go to an independent market-research outfit for their research. We barely break even on it and it takes too many resources. Human and financial.'

Swenson chipped in. 'We could recommend research outfits and claim a commission for the introduction.'

'We could, but we shouldn't. No more than we'd claim a commission from outside copywriters or artists. Let's just get shot of things that aren't our business.'

181

The research department came under Crombie and he defended it hotly but ineffectively. He claimed that clients would see it as a reduction in services, a contraction of the agency. When he finally came to the end of his diatribe, Collins said quietly, 'Which do you think clients would prefer, Steve, buying their market research from a specialist or doing what you suggested, paying increased fees?'

Schultz spoke before Crombie could answer. 'I'm for leaving the fees as they are with or without keeping an in-house research section.'

Swenson said nothing but Crombie knew that he would get no support from that direction. He shrugged angrily. 'You know, this having no president is totally negative. Any one of the four of us says "no" and that's it. The "no" guy always wins.'

Swenson only barely concealed his anger as he said, 'If we had a president it wouldn't be you, pal. Maybe you're better off as we are now.'

Collins said quietly, 'We could take a vote on it. How about it, Steve? A vote on fees, a vote on disposing of research.'

Crombie threw his pencil on the table, and leant back in his chair as if to withdraw from the discussion. But Marvin Swenson wasn't going to let him escape.

'I vote no on hiking fees and yes for getting rid of research.' He turned to look at Schultz. 'How about you?'

'The same, I guess. It makes sense all round.'

Collins waited for Crombie to respond and when he sat silent said, 'Me, too, Steve. We'll leave it to you to wind up research. What's next on the agenda?'

Crombie reluctantly looked at the agenda on top of his pile of papers.

'The lease. We have to decide whether we should renew it. They want an increase of fifteen per cent. And they've given us another seven years with a break half-way for a rent revision either way. I suggest we take it.'

For once they were all in agreement. Even Swenson.

There were two or three other items of routine business then Crombie looked around the table.

'Any other business?'

Collins was never able to decide what made him raise the issue at that particular meeting when he thought about it afterwards. It wasn't premeditated. He was almost surprised to hear his own words.

'I'd just like to notify you all that I'm applying to take up my option on the rest of my shares.'

Schultz grinned. 'You reckon we're still on the up and up then, David?'

Collins smiled. A routine smile. 'Never had any doubts, Jack.'

'Why now?' And Crombie looked genuinely puzzled.

'No particular reason, Steve.' He shrugged. 'Just feel it's time to take up the offer.'

'I don't remember ever seeing the agreement.'

'It was never put in writing. It was part of the deal when I came here. I assumed that Harry Parsons had told you.'

'He did. I'm not querying it. Parsons is due here next week isn't he? We could deal with it then.'

Collins nodded. 'He's arriving on Thursday morning. It's not very complicated. Just issuing share certificates from the merger issue that weren't taken up.'

Crombie looked around at the others. 'Anything else?'

There was nothing, and the meeting broke up, Collins walking back to his office with Schultz.

Jack Schultz didn't like board meetings. He felt they were not only a waste of time but a constant source of quarrels and the airing of rivalries.

'Those two make me sick.'

'Who?'

'Crombie and Swenson.'

'They both contribute their fair share to the agency. Crombie's a good finance man and Swenson's the best production man I've ever worked with.'

'Maybe, maybe . . . but they behave like kids at board meetings and their tensions go right through the whole shop. Every time we have a meeting the tension's around for days.'

Collins laughed. 'It's not as bad as that, Jack. Don't dwell on it. They only half mean it and it's up to us to stop the boat from rocking.'

'Huh. I wouldn't trust those two bastards as far as I can spit. I should have got the hell out and run my own show when I had the chance.'

Collins laughed as he turned into his office.

As he reached for the telephone he hesitated and decided to make it a person-to-person call. He gave the operator the Amarillo number. It seemed strange to be asking for a call to Mrs Harris.

The operator rang back in a few minutes.

'Your Texas party on the line, caller.'

'Thank you . . . is that you, Mary? It's David.'

There was no reply and he said, 'Can you hear me, Mary?'

'Yes, I can hear you. What do you want?' Her voice was cold and aloof.

'I'll be in Houston next week on business. I thought maybe when I was through I could fly up to Amarillo and see Jimmy. I've got a few things for him.'

'No. Lew wouldn't like that.'

'It's not really Lew's problem, Mary. *I'm* Jimmy's father and nothing can alter that. It's between you and me.'

'If it's between you and me then the answer's the same. No.'

'But why? Why shouldn't I see him?'

'Why do you want to see him, anyway?'

'I'd just like to see him.'

'Exactly. Your normal selfish attitude. *You'd* like to see him. You just happen to be coming down here on business. It never enters your mind that it's six, seven months we've been here and he's settled down. You don't give a damn if you disturb him. No matter what *you* might think, so far as Jimmy's concerned Lew is his father now.'

'But I'm . . .'

He was cut short by a man's voice. 'Mr Collins, this is Lew Harris. I won't have you disturbing my wife. Just leave her alone. You've done enough damage already. And the boy too. Just keep out of our lives.'

And Lew Harris hung up.

Collins put back the receiver and stared at the framed award on the wall opposite his desk. But he didn't see it.

The harsh words and attitude left him in a mood of mixed anger and depression.

It had taken days to find the courage to call her. There had been no meeting in Houston, it was just an attempt to make it seem casual. He had expected a cool response but nothing like the one he had got. And the final humiliating rebuff from Harris. Harris, the friendly welcomer of newcomers to the neighbourhood. The amiable widower with a wallet-full of Polaroids of his late wife. Maybe he should get a private detective agency to do a bit of checking on Lew Harris.

It was almost ten o'clock and all the agency staff had left. He had a whisky at a bar near the office and then walked up Madison to 72nd Street and along into Third Avenue.

It was nearly midnight when he opened the door of his apartment and showed the girl inside. It was the first time he had ever been to a singles bar and he hadn't really believed the stories he had heard. They seemed to be true.

He put a cassette on the hi-fi and she sat with him on a stool in the kitchen as he made them sandwiches and opened a bottle of wine. She was a secretary at a computer company on Second Avenue. She was in her early twenties and very pretty, and it was hard to believe that she needed to patronise a singles bar to find a boyfriend.

'Can I help?'

'No, honey. You just sit right there and look beautiful.'

'What do you do?'

'I'm at an advertising agency.'

'A big one?'

'A major one but it's not big in number of staff.'

'D'you want me to stay the night?'

He turned and looked at her. 'For me the answer's yes. What about you?'

'Can I phone my girlfriend who shares with me?'

'Does that mean yes you'll stay?'

'That's why we were both in Lafferty's, wasn't it?'

He smiled sheepishly. 'I guess so. The phone's in the living room by the TV.'

They sat watching the late-night film on TV as they ate, and then he took her hand and led her to the bedroom. They walked there together as if they had done it many times before. She smiled as he undressed her and when they were both naked on the bed her arms went round him and her mouth was on his mouth as she turned her body to his.

He walked with her to her office the next morning, made a date for the Saturday evening, and then walked back to the agency.

Chapter 25

DURING THE following six months Collins led a strange double life. Long, hard-working hours at the agency where he seemed to be having that same magic touch with both creative work and with clients. His evenings in strange bars, and some nights with casual pick-ups and call-girls whose names he got from the agency's lists for entertaining out-of-town clients. He kept well away from places where he might possibly be recognised.

A girl he met in a singles bar but hadn't slept with had invited him to a party at her place a few days later. It was there he met Dolly Jones. She was very young and very pretty, with long blonde hair, green eyes and a beautiful body. She was obviously much in demand and seemed to know everyone at the party which was in a large apartment on Sutton Place.

He phoned the girl who had invited him to the party to ask about Dolly Jones. She laughed and said that he would have to find out for himself. She finally gave him the girl's telephone number but made very clear that Dolly Jones was a 'swinger', one of a group of wealthy young people who used New York as their playground. He wasn't sure whether the girl was warning him off or encouraging him, but whichever it was he fancied Dolly Jones. He phoned her and she had to look at her diary before she accepted his invitation.

He booked a table for two by the pool at the Four Seasons and she was obviously impressed:

'Who do you know that gets you a poolside table at this place?'

He shrugged dismissively. 'A friend of a friend.'

'Have you been here before?'

'No. It's not my kind of place.'

'So why are we here?'

He shrugged. 'I thought you might like it.'

'What made you think that?'

'You looked as though you might like a special sort of place. It was . . .'

'Where do you usually take girls for dinner?'

'Ma Bell's or the Gardenia Club in Manhattan Plaza.'

She reached for the embroidered handbag. 'Let's go to Ma Bell's.'

'No. Let's stay right here. I've heard they do a really beautiful dessert . . . a chocolate velvet. You look like a chocolate velvet girl.'

She laughed. 'You're right. The way they do it is beautiful, and I love it.'

'You've been here before?'

'Yes. I knew a guy once who thought this was the only place to eat.'

'Next time we'll go to Ma Bell's.'

'Who said there'd be a next time?'

'Nobody. I was just hoping. I can enjoy tonight even more if I know there's a next time.'

'You're a strange man, aren't you?'

'Why?'

'You just say things right off.'

'You don't like that?'

'Oh yes. I love it. But I'm not used to it.'

'What are you used to?'

She laughed. 'Guys who just take it for granted that there'll be a next time. If they want a next time. Like they're doing me a favour to date me a second time. And here's you. Good-looking, obviously successful, openly saying that you want a second date before you've even discovered if I'll hop into bed with you.'

'Is that good or bad in your book?'

188

'Oh, boy. It's better than good. It's unique and romantic. I love it.'

'There must be something wrong with the guys you meet.'

'Maybe it's something wrong with me.'

'I don't think so.'

'Why not?'

'You're young and beautiful and very alive, and despite appearances I'd guess you'd rather be loved than taken for granted.'

'Where do you come from? I can't make out your accent.'

'I'm English.'

'Are you married?'

'No. I was, but we were divorced about a year ago.'

'What went wrong?'

'It's hard to say. It would be a long story.'

'So tell me.'

'I will some day. Let's enjoy ourselves now. What's your fish like?'

'It's delicious.'

'What about Ma Bell's?'

She smiled. 'OK. When?'

'How about next Saturday?'

The green eyes looked at his face and she said softly, 'How about tomorrow?'

'D'you mean that?'

'Yes. I mean it.'

'That's great. Wonderful. But we'll have to make it the Gardenia Club. Ma Bell's is closed on Sundays.'

They ate at the Gardenia Club and then went back to his apartment. Unlike most girls she didn't admire the decor or the furniture. She didn't even seem to notice it.

He poured them drinks and switched on the hi-fi which he had loaded with a schmaltzy cassette, and they sat together on the soft, leather couch.

189

'Susie told me that you're in advertising.'

'Yes.'

'Which agency are you at?'

'Crombie, Swenson and Schultz.'

'I've heard that name somewhere but I can't think where. All those long lists of names of agencies and stockbrokers and attorneys all sound the same to me.'

'What do you do?'

She laughed. 'Nothing. Just a parasite living on my father's money. The last of the good-time girls.'

'Any brothers or sisters?'

'No. Just me and Pop. My mother died a few years back.'

'That sounds a bit lonely.'

She turned her head quickly to look at his face. 'What made you say that?'

'Well, you must miss your mother. Fathers can do their best but for girls they're not the same, are they? And there must be times when you're on your own. And you can't be a good-time girl without an audience.'

She looked at his face for a long time and then said softly, 'You're very perceptive. Do you like me? I like you.'

'Yes, I like you a lot.'

'Do you want to have me now?'

He hesitated for a moment. 'I'd be lying if I didn't say yes. But that wasn't why I brought you here. Or why I dated you.'

'Where's your bedroom?'

'Dolly, you don't have to . . .'

'I want to. It's not you. It's me.'

It was past midnight when they eventually lay side by side on his bed.

'Where are you going to stay tonight?'

'Do you want me to stay with you?'

'Yes. If you can.'

'OK. I'll stay.'

'Where's your home?'

190

'At Bridgeport. Do you know Bridgeport?'

'I've been there a few times. I've got a client there. But we generally meet in New York.'

'Who's the client?'

'It's an electronics outfit – Jones and Morrell.'

She leaned up on one elbow and looked at his face, and said quietly, 'Did you know? Please tell me.'

'What's the matter, honey? Did I know what?'

'Did you know that that's my father's company?'

'You mean Casey Jones is your father?'

'Yes.'

'Oh my God. Oh . . . my . . . God. No, I didn't connect the names. I had no reason to.'

'You're sure?'

'I swear it, kid. I had no idea.' He looked at her face. 'It may sound crass or crude but let me say that if I'd known, I doubt if I'd have dated you, however much I liked you. You don't need to do that sort of thing to keep clients and I never, ever, mix business and my private life.'

'Do you know my father?'

'Yes. I know him quite well. In fact we get on very well together.'

'He's never mentioned me to you?'

'He's often said that he's got a daughter but he's never mentioned your name. But even if he had I'm not sure I would have connected you with him.' He smiled. 'Casey Jones is Bridgeport, and you're New York as far as I'm concerned. I had assumed that you live in New York. Do you think your father would object to me dating you?'

'No. I'm sure he wouldn't. In fact I think he'd approve.'

'We'd better tell him if you think it's necessary.'

'Do you think it's necessary?'

'It doesn't really depend on me.'

'Why not?'

'It would only be necessary to tell him if we were going to see one another on a . . . what shall I say . . . a serious basis. And only you can decide that.'

'Why not you?'

191

'I'm serious about you. I don't know how you feel about me.'

'I'm crazy about you, Dave.'

He kissed her lovely mouth.

'So let's tell him.'

'OK.'

Casey Jones had seen too many men come and go in his daughter's life to take the news too seriously but he was pleasantly surprised that she should be so interested in a man who was so far from the type that she usually ran around with.

Chapter 26

IT SEEMED that Parsons had come in on an earlier flight than planned and Crombie had met him in. For some reason he had been booked in at the Sheraton not the Barclay where he usually stayed when he came over for the monthly meeting. And he had not appeared at the agency by lunchtime.

Crombie phoned Collins just after lunch and said that he was speaking from Parsons' suite at the hotel.

'Harry would like a meeting at the agency at four, David. Is that OK with you?'

'Sure. Shall I tell the others?'

'I've told them already.'

'What's the meeting about?'

'No idea. Just a run over the situation, I guess.'

'OK. See you.'

Crombie had sounded strange on the phone, his voice high-pitched. If he didn't know him so well he would have thought he'd had too much to drink. But it was more than that. He sounded . . . and as Collins searched for the right word it came: euphoric. He sounded euphoric.

Collins dialled Schultz on the internal phone.

'What's the meeting this afternoon about?'

'God knows. Crombie sounded like he was pissed or something. Couldn't reveal what it was about but vital that I should be there. He'll be grinding some bloody axe, that's for sure. He belongs in Washington not Madison Avenue.'

'Sounds interesting, whatever it is.'

'Sounds goddam suspicious if you ask me. He phoned

193

Parsons yesterday in London. And Parsons altered his flight. Crombie sloped off and met him at Kennedy and that's usually your little burden. Then they creep off to the Sheraton so nobody knows where Parsons is. They're holed up there for hours, and then all of a sudden he wants a directors' meeting. I'll be keeping my powder dry until it's over, I tell you.'

Collins and Schultz went into the conference room together. Crombie was on the internal phone telling the operator to hold off all calls to directors for the next couple of hours.

Collins overheard him and said, 'Not a couple of hours. I've got a client meeting at 5.15.'

'Can't somebody else take it, David?'

'That's for me to decide.'

Crombie shrugged and looked at Parsons with helpless resignation. Parsons grinned at Collins. 'We'll probably be finished in half an hour, David. Don't worry. If you want to leave, you leave.'

There was an awkward silence as they settled themselves in the chairs around the table, and it was Parsons who started the meeting.

'First of all, congratulations from the board in London on the half-year results. We've not done too badly ourselves but I'm not sure that it's going to last. The London agency business is in more than its usual flux and I've had two household-name agencies offered me in the last couple of months.'

He stopped and picked an imaginary thread from his jacket sleeve, looking down as he brushed at the expensive Dormeuil suiting. When he looked up his face was tense.

'I've been thinking about this operation. It's got momentum and inspiration but somehow it lacks direction. I think that's probably my fault. When we came to our original agreement we solved several problems by having no president. All you guys were vice-presidents with equal status.' He paused. 'I think on reflection that was an error of judgment. We solved a few problems by making another

194

problem for the future. And I think it's time to rectify that. I'd like to suggest that we appoint one of you president. I'd like to know what you guys think about that.' He looked at Swenson.

Swenson looked up at the ceiling. 'I'm happy as things are.'

Schultz said harshly, 'Me too.'

Parsons looked at Collins. 'David? What about you?'

Collins smiled. 'Depends on who it is, Harry. He'd have to be acceptable to the board as a whole.'

Crombie cut in. 'I think it's the only way, Harry. I said as much at a meeting we had . . .'

'Cut out the crap, Crombie, you don't fool any of us with this little ploy.' Swenson's hatred for Crombie was on his face and in his strained voice.

Parsons sighed. 'Let's not get personal, Marvin.'

'It *is* personal, for Chrissake. It's a put-up job by this bastard on my left. It's obvious what he's been up to. He's gone behind all our backs licking your arse to get himself made president.'

Swenson leaned forward, looking at Parsons aggressively. 'And let me make clear that if that asshole is made president you'll have my resignation two minutes later.'

Parsons opened his mouth to speak but Schultz got in first. He said quietly, 'That goes for me too.'

Parsons looked at Crombie's pale face and then at the others.

'Let me make clear what I said. I said that there were signs that this place needed some leadership. That we could best get that by appointing a president.' He paused. 'I didn't say that it should be any particular person. Now does anybody disagree with that basic premise? Does anyone really, genuinely, believe that having four guys with no leader is the best way to run a business? Doesn't that mean that the guy who says "no" always stops any innovation or new thinking? Three guys can approve but if one guy says "no" then it can't happen.'

Schultz and Swenson exchanged glances as they heard

Crombie's words quoted by Parsons. But Swenson looked calmer. 'Maybe it's up to the initiator and the other two to put a better case. To persuade the negative guy that whatever it is, it *is* for the company's benefit.'

'Fair enough, Marvin. Any other thoughts?'

Collins took a deep breath. 'I think that if we had a president whom we all respected, it would be beneficial. But we've worked together for a longish time now. We know each other very well. Perhaps too well.

'We could go for an outsider to break the log-jam but I don't think it would work. We've all got our own funny ways and we've made it all go pretty smoothly most of the time. We'd resent some outsider coming in to cash in on our hard work. That's reasonable enough.

'There's not a lot we disagree about and very little that's good that gets thrown out. Maybe we could vote on those issues in future. A majority and whatever it is goes through.'

Parsons said softly, 'OK. That makes sense. Let this be the first issue. Let's have a ballot on who's made president. Has anybody got any objection to that?'

Crombie intervened quickly. 'Maybe we should leave it, Harry. We can all think about it.'

Swenson laughed. 'Afraid you'll only get one vote?'

Parsons said, 'No. We can't just leave it. It's been raised. Let's settle it now, once and for all. Get some paper, Crombie, and tear up four slips. I won't vote. This is your thing and now it's been dragged out let's deal with it.'

All four of them noted the 'Crombie' and as Crombie tore a sheet of his pad into four pieces Parsons reached out, took them and gave them one each.

Collins said quietly, 'We ought to establish something, Harry. Like we said, these things can only be decided by a majority. If a guy gets two votes that's not enough. It's three or it's void. And if it's void I suggest we have one more vote. If that comes out the same then we forget the whole idea. Agreed?'

196

Parsons nodded. 'OK. Anyone disagree?'

Nobody disagreed and one after the other they wrote down a name and then handed over the folded slips. Parsons looked at them one by one.

'Two votes for Collins, one for Crombie, and one blank. That means we vote again.'

Swenson held up his hand. 'Forget it. Mine's the blank. I change it to Collins.'

Parsons looked at Collins, half-smiling. 'Congratulations, David. I wish you well. We all do, I'm sure.'

And Parsons looked àt Crombie who managed a smile and leaned across the table offering his hand to Collins. 'I'm sure you'll do a great job, David. You'll have my support, I assure you.'

And for the moment the tension was over.

Collins had tactfully taken the title of Chief Executive rather than President and there had been surprisingly little resistance from the others. Even Crombie seemed to accept the new situation.

He saw his extra responsibilities as being mainly concerned with easing the tension between the three Americans and creating an atmosphere where each could use his undoubted skill or talent for the agency's benefit. He put aside any prejudices he had for or against any of the others, and when there were tensions or conflicts of interest he was determinedly impartial. They seemed contented with the new structure, and, despite the fact that it was unsought and unexpected, the new responsibilities had brought the old zest for work back into his life.

He spent two or three evenings a week with Dolly Jones. Although he was the outsider in New York he took her to places where she had never been before. The group she ran around with were virtually unaware of New York apart from whatever were the most fashionable restaurants and night-clubs of the moment. Museums, art galleries, concerts, and even the Brooklyn Bridge, were as new to her

197

as to the first-time tourist. Whilst she was not noticeably impressed by where they went and what they did she seemed to enjoy being with him. She slept with him on those nights and sometimes at weekends when they explored the upper reaches of New York State, booking in at small country hotels.

There were odd occasions when he escorted her to parties given by her friends and he was conscious of her irritation that he wouldn't indulge in many of the activities they seemed to find amusing. There was a wide variety of drugs available, and casual couplings – in bedrooms and, as the evening wore on, virtually in public. On a couple of occasions he had left without her but she would appear not long afterwards at his apartment. No apologies but anxious to please.

It was one of those evenings when he had walked back alone from a luxury apartment on East 38th, where a party that had started with dope had by the time he left progressed to LSD on sugar lumps. The last vestiges of the yellow-stained snow were beginning to fade. There had been almost no spring, the weather had slid from the long winter to summer almost overnight. When Dolly was alone with him she seemed happy and contented but with her friends she was resentful of his indifference to them and his obvious dislike of their wild behaviour.

She had rung his bell about half an hour after he had got back. He was watching yet another re-run on TV of *Casablanca* when the bell rang, and when he opened the door she was standing there smiling, her head tilted as if to ward off reproof.

She sat on his lap on the big leather sofa, one arm across his shoulders, a cigarette in a long ivory holder.

He smiled. 'Who are you this time – Dorothy Parker?'

She looked at him, pouting. 'Why are you always such a creep when we go to my friends?'

'It just comes natural, honey.'

'Why not join in the fun?'

'It's not fun . . . they're too sad to have fun.'

198

'Sad? They're all having a hell of a good time.'

'They're not, kid. They're adults trying to be children again . . . and it's maybe not sad, but it *is* pathetic.'

'How do you know? You've never even tried a joint.'

'Why should I?'

'They make you really *see* everything. Colours, shapes, textures.'

'I see those things anyway. They're for morons who can't see . . . can't feel. Oafs with no imagination.'

'But it's fantastic, Dave. Reds that seem to shiver and cloth that kind of looks like a ploughed field.'

He laughed. 'You can see reds that shiver if you look at the sun across the Hudson when it's setting. All you need is a mind that's really alive and aware – you don't need a chemical to distort your brain.'

'You make it all seem so horrible.'

'They're just the adult version of spoilt brats, and they just aren't worth us arguing about.'

'D'you want to love me?'

And her eager mouth was on his as his hand went under her skirt.

Casey Jones swirled the brandy round in his glass and then cupped the glass in his hand as he looked across at David Collins.

'How do you feel about the agency?'

Collins smiled. 'It's the best in New York.'

Jones shrugged. 'How much of the action do you own personally?'

'Five per cent and an option on another five.'

'Did they give it you, or d'you pay for it?'

'The first five was given. Well, it was part of the deal when I moved over from London.'

'And the other five?'

'I'll have to pay for that.'

'When are you reckoning on buying it?'

'Quite soon but it doesn't affect my position. I'm chief

executive and I've got a contract. That's what matters to me.'

'You're wasted there, David. You're on the wrong side of the fence.'

'What does that mean?'

'How much are you making right now?'

Collins smiled. 'Enough.'

'What's that mean? Ninety thousand gross and nothing much from your equity because it has to go back into the business?'

'Something like that.'

'Another whisky?'

'No thanks. I've had my ration.'

'I guess you already know that my little gal's crazy about you?'

Collins laughed. 'I think I'm only one of a dozen. Don't worry about that. She'll settle down with one of her swingers and be the ideal wife and mother.'

Jones looked at his drink before he set the glass on the table and leaned back in his chair.

'She won't marry one of those assholes. She knows she'd be out in the snow as far as I'm concerned if she did. They'd spend every cent she's got and then light out. Or they'd screw me for a divorce settlement. No way. If she marries one of those creeps she's on her own.'

Casey Jones leaned forward, one big hand just resting on Collins' knee. 'She needs a guy like you, David. A real man. A mature man who'll rein her in. Show her what life's really all about. She's a great kid. All she needs – all I want for her – is a guy who'll care for her like I care for her. Any guy who will do that will find me on his side. I'll give him security and a good life.' Casey Jones paused. 'You and I understand one another, don't we, pal?'

And although Collins only nodded he was moved by the tears on the big man's craggy face. He stood up slowly. 'I guess I'd better get on my way, Casey. I've got an early meeting tomorrow.'

'D'you want my driver to take you back? You can leave

your car here and he can check it over for when you come down on Saturday.'

'I'd better take it. I'll probably need it before Saturday.'

'OK. Remember what I've said tonight, boy. I wasn't just gabbing.'

Collins smiled and nodded. 'I'll remember.'

As Collins drove back through the darkness he wondered what Casey Jones would have thought if he knew about those torrid sessions, the willing limbs, the sweating bodies and the undisguised lust.

He had always had the impression that Casey Jones encouraged the swingers who Dolly ran around with. Despite his business acumen the old man seemed something of an innocent in other ways, and since his wife had died he had tended to retreat into his business. His handful of cronies came from business and golfing contacts. Collins had heard from several people that Jones' courtship and marriage had been a real romance. The typical Scott Fitzgerald, Alabama society beauty, and the college boxer who happened also to have a good brain for business. But now that he was alone with just his business and the pretty daughter, he was ill at ease with both. Only habit drove him on in business and Dolly was a constant reminder of the pretty girl from Auburn, Alabama.

Her mother had loved parties and the social whirl, but it had been high-spirits and gaiety rather than her daughter's defiant wildness, and the old man was so obviously aware that he had neither the words nor the power to restrain her. His daughter loved him in her own way. He was a very masculine man compared with most of her men friends; the sons of rich men or untalented actors and writers and artists.

She treated Collins differently from the others and had said many times that he was just like her father. Desirable but square, an achiever but not driven, masculine but not macho. When they were alone she was very different from her public performance. Gone was the brittle chatter and the need to shock. All those attention-getting devices that

201

she used to make herself the girl they would all remember. Alone with him she talked intelligently about his work and the people she met. She gave him the impression that she wasn't entirely taken in by the self-styled swingers despite her apparent need to attract them. And she seemed to be genuinely disappointed when he sometimes couldn't see her at weekends.

As he drove across the bridge it was beginning to rain and by the time he got to the apartment it was dark. He poured himself a whisky and switched on the radio. They were playing a quiet, smooth version of 'Long Ago and Far Away' and he was aware of the words. He remembered singing them to some girl while they were dancing. All those years ago at the Masonic Hall in Birmingham. 'Long ago and far away . . . I dreamed a dream one day.' It was just a pleasant song in those days. The latest hit. No more. The girl had snuggled up to him as it went on '. . . and now, that dream is here beside me.' Had he dreamed a dream in those far-off days? He wasn't conscious of having dreamed any dreams. Not even of having any particular ambitions. Maybe that was why he never seemed contented for long. Why he always felt vaguely isolated from the rest of the world. Safely uncommitted. Untouched by human hand. Maybe it was time to settle down and make a new life. He had pulled down so many shutters in his mind. On Mary, his son, and Sally Major. Perhaps it was time to let in some fresh air.

He switched off the radio, undressed slowly and went to bed.

Chapter 27

CASEY JONES was watching in the mirror as his daughter stood behind him tying his dress tie. He had watched it done scores of times but he had never absorbed how to do it himself. He was tempted to buy one of those ready-made black ties, but Ruthie had always said that only the nouveau-riche and creeps wore made-up ties.

'Hurry up, honey, or I'll be late, and I'm acting president tonight.'

'Hold still, you great eejit, it's almost done . . . There. You look like John Wayne. You really do.'

He turned smiling to look at her proudly. 'And you look like your sweet mother the first time I ever saw her.'

'Tell me.' She smiled, because she'd heard it many times before.

'She was with her folks at the University ball. The graduation ball, and I'd just made it that year by the skin of my teeth and a bit of wire-pulling from the boxing coach.

'She was so beautiful. In a white lace dress and a kind of hood thing. And she was wearing a camellia in her hair. I just walked right up and asked her for every dance right there and then. She gave me that look. You know the one. Said I could have one dance and one only. I weaseled away trying for two dances but she wouldn't give in. So I chose the last waltz. I didn't dance with any other gal the whole night and she noticed. Best thing I've ever done. They played "Alabama Moon" and I drove her back to her house in my old man's Ford. No kisses on the porch or any of that stuff. So I shook her hand and then asked her to marry me. A year later to the day we got married.'

She looked up at his face. 'And when I get married?'

'You'll have the grandest wedding in the State, baby. You can rely on that.'

'I don't mean that. I mean how about you? How'll you be when I'm not here to drive you crazy?'

He looked at her face intently, and said softly, 'You mean this, don't you? You're serious.'

'Yes.'

'Who is it?'

'Dave Collins.'

'When did it happen? When did he ask you?'

'Tonight. He'll ask me tonight.'

'How do you know?'

'Feminine intuition. He would have asked me last night but I headed him off.'

'Why d'you head him off?'

'I wanted to keep up the family tradition.'

He nodded. 'He's a nice guy. He certainly is.'

She stood on tiptoe and kissed him.

'I'd marry you, old man, if I didn't know you so well.'

He laughed. As he drove to the Country Club, he wondered how he could persuade Dave Collins to come on his pay-roll. He was earning good money but it wouldn't be enough to keep Dolly happy. All those years ago he had boasted to Ruthie's father that he was making 10,000 dollars a year and the old man had smiled and said he'd put up the money for him to start his own business. It had been five years before he was making real money but Ruthie hadn't minded. But they weren't like her these days. Especially his pretty Dolly.

He sighed as he handed the keys of his Cadillac to the doorboy, but he was smiling and joking as he made his way through the early arrivals to the committee room. They might be in Connecticut but the band was going to play 'Alabama Moon' for the last waltz no matter what. For a moment he wondered if they had last waltzes any more.

The drive to the Joneses' house was a semi-circle of almost half a mile and Collins parked just inside the wrought iron gates with the hood down. There was the perfume of mimosa and lavender in the air as he turned off the radio. Dolly Jones looked at him, smiling.

'Why do you stick to this ghastly little Mustang?'

'I like it.'

'It's a typist's car not a chief executive's car.'

'You're a terrible snob, my love. Too much Scott Fitzgerald.'

'Zelda came from Montgomery, you know. Mother knew her well. They played tennis together sometimes.'

He smiled. 'I can't imagine Zelda playing tennis.'

She pouted. 'You're an old square.'

'That's something I want to talk to you about.'

'What? Being a square?'

'No. Being old.'

She frowned. 'I don't get it.'

'I'm twenty years and two months older than you.'

'So what? Most of the men I go around with are older than me.' She shrugged and smiled. 'I like it that way.'

'Are you sure?'

'Of course I am.'

For long moments he looked at her beautiful face. Then he said quietly, 'Will you marry me?'

She laughed. 'I thought you'd never ask.'

'Does that mean yes?'

'It means yes, a thousand times yes.'

It was an hour before he drove the car to the entrance of the house and he was aware of their dishevelled appearance as he opened the car door for her.

'Maybe we should leave it till tomorrow before we tell him.'

205

She laughed as she looked up at him, her body pressed close to his. 'Why, honey? He'll know you screw me and if we can't screw tonight, when can we?'

She combed her hair, straightened her dress and turned smiling to wipe the perspiration and lipstick from his face with a Kleenex. She laughed softly and said, 'I love it when you have me like that.'

He half-smiled and took her hand as they walked to the steps and the white marble portico.

Casey Jones was in his shirtsleeves when the butler ushered them into the library. The old man stood in his stockinged feet, just a little the worse for wear, and held up his whisky glass.

'A drink, David?'

'Thanks. But we really came in to have a word with you.'

Casey Jones was a tactful father and he looked at his daughter and said, 'What have you been up to this time?'

'David's asked me to marry him. And I've said yes.'

Casey Jones turned his head slowly to look at Collins, trying in vain to subdue his obvious pleasure.

'Congratulations, my boy. She's a nice little lady, my Dolly. I hope you'll both be very happy. I'm sure you will.' He turned to look at his daughter. 'And you look after this man.' She smiled. 'Like the song says, "A good man's hard to find." Give me a kiss and I'll get Mayhew to bring in some champagne.'

They drank two bottles of Veuve Cliquot but it was a slightly stilted celebration. The old man was aware that he was going to be lonely without her despite the worry she gave him. Collins was still rather shaken by the suddenness of his proposal and its acceptance. And Dolly, aware of her commitment, and despite the fact that it had all worked out as she had intended, was suddenly faced with the reality that both men would take it for granted that she was willing to change her whole lifestyle. There would be disbelief and amused smiles from the swingers but there were several of her girlfriends who already envied her her capture of David Collins. In the circle of friends he was an odd man out. Unintentionally a wet-blanket on any party, but highly desirable as a husband when you'd had your fling. There was just that vague lurking doubt in her mind as to whether the fling wasn't over too soon.

He stayed the night and was given the main guest bed-room but she slid into his bed while he was still in the bath.

The next morning he sat with Jones at the side of the pool sipping an orange juice. It was warm and the old man was in his towelling bathrobe and slippers.

'Where are you going to live, David?'

'I guess we'll find ourselves a place downtown.'

'The guest house by the stream is for you two. I'll close it to guests. It's yours alone. It's furnished, and my people will keep it serviced for you.' He screwed up his eyes against the sun as he looked at Collins. 'Have you thought any more about coming to work with me?'

'I was very grateful, Casey . . . I think I should carry on at the agency for the moment. There's a lot still to be done.'

'Have it your own way, my boy, but let me say this. If you moved over I'd stay president but you would be chief executive. I'd double your present salary whatever it is. You'd get twenty-five per cent of the equity when you join and you and Dolly would get the rest when I die.'

Collins put out his hand and touched the old man's shoulder. 'You're a generous man, Casey. And a good man. I shan't forget, I promise.'

'Another thing, Dave. Those people you work for at the agency. Remember they're strangers. Out for themselves. They employ you because they need your talent. But they'd cut your throat if it suited them. You'd be family here. And that makes a hell of a difference, believe me.' He turned at the footsteps and smiled. 'Here she is . . .

looking more beautiful than ever. You want a drink or something, baby?'

It was a beautiful, late spring day the day they were married. The ceremony was at Casey Jones' house and David Collins got up at six and walked from the guest wing to the house that was to be their home.

It was called the guest house but it was bigger and grander than some of the mansions on the outskirts of Bridgeport. The long elegant front with its Palladian pillars was bathed in the early sunlight and the dogwood trees at the side of the house were already in bloom. The carved front door was open, and as he walked inside he could hear the sound of voices upstairs and a vacuum cleaner. And there was a pleasant smell of floor polish in the big hall that led to the stairs and the ground floor rooms.

Except for the contents of two tea chests in the study there was nothing in the house that was his, but Casey had spared no expense to make it comfortable for the two of them and impressive to visitors.

He walked back into the garden and over a rustic bridge to a stone bench on the bank of the stream that ran through the estate. For the last twenty-four hours he had had terrible doubts about marriage itself. And the doubts about marriage were not about its pleasures or disadvantages but the all-pervading fear that he was doing something more than just marrying for the second time. He seemed to be closing the door on everything that had happened in his life before that day. His first marriage, his son, his background. And Sally Major. Everything. He wasn't just putting down new roots but acknowledging that he had no roots. He didn't belong to anybody and he didn't belong to any place. It seemed suddenly to be a gamble. Like the cliché in those old Westerns. All his life on the turn of one card.

There were fish feeding by the wooden bridge over the stream, the circles widening and mingling together, and in the still, morning air he could hear the dull roar of trucks far away on the highway. He could walk out right now. Back to his routine. To the familiar insecurity of his present life, with no responsibilities and no obligations. But why should he? Why should he leave a beautiful girl whom he loved, and all the financial security that a man could wish for? A father-in-law who admired and respected him. Nothing would really change. It didn't have to. These were not changes, they were wonderful extras bolted on to his old routine. For a moment he closed his eyes and prayed a prayer. There were no words, no pleas, no requests. Just a silent message. A stone thrown into a mental wishing-well.

There were over two hundred guests and an extraordinary atmosphere of friendliness and goodwill that warmed his soul like a long slug of brandy. The ceremony itself had been more moving than he expected and Dolly looked even more beautiful than usual.

Casey Jones stayed behind with the guests as his driver took them to New York and La Guardia.

There was a bunch of red roses on Dolly's plane seat from the agency and a small present from them on Collins' seat, too. When he unwrapped it it was a Rolex watch and on the back was inscribed 'To mark all the happy hours' and the date.

Suddenly his doubts had gone. All was going to be well. He knew it. He could tell.

They had three happy, lazy weeks in Miami and came home tanned and contented, eager to get back to their new life.

Chapter 28

It SEEMED strange being in London again and faintly disturbing to realise that he had no home or roots in England any more. When he had gone to New York he had never felt that he would stay permanently in the United States, and although he found his life there pleasant enough he still didn't see it as his home ground. Maybe it was time to change his thinking. He had to belong somewhere.

The meetings with Harry Parsons and the London board had been routine and successful. They met quarterly and he reported on the agency situation in New York and the advertising business in general in the USA, and Parsons detailed the London position.

They discussed the exchange of creative and media-buying staff between London and New York and Collins gave an informal chat to the Creative Circle and was paraded to meet half a dozen of the agency's more important new English clients.

Parsons drove him to the airport for the afternoon flight and as they stood having a last drink at the bar he remembered and said, 'By the way, Harry. I wrote to you about taking up my share option, months ago. I never had a confirmation.'

'I phoned it to our solicitors to sort out. I should have told you. I'll liven them up tomorrow.'

'There's no problem, is there?'

Parsons pursed his lips. 'Not a problem, exactly, but Crombie was a bit touchy about it. Anyway. Don't worry about it, I'll get the solicitors to write you direct.'

'Crombie was glad enough to make it part of the deal at the time.'

'Too true.'

'And they've all made a hell of a lot of dollars more than they would have made if they'd gone on alone or split up.'

'Sure. Sure. People have short memories when it suits them. That's your flight they're calling. Good trip and love to the new lady.' Parsons patted his shoulder as he picked up his briefcase.

As Collins walked alone to the boarding gate he felt glad for the first time to be going back. London was a dull place, really. It was like somebody had switched all the lights off. And New York was all lights. Neon and brash they might be, but it was alive and energetic.

There were lights on all over the main house and there was a white Jaguar parked by the line of garages. He parked his own car with the keys left in the ignition and gathered his travel bag and the flowers and the packages for Dolly and walked across to their own house.

There was a light on under the porch and in their bedroom and as he walked from the hall to the open living room there was a faint incense-like smell in the air. He poured himself a drink and walked with it in his hand to the foot of the stairs and called her name. There was a radio on quite loud and he guessed she couldn't hear him.

He went back for the flowers and went slowly up the stairs. As he opened their bedroom door he couldn't take it all in at first. There were three people on the big bed. A man and two girls and they were all naked. And one of them was Dolly. The other girl he knew as Georgie and the man was Dwyer, who had the Jaguar franchise in Bridgeport. They were too intent on what they were doing to notice him. Georgie's mouth was on one of Dolly's breasts and Dwyer's hand was moving avidly between Dolly's long legs, his mouth on hers.

For a moment he stood there in disbelief. Then he

211

moved round the bed, grabbed Dwyer by the hair and dragged him off the bed. He was never clear about what happened in the next few minutes but he could remember shouting at Dwyer and the girl to get the hell out, and both of them screaming obscenities at him as they grabbed their clothes. And as he stood there panting he realised that the smell in the living room was marijuana.

When he turned to look at Dolly she 'had put on a dressing gown and was calmly tying the belt. She looked up at him coolly and said, 'Well you certainly made an entrance, lover boy. The guy in the white hat rides again.' She paused and grinned. 'How was swinging London?'

'What the hell are you up to? What's going on?'

She smiled. 'For God's sake. You don't want me to spell it out, do you? You've got eyes. You saw what was going on. A couple of old friends came a-calling. That's all. Just a little cuddle.'

'Is that what you call just a little cuddle?'

'Oh for Christ's sake, he was only having a feel. He wasn't screwing me.'

'He would have been if I hadn't come in.'

'So you saved your little girl from a fate worse than death.'

'And that's all you've got to say.'

'Don't be a complete asshole, honey. There's half a dozen of my girlfriends who'd be glad to let you do the same if you want to square the accounts. Just say the word and I'll fix it for you.'

'Why did you let it happen?'

'I was bored, honey. You've been away nearly a week. I needed a bit of fun.'

'You call that fun?'

She smiled. 'You used to think it was fun, old boy. You had your hand up my skirt the second time we went out together.'

'But you're married now. You're my wife.'

'So what? Why all the fuss? We're still married. I wasn't

212

alone with Tom. His girlfriend was there too. You could have had her while he was having me.'

For a moment he stared at her, then he walked to the door and as he got there she said, 'David.'

He turned. 'What?'

'I'm sorry,' she said quietly, 'I was a fool. I shouldn't have done it. And I won't ever do it again. I promise.'

For a moment he hesitated, tempted to walk across and take her in his arms, but he nodded and just looked at her before turning away and walking down to the living room. He poured himself a drink but he didn't drink it. He walked to the stairs and then stopped, his eyes closed. And then he opened his eyes and hurried out to his car.

He drove back to New York, garaged his car and walked to the apartment. The telephone was ringing as he went in and there was only one person who could guess that he was there. He let it ring and walked down to the Waldorf for a drink, and then moved on to a bar on 42nd Street. By the time he got back to the apartment it was beginning to get light. It was nearly ten o'clock before he woke. He bathed, shaved and walked to the agency, his mind in a turmoil of indecision and depression. He had no idea what he should do.

He had expected a telephone call from Dolly but no call came. He had a sandwich-lunch meeting with Schultz and Swenson and the routine began to give him back his equilibrium. She was waiting for him when he got back to the apartment. Contrite and apologetic. And he was aware that he had missed her.

His life with Dolly was not easy after the incident with Dwyer. It wasn't something he could forget, and his inclination was to keep them both well away from her old circle of friends. But he recognised that any overt restrictions he placed on what she could do would be bitterly resented or could even be defied. He didn't want to put his authority to the test.

He saw that they spent as much time as possible in New York, and his position at the agency made it easy for him to get tickets for all the most popular shows and concerts. They both joined the local Country Club and took lessons from the golf professionals. She was already a good tennis player. Far better than he was. She had made the semi-finals in the mixed doubles at the end of the season with Jimmy Wheeler as her partner.

Wheeler owned and ran the leading gallery in Bridgeport and was much the same age as Collins. With an attractive wife, two pretty daughters and a thriving business, Jimmy Wheeler was a happily married man. He liked Dolly but he was immune to fluttering eyelashes and plunging necklines, and he and Collins became good friends, the two families often going for picnics and boat-trips together. Julie Wheeler was older than Dolly but she was an extrovert whose cynical wisecracks hid the thoughts of a very perceptive lady. Having a French mother, she always looked chic and stylish.

Collins felt that Julie, who was lively without being outrageous, would be a good influence on Dolly, and Jimmy was an ally inasmuch as he was charming and attentive to Dolly but not interested in playing around. The Wheelers were happy to have Casey Jones along with his daughter and her husband, and Casey liked both the Wheelers and enjoyed the various expeditions that he was invited to. He particularly liked Jimmy Wheeler as a straightforward man who had a specialist knowledge of a world that was quite foreign to him, and frequently invited Wheeler over for a drink on his own. The relationship between the two couples gradually became genuine friendship and there was no need in the end for invitations. They dropped into one another's homes uninvited but always welcome.

They had been over to the Wheelers that afternoon and Casey had gone back to the guest house with the two of them for an early evening drink. A cold wind was blowing across the flats from the sea and somebody from the main house had come over and lit the log fire for them.

Collins poured them drinks and then joined them round the fire. He smiled at Dolly.

'I've been terribly extravagant today.'

Dolly laughed. 'Join the club.'

'What have you bought?'

'I went with Julie and bought two things. A white cocktail dress. That wasn't extravagant. Well, not very.' She paused and looked at her father. 'This is the part where Dave always says – "get to the point and tell me how you've sold the grand piano."'

The old man smiled. 'I know the feeling. So get to the point.'

'I bought some pearls. Real pearls. They're beautiful. Shall I show them to you?'

Collins smiled. 'Go on, then. Where are they?'

'I'll get them. They're upstairs.'

While she was away the old man said softly, 'I'm very grateful to you, Dave. Not only for what you've done at the company, but for your patience with Dolly. We were both very lucky to find you. Don't think I don't notice the efforts you've made to keep everything on an even keel.'

'Give her her due, she's responded remarkably well. It's not easy to give up the habits of years or the standards that your contemporaries judge you by.'

'Yes. I think she's tried. Just keep her well away from those bastards. They'd love to get her back in their clutches. Here she comes.'

Her eyes were alight as she opened the box to show them the pearls on their velvet cushion. They really were beautiful. Twin ropes, with a gold catch. She lifted them from the box and fastened them around her slender neck. They shone almost like opals in the flames from the fire and Collins realised again how beautiful she was. She turned, smiling, to face him.

'Aren't they beautiful, honey?'

'Not as beautiful as you. Let me do a deal with you.'

'What sort of deal?'

215

'Let me buy the pearls for you and you buy me my extravagance.' He smiled. 'It's not wildly expensive.'

She seemed to hesitate and he said quickly, 'Let me buy them for you, Doll. I specially want to.'

'Why?'

'Two reasons I guess. First because they're really "you". And secondly because I love you. I'd like to buy them for you.'

She pouted her mouth, smiling. 'You don't know how much you're letting yourself in for.'

'It doesn't matter. Really it doesn't. Please me. Let me do it.' She slid her slim arms around his neck and kissed him. A long lingering kiss that aroused him.

Later that night when they were both naked on their bed she wore just the pearls while they were making love.

It was when they were lying side by side afterwards that he said, 'Nobody even asked me what my extravagance was.'

She leaned up on one elbow. 'Tell me what it was.'

'It was an oil painting. Victorian and English. A small girl in a pinafore in a field of daisies.'

'Did you buy it from Jimmy?'

'Yes. He even gave me a reduction and he never does that. Like your pearls, he said it was very "me". You'll like it.'

'I'm sure I will. I'll phone him tomorrow.' She smiled at him. 'Can you love me again?'

There was a London phone call for him mid-afternoon.

'This is Guy Hampton, Mr Collins. I'm a partner at the agency's solicitors. I had to look into the question of your share option.'

'Should be no problem, Mr Hampton. It was five per cent.'

'Oh yes, there's no problem about that, it was the question of *quantum* and that has meant waiting for the accountants to come back with a figure.'

'Why are they involved?'

'They have to establish the value of the shares.'

'I don't understand. We bought at seventeen dollars a share. The three American directors, myself and Mr Parsons received our initial holdings for a nominal five dollars for the package.'

'Yes, I've got notes of that, but your option shares were for you to purchase.'

'Sure. At seventeen dollars a share.'

'That was the value a long time ago, Mr Collins. It's a different picture now. That's why I'm phoning you in case you have your own solicitor to advise you.'

'On what?'

'The current value per share is 120 dollars, that would mean just over a hundred thousand dollars for your option shares. I just wanted to check that you were aware of that.'

'That's crazy. That would mean I've been sweating away here to jack up the price I have to pay.'

'I'm afraid that's how it is, Mr Collins. D'you still want to go ahead?'

'Of course I do. But not at that price. I'll speak to Mr Parsons and get him to have a word with you.'

'I've already spoken to Mr Parsons. It was he who gave me my instructions.'

'I'll speak to him myself. Leave it to me.'

'Right you are, sir.'

Blazing with anger, Collins told the operator to get Parsons in London for him. There was an hour's delay because Parsons was on his way home and then he eventually came through.

'Hello, David. What can I do for you?'

'The option shares, Harry. What's all this crap about me paying 120 dollars a share?'

'That's the current value, David. You had an option to buy an additional five per cent any time during the period. Seven years.'

'That means I've been working my ass off here to make sure I pay a high price.'

217

'Not really. The choice of waiting was yours. If you'd bought on the first day you'd have paid seventeen dollars. You chose to wait until now when they're worth a lot more.'

'I find it outrageous, Harry. I really do.'

'It's not, I assure you. They were worth seventeen dollars years ago. No more, no less. They're genuinely worth 120 dollars at this moment. It's not some made-up figure, it's what the accountants have worked out.'

'And you're sticking to that despite my – my protests?'

'It's not a question of sticking to it, David. It's what was agreed.'

'We're a private limited company; those shares could be issued at a dollar a piece if the board said so.'

'Maybe. This is business, David, it's not personal.'

'And you wouldn't recommend the board to go my way.'

'My dear boy . . .'

'Yes or no, Harry?'

'If you put it like that, David, you give me no choice. The answer has to be no, and you should bear in . . .'

Collins hung up on Parsons who gave him the chance of an out by phoning back to the agency to say the line had been cut off, and would Mr Collins phone him back. He didn't.

He asked the girl to get Casey Jones and when he came on the phone Collins asked if he could see him alone at his office and Casey agreed straight away.

It was nearly two hours later when Collins was led by the works security guard to Casey's office.

The old man was already having a whisky and another was on the silver tray for Collins.

'What's the matter, Dave? You look all-in.'

Collins took a deep breath. 'I need some advice, Casey, I've nobody else to turn to.'

'I'm flattered, boy. Tell me the problem.'

Collins outlined the history of his life at the agency in both London and New York and then explained the conflict on the share option. The old man listened carefully and when Collins had finished Casey closed his eyes for long moments, opened them and turned slowly to look at the younger man.

'That's not your only problem, is it, boy?'

'I don't understand.'

'You young people think I'm some sort of dinosaur, don't you? You think I don't know what goes on in this town. Or maybe that I'm not old enough to know what the young people are up to.' He shook his head slowly. 'You're wrong. I know about most of it. I could ruin half the people in town if I passed on all the gossip I hear. And most of it ain't just gossip. It's fact . . . with a bit of decoration here and there.' He looked towards the window and the bowl of roses and said nothing for several minutes before turning back to look at Collins.

'I heard about what went on at your place. I heard it on the grapevine at lunch-time the next day. They didn't mention any name except Dwyer's or I'd have knocked their teeth out. But I saw Dwyer's car parked outside the house that day and I saw him and his girlfriend come out of your place half-dressed. It doesn't shock me. It doesn't disgust me.' His voice faltered and he said softly, 'It breaks my heart, Dave. It makes me wish I was dead. But if I was dead I couldn't try to help her. Or you, for that matter.'

'I'm sorry you had to know, Casey. I really am.'

'Look, boy. Let's face the facts of life. You and I are very like one another in many ways. I think the word is "square". And if being square means that I don't take drugs or screw everything in sight then I'm proud of being square. If her mother had been alive these last five years it would have been a lot different. I've done my best but my word never carried like her mother's. And I console myself that even with her mother around there would still have been some wildness. It's there and there's no denying

219

it. I went across to see Dolly this afternoon, and I read her the Riot Act. I've told her that until she's twenty-five all her allowance comes through you. She may get it all or she may not get a cent. It's entirely up to you. You'll be the boss. It's a crude way of dealing with it but it's the only way I can think of. She's been scared that she wouldn't get back in your good books but you seem to have dealt with it well, and I guess she's learned some lesson or other.

'But let's come to you, boy, and your agency. It's a poor return for sweating your guts out for them. But it's legal and they're entitled. They sound like mean bastards to me. I want you to come here and take over. Salary 150,000 a year and share of profits that aren't ploughed back. Fifty per cent of the equity right away and as soon as you're broken in you're the boss. What do you say?'

'It's very generous, Casey, but I'm not an electronics man. Do you think it would work?'

'I'm not an electronics man. But I know how to run a business and so do you. It'll work. I wouldn't suggest it if I wasn't sure.'

'OK. When do I start?'

'Tomorrow.'

'I'll have to give them at least a month's notice.'

'Tell 'em to go screw themselves and threaten to sue for fraud on the option if they kick up a stink. They'll soon climb down. I know those birds. I've dealt with them all my life. But I had something you haven't got yet. A lot of dough. And believe me, after a certain amount, the only value of money is to say "go screw" when you want to.' He sighed. 'Do you want to come back to my place for the night or what?'

'No. I'll go and tell Dolly what we've talked about.'

'Don't think I'm condoning what went on. I'm not. I'll settle the score with Dwyer in my own good time and my own way. But as far as Dolly's concerned I rate it as crass stupidity and a need to show off. She's not evil, son. I'm sure of that.'

220

'Of course she's not. How about I bring her across to you for dinner?'

Casey smiled, but there were tears in his eyes as he said, 'I love you, fella. I really do.'

Chapter 29

IT WAS past 9.30 by the time the last of the agency's staff had left and Collins started collecting up his personal things from his desk, and it was almost midnight when he had finished. He laid out his office keys on the bare desk-top and it reminded him of all those years ago when Parsons had left the old agency. He reached for the telephone and asked the White Plains operator for a person-to-person call to Parsons in London.

Ten minutes later he was put through. Parsons sounded amiable and lively.

'How are things, David?'

'Fine. And your end?'

'We've just landed Walker Food Products and we're having a celebratory meal with our team tomorrow.'

'Congratulations. Enjoy yourselves.'

'Was there something you wanted me for?'

'Yes, Harry. I've posted a letter to you today. It's my resignation. I didn't feel it was suitable material for putting on the Telex . . . I thought you should know straight away, though . . . so that you can deal with making a replacement.'

There was a long silence and then Parsons said, 'You're kidding me. Aren't you?'

'I'm afraid not, Harry.'

'But why, for God's sake? Why?'

'I guess the fact that you have to ask is reason enough.'

'What the hell does that mean?'

'You honestly mean you've no idea why I'm leaving?'

'Of course I haven't. How could I have known? You've never even hinted at such a thing.'

'I didn't like the agency's attitude about my option shares.'

There was a pause at the other end then Parsons said slowly, 'Are you telling me that that's the only reason you're resigning?'

'More or less. The agency's attitude was typical of what I most dislike in business.'

'So why didn't you discuss it with me personally?'

'I did, Harry. You agreed with the agency attitude. You said so. Quite positively.'

'But that was just an initial reaction. We could have discussed it again. You could have put your case to the combined board.'

'As far as I'm concerned, a "no" from you, Harry, is a "no" from the board. It wasn't just the "no", it was the indifference to my feelings.'

'Oh come on, Dave. We're not Girl Guides, for Christ's sake, we're business people. You are, I am, we all are.'

'I'm not, Harry.'

'Dave, you're one of the most successful businessmen I know.'

'I'm not really, Harry. I can play the game but I'm not a businessman.'

'What's that mean?'

Collins laughed softly. 'Just what I said.'

'Has somebody been getting at you, Harry? Some other agency?'

'No.'

'Are you sure?'

'Of course I'm sure.'

'What are you going to do?'

'I'm joining Dolly's father in his business.'

'That's crazy, man. Fatal. The son-in-law in the family business. They'll have you by the short and curlies. My God. I can't believe it. You'll be for ever dancing for two masters. The old man on one hand and Dolly on the other. Jesus.'

'It won't be like that, Harry. But thanks for the comment.'

'Suppose I fly over and we talk about it? We can sort this out in five minutes face to face. I'll tell the board that you're buying those shares at seventeen bucks and that's that. They can like it or lump it.'

'Thanks for the thought, Harry, but it's too late, I've made up my mind.'

'We'll see, boyo, we'll see. Uncle Harry's going to put his thinking cap on. I'll contact you tomorrow. Take care of yourself and keep an open mind just for a couple of days.'

'Have a good lunch, Harry.'

'See you, Dave.'

When the telephone roused Casey Jones from his sleep at four a.m. he was not best pleased. He was even more annoyed when he realised it was Parsons on the other end.

'Sorry to call you so late, Casey, but I've got a problem. I guess you know what I'm referring to.'

'Maybe. But carry on.'

'I gather that Collins is leaving us and joining you. What's more, I gather that he's physically moved out. Now that's not on, Casey. Really not on. His contract calls for six months' notice on either side.'

Parsons waited for Jones to respond but he didn't, and Parsons went on. 'I'm sure you wouldn't condone this sort of behaviour.'

'He's a grown man, Parsons. I guess he does what he thinks is right.'

'It's breaking a contract, so how can it be right?'

'I'm not well up on these problems of business ethics, Parsons. You'd better talk to Dave himself.'

'But you could influence him surely, Casey.'

'I wouldn't try, old friend. I wouldn't try. I think you

shouldn't try either. You might lose more than you gain.'

'How, Casey, how?'

'Our account with your folk in New York is substantial. If you go along with him I guess he'll leave it with you. If you hassle him he'd probably move it elsewhere.'

'And you'd back him in that?'

'He doesn't need my backing. He can do what he thinks best.'

'I see. Ah well, I thought I'd better talk with you anyway. How's business?'

'Fine. Real fine. I guess you'd better let me get back to sleep, old chap.'

Casey didn't wait for a reply. He hung up and was asleep again in a few minutes.

Chapter 30

FOR SIX months Collins probed into every detail of the electronics company's operations. The work-force was quite small. Fifty per cent of them were high-technology specialists and the rest of the staff were skilled assemblers working to fine limits. The products covered every aspect of electronic communications from computers to defence projects and radio transceivers. Jones and Morrell Electronics had a first-class reputation as innovators and manufacturers of reliable equipment. The electronics press suggested that their reputation had been achieved not only by the large investment in talent right from the start but also by avoiding the usual pitfalls of putting products on the market before they were properly 'de-bugged', just to ease cash-flow problems.

A further two months were spent in formulating his recommendations. It was a comparatively brief report of less than fifty pages and when he and Casey had met to discuss it Collins was aware that this could be the first time that his apparent authority could be questioned. He was tramping around on another man's dreams. Casey Jones had insisted that they held the meeting at their house rather than in the formal surroundings of the plant office.

Casey was wearing an open-necked shirt and denim jeans. He pointed at Collins' bound report.

'I've read it, Dave. It's first-class. You don't need my approval.'

Collins smiled. 'There are things I want to discuss with

you, all the same. Things where I need the benefit of your experience. And another opinion.'

Jones shrugged. 'OK. Fire away.'

'There are two main things. The R. & D. budget covering microchips . . . and the erratic supply of casings. I think we should keep our research budget on chips just to keep us ahead of the game but I think we should buy in. Producing our own was fine way back when supplies were erratic, but there are a dozen first-class outfits clamouring for our business now. Our production costs are more than we would pay for bought-in chips. And we can sell our manufacturing plant as part of a deal.'

Jones nodded. 'I think you're right. And we'd get the benefit of somebody else's research to add to our own. We'd free space and cash. Just go ahead.'

'The other thing is more down to earth. As of yesterday, we've got a quarter of a million dollars' worth of high-tech equipment that we can't invoice or despatch because we haven't got the simple, metal cases that the equipment goes in. Cases that only cost us fifteen thousand bucks all told. That's crazy. We've got a metal basher virtually controlling our output. We've got products sitting there where we've spent ninety-five per cent of the manufacturing costs, all held up for something that represents only half of one per cent. But it happens to be the last stage of production. And to make things worse we own fifty per cent of the equity of the company that's holding us up. I think we should buy the other half and take control.'

'More coffee, Dave?'

'No thanks.'

'It's a long story. There were a lot of companies making metal cases for hi-fi equipment, radios and the like but none of them produced to a standard I would accept. So I gave Gus Maddox the cash to convert his plant and up-grade his products. When we first started we couldn't fill his plant capacity by quite a margin. He had to look for other people's work to top it up. In those days our competitors didn't like buying from a company half-owned by me, a competitor. And they refused to give him orders on the grounds that they'd always be the Arse-end Charlies, with us taking what we wanted and them being left high and dry. It was a reasonable argument so we agreed, Gus and me, to a limitation. We could have half the capacity and no more. That's why we've got this problem now.'

'So we buy Gus out at a fair price.'

Casey Jones grinned. 'I wish we could, Dave. But old Gus likes running his own ship. He'd just as soon buy our half back.'

'So let him and we'll produce ourselves on more modern plant than he's got. And we'll be independent.'

'Gus would know that buying us out would mean having to find new customers for half his production. I doubt if his sales people could do that right away. Could take a couple of years before he's made up the loss.'

'So if we offer to buy him out he'll refuse. And if we offer him our half he'll hesitate.'

Casey laughed. 'I guess that's about it. But I agree with you. We should do one or the other. It's costing us money and goodwill at the moment.'

'You've no inclination either way? Us buying or us selling?'

'No. But he's going to delay and delay a decision.'

'Is it OK if I negotiate with him? To buy or to sell.'

'Sure. He's tough but he's straightforward.'

Maddox Metal Fabrications was on the edge of the Huntingdon Turnpike. A neat modern building with its offices in a separate block.

Gus Maddox came out himself to greet him as he parked his car in the visitors' lot, and Collins realised that he had seen him several times at the Country Club.

'Welcome, Mr Collins. Do you want to look around the plant before we start?'

228

'I don't think so, Mr Maddox. I've seen all the metal bashing I ever want to see.'

'Casey tells me you started off in an iron foundry.'

'Yes. Sounds a bit old-fashioned now.'

Maddox laughed. 'I like old-fashioned things. They always worked. Let's go on in.'

The older man took his arm and led him down a short corridor to a modern office that ran the whole width of the building.

Maddox pointed to a leather armchair and took one himself. As he sat down he said, 'You know, I've racked my brain for hours about our talk on the phone and I'm damned if I can see any solution.'

'Well. Let's go over all the pros and cons.'

'OK. Let's do that.'

They talked for five hours, going over every aspect of a possible deal both ways. Buying or selling. By five o'clock it looked like deadlock.

'Can I ask you, Gus, what your own personal feelings are? Forget the company aspects.'

Gus Maddox leaned back in his chair and looked up at the ceiling. When he eventually looked back at Collins he said, 'You know, I really don't give a damn one way or the other. I could be happy buying you out and going it alone. Provided the price was right. Or I could happily sell out to you guys and enjoy my garden, a bit of golf and the boat.'

'You know what the real problem is, Gus?'

'Tell me.'

'It's the price. There's kind of two different prices, depending on who's buying and who's selling.'

'Yeah. If I'm buying I've got to take into account certain things, and if I'm selling I've got to have other things in mind.' He grinned. 'One way I want the price low, the other way I want it high. So what's a fair price? We could haggle about that for years.'

'Can I suggest a way out that's fair either way it goes?'

'Sure. Go ahead.'

'We take two pieces of paper. On one of them it says "buy or sell" and on the other it says "price per share". We put them face down on the table here and you take one. I get the other. Whichever one we get we have to write down what we choose. So if you got the "buy or sell" paper you write "buy" or "sell" according to what you want. If I get the "price per share" paper I have to write the price down. If I put the share price low I could be selling at that price if that's what you've written on your piece. If I make it too high I might be buying at that price. Neither of us knows what the other has put until we turn the papers over. Whatever we come up with that's the deal.'

'And if I get the "price per share" paper I decide what price I'll either have to sell or buy at according to whether you've put "buy" or "sell" on your paper?'

'Yes.'

Maddox closed his eyes for long minutes, thinking. When he opened his eyes he was smiling. 'You know this idea is so good, so right, but it makes me ashamed.'

'Why?'

'Just because it *is* fair. Fair to both parties. And in business we're never really looking for a *fair* deal. Our idea of a fair deal is one where we come out better than the other guy.'

'This isn't a normal business deal, Gus.'

'Why not?'

'Neither party is really going to lose, whichever way it goes. We shall either be making our own containers here at our own plant with you in charge if you want, or at our existing plant over the river. You'll either be going it alone or you'll have enough to retire on in peace.'

'Let me talk to Cassie.' As he stood up he said, 'You know, this is like those old stories of fellows gambling away their inheritance at blackjack or something.'

Collins laughed. 'We're not gambling at all. I'm not the gambling kind. We're just sorting out a problem in a way that won't harm any of us.'

As Guy Maddox left the room Collins wondered if he would have had the courage to settle the deal in this unorthodox way if he had been Maddox. He wasn't at all sure. He couldn't see why he would have doubts and perhaps it was only the untraditional approach that disturbed him. And he smiled to himself as he realised that he was beginning to think like a so-called businessman at last.

Ten minutes later Maddox came back, beaming. 'She says get on with it. Says it's crazy but right.' He handed two cards to Collins. 'I've brought two cards. You write the words.' He paused. 'What did Casey think of all this?'

'I didn't discuss it with him.'

'But you'd thought of the idea before you came here?'

'Yes. As a last resort, and only if I was sure that you genuinely didn't mind which way it went so long as it was a fair deal.'

'Have you seen our accounts? Yes, of course you have. You get them monthly. OK, let's do it.'

Collins wrote on the cards then placed them on the desk face down.

'You go first, Gus.'

'I can't bear it.'

But he reached out and took a card and Collins took the other. Collins' card said 'Buy or Sell'.

He had already worked out in his mind that it would be better for them to buy out Gus Maddox. He would get a decent sum of money and could carry on at a salary if he wanted to. The only snag was the share price that Gus would write on his card. The shares stood at thirty-eight dollars on present accounts. To buy control meant you had to pay higher. He reckoned that if they paid sixty dollars a share they would be lucky. If they paid sixty-five to seventy it would be fair, and above that they would be paying well over the odds.

When he looked at Gus Maddox he had already finished writing but he still held his card.

'Let's put them down together, Gus.'

The two cards went down and Collins saw what Maddox had written. It said 'Seventy dollars per share'.

'Are you happy with this, Gus?'

'I guess so. A bit sad, but we couldn't have gone on in the old way.'

'Can I meet you tomorrow and go over a contract for you being chief executive at your present salary and general conditions?'

'It'd be a bit of a consolation for me, Dave.'

'Shall we give Casey a ring and we all have a drink at the club?'

'Why not? A great idea. There's the phone. You ring him.'

Collins' meetings with the agency could have been embarrassing all round but he made great efforts to see that they were not. Despite his experience he never made any attempt to take over agency functions. He gave them good briefs on what had to be achieved in results and made no suggestions as to approach or media. And for their part the agency made sure that their best brains were put on the account.

Crombie had joined another agency and Swenson was now the agency's president. Schultz handled the account and led its creative team.

It had been after a briefing meeting when the others had gone that Schultz said, 'Seems a long time ago, Dave. How's it all turned out?'

'Very well.'

'You don't miss this place?'

Collins smiled. 'Let's say I sometimes miss being in the advertising game but not very often.'

'You don't have any hard feelings about the agency?'

'I never think about it except when I'm due for a meeting.'

'Any hard feelings about Harry Parsons?'

'No. As you said: It's all a long time ago. I just don't think about the place, period.'

'He's in New York at the moment. I know he'd like to see you again.'

Collins laughed. 'What makes you think that?'

'He often says so.'

'What's the object of meeting me?'

'None, so far as I know. Just Old Lang Syne and all that crap.'

'Why doesn't he give me a call?'

'I'd guess he's scared he'll get a flea in his ear.'

'Tell him to call me. If he wants to.'

Parsons called him that evening at home and he invited him over to dinner the next day. He rang Casey Jones to invite him too.

Harry Parsons arrived in a chauffeur-driven limousine, with an extravagant bunch of red roses for Dolly. His handshake and greeting were effusively American and Collins was amused at the act.

During dinner Parsons went out of his way to praise the work that Collins had done at the London agency and in New York. He ventured to suggest that Collins might be missing the creativity of agency life.

Casey Jones pursed his lips. 'I've never quite understood what you advertising guys mean when you talk about creativity. What the hell is it, apart from having a few bright ideas that work?' He paused and added drily, 'And of course a few bright ideas that don't work.'

'It's more than that, Casey. It really is. Take David, here, for example. He had a knack, a talent, call it what you will, for taking the facts, the research figures, and translating them into pictures and words that were in everyday terms rather than business terms. He used to . . .'

'That's what he's still doing, Harry. Running a modern

233

business isn't just computers and production lines for God's sake. It's understanding people. People who work for you. People you sell to and people who use your products or service. And you get that understanding because you actually care about people. It's not a talent and it's no mystery either. This fellow does it as naturally as breathing. And he does it for one simple reason. He was brought up in the back streets of wherever it was and he saw how real people live.'

Parsons smiled. 'So what has he got that you and I haven't got?'

'He's got the guts to say out loud what most of us know and feel, but don't want to admit to. We haven't got the guts to say we're scared or greedy or loving or gentle. He does.'

'But loving and being scared doesn't sell industrial goods, Casey.'

'That's where you so-called business people make a great mistake. You live in those ivory towers in Manhattan, surrounded by artists and writers and film people, and conjure up this magic world for the average housewife. And then you have to turn your fine minds to the dreary world of industrial advertising. So you put on long, serious faces, and dark blue suits, and you do what you call technical advertising. And that's where you're wrong. All of you.' Casey smiled and pointed at Collins. 'All except this fellow. And why is he the exception? Because he's worked in a plant. Got his hands dirty. Not the boss's son "going through the works" so he can end up boss. But because it was the only job he could get. And he knows something you guys won't ever learn. When you're selling industrial goods you're still selling them to an individual. A man or a woman. And they're going to be used by an individual. Industrial advertising should be the same as any other advertising . . . aimed at people. Technicians, scientists, toolmakers . . . they're men not goddam robots.'

Parsons said amiably, 'Are you sure you're not exaggerating, Casey? Most of our industrial clients demand a technical approach.'

'Exactly. And because their products bore you you go along with it. It's the easy way out.'

'Can you give me an example?'

Casey Jones was silent for a moment. 'Yes. Right up to date. You look at any of the ads for office computers. They talk about modems, bits and bytes, memories, all the peripherals that are available and the rest of it. All that tells you is that they're proud of their damn machine and in love with its technology.'

'And what should they tell you?'

'They should tell you what use it is to *you*. What you can do with it. A chief executive, a sales manager, an accountant doesn't know the difference between random access memory and read only memory. And why should he? All he wants to know is what he can do with the damn thing when he's spent his dough. Does it provide him with more information, faster? Does it help him increase his profits?'

Parsons laughed. 'Maybe you're right, Casey. Maybe you're right.'

When, later, Collins walked with Parsons to his limousine Parsons stopped. 'How old are you now, David? Must be forty-six or forty-seven.'

Collins laughed. 'I'm forty-nine, Harry.'

'Is this what you want to end up doing?'

'I've never had any idea *where* I was going or where I would end up.'

'Why not?'

'I haven't got any qualifications of any kind. I've had to take what opportunities came my way. And then just get on and do my best. That doesn't lead to planned progress, I'm afraid.'

'Or is that just you?'

'I've no idea, Harry.'

'Thanks for a delightful evening.' He held out his hand. 'Keep in touch. I mean that sincerely.'

As Collins watched the tail lights of the car disappear at the bend in the drive he wondered why for him the word 'sincerely' always sounded superficial and insincere. An advertising man's word. A weasel word. Like 'darling'.

Chapter 31

HE HAD planned the holiday in Europe as an acknowledged reward for Dolly's obvious efforts to make things right between them.

They had a week in Rome, a week in Paris and a week in London. It was on their third day in London when Dolly said she would like him to take her to see where he had grown up.

Collins smiled. 'There's nothing beautiful there. Birmingham's rather like Pittsburg. It's all heavy industry. A bit grim.'

'So what? I'd like to see where you came from.'

He was vaguely pleased at her insistence. He had hired a car and after they had booked in at the hotel in Stratford-on-Avon he drove over to Birmingham.

Very little had changed and as they sat in the car looking at the row of terraced houses he smiled as he saw the net curtains still twitching as they were furtively observed.

'Which was your house, Dave?'

'The one with the brown door.'

'Did you mind living here?'

'I never thought about it. Nobody did. You just considered yourself lucky to have a roof over your head.'

'You didn't envy people in bigger houses?'

'No. You just accepted it all.'

'But you had enough ambition to want to do better for yourself.'

'Not really. It's hard to explain. It just sort of happened. One thing after another.'

'I can't imagine you just letting things happen. You're not that kind of man.'

He smiled. 'I am, you know. I'm just lucky. Let me take you up to Erdington and I'll show you my old haunts.'

He showed her where the church tennis club had been and stopped in the High Street at the Palais. There was a large white board that said it was going to be pulled down to become a Safeway Store.

She smiled. 'I can't imagine you going dancing every week. Was it the girls you were after?'

'I suppose so. Basically. Boys went in pairs or in a gang. The girls went with their pals but separately.'

'Did you screw girls in those days?'

Collins laughed. 'They didn't give you the chance, honey. There were always wild rumours that some girl let guys play around but I doubt if they were ever based on fact. Just wishful thinking.'

They were drinking their coffee after dinner in the residents' lounge when she turned to look at him. When he looked back at her she said, 'Do you want us to have children?'

'What made you ask that tonight particularly?'

'I guess just thinking about when you were a boy.'

'What do you feel about it?'

'I don't think I'd make a very good mother. I don't really like kids. But it seems a waste for you not to have a child. It could be bright, like you are.'

He smiled. 'Or she could be beautiful, like you are.'

'What was your son like?'

'He was bright. Gentle. I didn't see much of him because I was always at work.'

'Do you think about him?'

'Yes. I think about him a lot.'

'You've never told me that before.'

'There was no point.'

'Do you miss him?'

'Yes. I miss him. I'm ashamed and sad that I didn't do more when he was there.'

238

'Why don't we have him home for holidays?'

'His mother wouldn't let him come.'

'Why not?'

He sighed. 'She hates my guts.'

'Why?'

'I think basically she resented me getting on in business. Leaving Birmingham behind.' He smiled. 'She thought I was a sort of traitor for leaving here and not wanting to keep up the connection. And I guess she felt that if I really cared I'd give it up and come back here and live what she saw as a normal life.'

'Was she attractive?'

'Yes.'

'What do you feel about us having a child?'

He looked at her lovely face and then looked away, hesitating.

'Say what you really think, Dave.'

'In a way I'd love it. But part of me would feel that I was writing off my son. Not *her* making it so, but me. Closing him out. Saying it's all over.'

'So why don't you see your attorney and force them to give you access?'

'I guess for two reasons. Firstly I think I've left it too long and they've got it tied up. Her and her new husband. And secondly I think it could disturb him. I'm sure that he's being looked after properly and I expect he's settled into the new life long ago. I just don't want to disturb him, by giving him divided loyalties.'

'Let's have one last drink and go to bed, honey.'

It had been a long hard winter and the snow had lingered until mid-April but it was a winter that established his value at the company. He had increased turnover by seventeen per cent but profits were up by just over thirty per cent. He was paying almost as much in taxes as he had earned at the agency.

It felt strange to know that he was actually a wealthy

239

man, with a future that was secure and stable. He might owe his job to Casey Jones but his earnings came from his own efforts and skills.

He had bought a thirty-six-foot Hatteras on a fifty-fifty basis with the old man and they spent all their spare time on the boat that summer. Casey used it mainly for fishing and they used it jointly for exploring the coast and the offshore islands. During the summer the Wheelers sometimes joined them on a day cruise up to New Haven with lunch at the Colony Inn.

It was on a fishing trip with Casey Jones that it really came home to Collins how lucky he was. It was just him and Casey, and they had anchored for the night off Oyster River Point so that they could go after the striped bass early the next morning.

The sea was calm and as they sat having a last drink on the after-deck Casey had said, 'Are you happy, Dave?'

He turned his head, smiling, to look at the older man.

'What made you ask that?'

'I just wondered.'

'What about?'

'My life's been very easy compared with yours. Apart from when my wife died I've had no real troubles. I always had my father to back me up and although we weren't wealthy we weren't poor either.

'You've had to struggle. You were a soldier in a war. An unhappy marriage. And now you're in a foreign country. I sometimes wonder if I wasn't selfish persuading you to leave that agency job.'

'Why selfish, Casey?'

'Seems like I was just one more person who made you change your life, gave you one more set of problems to contend with.'

Collins smiled. 'Do you feel I'm not coping too well?'

'Of course I don't. I think you must know how I feel about you. If I'd had a son and he'd turned out like you I'd be a very happy man.'

'Is it Dolly you're worried about?'

'I do worry about her. I always have done and I suppose I always will – but no – I was thinking about you and how you've always beaten the odds. No family behind you, no money, no formal qualifications. It's a real success story.'

'It's just luck. And some of the disadvantages can be advantages.'

'Like what?'

'Qualifications, for instance. If you don't have any qualifications you have to take any chance you're given. People with real qualifications wouldn't have touched the jobs I had with a long pole. When I took them on I had to make a success of them . . .' he laughed softly, '. . . so that I could move on to some even bigger potential disaster. Don't worry about me, Casey, I'll survive.'

'I pray that you do, boy . . . I really do.'

One of the maids from the big house was using the polisher in the hall. She switched off when she saw him.

'Is it OK to carry on, Mr Collins?'

'Sure it is, Jose. Where's Mrs Collins?'

'She's gone shopping. Said she'd be back around seven.'

He looked at his watch. It was three o'clock. He said to the maid, 'If she phones tell her I've gone downtown to look for her, and I'm taking her out to dinner at the Holiday Inn.'

'OK, Mr Collins, I'll tell her.'

He parked his car near the Museum and walked back to the main shopping street and headed for Jimmy Wheeler's gallery.

The receptionist went in the back office for Wheeler and he came out smiling.

'Hi, Dave. D'you want a guided tour or are you just browsing?'

'I'm looking for Dolly. She's shopping and doesn't know we've got an early dinner engagement. Have you seen her around?'

241

He saw Wheeler nod almost imperceptibly to the girl, who got up and walked into the back office.

'I saw her way back. I've no idea where she is now.'

Collins smiled. 'I guess dress shops first, then shoe shops, then hairdressers.'

'How about I send my girl out to hunt for her while you and I have a coffee?'

Collins saw the tension on Wheeler's face and a pulse beating beside his eye. There was something wrong. He knew it from Wheeler's strained voice and the look on his face.

'What's going on, Jimmy? Has she been hurt or something?'

Wheeler looked away towards the window and the street. And then back at Collins' face.

'Don't go looking, Dave,' he said quietly. 'Just let me send my girl.'

'You know where she is?'

'I think so,' Wheeler said flatly.

'Where is she?'

'Do you love her, Dave?'

'Of course I do. What the hell is going on?'

'You've got no idea?'

'Of course not. Tell me what's happened, for Christ's sake.'

'She's at Jerry Adams' place.'

'Where's that? And who's Jerry Adams?'

'It calls itself a hairdressing salon. Adams owns it.' He looked at Collins' face. 'It's a dump for so-called swingers. She used to go there a lot before you were married.'

'So maybe she just wants a hairdo.'

Wheeler nodded. 'Maybe she does. I'd guess not. And I beg you to stay here with me while I send my girl.'

'Where is this Jerry Adams dump?'

'I'll go with you,' Wheeler said quietly.

The shop was two blocks away in a secondary street parallel to the main street. There were photographs of model hairstyles in the window and lace curtains. It looked far too sleazy for swingers to patronise. He stopped and looked at Wheeler.

'You mean to tell me that Dolly patronises this place?'

'It's not patronised for shampoos and sets, David.'

'What then?'

'Drugs. The lot.'

Collins pushed open the glass door and a man in shirt sleeves said, 'What you want, buddie?'

As he reached for Collins' arm he shoved the man away, pushing between the long bead curtains into a short corridor. There were voices coming from a room at the far end and Collins turned the handle but the door was locked. The door was flimsy and it gave easily to the thrust of his shoulder.

Dolly was on a leather couch, naked except for a white suspender belt and stockings, her long legs over the man's shoulders. Her eyes were closed as the man had her with a frenzied animal thrusting of his body and another man was fondling one of her breasts. A third man was sitting naked. Just watching.

Collins was vaguely aware of his own voice shouting as he tore at the man's long hair, pulling him backwards until he was on the floor. The man groaned as Collins' foot took him in the ribs and then a man was coming at him with a chair held high. He staggered back as Collins rushed at him wrenching the chair from his grip, smashing it down on the man's head again and again.

Then Wheeler was holding his arms from behind.

'That's enough, Dave. No more. Cool it. Let's go now.'

There was blood on Collins' face but it wasn't his blood. He stood panting, his chest heaving as he looked around.

'Where's Dolly?'

'She's gone, Dave.'

Collins looked around the sleazy room. He wanted to smash things but there was nothing to smash.

Wheeler took his arm. 'Let me drive you home, fella. I'll get my girl to follow us in your car and I'll take her back.'

As they drove back, Collins said, 'How long has this been going on?'

'Wait till you've cleaned up and calmed down then come over to my place and we'll talk.'

'I need to know now, Jimmy. I've got to know.'

'I guess it's been going on most of the time, David. Maybe not more than once or twice a week.'

'Do people know about this?'

'Some people do.'

'And nobody had the guts to tell me?'

'It's not a question of guts, David. Short of going in there like you did today, it's just rumours and gossip. Some wise-ass attorney could go for a couple of million bucks for slander and you couldn't prove a thing.'

As Wheeler stopped at Collins' house he saw the lights on all over and he guessed that Dolly was back. As Collins got out Wheeler said, 'Walk round the house just once before you go in, Dave. Try and stay cool.'

'I am cool, Jimmy. The other's gone. I'm cold not cool. Believe me.'

'Come over to us later. You or both, whichever way it turns out.'

Collins nodded. 'Maybe. Thanks all the same.'

Wheeler sighed as he watched Collins walk to the house and then he started the car and drove slowly back to town.

A radio was blaring away upstairs and as he walked into their bedroom there were clothes, shoes and hats strewn everywhere and two large travel cases open on the bed. When she saw him she stood glaring at him, hands on hips and he saw the anger bordering on hatred in her eyes.

'What do you want, you bastard?'

'What are you doing?'

'What does it look like? I'm packing. I'm getting the hell out. I've served my sentence with you and I'm off.'

'D'you want to talk?'

'About what?'

244

And the sheer effrontery cracked his calm. 'About your performance downtown.'

'What about it?'

'You don't feel called on to explain or apologise?'

'Why should I? Who the hell do you think you are . . . God?'

'You're not sorry about what you did? You don't regret it?'

She laughed harshly. 'You must be out of your mind. It's only those guys and others like them who've kept me alive and sane while I've been married to you. I told you that first time, if you want girls to screw on the side I've got plenty of girlfriends who'll oblige. Screwing's not some big production. Men have been screwing me since I was sixteen. Every guy who looks at me wants to screw me. I bet there's plenty of my girlfriends you'd like to screw, but you haven't got the guts. For you it's always got to be soft lights and sweet music and red roses. All that song and dance just to get your dick between some girl's legs. You're a bloody hypocrite like the rest of them. You're not a real man. You sicken me, Collins, you really do.'

'Where are you going now?'

'It's none of your business. You and I have had it. I'm going to see my attorney and file for a divorce.'

'On what grounds?'

'He'll find some grounds. Mental cruelty. I don't care what. Just so long as I'm free.'

'And when those creeps get tired of you?'

'They won't. I'll see to that. And there's plenty more where they came from.'

'Are you back on drugs?'

'I've never been off them, lover boy. That's what's made living with you just bearable.'

'Why didn't you tell me all this before we married?'

She shook her head slowly in disbelief. 'You'll never get it, will you? There's nothing to tell. It's normal. I've always put out for you whenever you want it. What difference does it make if a few other guys have it? We could have

been OK. Married and all the rest of it. And we enjoy
ourselves on the side. No harm done to anyone. But no
. . . not for the great David Collins. He's different. He's
special. Nobody shares his toys. You are my all-time asshole and I hate your guts.'

For a moment or so he stood there trying to think of
something to say but there *was* nothing to say.

He turned and left the room, walking back down the
stairs and out to his car.

He drove heedlessly, compelled to get away from it all
and it wasn't until he saw two helicopters landing at the
Sikorsky plant that he realised where he was. He slowed
down and then stopped at the next lay-by on the Parkway.

The rainclouds coming in from the east were bringing
the first gusts of rain and the vehicles on the Parkway were
switching on their lights although it was only seven o'clock.
Trucks heading for Hartford and Boston, and men driving
home to wives and families. Men whose only worries were
keeping up the payments on their homes and cars, whose
wives were normal and whose lives were uneventful.

He had no doubt about what he had to do but he felt
too exhausted to do it. It was a grim shambles that he
couldn't cope with. He could never fit in with her kind of
life and he had no inclination to even try. She was sick,
but instinct told him that he wasn't the cure. She wanted
her sickness. It was compelling and overwhelming, primitive and uncontrollable. How stupid, how naive he had
been to imagine that the life he gave her had wiped out
the old habits so easily. There were half-smiles and silences
that he remembered now, that had been such obvious clues
if only he had recognised them. They must have been
amazed at his apparent complaisance or indifference. They
would have taken for granted that he knew what was going
on and the more cynical would have assumed that he
looked the other way because of his father-in-law's great
wealth.

He shivered as he thought of the things he had to do, and closed his eyes as he tried to shut out the thought that there may be some other way. There was just one last check he could make and he started up the car and drove on to the next gas station and used the telephone. As he dialled the number he wondered if perhaps even the Wheelers wouldn't want to help him.

It was Julie Wheeler who answered the phone.

'Is Jimmy there, Julie? It's David.'

There was a moment's silence and then she said, 'Yes, he's here, Dave. D'you want to speak to him?'

'Could he spare me a few minutes if I came over?'

'I'm sure he would. Come on over.'

'You'd better ask him.'

'There's no need to, Dave. Where are you?'

'I'm just past the Sikorsky plant at Stratford.'

'What are you doing up there?'

'God knows. I just drove around. Something happened. You probably haven't heard yet.'

She sighed. 'I heard all right. Just get over here as soon as you can.'

'You don't mind?'

'Don't be silly, we're friends.'

The rain was sweeping across the highway as he drove back towards Bridgeport.

There were lights on all over the Wheelers' ranch-style house and Jimmy Wheeler was standing at the door as he made his way through the rain. Wheeler led him through to their sitting room where a fire blazed in the stone fireplace. Julie Wheeler was pouring out drinks for the three of them.

As Collins lowered himself shakily into one of the armchairs, Jimmy Wheeler said, 'The kids have gone over to friends so there's nobody going to disturb us.'

'Did you know about what was going on before today?'

'I had my suspicions but I didn't have more than that until about a month ago. And then only by accident. I saw

247

her with Jerry Adams when I knew she had told you she was with us. Knowing what went on way back and what Adams was like I assumed that things were . . .' he shrugged, '. . . not OK.'

Collins took a deep breath. 'I'm going to get out, Jimmy. I can't cope with this. It's beyond me.'

'What happened when you got home?'

'She was angry and defiant. Angry at what *I* did, not at what she was up to. She told me it had virtually never stopped and that it wasn't going to stop in future. It was her life and she was going to live it as she chose. Said she was going to divorce me. I could like it or lump it. She was packing two cases and I drove off. I don't know where she's going to.'

'We're both terribly sorry, Dave, you know that. What can we do to help? What are you planning to do?'

'I'm walking out on her and Bridgeport and the job. That's as far as I've got.'

'What about Casey? He'll be absolutely struck down by this.'

'What can I do? I can't go on working for him. I don't want to anyway. I don't think I shall stay in the States. I'll go back to England.'

'Are you going to divorce her?'

'I don't know. I suppose so. There's no point in hanging on.'

Julie leaned forward. 'Do you still love her, Dave?'

'No.' He shook his head slowly. 'I'm sorry for her, but that's about all.'

'How can Jimmy and I help you? What can we do for you?'

Collins sighed. 'I guess I just wanted to see if you thought I was crazy in walking out.'

Jimmy Wheeler shook his head. 'No, you're not crazy. Most men would walk out on her. But I'm not sure you're wise in walking out on the job. Casey won't change his mind about you just because you've had enough of Dolly. He won't like it but he'll understand. I'm sure. And it won't be easy to find an equivalent scenario somewhere else.'

'There'd be too much to remind me. And there won't be a soul in town who doesn't know what a fool I've been.'

'It's been going on a long time, Dave. I haven't noticed people changing their attitudes towards you. Dolly's circle will be amused but the amusement won't last long. There will be other scandals to occupy their minds. Most people who matter will be hostile to Dolly and sympathetic towards you.'

'What will happen to Dolly?'

'Is she back on the drug kick?'

'I think so. I'm not sure.'

'She'll either marry some bum who doesn't care how many guys screw her so long as he has her money and his own girls. Or boys. Or she'll end up in some mental hospital. She's not a kid any more. She's what – twenty-six or twenty-seven? And like she said to you – she's got her own life to live. You can't play God to those kind of people. They're self-destructive. Sad to watch, but in my experience incurable and doomed.'

'Do you think she ever loved me?'

'Love's a big big word, David. She certainly admired you. And there's no doubt she wanted you. She's never set her cap at a man as she did at you. But love . . . no. I don't think Dolly *loves* anybody. Not even Casey. Not even herself.'

'What made her like that? Was it her mother dying?'

'I doubt it. Dolly was playing the sex game before her mother died. Heavy petting in cars, groping at dances. And at fifteen years old that's way ahead of the local record. Her mother might have known how to dampen her down to some extent but Dolly's no fragile flower. Let's not kid ourselves, she's a very tough lady, is Dolly. Maybe a psychiatrist can help her but I wouldn't bet on it.'

'How about your relationship with her?'

Julie interposed. 'What Dolly got up to before you came on the scene was none of our business. She was a welcome guest and we've never provided empty bedrooms. I guess she'll stay away for a few weeks and after that, well, we'll see. She won't be excommunicated but I guess we'll keep our powder dry. Most people will be much the same.'

The telephone rang and Jimmy Wheeler walked into the next room to answer it. When he came back he said, 'That was Casey. He wanted to know if we'd seen you or knew where you were. I told him you were with us. He asked if he could come across and see you. I said yes. In an hour.' He looked at his wife. 'Run him a bath, honey.'

When she had left Wheeler said, 'There's nothing useful anyone can say when these things happen, David. If things are worth saving you can try and put together the pieces. In this case I think you're damn lucky to get out of it. I didn't want to say anything while Julie was here but Dolly Jones screws around because she likes it and it feeds her vanity and ego. I love old Casey, but don't change your mind, whatever he says.'

'I won't, Jimmy. I couldn't.'

'When you've finished talking with Casey we want you to stay the night with us. And we want you to stay with us until you've worked out where you're heading for next. There's no hurry. You look all in so have a bath before you see Casey. Julie and I will be eating out. We'll be back around midnight.'

'Thanks for everything, Jimmy. Thank you both.'

Casey Jones looked old and worn as he settled himself into one of the big armchairs. He looked at Collins and then said gruffly, 'You must know what I feel, Dave. I'm terribly sorry. Thank you for being willing to see me. I badly needed to see you.'

'I wanted to see you, too.'

Casey shrugged his shoulders helplessly. 'What can I say, David? I'm lost for words. It's bad enough for me but it's nothing compared with what your feelings must be. You must hate my guts.'

'I don't, Casey. Nothing will alter my opinion of you. You've done everything you possibly could. It's not your fault any more than it's mine. We tried. Maybe we didn't try hard enough or the right way but . . . well . . . it wasn't in our power to succeed.'

'Would you forgive me if I suggested something outrageous?'

'I'm sure I would.'

'Would you give her another chance? Just one more, boy. Three months, six months. And she's on trial.'

'Has she spoken to you since it happened?'

'I suppose you could call it speaking. More like the ravings of a crazy woman.'

'She doesn't want another chance. She wouldn't take it if she was offered it. She wants those creeps like Jerry Adams. She hated her life with me.'

'She's just a stupid kid, Dave. She'll be in tears next week.'

'She's twenty-seven, Casey. She's not a kid; she's a grown woman.'

Casey Jones reached for an envelope he had put on the coffee table, picked it up and handed it to Collins.

'I brought that to show you.'

Collins slid out the photograph. It was Dolly aged about seven or eight. Already very pretty. Smiling into the camera, her head coyly to one side, one hand holding a rag doll. She still had that rag doll. All the promise of her future beauty was in that face and no sign or hint of disaster. He slid it back into the envelope and when he looked back at Casey Jones' face he saw that the older man's cheeks were wet with tears.

'Is there anything I can do to help you, Casey?'

'Just give her one more chance,' he said softly, his voice quavering, his eyes pleading.

'It isn't on. I'd end up killing somebody.'

'You're going to leave her?'

'She's left me already, Casey.'

'I mean permanently.'

251

'Yes.'

'D'you want a divorce?'

'She does. She said I'd be hearing from her attorney. I shan't oppose it unless her guy tries playing games.'

'You don't want to put her through a scandal, do you?'

'No. Just as quiet a divorce as can be arranged.'

'I'll see to that. Leave it to me. And what about you? What are you going to do?'

'I'll resign and hand you back my shares. I've got enough money to get by on for several months. I expect I'll go back to London.'

'Will you keep in touch with me?'

'I'd better not, Casey. Whatever we said or wrote we'd be thinking of something else.'

'I'm there if you want me. But you understand I've got to stick by her. When the chips go down on the table those shits will leave her in the gutter. I'm all she's got now.'

'I understand.'

The old man stood up slowly. 'Don't get up. I'll see myself out.' He stopped at the door. 'If you change your mind I'll be there. You can have everything I've got. The lot.' And he turned and shut the door behind him. Collins heard his car start up a few minutes later.

Chapter 32

A SUITE of rooms had been taken at the Waldorf Astoria. Present were Jimmy Wheeler and his attorney, an attorney representing Casey Jones, and David Collins himself.

Jimmy Wheeler ran the meeting and started briskly.

'As a friend of both Mr Jones and Mr Collins I've been asked to conduct this meeting. I want to emphasise right now that this is an informal meeting. And it is a private meeting whose details will not be discussed outside this room. Are we agreed?'

There was no dissent as Wheeler looked at the others round the table.

'OK. Let's start. David, you have signed transfer documents for 261,452 shares in Jones and Morrell Electronics and you have asked for no payment as they were originally given to you by Casey Jones. I accept those shares on Casey's behalf but I have a cheque here for 200,000 dollars. This represents only one-tenth of the value of those shares.

'You gave me authority to deal with this matter on your behalf and I have accepted the 200,000 dollars as representing a generous action on your part out of friendship for Casey Jones.

'You had no contract of employment as chief executive of Jones and Morrell but in normal circumstances you would have been in breach of your contract in walking out. Such breach is waived unconditionally and I have here a cheque for 50,000 dollars in your name representing the overriding commission you earned for the second quarter of this fiscal year.

'Next I have a reference in glowing terms signed by Casey Jones regarding your work at the company. Maybe that could be of use to you.' He paused. 'Lastly, the house. Mr Viner, will you say your piece?'

Viner, a neat, slim man, was Casey's attorney.

'The deeds of the guest-house, Mr Collins, were made over to you and Mrs Collins jointly. It would save a lot of embarrassment for my client if you could sign a transfer deed back to him.' He passed a single sheet across the table towards Collins. Wheeler reached out, intercepted it and passed it to his own attorney who read it, shrugged and nodded as he handed it to his client. Wheeler passed it to Collins who signed it without reading it and passed it back to Viner.

'Anything else?' Wheeler looked around and as the two attorneys shook their heads Wheeler said to his man, 'Paul, take Mr Viner for a drink, yes?'

As Viner stood up, fastening his briefcase, he looked at Collins. 'My client has really appreciated your attitude to everything, Mr Collins. I'd like to add that it makes a pleasant change in my profession to witness civilised behaviour.'

He held out his hand and Collins shook it briefly, half standing as he reached across the table.

When the two attorneys had gone Wheeler took off his jacket and looked at Collins.

'It's been a bad few weeks for you, old pal. But it's helped all round in straightening things out.'

'How is Casey?'

Wheeler shrugged. 'Not good, not good. He never used to look his age, but he does now. He's worn out, physically and mentally. And he's lonely in that damn great mansion of his. What about you?'

'I'm leaving tomorrow for London.'

'What are you going to do?'

'God knows. I'm out of touch with the agency scene over there. I'll just see what turns up.'

'I hope all goes well for you, David. You know you can

call us any time.' He stood up and held out his hand. 'Take care of yourself.'

'Thanks for all you've done. And love to Julie and the girls.'

It was raining when Collins landed at Heathrow. And it was six a.m. He told the cab-driver to take him to the Hilton, then he remembered going there with Dolly and he told the driver to go to the Cumberland instead.

He booked a double room and after he had bathed he lay on one of the beds. He had just over a quarter of a million dollars in his account at the Chase Manhattan in Berkeley Square. It sounded a lot but it was only a little more than he had earned in the last fiscal year. Still, it was enough for him to bum his way comfortably around Europe for a few years if that's how things turned out. But what he really wanted was a job. A job that would fill his mind to the exclusion of everything else.

He looked up O'Brien's number in the book, called him and made an appointment for later that morning. Arthur O'Brien ran a specialised placement bureau for creative and top advertising people. He had often used the bureau himself to recruit people in the old days. And Arthur O'Brien knew the London advertising scene better than the people who were in it.

The office was in a small block in Regent Street and O'Brien shook his hand and waved him to a chair.

'What are you after this time, David?'

'A job.'

'A job? You mean for yourself?'

'Yes.'

'Tell me about the New York agency bit.'

Collins filled him in briefly about his time in New York and O'Brien sat silent for long minutes before he spoke.

'That wasn't quite the story your old friend Harry put around, David.'

'What did he say?'

'Nothing very definite. Just a vague picture of you not fitting in. The usual agency in-fighting and then you were edged out and went to the electronics firm. I'm not saying that anyone takes much notice of what old Harry says, but it certainly doesn't help.' He paused. 'What are you after?'

'Creative director – something on those lines.'

O'Brien shook his head. 'Forget it, David. Creative directors average twenty-seven to thirty these days. Anybody older than that who's an agency director has got a majority shareholding from way way back.' He sighed. 'It's a tough time right now, old man. I've got real whizzkids with bundles of awards who've been on my books for seven or eight months looking for a place. Top guys who used to be in *Campaign* every other week.'

'What could you get me?'

'D'you want it straight or soft?'

'Straight.'

'I'd be wasting your time and mine if I said I could offer you anything. For the agency business today you've been away too long and you're too old.'

Collins half-smiled. 'I'm younger than Harry Parsons.'

O'Brien shrugged. 'Sure. But he stayed put. You went off into the wild blue yonder.' He shook his head. 'I'm sorry, David, but it's no good me bullshitting you. Try Parsons. He's not got anybody of your experience. And he knows your track-record.'

As Collins sat in the taxi on the way to the Cumberland he knew that what O'Brien had said was a fact. He was too old for the only business that he was really good at. Not actually too old but too old to match the phoney swinging image that agencies so desperately built up. They were show-business now not mere producers of first-class ads.

He ran a bath and lay in the warm water until it was cold. He felt low and dispirited as it slowly sank in that he had been relying on something that didn't exist any longer. The sunny dream-garden of a top creative job was just that. A dream. He had imagined himself choosing carefully from two or three offers from big agencies. Picking the one where he could plunge in and involve himself. Getting new business, winning them awards. It wasn't crazy. He had the talents and he had the experience. But he was fifty and for them he was over the hill. That look on O'Brien's face had said it all. Embarrassment, pity, sympathy and the awareness in his eyes that he was looking at a loser. But he'd got money in the bank. To hell with them. He'd buy a boat and beachcomb around the Med. And as he climbed out of the cold bath he knew that he wouldn't. It was all crumbling away. He was a loser. All the others were winners. The Marys, the Dollys, the Harry Parsons. The people who had worked out long ago what the world was all about.

He dressed and took a taxi to the bank. There was a cable for him there from Wheeler. He read it twice before he could take it in. Casey Jones had died the previous day of a massive coronary. While they had been sitting around that table in the Waldorf, Casey Jones was living out his last few hours on earth. He was sixty-eight and could have reasonably expected another eight or ten years.

Collins drew out two thousand dollars and as he stood in the Square looking for a taxi he was seized with a depression that made him feel faint. He leaned back against the railings around the bank's basement as all his strength seemed to flow out of him. It was an hour before he made it to the hotel and he undressed and slept the rest of the day and through the night.

When he woke he felt as tired as if he hadn't slept and his limbs seemed heavy. He shaved and dressed slowly and then phoned Parsons at the agency.

Parsons was amiable. He'd call at the hotel around five o'clock for a drink on his way home. And Collins remembered Parsons' old strategy. If there's a meeting you don't really want, have it at their place. Then you can leave when you choose. If they're at your place it's not so easy to get rid of them.

257

Reception phoned and announced Parsons and he asked for him to come up.

Parsons looked tanned and prosperous. More American than British.

'Glad to see you back, David.' He paused as he lifted his glass. 'I gather things got a bit shambolic towards the end.'

Collins nodded. 'And how's the agency?'

Parsons made himself comfortable on the edge of one of the beds. 'We can't complain, really, David. We're keeping our heads above water. New York's turning in a good contribution and we're opening an office in Hong Kong at New Year.' He smiled a self-satisfied smile. 'Keeps us all on the go. And what about you?' He looked solemn for a moment. 'Sad news about old man Jones – the agency Telexed me this morning. But I guess he'd had a fair run for his money. Can't live for ever. None of us. So what about you?'

'I'm looking over the job market before I decide what to do.'

'Quite right, too.' Parsons grinned. 'Glad to hear you've given up leaping from frying-pans into fires.' He turned and put his empty glass on the bedside table before he stood up. 'Well, nice seeing you again, Dave. We must have a meal some time.'

'I was thinking of going back into advertising. What d'you think?'

Parsons pursed his lips. 'It's tough now at your sort of level. Problems of shares, pensions and all that crap. The agencies are going for kids. They reckon you're old at thirty and one foot in the Jordan at thirty-five.'

'Do any of your shops need help?'

Parsons looked at his shoes and then back at Collins' face. 'Wouldn't work, David. Too much water gone under the bridge.' He put his hand on Collins' shoulder. 'We must have a meal together one of these days.'

After he had left, Collins sat alone in his room, unmoving and breathing shallowly. Parsons' words went trailing through his mind like the news lights in Times Square. The crude brush-off of 'we must have a meal sometime'. The code phrase that put unwanted acquaintances in their place. The crack about frying-pans and fires and its obvious reference to the zig-zags of his career. The old agency had seemed like a last small piece of firm land in his present mental quagmire. But it was sickeningly clear that Parsons wasn't going to have him back.

He sat in the cramped hotel armchair all night. Unthinking, sometimes nodding off, but he couldn't engage the gears of his mind. The whole weight of his life bore down on him.

It was dawn when he reached for his pocket-book and then asked the operator to get him the call. Half an hour later the phone rang and he picked it up.

'Amarillo 7904. Mary Harris speaking.'

'Mary.'

'Who is that?'

'It's me, Mary. Dave.'

'What is it?' Her voice was as cold as ever. Cold and wary.

'I don't feel good, Mary. I just wanted to talk to someone.'

'You're drunk, David. For heaven's sake go to bed or something.'

'How's Jimmy?'

'He's OK.'

'Tell me something about him.'

'Don't be ridiculous. Jimmy's fine.'

'And how're you?'

'What is all this, David? What are you up to?'

'Say something nice, Mary. Just something nice . . . anything . . . tell me that . . .'

The phone clicked as she hung up and in slow motion, with great effort he put the receiver back on its cradle.

He leaned forward, his face in his hands, tears running down his face and through his fingers. An hour later he slowly opened his toilet bag, taking out the soap and the

259

razor and bits and pieces until he came to the bottle. Unlocking the small refrigerator of the self-service bar he took out the bottles of whisky, gin and brandy. His hands were trembling as he prised off the metal caps and carefully ranged the open bottles side by side on the bedside table.

He lay back on the bed and one by one he swallowed all the blue-green capsules and drank from the bottles. He lay on his side with his head cradled on his arm and closed his eyes. The slow blue waves in his mind became green then red and then the orange of molten iron as it poured from a cupola and he could smell the warm dank smell of foundry sand. It was the last thing he was conscious of as the great beats of his heart subsided, slowed, and then finally stopped.

PART III

Chapter 33

As HE turned the corner he looked at his watch. It was twenty past two. He had walked for only half an hour or so, but it had seemed like a lifetime. Some instinct made him go to the front door. For a moment he stood there with his eyes closed. Then he opened them and pressed the bell. The hall lights came on and he saw her shadow on the leaded lights in the door. Then it opened and she was standing there. He looked at her face and said softly, 'I'm sorry, Mary, but I can't give up Sally.'

For a moment she stood looking at him but there was no indication of her feelings on her face. Then she pointed behind her.

'I guessed you'd do that. I've packed your bags.'

She turned and dragged forward the two big cases until they stood between her and the open doorway.

'What about the rest of my things? We ought to talk about all this.'

'There's nothing to talk about. If there is then you can talk to my solicitor. You can send him a list of anything you claim.'

'Who's your solicitor?'

'Phil Lomax.'

'You've already talked to him?'

'I asked him for advice about my situation.'

'What about Jimmy?'

'What about him?'

'I shall want to see him. And I shall want to explain.'

'Explain what?'

'Why we're splitting up. And that I shall still be his father and that I'll be seeing him regularly.'

'That's up to the court to decide. I shall tell him myself what's happened.'

'You've got this all cut and dried haven't you?'

She shrugged, and for the first time he saw the hatred in her eyes.

'I'm sorry, Mary. I really am. Believe me. I didn't mean to hurt you, it just happened.'

'These things don't just happen, David. If you don't want to do something you don't have to do it. You've done what you've done and now you've made your choice you'd better get on with it.'

She pushed one bag forward with her foot and as he reached for the two heavy cases and swung them over the doorstep she closed the door before he was standing upright again. He heard her footsteps receding and then the hall light was switched off. He was trembling, stunned by the speed of it all. The terrible contrast from coming home like any other night to finding himself standing on the front porch of his own house, his marriage over and done with in a couple of hours.

Slowly he walked back to the garage leaving the double-doors open as he started the car and drove round to the front of the house. He looked up at the bedroom windows as he loaded the cases into the boot. There were no lights, just the reflection of the moon on the diamond panes.

There was little traffic on the roads but he drove slowly as far as Chelsea Bridge, where he stopped the car. Chelsea Bridge had always been, subconsciously, the frontier between his two lives. South of the river was the routine normality of his home life, north of the Thames was the excitement of his work and the girl. But like some political refugee he no longer had that dual nationality. From now on he belonged north of the river alone. And 'belonged' was an exaggeration. He didn't 'belong' there. He didn't belong anywhere.

He watched as a River Police patrol boat pulled into the

floating landing-stage at the foot of the bridge on the north bank, the lights in its wheel-house glowing orange in the darkness. He watched for several minutes as the shadowy figures of the policemen tied up the launch and stooped, kneeling, on the landing-stage. And then he realised what they were doing as one of them shone a torch on the corpse they were wrapping in a canvas shroud. A police car with its blue light flashing, and an ambulance, drew up on the embankment and he walked back to the car, trembling again as he had when the door closed on him at his home.

He turned the key in the agency door and carried his bags up to the small flat before he parked the car in the square. Back in the flat he lit a cigarette and sat in the dim light from the moon and the street lamps. Already the heavy lorries were moving into the city to pick up their loads from Covent Garden and Smithfield, but he barely heard them as he tried to collect his thoughts.

It was in this room that he had first made love to Sally. It seemed a long, long time ago. And for the first time he wondered how much had been love and how much had been lust. In reflex he stood up quickly to brush away the thought. And the answer. He reached for the ashtray to stub out his cigarette.

He slept in his clothes, sitting in the armchair, and woke just after six to the wail of a police car's siren as it swept up Lower Belgrave Street towards Hyde Park. He opened the cases to check if there was a razor. Both cases had been carefully and scrupulously packed. Shirts, underwear, shoes and suits neatly folded. He realised that the bags must have been packed even before he had got home.

It was already warm as he walked through the dusty streets to the snack bar at Victoria Station. He bought a *Daily Express* and started to read it as he ate the buttered toast and sipped the weak, hot coffee. He gave up after a few minutes. Nothing would take his mind off his immediate problems. He had to put on an act for Harry Parsons and the agency. He would have to choose his moment carefully when he knew more about what was going to

265

happen. He would have to choose his moment to tell Sally, and he realised that he wasn't absolutely sure what her reaction would be. Almost sure, but she could feel differently now that it had happened. And because of the way it had happened.

He was back in his office by nine o'clock looking through his appointments for the week. It was going to be a busy week but he'd have to find time to see a solicitor.

He had known Phil Lomax for years and had used him for the few small legal problems they had had from time to time. An action against a builder for poor work when they had extended the bathroom, a threatening letter to a book-club that kept invoicing them for books he had returned and a civil action brought against him when a cyclist had collided with his car.

Just before lunch-time he impulsively dialled Lomax's number and was put straight through.

'It's David Collins, Phil. Mary told me that she had spoken to you about our domestic problems.' He paused but there was no response. 'Can you hear me, Phil?'

'Yes, David. I was waiting for a question.'

'Does this mean you'll be acting for her? I'm afraid it's kind of come to a head.'

'Yes. She came to see me this morning. I've dictated a letter to you but it'll be a couple of days before it gets typed.'

'Does that mean she's going ahead with divorce proceedings?'

'I'm afraid so. Look, David, I can't discuss this with you. I've had certain instructions from my client and I shall be carrying them out. You'd better get someone to advise you properly.'

'Can you suggest somebody?'

'It wouldn't be ethical for me to do that, David. Try the Law Society or ask a friend for a recommendation. OK?'

'OK. I'm sorry about all this.'

'I'm sorry too, but I can't discuss it any more.'

266

'Thanks. See you.'

'Bye.'

As Collins hung up he realised that he had been snubbed. Phil Lomax was no longer his friendly family solicitor. He was the man who would make sure that he got the roughest ride that the law allowed.

He said nothing of the new situation to Sally until they met at the Hilton that evening. They sat in the first-floor lounge and after the drinks had been brought he looked across at her face. She held her head to one side listening to the pianist against the clatter of plates and glasses and she smiled when she saw him looking at her.

'Can you hear what she's playing?'

He turned his head and listened intently, smiling as he turned his head back to look at her. The pianist was playing 'Love is the sweetest thing'. He took a deep breath and plunged in.

'I've got something to tell you.' He saw the fear in her eyes and he went on. 'Mary's sueing me for divorce.'

'What? When did this happen?'

'Last night. When I got home last night she told me that she knew about us and I had to choose between you and her.'

'You mean you had to decide on the spot?'

'More or less.'

'And what did you say?'

'I said it was you.' He shrugged. 'She'd already packed my bags. I slept in the flat at the office.'

'Oh, Dave. Why didn't you phone me? I'd have come up. You must have felt terrible.'

'I didn't get to London until nearly three o'clock in the morning.'

'So what? You should have called me.' She leaned forward. 'Are you sure about this? Are you sure it's the right thing?'

'I'm not sure it's the *right* thing. I'm sure it's what I want.'

'Oh God what a mess.' Then she shook her head. 'No,

it's not a mess. We won't let it be a mess. Where are you sleeping tonight?'

'At the office.'

'I'll stay with you. I don't want you to be on your own.'

They walked back to the office and for some inexplicable reason his depression lifted. There were problems, but nothing that couldn't be solved. And there were benefits too. His relationship with Sally could be open now and uncomplicated. She loved him and was supportive and they would be happy together. There was nothing to be gloomy about. The shock would wear off and there would be a new life. The late evening sunshine matched his mood.

Not even the letter he received the next day from Lomax dampened his new confidence. The letter, addressed to him at his office, was marked 'Private and Confidential' and it notified him that his wife was applying for a divorce and maintenance for herself and their child. He was asked to confirm that he had received the notification. A copy of the plaintiff's application and statement would be forwarded in due course. Meanwhile, could he keep his wife in funds until a hearing could be arranged.

There was a solicitor's brass plate in Ebury Street and he phoned for an appointment with one of the partners.

Jack Villiers was an elegantly dressed man but his office was old-fashioned, a typical stage solicitor's office. Hunting prints on the wall, black tin boxes on the floor and a pile of briefs on the big partners' desk.

'Do sit down, Mr Collins. I gather that it's a domestic problem. Wife sueing for divorce. Tell me all about it.'

Villiers sat impassively, listening intently as Collins talked. When he had finished Villiers said, 'What on earth made you agree to all this, Mr Collins?'

'To what?'

'To leaving your house at a moment's notice. To giving an answer to a vital question in a matter of half an hour.'

'I didn't have much choice. It seemed the only thing to do.'

'I assume that you have, in fact, given her grounds for an action for adultery with the woman named?'

'Yes.'

'Why did you admit it?'

'She said she already knew.'

'What rubbish. She may have had her suspicions but unless she was in the room at the time she couldn't possibly *know*.' Villiers pursed his lips. 'Do you want a divorce?'

'I think it's inevitable in the circumstances.'

'You could give up the girl, go back to your home and there's little they could do. They might try but they wouldn't succeed.'

'It would be a pretty unpleasant atmosphere.'

Villiers shrugged. 'So what? It's going to be pretty unpleasant for you anyway. They've got you over a barrel. They'll squeeze every penny out of you that the law allows. And the law allows a lot. A hell of a lot.'

'She won't be vindictive – she's not that kind of person.'

Villiers sighed and smiled coldly. 'She will be when her solicitor gets going. She'll claim that it isn't her doing of course. She's just doing what her solicitor advises her to do. They always do.'

'I think you'll find she's an exception.'

'Let's hope you're right, Mr Collins. So. What do you want me to do for you?'

'Just handle it for me.'

'All right. What about the child. Do you want access? Do you want to see him or would you rather make a clean break of it?'

'I want to see him but not until things are a bit more settled.'

'And the girl, Sally whatever her name is, is she going to deny the relationship?'

'You mean as co-respondent?'

'As what the law calls "the woman named", Mr Collins.'

'No. She won't deny it.'

Villiers nodded. 'Right. Leave the letter with me. Don't

269

reply to it. Don't contact your wife or go to your house without checking with me first.'

'Right.'

'I'll keep in touch. When it's necessary.'

Harry Parsons was sitting in his shirtsleeves fanning himself with the last few pages of a layout pad.

'Where were you last night, my boy? I phoned your place and got a very frosty reception from your good lady. No idea where I could contact you. No idea when you would be home and a distinct crackle of icicles in the voice.'

'We've called it a day, Harry. We're getting a divorce.'

'When did all this happen?'

'A couple of nights ago.'

'Is it Sally?'

'Partly. I'd rather not discuss it.'

'You got a good solicitor?'

'A chap named Villiers. They're round the corner.'

Parsons smiled. 'Oh, I know Villiers. Quite a smoothie. Got a reputation with the ladies himself. Ah well. As long as you're getting the right advice. Are you in the mood to discuss work?'

'Of course I am. I've been discussing work all day.'

'OK. OK. Don't get all defensive.' He leaned back in his chair. 'I've heard that Martin Chemicals are up for grabs. I'm seeing Hargreaves, their MD, tomorrow afternoon. Would you like to come along? It's three o'clock at their place in Piccadilly.'

'Sure. Do you want me to do any research?'

'No. It's just a preliminary skirmish. I've had the file on them brought up to date. Have a look at it tonight. It's on my girl's desk.'

Collins stood up. 'I'm using the flat until I can find a place: is that OK with you?'

'Just you?'

'Most of the time.'

'Fine. But for God's sake be discreet.'
'I will.'
As Collins opened the door Parsons said, 'David.'
'Yes?'
'I'm sorry it's happened. I hope everything works out well for you. Anything I can do you've only got to ask.'
'Thanks, Harry. See you tomorrow.'
'OK.'

They ate that night at Franchi's, a small Italian restaurant in Victoria. A place that was to become a regular eating place. It was family-run and the food was good and inexpensive and Collins enjoyed using his few phrases of wartime Italian. They found a small two-roomed flat in Pimlico and spent their evenings decorating and furnishing it from second-hand shops.

It was nearly four weeks after he had left home when they finally moved into the flat. She had had some of his photographs framed and hung them on the wall of the stairway that led up to their rooms. Landscapes and still-lifes that had won prizes at the Camera Club. They had spent a day at Austins of Peckham Rye buying second-hand furniture, and their only extravagance had been fitted carpets in their sitting room and the bedroom. He had recalled how, when he was first married, and Mary and he were buying furniture and carpeting, how long they had had to wait, saving up and buying things one at a time. And he felt guilty about being able to buy what they wanted in a matter of hours without thinking about the cost. But he felt safe and secure in the small flat and as the days passed the guilt faded and he referred to it naturally as 'home'. His old home became 'the place at Streatham'.

A month after they had moved in, his solicitor phoned him at the office. An enquiry agent was to visit the flat to

271

provide 'independent' evidence that he was living with the girl. And the girl must be there too. When would it be convenient for the man to call? Collins had suggested the next Saturday morning.

The thought of the man's visit and the intrusion of the divorce proceedings into his new life had depressed him but Sally had laughed when he told her about the man.

He had had vague visions of a hard-faced, hard-eyed private eye, a vision that belonged more to Hollywood films than the reality of the man who rang the bell on the Saturday morning.

He was a balding, elderly man, stoop-shouldered and dressed in a crumpled brown suit and well-worn black shoes. As Collins opened the door the man straightened up painfully, holding out a well-used card.

'Arthur Lewis, squire. At your service.'

'Do come in, Mr Lewis. We were expecting you.'

The man winked. 'No, no, Mr Collins. I much regret butting in on you like this, all unannounced.' He looked at Sally. 'And this is the new lady. Don't be worried, dearie. I do this every day. Two in the morning, and three after lunch.'

'Would you like a cup of tea?' she asked.

'No, I won't indulge on duty, ma'am . . . Now, just a couple of routine questions . . . you live here, young lady?'

'Yes.'

'And you're . . .' he looked at his notebook, '. . . you're Sally Ann Major, yes?'

'Yes.'

'And you live here all the time?'

'Yes.'

The old man turned to Collins. 'I'll just have to see the bedroom, guv'nor. Just a glance.'

Collins walked to the bedroom door and opened it wide as the old man peered inside.

'And that's the "*coucher*" as they say, is it?' he said pointing to the bed.

'The what?'

'The "*coucher*",' the old man repeated winking broadly again at Collins. 'Well, that's it. I'll be in court . . . you can always rely on Arthur Lewis . . . people are people I always say . . . sinners and angels, they're all the same to me.' He turned smiling to Sally. 'Well . . . take care, duckie. *C'est la vie* and all that.'

And then he was gone. Nodding to himself as he creaked slowly down the narrow wooden stairs. And the visit of Arthur Lewis had brought a touch of light relief to the grim reality of the divorce.

Its routine formalities were like some watershed in his life. He was no longer responsible for what was happening. It was Mary who was sueing for divorce, not him. It was her conditions that made it impossible to see his son. Apart from finance she was no longer part of his life. It was she who had decided the issue not him and it gave him a strange feeling of relief and release. He could enjoy his life with Sally without any qualms. The solicitor was obviously right. She'd dug a nice deep hole for him to fall into and he'd fallen. So OK. So be it.

They went to cinemas and concerts and theatres, and at weekends they drove into the country and ate at small pubs. They had a weekend at Stratford and saw *Falstaff* and *Hamlet* at the theatre. And they had a weekend in Ostend with visits to Bruges and Ghent.

People at the office noticed his new look and the more relaxed attitude to his work. There were the usual divisions between those who said nothing but obviously wished him well and those who took a high moral tone and also said nothing but showed their disapproval in aloofness and formality. He was amused at the various reactions but was relieved when, as time went by, his relationship with Sally was no longer of interest to any of them.

For Collins, although he never analysed his feelings, it was like being released from jail. His childhood and his marriage were in the limbo of the past and could never touch him again.

He sometimes had the feeling that it was too good to be

273

true, or too good to last, but he knew that was irrational thinking. It was there every day. An easygoing life, loved and cared for by someone who shared his interests and admired his talents. He'd had more love and affection in those sunny months than he'd had in the whole of his life. But nobody escapes that easily from a lifetime of indifference and resentment. David Collins at forty was living the life he should have had in his late teens and twenties. His childhood, the war and his marriage had robbed him of those years, but circumstances had made a gap in his time-scale that nature had filled automatically. David Collins was living as if he were twenty years old. Free of all responsibility for the first time in his life. And Sally Major was delighted by the changes she was sure she alone had wrought.

Collins' escape from reality ended with a call from his solicitor.

Villiers waved him to the chair in front of his desk, and then looked across as he pushed aside a pile of papers.

'I thought it was time to tell you the position, Mr Collins. I've had several telephone conversations and some correspondence with the other side. They want a statement of all your income covering the past five years. Your wife is claiming the matrimonial home. Plus substantial maintenance for herself and the child of the marriage.'

Collins shrugged. 'I'll get my accountant to send you the financial records. How much maintenance will it be?'

'I'd imagine it would be at least half your gross income. Might be a little more.'

'What about access to my son?'

'They ask that there should be no access until after the divorce hearing.'

'When will that be?'

'Between four and nine months. The lists are pretty full at the moment.'

'Can they stop me from seeing him?'

'They have produced a statement from the family doctor saying that he thinks it could be prejudicial to the boy. And there's an affidavit from your wife claiming that you saw little of him even when you were living there. It quotes dates and times and so on.' He shrugged. 'The usual stuff that they put forward when they've got the husband where they want him.'

'Is that my position?'

'I'm afraid so. You gave her all the cards she needed. You admitted the adultery and you walked out of the matrimonial home of your own free will.'

'Hardly my own free will.'

Villiers sighed. 'She didn't call the police. She made no threats. As far as the court is concerned you left of your own accord.'

'Can you do anything about access?'

'I can try, but we shall be wasting our time I'm afraid. They've got it all cut and dried. I don't like to say it but this woman obviously hates your guts and she's going to stick the knife in every chance she's got. The more you protest the more she'll enjoy it. If you take my advice you'll do nothing, then the satisfaction for the other side tends to cool down. Keep up the payments and stay out of the picture.' He looked at Collins. 'How is all this affecting you?'

'I find what you've told me now very disturbing. When I think about it I realise that I was very stupid. Naive maybe. I left myself open to all this.'

'How's your new life turning out . . . the girl . . . Sally Major?'

'That's fine. She's very supportive and calm. I'm doing my best not to think about it all, but . . .' he shrugged. 'With all this, it creeps back in.'

'Any chance of getting away for a bit? A holiday. A couple of weeks in the sun?'

'I'm afraid not. I'm too busy.'

'Is it affecting your work at all?'

'I don't think so.'

275

'Don't let it. Remember you'll have two lots of people to support when the divorce is through.'

Villiers stood up and escorted Collins to the door. 'Take it all as calmly as you can. Worrying won't help. But you know that, I'm sure.'

When Collins was at work his mind was entirely occupied and engaged. When he was at their flat he was happy and relaxed. But there were spaces in his day when the black dog of guilt and uneasiness stalked through his mind. In a taxi on the way to a client, waiting to be served in a shop, a few moments alone in a restaurant waiting for Sally to come back.

Chapter 34

As THE months went by it was obvious to all those who worked closely with him at the agency that despite the long hours he worked he was no longer functioning as the mainspring of the agency's creative thinking. From time to time there were flashes of the old genius but the inspiration was no longer available consistently. He was doing a job but not his old job. He was becoming more an administrator than a source of creative thinking. As an administrator he was efficient but it wasn't what he had been hired for, nor what he was paid for. There were plenty of good agency administrators available but few really good creative directors. Parsons would have been prepared to leave him as an administrator, but he needed a top creative man, and the blow both to Collins' pride and the agency's reputation which would come from him appointing a new creative director could create new problems that could be even more damaging than the existing ones.

It was just before the Christmas holidays when Parsons sent for Sally Major while Collins was supervising photography at an outside studio.

He had asked her to see him in that small flat at the top of the agency building where she and Collins had first made love.

When she was settled in the armchair he said, 'Tell me about David, Sally. How's he making out?'

'I'd rather not talk about him, Mr Parsons.'

'Why not?'

The girl shrugged. 'I don't think it's right to talk about him behind his back.'

Parsons nodded. 'I know that, but I'm not criticising him. Just trying to help.' He paused as he looked at the girl. 'You must already realise that he needs help, Sally. Isn't that so?'

'I know he's sometimes unhappy, but he's had a lot to cope with.' She sighed as she looked across at Parsons. 'Does this mean you're gunning for him?'

'Why should I be doing that?'

'Because you think he's not coping as well with his work.'

'Honey, you're a smashing girl in every way. I'm very fond of you and I admire your guts with David. But I knew him when you were still in nappies. He's got great talents and an exceptionally creative mind. He was the first senior man I recruited. He played a tremendous part in getting this agency off the ground. The agency owes him a lot. So do I.' He sighed. 'So I'm not likely to be gunning for him as you put it. But there is a problem. You must know that, you work here. It's getting worse as the weeks go by. It's not just David, it's the whole agency. His problem is going to drag all of us down with him unless I can find a solution.'

'Why are you telling me this?'

Parsons shrugged. 'I'm not really sure. Desperation is part of the reason. We're both on his side. You love him and I admire him, but we'd both have to be pretty stupid if we didn't realise that he's making a terrible hash of things, and has been for the last nine months or more.'

'You think it's my fault?'

'No, love. It's nobody's fault. Not yours. Not his. Not mine. It's that whole bag of genes that make up Dave Collins. And his upbringing. And his marriage. Neither of them did him much good.'

'Why? Why do you say that?'

'You know why I say it, Sally.' He shook his head slowly. 'You and I both know it. He's walked a tightrope all his life. He never fell off because he never looked down. Now he *has* looked down. And he doesn't know what to do. Walk back or walk forward. And he hasn't got the equipment, the mental equipment, to help him decide. He's a small boat in heavy waters without a rudder. Just wallowing . . . taking on more water as the hours go by. Sinking. Very slowly. But still sinking.'

'What do you think he should do?'

'If I knew, my love, I'd not be sitting here talking. I'd have done something about it. I'm not talking as the boss right now. We're equals. Your views are as valuable as mine. Maybe more so. Every way I look at it the solution is worse than the problem.'

'Tell me what you think. Honestly.'

Parsons looked towards the window and then back at her face.

'OK. Let's ignore our own feelings as persons for a moment. The problem. My right-hand man has ceased to function. The more ruthless talents in the agency are hacking their way through to get his job. Those who are more human are standing aside. Mainly his own team. But even they're demoralised. They're not functioning either. The whole damn place is in a kind of limbo. Holding their breaths until something happens. So what can happen? I could sack him and have every justification for doing so. But that won't solve his problem . . .'

'What *is* his problem?'

Parsons leaned back in his chair, staring at the ceiling before he leaned forward again and looked at the girl.

'Guilt. Guilt is his problem. He's got a guilt complex a mile wide. He left his wife. She made him decide between herself and you. And that was either very shrewd or very wicked. The choice should have been years ago, and it should have been between her or not her. From what I've seen of her she didn't love him. I doubt if she had any real feeling for him. She was too unimaginative to wonder if his relationship with you might have been because of her own lack of warmth and affection. That kind of person tends to be very self-righteous.

279

'So he chose you. And what man in his right mind wouldn't have done the same? But Dave Collins was never really in his right mind. He never was a normal man. He'd been programmed all his life to get on with his work because that was all that he deserved. He never looked for love and warmth. That was for other men, not him. Then you came along. And . . . the music played. You were not only young and beautiful but you loved him. Not as a talent. Not as a creative wonderboy, but just as himself. And before he got used to the idea . . . before he's worked out what it all means, she puts him on the spot.' Parsons leaned forward. 'So he's riddled with guilt. Guilt for leaving his wife and son. Guilt for having a prize like you as his reward for doing the wrong thing. The fact that he never got a reward for doing the *right* thing will never enter his mind. For him he probably feels that he ought to go back to that arid life with her. He'd never seen it as all that bad before. But the choice isn't that. I doubt if she'd have him back anyway. As I said, she never really wanted him. Even she's not all that much to blame. She's just another victim. But the difference is that she's a victim who knows how to survive. She's got her lifebelts all around her. Her parents, her son, her friends and now her self-righteousness. Look what my terrible husband has done to me.

'So we come to his reward . . . you. I've no doubt he loves you just as much as you love him. But for him it's a new experience. One he thinks that he doesn't deserve.' Parsons leaned forward to emphasise his words. 'That man's mind is in a turmoil, Sally. I wish I didn't care about him, that he was just a senior employee. I wouldn't hesitate. I'd sack him right now.' Parsons saw the tears in the girl's eyes and he said softly, 'Don't worry. I shan't sack him. But you've got to think hard about your part in this.'

'What *is* my part?' she said softly.

'I'm not sure. But I am sure that he's not just feeling guilty about leaving his wife. He's guilty about doing that and getting a reward for doing it.' He paused. 'If he'd met you after he had left her there'd have been none of this trouble. Not to this extent anyway.' He paused and looked at her. 'And remember. If there's any way you think I can help you both, then let me know. On this thing we're pals. Not bosses and secretaries. OK?'

She nodded as the tears slid down her cheeks, and managed a watery smile before she stood up and headed for the door.

Chapter 35

SALLY HAD wondered for days which one of them she should talk to. They were a wonderful pair but very different from one another. She knew that her mother's advice would be down to earth and practical. Inclined to see everything as entirely black and white, she would have no doubts and would ignore all side issues. But it seemed cowardly to choose her father as her confidant. He was the gentle, tolerant one of her parents. He would understand but he would be upset by her predicament. He had always been gentle and loving, tolerant of her misdemeanours and not given to overt criticism of her or other people. It wasn't assurance on moral wrongs and rights that she needed, she had sorted those sorts of things out for herself long ago. Her mother would be brisk and concerned only for her daughter's well-being and she needed someone who would put David Collins' interests before hers.

It was a Saturday morning when she finally spoke to him. She would have preferred later in the day because it seemed a later in the day sort of subject. But on the Saturday morning they were alone.

For nearly twenty minutes she talked without interruption as he sat there listening, his arms folded, sometimes closing his eyes as he tried to absorb the details, and when eventually she had finished she dreaded what his first words would be. Fearing mild condemnation or even outright disapproval.

He reached out for her hand and said quietly, 'You must love him a lot, my dear.'

'I do, Daddy.' She shrugged. 'It's not an affair. Not for him, not for me.'

'You must be very unhappy right now.'

'I suppose I am. But I want to stay calm. I want to help him. Maybe save him.'

'And what do you think his reaction would be if you did this . . . walked away?'

'He'd be unhappy. He'd miss me terribly but he's so confused, so depressed, I don't think it would have all that much effect. He's only half in the world. I think he'd get over it. I think he'd stand more chance of sorting things out if I wasn't around.'

'Would you go on seeing him from time to time?'

'No. But if he wanted me after he'd sorted it all out I'd go back like a shot.'

'You say you were both very happy together for quite a long time. What changed all that?'

She sighed. 'I'm not sure. But there was nothing much happening with his divorce. Then he had to see his solicitor and I think that was the start of his depression.'

'Any particular reason?'

'I think it came home to him what he'd done. That and not being able to see his son.'

'Have you suggested you leaving while he sorts it all out? Even obliquely?'

'No.'

'Why not?'

'Because he'd only think about it from my point of view.'

'He sounds an exceptional man. A good man.'

'He is, Daddy. I haven't painted an exaggerated picture because it wouldn't help.'

'So why not stay and just see it through with him?'

'I'd love to. All my selfish instincts tell me that that's what I should do. But it *would* be selfish. He's like a drowning man and if I stayed I should be just jumping into the water with him. I'll do more good standing on the bank trying to help him out.'

'How would your leaving help him?'

283

'It would take me out of that terrible equation in his mind.' She sighed. 'And if it works I'll have my reward.'

'And if it doesn't work?'

'If in a year it hadn't worked for him I'd go back if he wanted me to . . . and get in the water with him.'

'Why did you want me not to tell your mother about this? She's a very sensible woman.'

'I don't want somebody sensible. I want somebody loving. Somebody who'll love him as well as me. Mummy won't be like that. She'll be all for me.'

He smiled. 'You sound wiser than I've ever been. Are you sure you haven't already made up your mind?'

'I have . . . almost. I just need edging over the line or told that I'm being a coward for not staying on.'

'You'll never be a coward, little girl. Never. I see only one problem.'

'What's that?'

'I think you're almost certainly right about what you should do. But have you thought about the doing of it? The rooms you won't see any more. The face that won't be next to yours on a pillow when you wake up. All of that.'

For long moments she looked at his face and then she said softly, 'You *do* understand. I knew you would. I even prayed that you would.'

'Where will you go? It would mean leaving your job.'

'I was thinking of going to France. Working there for a year.'

'Why not go to a university? I'd finance you.'

'No. I'd love that. But I don't want to have a treat or a consolation prize. I just want to go into cold storage for one year.'

'Can I say how sad I am that it's turned out this way. And can I say how much I hope that it all works out and you get your reward. And David too.'

She shook her head and her voice quavered. 'Don't say any more or I'll cry. I don't want to do that.'

And she reached out for him, his arms going round her, and she sobbed as if she would never stop.

She made a list of the things she would take and then tore it up. She would take nothing. It would hurt him more for all the familiar things to suddenly disappear. She left everything except the clothes she was wearing and her toilet things.

She wanted not to take one last look but she stood at the door, shivering despite the heat, wondering if she would ever see any of it again. Conscious of the white envelope propped up against the little red leather travelling clock on the mantelpiece. Then she turned, pulling the door to behind her. For a moment she stood in the sunshine on the landing, her resolution draining away with every second, then she shook her head and made her way down the stairs. She stopped a taxi on the Embankment and an hour later she was at the hotel near the airport. It was going to be the unhappiest night she had ever spent and she guessed that there were going to be many more like it to come. She had a seat booked on the early flight to Paris the next morning.

Chapter 36

HE HAD to catch the late train back from Manchester after the client meeting and it was almost midnight when the taxi dropped him outside the flat. The client was in the rag-trade and he'd brought her back two cotton summer dresses. One with daisies round the hem and one with a red oriental poppy motif.

As he let himself into the flat the living room was in darkness and he guessed that she had been tired and gone to bed. He switched on the light and put down his briefcase and the packages with the dresses and stood there, wondering if it would wake her if he made a cup of tea. He smiled to himself. She'd want him to wake her anyway. It was then that he saw the envelope on the mantelpiece. Instinct told him that it was bad news. She'd been called away. Perhaps one of her parents was ill. But as he reached for the envelope, the stillness, the emptiness of the flat, told him that it was more than that. His hands were shaking as he tore it open.

He read the note a dozen times, weighing each word as if it were some legal document with hidden meanings in a word or phrase. Searching for some clue that would tell him one way or another what he had done to deserve it. He looked at the torn envelope again but there was still only the one word in her round schoolgirl handwriting . . . 'Davie'. He went through the shades of meanings and emphasis on all the variations of his name. David represented distance or formality. Or on the other hand it could be respect. Dave implied a kind of wildness. Even juvenility. Friendly to the point of being too friendly. And

Davie. Davie was what she always called him when they were on their own. He'd always liked it when people called him Davie. Maybe it meant that like she said in the letter she really did still love him. And when he had sorted himself out she really would come back.

He folded the letter and put it in his wallet, and reached for the sleeping pills that the doctor had prescribed two days ago. The doctor had listened to the first few words and then reached for his prescription pad. As he passed over the prescription he stood up to end the conversation. A brief, dry handshake and he was out in the marble hallway.

He hadn't wept. The letter was just one more blow in a series of blows. The loving was over. He slept that night as he had slept for weeks, in a nightmare that had people but no threats. They couldn't see him as they walked by and they couldn't hear him when he spoke or shouted to them. Nothing threatened him but he always woke up soaked in sweat, his fists clenched and the soft thudding of an artery somewhere at the side of his neck.

The next day at the office he held meetings with the creative teams, briefed photographers and dealt with his paperwork and had no recollection in the evening of anything that he had done. To have got through the day was enough. The next problem was to get through the night.

It was late one night, just over a month later, when he drove south across Chelsea Bridge to Streatham and pulled up at the house. He had actually put his hand on the latch of the garden gate before he realised what he had done. He had forgotten that it was no longer his home and that he didn't belong there any more. There were lights on in the house and he stood there for a moment his head bowed and his eyes closed. Then he walked back slowly to the car and drove off.

He was in a white room when he came to. Looking at a white lamp in a white ceiling, and a man was holding his hand. He turned his head to see who it was and he could hear the crackle of the joints and sinews echoing in his head as he moved.

'Don't move about, David. Everything's all right.'

He closed his eyes and slid back into the warm comforting water in which he was floating.

It was a few days later when Harry Parsons came to see him again.

'How're you feeling, David? Are they looking after you well?'

'They think I'm mad.'

'What makes you think that?'

'I ask them questions and they just smile and give me another pill.'

'You don't remember what happened?'

'No.' He shrugged. 'Nothing happened.'

Parsons drew up a chair and put a small parcel on the bedside table.

'They found you wandering on Chelsea Bridge. You'd left the car at Clapham Common. I guess you walked the rest of the way. You were in a bit of a state when they contacted the police. They eventually contacted me and I arranged for you to come here.'

'Who's "they", the people who contacted the police?'

'A milkman and a taxi-driver. They thought at first that you were drunk and then they realised you were ill.'

'Did somebody beat me up or what?'

'No. You'd just had enough of the world for a bit and you opted out.'

'I don't understand.'

'You had a nervous breakdown. Too many pressures. I ought to have stopped it. Anyway, all's well that ends well and all that crap.'

'When can I leave this place?'

'Say a couple of days more rest. It's up to you. You're not fit but you'll be OK.'

'How long have I been here?'

'Not long. About ten days.'

288

'Ten days? For Christ's sake what's happening to my work?'

'Which work are you thinking of?' And Parsons was looking at him intently.

'Any of it.'

'Nothing in particular?'

Collins was breathing shallowly and his eyes were agonised as he looked at Parsons' face.

'The airline account. What about the airline account?'

Parsons stood up. 'That's all under control. Phone me at home as soon as you're out. Come and spend a weekend with us. It'll do you good, a change of scene.'

When Parsons left Collins opened the small package. It was four paperbacks and he left them lying on the bed.

Harry Parsons drove to the Savoy where he was meeting his wife. He'd have to see Ritchie and work out some severance deal. It was time to clean up the shop. The poor bastard couldn't even remember that he had lost them the airline account six months ago. A series of small errors. Wrong addresses and phone numbers in expensive press ads. Various pieces of careless administration. He had pleaded himself with the airline's president for a second chance but it was too late. They had already appointed another agency.

Collins discharged himself from the private clinic that evening and took a taxi back to the flat. He wrote out a short letter of resignation from the agency and a separate long letter to Harry Parsons thanking him for all he had done, both in the last few days and over the years. After he had posted the letters he walked slowly and carefully to the small Indian shop on the corner and when he had gone round the shelves one of the assistants carried the heavy cardboard box back for him. The clinic had given him two bottles of capsules. One lot to see him through the day and the other to get him through the night.

It was about midnight when he grilled a couple of sausages and ate them, still hot, in his fingers. He was barely aware of what he was doing. Then he lay on the bed, still dressed. He lay there for several hours, staring up at the ceiling, before he reached for the sleeping pills. He took two but it was getting light before he slept.

For ten days he lay on the bed, his clothes unchanged, sleeping and waking, oblivious of the days or the time. He didn't think. He wasn't capable of thinking. Fleeting visions like short pieces of film went through his mind. Places and people that he never recognised. Red sunsets, snow on the bark of a tree, a flower opening like one in a time-lapse film, a cottage with roses and golden sunflowers in the foreground and a naked girl running alongside a horse at the edge of a cornfield. He ate small snacks from tins and made endless cups of tea. Sometimes the telephone rang but he didn't answer it, he scarcely heard it. And as the days went by he spent more and more time just lying on the bed. Unthinking and uncaring. Both awake and sleeping he lay with his legs drawn up, his body curled up like some untidy rag-doll foetus.

He had been aware of the knocking for some time and a voice calling his name. He wasn't sure where it came from but he had no will to move from the bed. He closed his eyes and sank back under the waves of his exhaustion once more.

When he woke again there was a man sitting on the chair beside his bed. A man with a beard. A man he vaguely recognised.

'I'm sorry I had to bust the lock to get in but I thought you might be ill or something.'

When Collins didn't respond the man said, 'I was a bit worried about you, David. I phoned several times but I couldn't get an answer.'

Collins heard the dryness of his own mouth as he spoke.

'I'm sorry. I'm sure we've met but I don't remember the name.'

'My name's Trevor Amis. I worked with you at the

agency. You hired me. I'm senior copywriter. Just been promoted group head.'

Collins nodded slowly. 'Yes . . . Trevor . . . I remember that name. Did he send you?'

'Did who send me?'

'I don't remember his name. The boss.'

'You mean Parsons? Harry Parsons?'

'Yes, that's the one.'

'No. He didn't send me. Nobody sent me. I just wanted to check myself that you're all OK.'

'Yes. I'm OK. Tired but OK.'

'I'm going to move in with you for a couple of days, David. Straighten up the place a bit. Get it ship-shape. It looks like it's got a bit out of hand.'

But David Collins was already asleep.

When Collins woke he saw Amis there with a girl who smiled at him when she saw his eyes open. She nudged Amis and he turned to look at Collins.

'Welcome back. This is Connie, my wife. She used to work at the agency doing paste-ups in the studio.' He waved his hand around the room, smiling. 'We've given it a going over. Brightened it up a bit.'

Collins made the effort, swung his legs off the bed and sat there looking slowly round the room. All the rubbish had been cleared away. Tins and packets were neatly arranged on shelves and there was a bunch of Michaelmas daisies in a vase on the small table. Ranged along the mantelpiece were half a dozen postcards. Pictures of paintings in the Tate.

'Hope you approve, Dave,' Connie said.

'I don't understand. What's going on?'

The girl smiled. 'You're going to have a nice grilled steak and so are we. I've put clean clothes out for you in the bathroom and the water-heater's on, so have a bath.'

He staggered as he stood up obediently and Trevor Amis caught his arm and led him to the tiny bathroom. Amis sat on the toilet as Collins undressed, and read an evening paper as Collins lay in the warm bath.

When they had finished the steaks and they were sipping the coffee Amis said, 'I'm going to stay with you tonight, old man, and tomorrow we'll work out a bit of a programme. You look better already.'

Collins nodded. 'I am better. I'm sorry if I've been a bloody nuisance.'

Amis laughed. 'You haven't. We all get the heebie-jeebies from time to time and that's when we need a mate.' He grinned. 'I'm your mate for this time.'

'Why bother?'

Amis shrugged. 'Don't want to see a good talent thrown away. Not enough of it around to be able to waste it.'

'What particular talent are you thinking of?'

Amis looked at Collins' haggard face. 'Truth or fairy story? Which do you want?'

'Truth. I think.' And he smiled wryly.

'Thank Christ for the smile. OK, the truth. You've wasted your time for years at the agency and if Harry Parsons was as bright as he thinks he is he'd have noticed and stopped it. You're not the best copywriter I've ever met or even the best graphics man but you've got a talent for knowing how to touch people's minds with an ad. I've never met anybody half as good at that as you are. And that's the bit that matters. There's plenty of copywriters as good as I am and dozens of artists and photographers who can translate the idea. But it's having the bloody idea that's difficult. With you the agency grew, but over the last months you did less and less creative work and more and more admin. You did it OK, but a decently educated clerk could have done it just as well. That's all that's the matter with you, mate. Seriously.'

Collins sighed. 'You could be right, Trevor. So what do I do?'

'Are you broke or have you got enough bread to live on for a bit?'

'I guess I could get by for a year or so.'

'You remember when the agency first started and we hadn't got much capital you used to do some of the photography for us yourself.'

Collins nodded. 'Yes. I remember.'

'Those were some of the best photographs we ever had. We're still using some of them in the pharmaceutical ads and the insurance company ads. I want us to find you a small place for a studio and set you up as a freelance. I can pass you work and I can put the word round at other agencies. We've talked about it, Connie and me. We've got a bit in the bank and we'd be prepared to buy a stake in you up to a thousand quid.'

Collins looked away for a moment and then back at the two faces at the other side of the table.

'You don't know how much good you've just done me. You can have the stake in any business that's mine but I don't need the money.' He paused. 'You know, for months people have been saying to me that I should put all my mind into my work. I never realised before why I couldn't do it.' He sighed and was silent for long moments. 'Apart from my personal problems my work bores the hell out of me. I'm sick of meetings and admin. I can do it all right, but by God it bores me. I really enjoyed doing that photography but I never saw myself as a photographer. I'll think about it. I'm tempted but I want to feel I'll be good at it. More than just competent.'

'You'll make a pile, David. Take my word for it. We'll get moving on Monday.'

'What day is it today?'

'It's Saturday.'

'What month is it?'

'It's September. The 15th of September.'

'How did you find me?'

'Had a sneaky look in the old files at the agency for your home address.'

'You know about Sally?'

'Yes.' Amis reached out and touched Collins' arm. 'But David, I can't help you on that. I haven't got any experience that way. All I want is to get you on your feet, get you moving, and what you do then is up to you. You'll be OK once you're standing on firm ground.'

'You must have spent a lot of time thinking about all this.'

Amis shook his head. 'No. Not really. It all seemed pretty obvious to me. You're a creative guy and you should have stuck to it.'

Connie cooked them a liver and bacon supper to celebrate the signing of the lease for the studio. It was part of a condemned property in Pimlico owned by the local council. It was due to be demolished as part of a rehousing and rebuilding plan but the plan covered a period of ten years and the part that Collins had rented had a potential life of at least another five years.

The effect on Collins of being taken over by the Amis couple had been dramatic. He still became tired quickly, but the strained look round his eyes and mouth was beginning to go. He spent hours checking equipment and working out a budget. When they got to the coffee Amis said, 'When can you start functioning?'

'Two weeks, I guess.'

'Make it ten days and I can give you your first job.'

'D'you mean that?'

'Of course I do. I've got a car accessories shot that needs to be good but I can't wait two weeks for it.'

'That's great, Trevor. Thanks.'

'What are you doing about equipment?'

'I'm buying a Hasselblad and three lenses. I'm hiring a 5 x 4 and a full studio flash outfit, and I'm going to put all my processing out until I know I'm really in business.'

'Sounds sensible . . . I had a word with an old mate of mine at JWT. He'd give you a whole mail order catalogue if you'd take it. Crap, but it's worth £10,000 at least.'

'I'll take it, Trevor. I'll take anything until I've built up the business.'

294

Amis smiled. 'That's my boy. When are you moving in?'

'Tomorrow. I'm going to live there. In the two rooms at the back.'

'I'll come round in the evening after work. We'll both come round and lend a hand.'

'Can I take you both out for a meal on Saturday?'

'You bet.'

'Nothing posh. Just jeans and sweaters.'

Amis smiled. 'You know me. That's posh as far as I'm concerned.'

The old building had been a warehouse and now it had been cleaned and re-decorated it was almost an ideal studio. Its high roof and double-doored access to the street was a great advantage. There was far more space than he needed and he spent a few hundred pounds on partitioning off the area he needed for the studio itself.

In the first few weeks most of his work came from Trevor Amis. Routine shots which he did with all the caring and talent he had. There was little room for inspiration or creative touches but the care was visible in the lighting and the treatment.

What surprised Collins was that, excluding the capital outlay for equipment, the company was breaking even in the first few weeks. Not that money was a pressing problem. He had received a formal and impersonal reply from Harry Parsons to his letter of resignation. A cheque was enclosed that covered two months' salary and the price of his reverted shares in the company. He had made a few hundred pounds profit on giving up the lease of the flat and after all the equipment and refurbishing of the studio had been paid for he had just over £9,000 in the bank.

Trevor and Connie Amis frequently dropped in on their way from work for a sandwich and a drink, and after they left he carried on working to midnight or beyond. Despite his solicitor's advice he had refused to go to the divorce hearing. He had deliberately shut his mind to his past life.

295

All of it. He knew now that that particular ice was far too thin to carry his load. There were brief seconds sometimes when it seeped into his mind like a swirling rush of angry floodwater and he would consciously stop and close his mind as if he were closing the bulkheads of a foundering ship against the raging ocean. He had learned too painfully how to make it work to take any risks, and he avoided anything that would remind him of his old life. People, places, incidents were not to be remembered.

For three months Collins worked without counting the hours. He had more work than he could handle and he hired a girl assistant and set up his own darkroom and processing unit. Laura Mason had had three years at the Guildford School and knew more about the technicalities of photography than he did, and they made a good combination. It was through one of Laura's Guildford School contacts that he was asked to do an emergency fashion session for an Italian magazine.

The photographs were of a range of woollens, and because they were for editorial use rather than for advertisements the fees were not top-scale. But the series marked a turning point for Collins and the studio. Instead of the standard lighting which would show up the manufacturing expertise, Collins had lit them with a soft lighting that was almost shadowless. The photographs were like pre-Raphaelite paintings. He had done the personal treatment at his own expense in addition to the standard shots that the magazine had commissioned.

He was phoned by the features editor within hours of the photographs being delivered. They wanted his own version. They would pay top rate and a retainer for another six commissions. He refused the retainer because he didn't want to limit his outlets but agreed to taking any commissions they cared to give him.

It was another three months before the issue appeared with his photographs and the response was instant and positive. The manufacturers came back for advertisement shots and when, tongue-in-cheek, an Italian magazine had shown them, framed, in their beautiful reception area, they had had hundreds of offers to buy them, and an observant editorial girl noticed that sixty per cent of the offers were from men. Fashion photographs that could induce macho Italian men to want to buy them were obviously special.

Assignments came in from France, Italy and America and Collins decided to appoint a commercial director for the studio. He chose a woman in her mid-thirties from one of the top London fashion magazines. She was handsome rather than pretty, and with the good looks had an elegance that concealed a tough and competent business mind.

Collins wanted to avoid getting involved again in the commercial aspects of a business and the woman was looking for a chance to make both money and a reputation.

He still lived in the two rooms in the studio building. There was a good-sized living room and a small bedroom. The living room was furnished a little better now that the studio was making good money, but it was essentially masculine. Teak and black leather and glass. The floors in both rooms were still the original brick, from when that part of the building had been a workshop. The bedroom was even plainer. A single bed, a wardrobe and a small chest of drawers. A table by the bed held a reading lamp and a pile of books.

It was a Friday night after a long hard week and as he poured her a gin and tonic Carmen Friedman said, 'How much do you think the company's got in the bank, David?'

'Two or three thousand. Something like that. D'you want a sandwich?'

'No. I'm eating out. We've got £15,000 on deposit and £653 on current account. And we're owed just over £10,000.'

'Sounds good,' he said, as he sat down facing her.

'My God. You really are the limit. It's bloody marvellous. Most studios in London have got thumping great overdrafts.'

'It's keeping things small that does it.'

'You must be psychic.'

He laughed. 'Why?'

'I was going to suggest we expanded. Took on an assistant to do the routine photographs.'

He shook his head, 'I won't ever do that.'

'Why not? Some of the stuff we get is only because they want to cash in on your name. They'd be happy enough with routine shots. At the moment we're even turning away high-grade assignments because you're overloaded yourself.'

'I just don't want the responsibility.'

'What responsibility, for heaven's sake?'

'The responsibility of employing people.'

'But you employ me. And young Laura.'

'I wish I didn't have to.' He smiled. 'Sounds terrible but I don't want responsibility for other people. I console myself that you and Laura could get jobs in a couple of hours if I went bust.'

She put her glass on the low table and he was suddenly aware of her long elegant legs. She looked across at him.

'You know, you're a very deceptive man, David Collins. You look as if you could take on the world. You've got a fantastic talent. And yet you're insecure. Why? Who did what to you? A woman?'

He laughed. 'Nobody's done anything to me. I just don't want the responsibility of employing people. It makes me responsible for their lives and their families. I'm content as I am. And I don't want to be a businessman. I just want to earn a living.'

'Don't you want to be rich?'

'I don't really know. I suppose I'd like a lot of dough in the bank. Security and all that. Independence. But I don't want to swim around in the great big waves to get it.'

'But you were number two man in a first-class agency.'

'But I ought not to have been. Anyway, the other guy was the real businessman.'

'You didn't mind that?'

'No. Suited me fine.' He leaned forward smiling. 'It's

funny. I can remember him asking me that. If I minded. And when I said "no" he looked at me just like you're looking at me now. Pleased but wondering. Wondering if I really meant it.'

'Maybe I'll change your mind some day and I'll make you really rich. Can I ask you something? Something personal?'

'You can ask.'

'Somebody told me that not too long ago there'd been a girl in your life. A young girl . . . what happened to her?'

He shook his head and she saw the sudden tension on his face.

'I'm sorry, David. I didn't mean to probe.'

'What time's your dinner date?'

'OK. I can take a hint. It's an Israeli fashion guy. It ought to be me taking him out but you're so much in demand the meals are usually on them.'

'We can pay our own way surely?'

'Why the hell should we? Let the bastards pay if they want us that much.'

He laughed. 'I'm glad you're on my side.'

As she stood up she smiled. 'I *am* on your side, David. All the way.'

Collins looked up at the blue sky trying to locate the plane that was holding up the session. As its sound faded he bent back to check the viewfinder of the Arriflex.

'Move the reflector over, Laura. No, the other way, you're casting a shadow . . . that's fine. Hold it there.' He lifted his head and looked at the model. For a moment he wondered if she was not too young. It was young fashion he was shooting but although she was in her early twenties she had almost too youthful a face.

'Debbie, when we take this last section the lens will be in close-up on your face. I want nice sweeping eyelashes so don't shut your eyes too tightly. Then you lift your head, counting four. Mouth opens slightly and you lift up

299

the poppy. Just touch it to your mouth, lower it and then turn full face to the camera. Big eyes, head slightly back to show your nose, and your lips just slightly apart. Just a glint of front teeth. OK?'

She nodded and Collins said, 'OK. Let's have a dry run. No camera, no sound. OK, head slightly down. Right. Carry on. Good . . . good . . . lovely . . . face to me . . . wonderful. OK, relax.'

Collins took one more meter reading from the model's face and another from the white cotton dress with its border of red poppies. Then he walked back to the camera, his head bent to the viewfinder.

'OK, everybody. Quiet please. OK, Debbie . . . starting . . . now.'

Then there was nothing but the sounds of the countryside and the soft whir of the camera.

'OK, Debbie. That was marvellous. I want to do it once more without the poppy. It's going to look very pale against the poppies on the skirt. Could make them look a bit loud. OK.'

The girl nodded and they went through the routine a second time. It was for a forty-five second TV commercial. The first he had been asked to do, and he was being paid half-fee on an experimental basis. If they used it he would get the full fee. Carmen Friedman had been reluctant to let them get away with the half-fee basis but Collins had said he wanted to do it and that was that.

He stayed up all night, waiting at the lab for the film to be processed, and then spent the whole weekend editing. He had been asked only for the photography but once he had seen the finished version he wrote a script and phoned an actor friend who did a speculative voice-over for him. And finally he recorded the few bars he wanted from Beethoven's *Pastoral*, the third movement, after the storm.

On the Monday morning he spent four hours at a recording studio, mixing the voice-over and the music and having it laid on the stripe.

300

In the afternoon he ran it in a darkened corner of the studio for Carmen and Laura and when he switched on the lights again they were still sitting there silently.

'You don't like it?'

'It's fantastic, David. I just wished it went on and on.'

Collins smiled. 'And you, Carmen?'

Carmen Friedman sighed. 'I'll never cease to be surprised by you. It's bloody marvellous. It really is. And your bloody cheek in ignoring the client's script for the voice-over . . . well. They'll rave; David. They really will. You've turned a line of cheap cotton dresses into a glamorous line in forty-five seconds. When can I have it to show them?'

'Tomorrow afternoon. Shall I pay to have the sound put on opticals?'

'You bet. They'll pay all right.'

Carmen Friedman came back with the fee doubled. When the TV ad was first shown the response was immediate and overwhelming. Sales of the line went far beyond the client's most optimistic expectations. Debbie, the model, had a diary crammed with bookings, and even the sales of LPs of Beethoven's *Pastoral* went up. And suddenly David Collins was a name to be conjured with for TV commercials that had to be 'different'. That first TV ad had been against all the trends in fashion advertising, it was the softest of 'soft-sell' which in itself was against all the current thinking on TV advertising. But it worked. As Collins had known it would.

He had been amused that the agencies and clients who pressed him to do their TV commercials wanted that same ad no matter how inappropriate it might be to their products. The same model, the same setting and perhaps some other Beethoven symphony to prove that it wasn't just a crib.

He talked for hours with Carmen about what their policy should be, and eventually they compromised. He would only do one TV commercial a month and the fee would be as high as Carmen could get.

In the next six months he produced only four more TV ads, two of which won awards in both London and Europe. It was then that Carmen asked for an evening meeting with him.

She refused the offered drink and looked at her notepad impatiently as he settled in the leather armchair.

'I want to make a suggestion, David. A business proposition. We're wasting literally dozens of opportunities every week of earning a hell of a lot of money.

'It comes to us because of your reputation. Some of it has to be your work and we get top fees when we can take it on. But a lot more just want the studio name. It doesn't have to be you. Those jobs already represent at least twice what you can earn the studio by yourself. Now that's crazy. It's just throwing money away and I want to suggest a compromise. Will you hear me out?'

Collins smiled and shrugged. 'I'm not stopping you, my dear.'

'OK. It's this. You go on as you are. In this place with me as your business manager. We have plenty of space for another studio in the other part of this building that's standing empty. I'll finance it myself and you'll take an agreed share of the profits for the benefit of me using the studio name. You can lay down the creative guidelines or not. Whatever you wish. We'll get a good guy or even two and they won't trouble you in any way.'

'You sound as though you have been thinking of this for weeks.'

'Six weeks, that's all.'

'How much will it cost to set up?'

She glanced at her notes, and then back at his face. 'I reckon £15,000 capital costs and maybe £3,000 to cover cash-flow until our invoices are paid. Say £20,000 in all.'

'Where are you getting the money from?'

'I've got ten grand in the bank and a bank loan with my flat as security for the rest. No problems.'

302

'Have you talked to them? The bank?'

'Yes. Like I said. No problem.'

'Let me think about it for a couple of days and we'll talk again.'

'I need to know now, David.'

She saw him shiver as he heard those words and frowned. 'Are you cold?'

'No.'

'Somebody walked over your grave.'

'Perhaps.'

'Ask me anything you want to know.'

'Is this what you want? Really want?'

'Yes.'

'You could make a lot of money without any investment if we just carry on as we are.'

She shrugged and smiled. 'You know what that American said to you the other day – "Too much ain't enough for me."'

He shrugged. 'OK. Go ahead.'

'You mean that?'

'Of course I do.'

'I won't ever forget, David. I promise.'

Connie Amis was coming out of the small local supermarket when the girl spoke to her.

'Connie.'

'I'm sorry, I don't . . . my God. What on earth are you doing here?'

'I wanted to talk to you.'

'What about?'

'I think you know, don't you?'

'Maybe. My place is just round the corner, you'd better come and have a coffee with me.'

'Thanks.'

Connie waited until the coffees were poured and then she said, 'How did you know I'd be at the supermarket?'

'I got your address from the telephone book. I followed you. Trying to pluck up my courage.'

'Is it David Collins?'

'Yes. Will you tell me about him?'

Connie sighed. 'He's back in the world, if that's anything. He had a nervous breakdown. Was in hospital for nearly two weeks. He resigned from the agency and Harry Parsons has never gone near him since. He's got a photographic studio that he owns entirely and he must be making a lot of bread. That's David Collins so far as I'm concerned.'

'Has he ever spoken about me?'

'I've never heard him utter one word that was anything other than business. I shouldn't think anyone else has either. He doesn't talk about himself at all.'

'Is he happy, do you think?'

'I shouldn't think so for a moment. His wife screwed him for all she could get. He sees his boy once every two weeks when she can't find an excuse to prevent it. Anyway, I don't think David Collins is built for being happy. All Trevor and I care about is that he survives. That, he does.' She paused and looked at the girl. 'What about you?'

'I've got a job at an agency in Geneva.'

'What are you doing over here?'

'I saw a piece in an Italian magazine about David. I wanted to know how he really is.'

'You still love him?'

Sally shrugged. 'Yes.' She hesitated. 'Perhaps not the same way, but I love him.'

'In what way different?'

'It's been nearly two years. I suppose one gets a different perspective.'

'What's that mean?'

'I suppose I feel more . . .' she shrugged, '. . . detached. Calmer. More mature.'

Connie smiled. 'You always were mature, Sally. It's just time the great healer and all that jazz, isn't it?'

'What makes you say that?'

'Your face, honey. You were always very pretty. You're even prettier now. Maybe lovely's the word. David Collins' face used to be quite handsome but he ain't handsome now, I assure you. Attractive maybe, if you like the haggard well-worn look. I don't think anything or anybody is ever going to change that. He belongs in that face.'

'You like him, don't you?'

'Trevor likes him. Loves him even. Like a long-lost brother. For me . . . well, I'm sorry for him. Sympathetic. That's about it.'

'You don't think I should see him?'

'That's up to you, love. It won't do *you* any good. It would probably destroy *him*.'

'You don't think he'd want me back?'

'Who's the lucky man?'

'I don't understand.'

'You've got a man, haven't you?'

'How did you know?'

'Because if you hadn't you wouldn't be sitting here. You wouldn't have contacted me. You'd be round there now. It would have been a disaster but you wouldn't have known that. So who's the lucky guy?'

'He's an Italian. He wants me to marry him.'

'I should catch the next plane back. Forget David Collins, and with that ghost out of the way decide whether you want your Eyetie or not. Is he a bottom-pincher?'

Sally smiled for the first time. 'He's a Count and he doesn't pinch bottoms.'

'They're all bloody Counts out there. And they're all bottom-pinchers. I wouldn't mind one myself, sometimes. Make a change from my faithful Welsh sheepdog anyway. More coffee?'

'I'd better go. Thanks for being so kind, Connie. And so sensible.'

'Me? Sensible? That'll be the day.'

Chapter 37

'D'YOU WANT a Coke or an orange? Fresh orange?'

'A Coke, please.'

Collins poured the Coke and a small malt whisky for himself.

'Which did you like best, the ballet or the football match?'

'The ballet. The football was OK, though.'

'Why the ballet?'

'I don't like games, especially football.' The boy looked at his face. 'Momma says it's sissy not to like games.'

'Why don't you like them?'

'They're rough, and anyway I'm not any good at them. And I think it's silly to get hurt for no reason.'

'Sounds good common sense to me. Why do you like the ballet?'

'I love the music and the lighting and the costumes. Everything. It's like in a dream when you can float. I'd like to be a ballet dancer when I grow up. You have to be very tough, you know. Just as tough as a footballer.'

'You have to start early, too. Would you like to go to a ballet school and see what it's like? Try it for a year, say, and see if you like it?'

Jimmy sighed. 'She wouldn't like it. She says if you don't have a father you should go in the army or the police. Something with men.'

'But you have got a father. I'm your father.'

The boy blushed. 'You know what I mean. It's . . .'

'Don't be embarrassed. I know what you mean. Having

a father or not having a father doesn't make any difference to what you want to do. I didn't have a father. He died when I was a baby but I tried various things before I decided what I wanted to do.'

'Why didn't you two like one another?'

'What did your mother tell you?'

'She said you weren't interested in us and you walked out. I don't really believe that.'

'Why not?'

'You see me every two weeks. If you weren't interested you wouldn't bother.'

'We'll talk about it one day. But you can take it from me that I care about you. I think about you a lot. You're my son. My boy. But things went wrong and not being with you was part of the outcome. And in those days I was so busy that I didn't see much of you even when I lived there.'

'Can I have another Coke before I go?'

'Sure.' Collins reached over and opened another can. 'Here you are. Would you like a sandwich or something as well?'

The boy laughed. 'No. All those chips filled me up. They like you, don't they, Trevor and Connie?'

'They've been good friends to me.'

'He showed me some of his drawings. It must be great to be able to draw like that.' The boy smiled. 'He said you're a genius.'

Collins smiled and shook his head. 'There's no such thing. Drink up.'

He drove the boy back to the house and sat in the car as he opened the garden gate, turned and waved before he made his way up the garden path to the front door. It was always left ajar for Jimmy to go inside. She was never there when he brought him back. The boy waved again and the door closed.

Despite the time that had gone by and his new equilibrium, going to the house always depressed him. Seeing the door close reminded him of that other time.

He always looked forward to seeing Jimmy but was tense all the time he was with him. There was so little they could talk about. If he asked what the boy did it was looked on as interference or quizzing. Almost everything was taboo. He tried to be bouncy and cheerful but he felt it was a sad, ineffective performance. That was why he always tried to see that they spent some time with Trevor and Connie. It was neutral territory and they could both relax. He looked forward to those Saturdays but he knew that they weren't successful. A strain for both of them. But they were a contact and that was what mattered.

He brightened up as he remembered that he would be seeing Penny that evening. Penny Goodhew was a friend of Debbie, the model in that first TV ad, and they'd met at Debbie's engagement party – she'd had several engagement parties since she became a top model. Penny was a model too. Her father was a barrister and an MP, with a thousand acres or so in East Anglia. The manor house and the land had been in the family for generations and he was expected to be the next Lord Mayor of the City of London.

Despite her good looks, Penny had not been a successful model financially. Her attitude to both clients and photographers hadn't helped: she made it quite clear that they were very lucky to be photographing Penelope Goodhew. But her pictures were easy to place in the high-society magazines in London, Paris, Rome and New York. And they had to admit that she not only photographed well but wore *haute-couture* as if it were her usual wardrobe. Which of course it was.

He had driven her back to her father's town house in Eaton Square and she had invited him to call in at her own flat in Chester Mews the next afternoon. Away from studio lights he realised that she had one of those rare faces that are actually as beautiful as they photograph. She had large grey eyes, a neat well-modelled nose and a soft full mouth. It was a cool, calm face and the wide eyes were not only beautiful but observant. Studio people had nicknamed her

The Iceberg and he wondered if it was because of her temperament, her looks, or her open indifference to their flattery and their profession. He had used her once or twice without remembering her name but her cool beauty wasn't what he was usually looking for. His young pre-Raphaelite lovelies were generally in their teens or early twenties. He needed prettiness rather than beauty for the effects he tried for.

He had been amused when he went to her flat for tea the next day to find that she had borrowed one of her mother's maids and that it was an almost formal tea: neat, triangular smoked-salmon sandwiches, buttered toast and Tiptree jams, and a choice of Indian or China tea from silver teapots.

As they ate she asked his opinion about various politicians and when she saw that he was bored had asked him questions about himself. He realised that they were back in the days of calling cards, salons and patronage. She was taking him under her wing. He stayed for an hour and when he was leaving he invited her to dinner the following week. She walked over to a beautiful antique bureau and after consulting a leather-bound diary she accepted.

There had been a number of dinner dates since then. Wherever he took her she seemed to be known by head waiters, and the service they got was remarkable. She knew about food and wine and tried in vain to improve his taste in both.

As he shaved in the small bathroom he wondered what Mary's life was like now. She had enough money from him to live well. He had to supply details of his earnings annually and her solicitors applied for appropriate increases which he never opposed. He was paying almost as much in tax these days as he had been earning gross at the agency. He had seen Harry Parsons once or twice but Parsons had always pretended not to see him. The agency never used him now for their photographic work. There had been the few routine jobs that Trevor Amis had passed him in the early days but they had stopped very quickly. He had never asked why. He took it for granted that Parsons was behind it.

He sometimes wondered how it was that so many people were antagonistic to him after the divorce. People who had known him casually for years seemed to go out of their way to avoid him. Those he met accidentally where small talk was unavoidable adopted a rather superior attitude, and he sometimes wondered what they had heard that had made them change their attitude towards him so quickly and so easily. But it no longer disturbed him. It just made him more determined not to rely on other people.

Penny and he ate that night at Leoni's and when he stopped the car at her flat she said, 'Why haven't you ever asked me back to your place?'

He smiled. 'It's a bit primitive for you, honey. You'd definitely be slumming.'

She shrugged. 'Rubbish. Let's go there. I'd like to see it.'

She stood looking at the books on the shelves as he made the coffee, then turned slowly, her eyes taking in every detail of the room and its furniture.

She sat down beside him as he poured the coffee and as he straightened up she said, 'Why don't you have some of your own pictures on the walls?'

'I like the bare walls. They're restful.'

'And your choice of pictures would give people clues about you.'

He laughed. 'They're not my pictures, Penny. They're pictures of my clients.'

'Why do you invite me out?'

'You're beautiful and intelligent and you give me an insight into people I don't understand.'

'My God. You make me sound like the *Encyclopaedia Britannica* in a special binding.'

He laughed. 'More like *Debrett* or *Who's Who*.'

'Can I ask you a personal question?'

'Try. I may not answer.'

'Are you a queer?'

'What makes you ask that?'

'Most men who date me more than once can't wait to get my pants down. You've never even kissed me. Not even a peck on the cheek. And you've got great charm in a special sort of way. You're very masculine in most ways but you're also very closed in . . . as if there's something you're hiding. Most men I know like that are homosexuals. Charming but aloof. Charming because they aren't trying to get me into bed.'

'So why don't you just accept your diagnosis?'

'Because I've heard that now and again you've bedded one or two of your little girl models.'

He smiled. 'Confusing, isn't it?'

'Tell me, David.'

'Why do you want to know?'

'Because I want to sleep with you.'

'Sounds a pretty good reason to me. No. I'm not queer. Never have been. And I'm sure I'm not charming. You're confusing charm with friendliness. And I'm not knowingly hiding anything. But I'm flattered that you want to sleep with me.'

'I wanted to sleep with you the first time I modelled for you. You didn't even remember my name until you were doing the shots for Courrèges.'

He smiled and reached out for her hand. 'Just the dedicated professional at work. Let me show you my bedroom. Somebody once said it was "*nouveau* Wormwood Scrubs."'

She laughed as they both stood up.

She lay looking at his face, half-turned towards him, her arm across his chest.

'Can I stay with you all night?'

'Of course you can.'

'Did you know that I was supposed to be engaged to Piers Maitland?'

'No. Are you?'

'He asked my father who said it was OK by him and after that Piers told all and sundry that we're engaged.'

'Did he get round to asking you if you agreed?'

'Yes. Several times.'

'What did you say?'

'I said I'd think about it. What do you think of him?'

'He's a creep but I gather he's a wealthy creep.'

'He pretends he is. Most of the family goods and chattels are in hock to one of the merchant banks.'

'So?'

She smiled. 'Tell me what you want to do to me next. Something really wild. Something you've never done with another girl.'

'That's very cunning, my love.'

She laughed. 'Why?'

'If I come up with something routine you'll say it's old hat, and if I don't come up with anything you'll think I've been swinging from the chandeliers with every model in town. So you choose. This is the Ladies Excuse-me.'

Chapter 38

ON THE fifth anniversary of the studio starting in business, Collins took Laura, Carmen and her three staff, his accountant and Trevor and Connie Amis to a celebratory dinner at the Ritz. He had suggested the Connaught but they had all pleaded for the glamour of the Ritz.

It had been a pleasant evening and afterwards he took Carmen back to her flat. The flat was at Dolphin Square and when the taxi had left she invited him in. He saw the disappointment on her face when he said no, but he wanted to walk back to the studio and maybe do some work.

'I think you work too hard, David. It's crazy. Both studios are doing so well. You don't need to work like a slave. We're making pots of money.'

He smiled. 'I don't do it for the money, sweetheart. I know everybody says that . . . but I really mean it. The money doesn't mean anything after a certain point.'

'But you don't even buy yourself things. No treats, no anything. You're just like a mouse on one of those wheels.'

He laughed. 'Don't worry about me. Maybe that's what I was meant to be. Safe and secure in my little cage.'

'What do you think of Roger?'

'Is he the red-haired one?'

'Yes.'

'Seems pleasant enough. The work I've seen of his is competent but it isn't going to cause a sensation. Why? Why do you ask?'

'I thought of giving him a contract. I don't seem to be able to hang on to them for more than three or four months. They get themselves a bit of a name because people think they're part of your set-up. And then they leave and start up on their own.'

Collins smiled. 'That's why I don't like employing people. Remember what I said in the beginning? . . . Two years ago, when you started up.'

'What did you say?'

'I don't remember the exact words but what I was getting at was that I'm a photographer and I don't want to be an administrator, a personnel officer and all the rest of the problems you've got yourself.'

'I don't really mind the problems.' She looked up at his face. 'Don't you get lonely in that dump, David?'

'No. It's all I want.'

There was a pile of fashion magazines on a table beside the desk. Both the *Vogues*, *Harpers* and several copies of French, Swiss and Italian magazines, all marked at the pages where his photographs appeared. It wasn't easy for fast-run printing to show the delicacy of his photographs and he checked from time to time to see how they were being reproduced.

He was half-way through the pile, tossing them to one side after he had checked them, then he saw the photograph and the text.

A SON FOR THE COUNT

The Conte di Stefano leaving the Ospedale Vittorio with his English wife, the former Sally Major, with their new-born son. The new baby is to be named Alessandro after his paternal grandfather who died earlier this year.

When the duties of the family estate allow, the Count is to be found at his gallery in the Via Veneto where connoisseurs can . . .

He sat there with the magazine open on his lap, his heart thumping as he felt his mind go back into those days of depression and confusion. Forcing himself to his feet he let the magazine fall, and without thinking what he was doing he walked through the studio, across the cobbled yard to the street. There was a mist of fine rain as he walked to the Embankment and he stopped for the cars before crossing the main road. A squat tug was pulling a line of barges up-river against the tide, black smoke pouring from its stubby funnel, a light in its curtained saloon.

As he leaned against the balustrade his tension had already dissipated and his mind was clear as he looked across the river. She looked just the same as she smiled fondly at the baby cradled in her arms. If he had been sensible it could have been his baby. He should have behaved sensibly. Sorting out the problems one by one as they arose. And eventually they would have been married. A normal happy couple. An orderly straightforward life. A home that Jimmy could be part of. Weekends in the country. Holidays together. Theatres, the cinema, concerts and a small circle of friends. Wedding anniversaries and flowers to surprise her. Somebody to love and somebody to be loved by. He had been juvenile, panic-stricken and pathetic. And for no good reason.

He walked slowly back to the studio and his rooms. It was a mistake that he wouldn't make again.

Carmen Friedman was smiling across the table at him.

'This is your half-year cheque from my operation, David. Guess how much it is?'

'I've no idea.'

'Guess.'

'Somewhere between two and three thousand pounds?'

'Nineteen thousand pounds and it will be more for the second half.'

'You must have been really ripping them off.'

'No way. They got value for money. OK. It was your name brought the business but we didn't kid anybody.

Nobody thought you were taking the photographs yourself.'

'Are you happy?'

She smiled. 'Yes. Not as happy as I'll be when it's doubled.'

'You've done a marvellous job. I'm very proud of you.'

'By the way, I met an old friend of yours at a party last night.'

'Who was that?'

'A guy named Fredericks. Said you were officers together in the war. Said he saw you again in Birmingham years ago. After the war.'

'What's he doing now?'

'He wasn't wearing a uniform but I gather he's still in the army. Somebody told me he was a general. A brigadier. Is that a general?'

'Yes. What had he got to say?'

She grinned. 'He seemed to know you pretty well. Said he'd always known you'd be good at something, but thought you were too introverted to take risks. He was surprised to hear that you were divorced. Said it was out of character. Though maybe you were making a dash for freedom.' She paused. 'I didn't know you'd come from such a terrible background. He said you'd started in a foundry, whatever that might be.' She smiled. 'Is that why you never talk about yourself?'

'No. It's just that it's not worth talking about.'

'I loved hearing about you. You must have looked very dishy in your uniform. Have you got any photographs I could see?'

He shook his head. 'No, thank God.'

'Are you pleased about the cheque?'

'Of course I am. And I'm pleased for you that it's all worked out just as you planned.'

'Can I take you out to dinner tonight to celebrate?'

'I can't tonight. I've got a date.'

'Is it that Penny female?'

'Maybe. We'll celebrate some other time.'

'You seem to be seeing her an awful lot. I hope you're not serious about her. She's not your type.' She looked at his face. 'You always go for young girls, don't you? She's far too young for you. Anyway her family will be expecting her to land a title or at least some rolling acres.'

'Sounds like you're expanding into the match-making business.'

'Somebody's got to stop you from being an idiot again.'

'Again?'

She saw the look on his face and said quickly, 'I'm sorry, David. I shouldn't have said that.' She stood up. 'I care about you, you know. I'm not just the career woman busy making a pile.'

'I'm sure you're not. But . . .' He shrugged and reached for the telephone. 'If you see Laura, tell her I want her, will you?'

They were walking through the studio. There was only one light on and they had to thread their way carefully through the tripods and lighting equipment.

'This is new, isn't it?' Penny paused at the plasterboard offices that had been put up in one corner of the studio.

'It's been there about a couple of weeks.'

'That's Laura's new darkroom, I suppose. What's Friedman Enterprises, for God's sake?'

'That's Carmen's own company. Watch the cable, honey.'

When they were in his living room she walked about restlessly. They had a couple of drinks and then went to the Connaught for dinner. They were at the peach-flan and cream stage when she said, 'Tell me about Friedman Enterprises.'

'It's Carmen's own company. She financed it herself.'

'Does that mean that you work for her?'

'No. She's got her own staff. I'm a director, and although she does all the work I get half the profits. It's a generous arrangement on her part.'

317

'I thought she worked for you.'

'She does. She's business manager of my studio as well.'

'She always talks as if she's the one who matters. The boss.'

He laughed. 'She's probably right. If I was on my own, without her, I guess I'd be broke by now. She's got all the business sense, I just take a few pictures.'

'And if she walked out you'd be in the shit?'

'She won't walk out. Why should she? She loves what she's doing.'

'She wants you too.'

'OK. I do my part and she does hers. It's a combined operation.'

'I didn't mean that.'

'I don't get it.'

'I mean she *wants* you. Wants David Collins.'

'You're crazy. She's got dozens of men friends.'

'Do you sleep with her?'

'No. Of course I don't.'

'No, of course, my foot. She's very attractive.'

'Well I haven't, and I don't, so let's change the subject.'

'I saw Harry Parsons today. He asked after you. I told him that you were well on the way to your first million.'

Collins smiled. 'What were you doing at the agency?'

'Trevor Amis wanted to introduce me to a client and I saw Parsons in reception.' She laughed. 'There are half a dozen framed awards on the wall facing you. I looked at them. They're all yours and there's nothing after you left.'

'Did you get the job?'

'I don't know. He was a little creep from some food company. A brand manager I think he said. I think he had ideas well above his station about models. I gave him the ice treatment and I think he got the message. But Trevor thought I'd get it despite all.'

'I saw in the evening paper that your old man is about to become Lord Mayor.'

318

'Yes. Mummy's furious.'

'Why? I should have thought she'd love it. A knighthood into the bargain.'

'He could have got that anyway. But now she's got all those ghastly Livery men and their wives. And it costs a packet. Twenty thousand quid. You can buy a hell of a lot of clothes for that.'

'I saw your friend Piers today.'

'What had he got to say?'

'We didn't speak. I was in the Army and Navy. We just passed by one another. He looked as if he'd like to spit in my eye.'

She laughed. 'I gave him the push a few weeks back. Some busybody told him it was because of you.'

'And was it?'

She shrugged. 'Kind of. Let's say you were the catalyst.'

'I've always wanted to be a catalyst, honey.'

'Don't call me honey. It's vulgar even in America. It's meaningless, like, "Have a nice day, now."'

'What shall I call you?'

'Same as you always do. Just Penny will do.'

He had taken Jimmy to see the matinée of the Festival Ballet. They had tea in the Festival Hall cafeteria and then he'd driven the boy home. Penny was spending the weekend with her parents in East Anglia and he was to spend the evening with Trevor and Connie.

They were playing Rummy afterwards and as Trevor grinned and laid down his cards he said, 'By the way, your girl was at the agency yesterday. Closeted for over an hour with Parsons. What's going on?'

'Maybe he was talking about some modelling job.'

'Not that girl, dope. Carmen. Carmen Friedman.'

'Really? I'm surprised. Perhaps he's decided that the agency will use us after all.'

'They've been using her company for months. Not chicken feed, either.'

'It wouldn't come my way. I only work for my own clients.'

'I'd watch our Harry if I were you.'

'Why?'

'OK. Out. A rummy.' As he displayed his cards he said, 'Why? Well, I always go on the basis that if Harry Parsons says something or does something there are always two reasons. One is the obvious one, whatever that might be, and the other is something entirely different. Some little move on his private chessboard. Some little move that will turn up in a couple of months' time. He's changed a lot since you left.'

'In what way?'

'When you were there the agency bounced along very nicely. Successful. Staff reasonably contented. Top class work keeping clients happy or as near happy as clients can ever be. He could give all his time to being Machiavelli and he didn't have to do it too openly. Once you left he'd got the lot on his back. He tried various substitutes for you but none of them worked. Either he picked yes-men or if he chose talent he managed to grind it down to being a hack. He doesn't understand people. You do.'

'For God's sake, Trevor. My record in understanding people is abysmal.'

'That's where you're so wrong, old pal. Your record with people close to you ain't so hot but where you aren't directly responsible for their lives you've got a magic touch. I know. I was on the receiving end. A nod of approval from you could make my day. And you had an instinct for knowing when to nod and when not to.'

'So back to Harry Parsons.'

'Harry Parsons hates your guts. Make no mistake about that.'

'But why? I've never done him dirt.'

'People like Parsons can take being done dirt in their stride. What they can't take is being done good. Harry Parsons is a shrewd operator but it was you who made that agency grow. Those inside the agency knew that but it

320

didn't matter one way or another. But outside the agency Harry Parsons was the front man. It was his agency and his success. And suddenly you're not there any more and it really is his agency. It makes money, it's reasonably efficient, but it ain't got that sparkle any more. We do humdrum advertising for humdrum clients. There ain't no fun any more. So Harry Parsons doesn't love you, my friend, and you'd be wise to remember that.'

'There's nothing he could do to me, Trevor. I'll just go on taking photographs and doing a few commercials and I could live very happily on a tenth of what I'm earning now.'

'You may be right. All I'm saying is watch it, mate . . . your deal.' He turned to look at his wife. 'How about another beer, love?'

Collins stood looking at the 20 x 16 print. The girl was pretty, the jacket and skirt were well designed and well made. It was a grainy print, deliberately grainy. The girl was walking past a bus queue, pert nose in the air and all the male heads were turned to look at her. It was good of its kind but uninspired. Good photography, weak basic thinking. And it had been done before many times.

He turned to the man standing beside him. 'Have you got a pencil, Roger? A soft one? 4B would do.'

When the pencil was produced he turned over the print. He drew three faint vertical lines from top to bottom of the paper and drew the outline of a girl on the left hand vertical. She was looking back over her shoulder at her reflection in a mirror, her legs apart, straining the soft material of the skirt tightly across her shapely hips. On the edge of a bed the manufacturer's bag lay with its logo showing clearly. Then he turned to the young man.

'Have a think around this, Roger. A model not quite so young as the one you had. They sell to women from twenty-seven to thirty-five so let her be a twenty-five-year-old. Not that lovely blonde hair. Nice hair but in-between.

Good legs. Average bust. She could be just a tiny bit out of focus even. But the carrying bag and the logo crisp and clear.' He threw down the pencil and stood hands in jacket pockets. 'You know, it's a mistake to assume that women buy clothes so that they can be stared at by men. If anything, I reckon they buy to impress other women. But most of all they buy to impress themselves.

'Women will recognise that moment of truth when they go up to their bedroom to try on what they've just bought. What you've got to get over is that she's still happy with what she's bought. Have her nearly smiling. Not actually smiling. Just a second before it happens.' He grinned. 'Anyway, you guys seem to be doing very well without listening to old codgers like me.'

The young man said, 'We've got to present the print tomorrow morning, Mr Collins.'

'Great. That means you've got all night. Have a word with Miss Friedman, she'll know whether it's worth the extra effort.'

Collins was amused at the look of disbelief on the young man's face.

Chapter 39

A BIRMINGHAM advertising agency and the *Birmingham Mail* had jointly put on a small exhibition of his work in the newspaper's foyer and there was a small luncheon afterwards. He had taken Penny with him. In the morning he took her to see the outside of the foundry where he had started work, the house where he was brought up and the school in Slade Road. After lunch he drove her out to Sutton Park.

As they sat in the car looking down towards one of the small lakes he smiled and said, 'It's hard to believe that coming to this park used to be both an adventure and a treat. The Sunday School used to bring us here in the summer and that was a red-letter day to be looked forward to for months. It was Sutton Park, the Botanical Gardens or the Lickey Hills. The Lickey Hills was like foreign parts.'

'Did you like it when you were a child?'

'No. I hated it. I was hopeless at school. Just generally thick.'

'I can't believe you were ever thick.'

'I was. I'm not being modest. I blush to think about how dopey I was.'

'In what way?'

'Every way there is. I can't describe it. I lived in a dream world.'

'What were your parents like?'

'I don't know about my father. He died when I was a baby. My mother died a few years ago.'

'She must have been very proud of you.'

'For what?'

'For how you'd got on from such an unpromising start.'

Collins sat silent for a moment and then said, 'It's time we were heading back to London while there's still some light left.'

'Is there anyone you want to call on, old friends and so on?'

'I don't think so. Is your door closed properly?'

'Yes.'

They were having dinner with her parents that evening in the house in Eaton Square and he'd dropped her there before heading south to Pimlico and his own place to change. He had met them once at the Festival Hall during an interval. He wasn't looking forward to the dinner.

Penny's father was a heavily-built man with a smooth waxy skin. A small military moustache disguised his soft full mouth; his pale blue eyes were alert and lively. He gave the appearance of being the bluff and jolly businessman, but Collins soon realised that there was more to the man than that. His seemingly casual and disconnected comments and questions at dinner had been a skilful verbal reconnaissance of his daughter's guest.

There were only the two of them when they retired to his study, where port and glasses were already on a silver salver.

When the drinks had been poured Goodhew leaned back in the soft leather armchair and looked across at Collins.

'Your very good health, my boy.'

'Thank you, sir. And yours.'

'Penny tells me you've got a very flourishing business that you started from scratch. I must say I've always admired a man who could do that. A good business brain . . . worth a lot.'

Collins smiled. 'I'm afraid the business brain isn't mine.

I've got a girl . . . woman . . . who started as my business manager and is now our financial director. Left to my own devices I'd have probably ended up taking wedding photographs.'

'Well at least you can recognise talent in others. Not many can do that. And some who can't stomach it when it works.' He crossed his legs comfortably. 'What would you say are the qualities that make a good photographer?'

'It depends on the kind of photography. In the majority of cases all you need is technical ability.'

'And in your case?'

'An interesting question. I've never really thought about it.'

'Makes your answer all the more intriguing. Penny says your photography is very special.'

'It's probably individual rather than special.'

'Emotional? Wearing the heart on the sleeve?'

Collins looked surprised. 'How very perceptive. It's never struck me that that's what it is. But you're right. A kind of loving.'

Goodhew smiled. 'A lucky man to be doing what you so obviously care about. Most of us haven't got the guts . . . you used to be a senior director of an agency, I gather?'

'Yes. But that was some years ago.'

'But you've had some business experience.'

'Yes. I was entirely in business at one time. I worked for a group of iron foundries. I was sales director when I left. In fact I was in business longer than I've been in creative work.'

'But you didn't like it?'

'I wouldn't say that. I just got on with it. I only changed because of other people offering me a different career.' He smiled. 'Luck, I'm afraid. Not good judgment.'

'The woman . . . the financial director. She a shareholder?'

'Not in my own business. She has her own set-up as well

325

that benefits from my name. It does the work that doesn't interest me personally.'

'No chance of her walking off with the business?'

'She could walk off with her company any day she wanted to. And my personal income would go down on my own business. But I'd still get by.'

'Maybe you should get her on some sort of contract.'

'I don't think that's really necessary.'

'You trust her?'

'No. I avoid having to trust people. It's too . . . involving. She's got nothing to gain by walking out, and a lot to lose.'

'Remember . . . a woman scorned and all that.'

Collins laughed. 'I'm not likely to scorn her. I'm grateful for what she's done.'

'Of course, of course. We'd better join the ladies . . . another glass before we go?'

'Thank you, no.'

He saw a light on in the studio as he locked the car doors. He didn't remember leaving a light on. As he unlocked the small side door he looked up to the shadowy roof trusses where the solitary lamp shed a weak light over a corner of the studio. It was a light they seldom used. Then he saw her, sitting on one of the big aluminium boxes that housed their mobile flash units. He looked at his watch. It was almost one o'clock.

Her face looked white and strained as he walked towards her.

'What's wrong, Carmen? What's the matter?'

'I wanted to talk to you, David.'

'Go on into my place. Switch the light on.'

He followed her inside and pointed to a chair as he took off his anorak and walked over to the drinks cabinet.

'D'you want a whisky, Carmen?'

'Have you got a brandy?'

For a moment he turned and looked at her then turned

back and poured a brandy for her and a whisky for himself. As he handed her the glass he sat down facing her.

'What is it? What's gone wrong?'

She sighed, looked at his face then looked away as she said, 'Is it true about you and Penny Goodhew?'

'Is what true?'

'That you're going to marry her?'

'Who told you that?'

She shrugged. 'The word gets around. I heard it at a party tonight.'

'So why not tell whoever it was to mind their own business?'

'I need to know, David.'

'At one o'clock in the morning, for God's sake?'

'Yes.'

'Well, whoever I marry, whenever I do, it won't affect our relationship, if that's what's worrying you.'

'You don't understand, do you?'

'Doesn't seem like it.'

'I love you, David. I always have. That's why I did all this.'

He saw the tears in her eyes and realised that she was speaking the truth. For long moments he just looked at her, stunned, trying to collect his thoughts.

'Why on earth didn't you ever say anything about this before?'

'How could I, David? I thought maybe if I worked very hard and was successful that you would . . .' she shrugged, '. . . maybe notice me more. Come to like me, even.'

'I'm terribly sorry, Carmen. And I do like you. Always have done. I saw you as being a first-class business manager and then was delighted to find that I was right. The whole set-up owes so much to you. I don't know what to say to . . . to ease things for you. Would you rather leave or make some other arrangement?'

'Are you going to marry Penny Goodhew?'

'I don't know. We haven't talked about marriage. I'm

327

very fond of her. And I really shouldn't be discussing this with anyone.'

'Do you want me to leave now I've told you this?'

'Of course not. You belong here just as much as I do.'

She smiled. A tight sad smile. 'You're not interested in me as a woman, are you? I'm just an ambitious business-woman, yes?'

'Carmen, I asked you to come and work for me because I thought you were wasted at the magazine. You liked my work and you could make this place into an efficient studio. If I'd thought of you in any other way than that I'd never have asked you to work for me. It would have been stupid to mix business and emotion. You seemed to have a life of your own. You seemed happy and successful in what you were doing here and that was how I saw it.

'I admire you in many ways but for me the girls who work for me are untouchables. Out of bounds.'

'You won't be embarrassed having me around?'

'Of course not. How about you?'

'I want to stay if you'll let me.'

'It's not a case of just letting you. I want you to stay.'

He stood up and held out his hand to pull her to her feet.

'Let me run you home.'

He dropped her outside the entrance of the flat at Dolphin Square. She didn't look back as she walked inside and Collins was sorry for her and shocked by the declar-ation. He had genuinely never had eyes for her as a lover. She was attractive but he'd learned that grim lesson too harshly, about loving somebody who worked for him, to tread that path again.

He spent ten days in Cannes for the Film Festival. Although the Festival was not concerned with commercials it gave him a chance to see other people's work and meet people in the business. The weather had been bad and the films had been worse.

He had met a lot of agency creative people he knew. People from the old days and people who commissioned him now. At fifty-one he was treated with an amused respect by most of them. Amused at what they saw as his old-fashioned schmaltzy approach, and respect because he had been proved right so many times.

It wasn't until the fourth day that he saw Harry Parsons. Collins had been sitting with an American scriptwriter, drinking coffee at a terrace restaurant, when Harry Parsons came to the table. He was tanned and smiling, his hand held out.

'I heard you were here, David. Nice to see you. And Joe Grabowski isn't it? I saw your entry in Atlanta in the public service section. Should have taken an award.'

Without waiting for an invitation Parsons pulled out a chair and sat down, waving to a waiter as he said, 'Let me buy you both a drink. What'll you have?'

The American smiled. 'A Bloody Mary.'

Collins said quietly, 'A glass of red wine, thank you, Harry.'

They chatted about mutual acquaintances in London and New York and then the American took the hint and left.

'And how are you, David? You're looking remarkably well.'

'I'm fine, Harry. How about you?'

Parsons shrugged. 'So-so. The agency world's getting a bit boring these days.' He grinned. 'Not like those adventurous times when you and I first set up together.'

'I can't imagine you being bored, Harry.'

Parsons sighed. 'You'd be surprised. We're doing all right, of course. But I miss those days.'

'What do you miss?'

'Hard to pin it down. The excitement, I suppose. The battle to get new accounts. Nowadays when I pitch for an account and get it I come back in the taxi thinking, "Christ, now we've got to service the bloody outfit."' He smiled. 'In the old days I could leave all the washing up to you.'

329

'It probably wouldn't work these days. Advertising's for juveniles now.'

'You don't miss it yourself?'

'Some of it, I suppose. But not so that it matters.'

Parsons said softly, 'You wouldn't fancy coming back in, would you? Equal status with me. Name your own price.'

Collins looked at Parsons' face. 'Are you serious?'

'Never been more serious in my life, David.'

'Why, Harry? Why?'

'We could make a bomb together, David. We were a great team and because we've both got a lot more experience than we had before we could be unbeatable now.'

'Tell me something, Harry. When I had that breakdown you came to see me. The agency picked up the tab for the treatment. And then you never came near me again. When I sent in my letter of resignation you gave it to Hargreaves to deal with. Like I'd got some infectious disease. Why? I never understood.'

'I ran out of steam, David. I thought we'd all go down the pan if you came back to the agency. I didn't know how to handle it.'

'You seemed pretty decisive from my end of the telescope.'

'You still hold that against me?'

'Let's say it didn't help me at the time. You must have known the state I ended up in.'

Parsons shrugged. 'I'm sorry. I really am.'

'It wouldn't work. Second time around isn't ever the same. Despite what Sinatra says.'

'There must be something you want, David? Something that would really please you. Whatever it is it's yours. I promise.'

Collins laughed. 'I earn more than any agency could pay me already. I enjoy my work. I have a handful of friends. What more could I want?'

'You'd keep on with your studio. We could make you a

world name. Do a thorough PR job on you. Make you like Avedon or Parkinson. A household name.'

Collins smiled. 'You're really serious, aren't you, Harry?'

'By God I'm serious. And don't think we couldn't do it, David. I'd hire the best PR people in London, New York and Europe.' He leaned forward. 'Look. Take your time. There's no hurry. Think about it and we can talk again.' He stood up. 'Let me leave you in peace. Take care of yourself.'

'OK, Harry. You too.'

Despite what he had said, it wasn't easy after that evening, working with Carmen Friedman. He was aware of her in a different way now. She sensibly kept away from him most of the time but he was sometimes conscious of those brown eyes looking at him with affection as he turned from the camera or his drawing board.

He hadn't told Penny about the incident, nor his encounter with Parsons. He was tempted to tell Trevor Amis about both episodes but decided to wait. He gave no thought to Parsons' proposition. It had no appeal for him and even if it had he would never have gone along with it. Parsons was a businessman and he'd had enough of businessmen. He left it for two months and then composed a friendly but firm letter thanking Parsons for the offer but declining it.

It was almost exactly a year since he had met Harry Parsons at Cannes when the intercom buzzed and he lifted it as he waited for the model to sign the release form.

'Hello?'

'It's Carmen, David. Could you spare me a minute?'

'Where are you?'

'In my office.'

'OK. I'll be in in a few minutes.'

331

He walked with the girl to the studio entrance and checked that her taxi had arrived before he walked across the studio to Carmen Friedman's office.

He was surprised to see Harry Parsons sitting there with her, his briefcase open on the table. As he looked at Carmen she avoided his eyes.

'You two know one another, don't you?' she said.

Collins nodded. 'I didn't know you were here, Harry. Are you being looking after?'

Parsons smiled. 'Do sit down, David. We've got things to discuss.'

Collins just stood there. 'I don't interfere on Carmen's side, Harry. Whatever she says goes, so far as I'm concerned.'

'You'd better sit, old boy. Like I said, we've got things to discuss. Important things for all of us.'

As Collins pulled out a chair and sat down it was his first realisation that something was wrong. He looked again at the girl but she was ostentatiously fiddling with a couple of buff-coloured files.

'Carmen and I have been talking off and on for quite a long time about cooperating for our mutual benefit. In the last two months we've had several meetings to iron out the details. I know that you have no stake, no holding in Friedman Enterprises, but we both thought we should let you know what we have arranged.

'Today, the agency bought a sixty per cent holding in Friedman Enterprises and that creates some problems so far as Carmen's relationship with your studio is concerned.

'I feel that she should devote all her time to the company's business but she has this . . .' he smiled, '. . . gentleman's agreement let's call it, with your good self. She feels that we should know your views on that particular aspect. So tell us what you think.'

Collins looked at the girl. 'How much did he pay you, Carmen?'

Parsons interjected. 'David. I must point out that I have a controlling interest in this company now. I shouldn't want the company's business discussed with an outsider. Not even such a close associate as yourself.'

Collins looked at Parsons. 'I'll discuss it with Carmen, Harry. I'll let you know what I've decided.'

'I'm sure that you know I shall lean over backwards to give my approval to whatever you suggest. However, you'll understand that I have to consider the interests of the company and the agency first.' He stood up, closing his briefcase as he spoke. 'And I feel I have to point out that Carmen has signed a five-year agreement covering her services to the company.'

Parsons nodded to the girl and brushed past Collins to the door. 'Best of luck, David,' he said as he closed the door behind him.

As Collins sat there all the warnings about Parsons from Trevor Amis went through his mind. And old man Goodhew's comment about 'a woman scorned'. He looked at Carmen Friedman.

'Why did you do it?'

She shrugged. 'I felt I needed a new start. New fields. New faces.'

'And to put me down?'

'It didn't start in a way that would put you down. It just sort of escalated that way. And he made my position with you seem pretty fragile. No written agreement. No contract. You could have sent me packing at a moment's notice.'

'But you own Friedman Enterprises, lock, stock and barrel.'

'Without your name it wouldn't last long.'

'But it won't have my name now.'

'Parsons guaranteed all the agency's work and that will even things out.'

'And he's told you that you can't act as business manager for my own studio?'

'He made it pretty clear that he didn't want me to.'

'And what are you going to do?'

'Just carry on, I guess.'

333

'You're going to learn what real business is like, my dear. You'll be working for Harry Parsons now, not me. It's going to be very different from now on.'

'What will you do, David? How will you manage?'

He looked at her bleakly. 'I suppose I could sue you for breach of contract.'

'But we don't have a contract, David.'

'We do, my dear. Despite what Parsons told you. We have a verbal contract and that wouldn't be difficult to establish. A verbal contract is just as binding as a written one. Harder to establish, but the company's files would provide proof enough.'

'Parsons said that there was no contract, just a loose working arrangement. Why would you do that to me, anyway?'

'Just for the pleasure of exposing Harry Parsons in open court. Did he tell you that a year ago he'd offered me anything I wanted to go back as joint head of his agency?'

'No. You mean he's doing this because you turned him down?'

'That and other reasons. Did you tell him about your feelings for me?'

'Only about three months ago.'

'And he said you needed new faces and new fields to conquer and all that crap.'

'You make me feel I've been terribly stupid.'

Collins stood up. 'You have, my dear. You really have.' He nodded as he stood at the door. 'Goodnight. By the way, tell Parsons that I want you and your people out of these premises by tomorrow night. The lease of the whole premises is in my name and my studio's name. And like Parsons said . . . "Best of luck."'

Chapter 40

WHEN COLLINS walked out of Carmen Friedman's office his anger did not last long. He could manage without her. There were plenty of other people who would make efficient business managers. Especially now that his reputation was long established. And if necessary he could get by quite comfortably without a business manager.

Two hours later a small van parked outside and he stood watching as two men carried out the desk, chairs and filing cabinets from Carmen's office. They brought a small hand trolley for the box files and several small packages. And suddenly his confidence waned. Suddenly he felt sad. Not for himself but for Carmen Friedman, who had temporarily let her own disappointment about her relationship with him cloud her business sense. She was a fool, but she was at least a loving fool. She would already know that she was making a great mistake. She had already lost her independence and now she was leaving the company and surroundings that she had helped to build.

He saw the light go off in her office and as she came out she saw him standing there. She walked towards the door, hesitated, then stopped for a moment before turning back and walking towards him.

He saw the tearstains on her face as she stopped in front of him.

She sighed deeply. 'You must hate me, David. I'm terribly, terribly sorry.'

'I don't hate you, Carmen.'

'I've left your account books and your work schedules in my office. They're all up to date.'

'Thanks. I appreciate that.'

She looked up at his face, her voice quavering, her lips trembling as she said softly, 'Say something to me, David. Anything. Say something gentle.'

For a moment he hesitated, then he said quietly, 'Carmen Friedman. I thank you sincerely for all the good work you have done here. For all your kindness to me and your companionship. It doesn't diminish because of what has happened today.'

'Do you hate me?'

'No. I'm just sad. Sad for us both. I loathe the man who planned it all so carefully . . . we're both his victims in some way. But maybe we'll both survive him. I hope so.' He leaned forward and kissed the top of her head and she turned away, crying, as she walked to the door.

When she had gone he walked back into his room, poured himself a whisky and switched on the hi-fi. It was on radio, and as he walked over to the big leather armchair he realised that they were playing 'September Song'. His mind unconsciously absorbed the words – 'and the days grow short when you reach September . . .' And the words seemed to have a significance for him. He seldom thought about his age. He even had difficulty sometimes, remembering exactly how old he was. But what did it matter? He had a business that could support him for the rest of his days. Which was a lot more than most men had at any age. He knew he was lucky to be in that position. But the day's unhappy events suddenly seemed part of the pattern of his whole life. Things went along smoothly for several years and then, out of the blue, somebody did something that made it change. His ex-wife, Parsons, Carmen Friedman, the foundry people, the first move to an advertising agency. All the changes in his life were initiated by other people. But was it he who made them do it? Did he bring about his own crises? And if so – how?

He walked out into the studio, his drink still in his hand,

and he stood there looking at it in the dim light of the single fluorescent tube above the white roll of background paper. The tripods, the aluminium cases of cameras, lenses and meters, the big studio flash-lights on their stands, screens, reflectors, gold, silver and white umbrellas for the smaller flash units. And cables everywhere, plugged into control boxes, multi-socket trailing blocks and heavy-duty wall-sockets. And what had been a kind of home was now just a ramshackle building in a London slum.

In that moment he knew he didn't want it any more. It was going to be a burden, an albatross around his neck. Account books, negotiations, bills, incoming cheques, banks and taxmen. Whatever he wanted it wasn't that.

As he walked back into his room he looked at his watch. It was only ten o'clock but he was tired out. As if his half-formed decision had settled an issue, his mind was calm and he was ready for sleep.

He switched off the radio, undressed, and was asleep ten minutes later.

The phone was ringing insistently when he came back from the coffee stall at eight o'clock the next morning.

'Collins.'

'Is that David Collins?'

'Speaking.'

'My name's Alastair Forsyth, Mr Collins. I'm with the *Birmingham Mail*. We met eighteen months ago when you had an exhibition of your photographs in our building.'

'I remember you, Mr Forsyth. What can I do for you?'

'We'd like to discuss commissioning a book from you, Mr Collins. A book about Birmingham.'

'I'm afraid I'm not a writer, Mr Forsyth.'

'It's a book of photographs that we have in mind.'

'Sounds interesting.'

'When could we talk about it? I'm quite prepared to come up to London if that would help.'

'When would you like to come?'

'What about today? We'd like to publish the book in about six months' time.'

Collins hesitated then he said, 'OK. I'll be here all day. Come over as soon as you get to town.'

'Does that mean you *are* interested?'

'Yes. Definitely.'

'I'll look forward to seeing you again.'

'Fine. I'll be here.'

As he hung up he half-knew what he was going to do. The phone call fitted so neatly into his thoughts of the previous evening. It was a sign, a talisman that his thinking was right.

He made a dozen phone calls. Calls to his bank, his accountant, to two friendly rivals with good studios, to an estate agent, and he sent Laura to the bank with a note.

Alastair Forsyth arrived at midday and Laura got them sandwiches and coffee. At the end of an hour's discussion they had roughed out the heads of agreement of the contract and Forsyth had checked it with his office in Birmingham. The details were all acceptable to them and the assignment was firm. Forsyth was delighted that he had been able to commission a well-known photographer and as they waited for the taxi to arrive Forsyth said, 'I believe you've spent some time in Birmingham, Mr Collins.'

Collins laughed. 'I was brought up in Birmingham. I left when I was a teenager.'

'So you'll see it all with some affection.'

Collins smiled. 'Yes . . . but there was a time when I wouldn't have believed I'd ever say that.'

'Why?'

'Oh, things. I'll tell you when I've finished the book. Here's your taxi. He knows you're going to Euston.'

They shook hands and Collins stood watching until the taxi headed for the Embankment.

He walked back to his own rooms and buzzed the darkroom to ask Laura to come in.

She looked pale and worried as she sat down facing him.

338

'Did you hear that Carmen Friedman has sold the control of her company to an advertising agency?'

'She phoned me last night and said that she had left . . . she seemed very upset.'

'I think she was . . . but let's talk about you. I don't want to carry on this place on my own so I've decided to close it down . . . but I've taken the liberty of talking to two friends of mine, Tom Stopwood and Louis Machin. They both run very successful studios. I said that you might be available and they're both willing to take you on right away. See them both and choose the one you like.

'Next thing is money. I've made out a cheque for three months' salary.' He reached over to the table and took the cheque and handed it to her. 'Apart from that there's another cheque in this envelope. It's for five thousand pounds. We'll call it severance money so that you don't have to pay tax on it.

'And I want to thank you for all your hard work and loyalty while you've been with me. I really appreciate it.'

'Why are you doing this, David? What are you going to do yourself?'

'It probably sounds crazy, but I honestly don't know. All I know is that I don't want to run a business. I just want to take photographs.' He smiled. 'I'll get by . . . I've got enough money to just free-wheel for a bit. See the world and all that.'

'What will you do about the studio?'

'Tom Stopwood is going to take it over. I'll just take my own gear and leave the rest.'

She stood up. 'Thanks for the cheque . . . you've been very generous . . . I've liked working here. I'll miss this place . . . and you.'

'That's a nice thing to say. Thank you.'

'Can I take one of your prints for my room?'

He smiled. 'Take anything you want.'

*　　*　　*

339

He felt no regrets about leaving as he packed his gear that night. He no longer had any affection for the place. It was just a converted warehouse again and nothing to do with him. There were lessons to be learned from what had happened. He wasn't sure what they were but he would know in due course.

The next morning he loaded the three leather cases into the MGB, and left the studio key in an envelope at the coffee-shop as arranged with Tom Stopwood. He had already sent a note and a bracelet by hand to Penny Goodhew. He didn't look back as he started the car and moved out into the early morning traffic on the Embankment.

It called itself a hotel but it was, in fact, a boarding-house, even by Birmingham standards. There was only one room available with a telephone and he booked it for a month. It had once been the home of a local brewing magnate who had moved to the superior environment of Sutton Coldfield after he had received his knighthood. Solid and Victorian, the house had its virtues. High ceilings and a conservatory that was a masterpiece of ironwork and glass, still cared for, with its staging filled with clay pots of geraniums, calceolarias, cinerarias and a number of exotic lilies. The elderly widow who ran it was amiable and obliging and it was obvious that most of the patrons were regulars. Salesmen, service engineers and a few theatricals from the pantomimes in the town.

He phoned Alastair Forsyth at the *Birmingham Mail* who told him that a junior journalist had already been assigned to the project. It was a girl and it was suggested that he should meet her at the newspaper offices the following morning when she would be off-duty.

The evening meal was in the large living room on the ground floor next to the conservatory and Collins was treated with politeness at first and then friendliness when they discovered that he was a photographer. They were

340

the usual mixture that could be expected from a dozen or so men whose livelihood came from selling goods and services. Most of them obviously knew one another well, enquiring after families and ailments, O-levels and jobs, and it reminded Collins of a sergeants' mess from his army days. Quiet men, loud, jolly men, listeners and chatterers and the usual man who kept them up to date on the latest jokes. He went early to his room and was in bed, reading, by ten o'clock, with a pile of paperbacks on the small table at the side of his bed. He had chosen them to match his present mood. Standard reading that looked back rather than forward. The two he looked at that night were Palgrave's *Golden Treasury* and Arnold Bennett's *Diaries*.

He met Alastair Forsyth in a small interview room at the newspaper offices. He was a sharp, energetic Scot who had worked on provincial papers for years. He pushed his glasses up his long nose as he looked at Collins.

'I'd better tell you that originally I didn't hold out much hope for this project. If it hadn't been for your name I can't imagine that the management would have agreed to it.'

Collins smiled. 'We'll change their minds, Alastair. Meantime I'd like to get started if that's OK with you.'

'Well there's no problem there.' He smiled. 'She's a bright wee girl, the one they've assigned to you. Not much experience as yet, but she's competent. Would you like me to wheel her in? I'll have to leave you to it, we've got a by-election tomorrow and I've got to do a last-minute round-up of the candidates and all that.'

'That's fine. What's her name?'

'Patsy. Patsy Thatcher. She's twenty or thereabouts. A bit scared of the project so you'll have to break her in gently. I'll go get her now.'

A few minutes later Forsyth came back with the girl, introduced them and hurried off. She was tall and blonde and pretty and she stood just inside the door, her notebook in her hand.

'Why don't we go out for a coffee, Patsy? They probably need this room for other meetings.'

'Whatever you say, Mr Collins.'

'Let's go to the new hotel. What is it now? The Albany?'

She nodded. 'Whatever you want. I'll get my coat and meet you down in reception.'

It was only a short walk to the hotel and they talked about the newspaper's new building and he told her about the old days when you could stand on the pavement and, through the big windows, watch the presses printing the paper.

When the coffee had been poured he said, 'Whereabouts do you live in Birmingham?'

She blushed. 'In Alma Street off Slade Road in Erdington.'

He stared at her. 'What number?'

'Twenty-three.'

'I was brought up in Alma Street. Isn't that strange. It used to be . . . let me see . . . the Macleans lived at twenty-three.'

'They moved to Coventry just after the war.'

'Well now. That's a nice start to a project. Both from the same street.'

'Alastair Forsyth said you wanted to get started straightaway. Did he explain about my work arrangements?'

'No.'

'I've got to be in the office my normal hours and that means that I'll only be able to work on the project after five in the evening. Except weekends. I get Saturdays and Sundays off. I can do some research for you in office hours if I have spare time.' She laughed. 'But they keep me pretty busy most days. They're not slave-drivers or anything but they like to keep us all fully occupied.'

'So you'll virtually be working in your own time?'

'Yes. But that's OK. I volunteered. I wanted to do it.'

'Why?'

'A lot of reasons. Nobody's ever done a real book about Birmingham. Not like it really is. The people, and the skills, and the way they live. They deserve to be cared about. The sort of thing that *Picture Post* used to do.'

He smiled. 'Yes. You're absolutely right. That's a real inspiration. You shame me in the first hour.'

She smiled. 'In what way?'

'Because I was presumptuous. All I thought of was my pictures. And captions by my tame writer.'

'I'll do captions if that's what you want, but it'll only be a run-of-the-mill book if we tackle it that way.'

'We won't, I assure you.' He looked at her, smiling. 'You don't know how much you've cheered me up.'

'I'm glad.'

'Can I call you Patsy? I'm David.'

'Yes, I'm Patsy, but it wouldn't be right for me to call you by your Christian name.'

'God. I'm getting on but I'm not that old.'

She smiled. 'It's nothing to do with age. Just seniority. You're the leader of this project. I'm just . . . whatever . . . the "gofer".'

He smiled. 'OK. We'll see. When would you be ready to start?'

'I finish at five. I could meet you somewhere at five past.'

'What about here?'

She shook her head. 'This isn't Birmingham. This is for visitors. How about the cafeteria at New Street Station at ten past five?'

'Fine. Whoever gets there first orders two coffees.'

She laughed. 'OK.'

'Is the central library still where it was?'

'It's at Paradise Circus.'

'I'll do a bit of basic research to get us started.'

She was waiting for him, the coffee already on the table.

As he sat down he laughed. 'It's only five o'clock now, I was sure I was going to get here before you.'

'I escaped a bit early. Sugar?'

'Thanks. Three spoons please.'

'My, that's a sweet tooth. How did the research go?'

'I did very little. I couldn't stop thinking of how we could make this book something really special.'

'Have you got any ideas about where we start?'

'Just one. What about you?'

'I think we should start in an iron foundry.'

'What makes you say that?'

She laughed. 'I'm only teasing. Remember my name?'

'Patsy, Patricia. I don't get it.'

'My surname. Thatcher.'

'I still don't get it.'

'Think back. A long way back. Before I was born and you were just starting work.'

'Go on.'

'Sam Thatcher. He's my grandfather.' He smiled. 'He told me all about you.'

'My God. I don't believe it. Yes, I remember he had a son. He worked in the foundry at Witton. The GEC. He was just a few years older than me.'

She was still laughing. 'There's more to come.'

'Tell me.'

'My mother's name is Joan. Does that ring any bells?'

'Joan. No. Joan.' Then he looked up quickly. 'Not Joan Latham?'

'That's the one.'

'Why didn't you tell me this before?'

She smiled. 'I wanted a chance to look you over when you didn't know. To see if I agreed with what they had to say about you.'

'And what did they say?'

She grinned. 'Mr Collins. I'm a journalist. I couldn't reveal off-the-record conversations.'

'Sounds like it must have been pretty bad.'

'No. Not exactly. They were both wrong on some things. Different things. But right on others.'

'Tell me more.'

She shook her head. 'Not now. Some day, maybe. We'll see.'

'You sound terribly grown up. As if you were talking to a child.'

She smiled. 'Let's go back to our project. We don't have to start our work where the book starts. We can wait to see what we've got before we plan how it goes in the book.'

'So why don't we start in an iron foundry, as you suggested? The one I worked at with your grandfather.'

'OK. Tomorrow you go there and pick half a dozen people. People doing basic jobs. Foremen as well as moulders and the others. Get their addresses so I can interview them and you arrange to photograph them. And tell them I'll be contacting them to interview them.'

'Say they don't agree?'

'They'll agree. Nobody ever refuses to be interviewed or photographed by the *Mail*. Clear it with top management first and then there'll be no problem. OK?'

'OK. Can I give you a lift somewhere? Or what about a meal?'

'Mum will be expecting me. Thursday night is bangers-and-mash night. And I've got some ironing to do.'

'Same place, here, same time tomorrow?'

'Fine,' she said, standing up. 'And don't forget . . . I want lots of good leads.'

There had been no problems. Patsy was right: the fact that it was for the *Birmingham Mail* was enough. There had been very few changes to the buildings. The two foundries, the fettling-shop, the pattern-shop and the machine-shop looked much the same. But the new managing director was in his mid-thirties. With a degree in business management, not in metallurgy.

He talked with dozens of people and in the end came

345

up with ten to be interviewed and photographed. He was fifteen minutes late at the cafeteria and she was sipping her second cup of coffee. There were two cups waiting for him.

'Sorry I'm late. I couldn't park the car.'

'The one with the spoon is the hot one. They'll let you use our car park. Get Alastair to fix it.'

He pushed the paper across to her. 'Names and addresses and telephone numbers where there's a telephone.'

She looked at the long list. 'Good grief, this looks like the cast for *The Forsyte Saga*. What's that word?' She pointed.

'Fettling. The fettling-shop's where they take off the bits where the moulds join and the metal seeps through. It's a sort of tidying-up process. A bit rough and ready, before machining and finishing.'

She looked at his face. 'Did it seem strange going back there again?'

'I thought it would seem strange but in fact it didn't. I didn't see anyone I remembered, but . . .' he shrugged, '. . . no, it was easy.'

'You don't think we've got too many here for just one industry?'

'I don't think so. Anyway, better for us to have to whittle down than not have enough choice.'

'How many pages will we have?'

'Roughly two hundred.'

'How many for words as opposed to pictures?'

'Half and half.'

'D'you mean that?'

'Yes. Don't you agree?'

'Yes, I agree all right. It's very generous though on your part.'

'Can I talk business for a moment?'

'Aren't we already?'

'I mean personal business. The deal I've done with the paper is that they pay my expenses and I get seventy per cent of the profits after production costs and distribution costs come off. I think you should get a percentage too. For yourself.'

She laughed. 'They'd never wear that. They'll pay me NUJ rates for the time I work with you, and my expenses, but they'll say I'm lucky to have the chance to work on it and have my name on the book.'

'Would you let me talk to them about it? Very tactfully.'

'OK. But don't lose me my job. I need it.'

'Leave it to me. What do we do now?'

'How long do you need for this photography?'

'Two, maybe three days.'

'It's Friday today. That takes us up to Wednesday night. I'll need longer than that. How about we meet this time next week? Then I'll have broken the back of my part.'

'OK. Where shall we meet?'

She smiled. 'Where else? Here, of course. The beating heart of Brum.'

He worked long hours every day but it took him until the Friday morning before he was satisfied with what he had got. The newspaper let him use their darkrooms and he processed every roll himself. It had been a long time since he had done his own developing and printing and he ended up with just over a hundred 10 x 8 prints.

It was exactly five o'clock when he arrived at the cafeteria. He saw that he was first and collected their coffees and found an empty table. By half past five she had still not arrived and he was suddenly aware that he had been looking forward to seeing her. Looking forward to her approval of the results of his hard work. Looking forward to seeing her words that could enhance the pictures. But he knew in his heart that it was more than that. He was looking forward to seeing *her*. The lively mind and the friendliness put him at ease. He didn't have to play any part with her. Not even the top photographer bit. She accepted that he was good at his work, that he was some sort of a name and that she was the junior. And that was deference or modesty, because he guessed that she would be just as caring with her words as he was with his camera.

It was just after six when she arrived, breathless and apologetic.

'I tried to phone here but they don't have a phone. It seems that even for business they use one of the public phones. Crazy. I'm sorry. Terribly sorry. I had something I had to finish.'

He smiled. 'Not to worry. All four coffees are cold. I'll get us another.' He pushed across the two envelopes. 'Have a look at those. I'll be right back.'

She looked up at him. 'Can I have a piece of fruit cake?'

'You bet. Anything else?'

'No thanks.'

When he got back to the table with the coffees and cellophane-wrapped cake she didn't look up from the photographs until he sat down.

'You know . . . they said you were very good . . . but it's more than that. These are wonderful. There are a dozen or so where you seem to have looked inside them . . . as if you know everything about them. Especially this one.'

She pushed across one of the prints. It was a young moulder. Taken not in the foundry but in his small back garden with his young wife and their daughter.

'What do you like about that one specially?'

'All of it. It says so much. The man looking straight at the camera. All four-square and rather macho. The pigeon held so carefully in his hand. His wife beaming up at him and the little girl with her eyes screwed up against the light and her hand on his belt.'

'So what does it tell you?'

'Everything. The macho, four-square look because he's a man. A man who doesn't like being photographed but is letting it happen because he's proud of his family. And the clues that he's not really all that macho. Wives don't look at their husbands like that unless they're something special. His hand holding the pigeon very gently and the little girl. That's the give-away. That hand hanging on to his belt. A very trusting little hand.'

Collins sat silently for several seconds. 'You know, you're an extraordinary girl. You really are. Lots of people have admired my photographs. All kinds of people. Men and women. But they couldn't say why they liked them. Couldn't have described what they saw as you just did. Maybe you should be a photographer.'

She shook her head. 'No. Definitely not.'

'Why not?'

'Just one reason. I don't want to be. I'm a word person.'

'You're much more than that. Much more.'

She turned the compliment aside. 'I've only written out my basic notes. I wanted to see the pictures before I plunged. I'm glad I waited.' She smiled. 'I could write a poem about that picture.'

'So be it. Keep the pictures then.' He paused. 'How long will it take you to do your pieces?'

'You've got ten people and we only need six. Can I choose the six, write the pieces and then we decide together if I've chosen the right ones?'

'Yes. How long?'

She thought for a few moments. 'How about . . . how about meeting on Sunday? Spend the whole day working out a plan. A programme. And I'll bring along what I've written.'

'Fine. Where shall we meet?'

'It's up to you.'

'Come to my place. The Fentham Hotel off Chester Road.'

She looked surprised. 'Is that where you're staying?'

'Yes. Don't tell me it's a secret den of vice or something.'

She laughed. 'No. It's OK. I just imagined you'd be staying somewhere posh in town. A four-star hotel. Anyway a hotel, not a boarding-house.'

'Mrs Parkinson would tell you that The Fentham is a hotel.'

'What time shall I come?'

'Nine. Ten. It's up to you.'

'Let's make it nine.'

'OK. Do you want a lift?'

For a moment she hesitated then she said, 'No. I'll get the bus. Thanks for the coffee and the cake and apologies for being so late.'

'Not to worry. See you on Sunday.'

Mrs Parkinson was used to theatricals and their wicked ways but she was less sure about letting a nice local girl like Patsy Thatcher go up alone to a man's bedroom, even if it was more a bedsitter than just a bedroom. But she pointed the way up the stairs and gave directions to her prize boarder's room. She liked David Collins. He was obviously well-off despite the faded blue jeans and the denim jacket, and several of her bridge friends had heard of him and seen his pictures in respectable magazines.

'I'm sure he's up, dear, but give him a knock before you barge in. You know what I mean.'

'I will, Mrs Parkinson. And Aunt Ada said to give you her regards.'

'Oh how nice. How is she? How's that back of hers?'

'Still playing her up, I'm afraid. But she's got her new pills so we've all got our fingers crossed. Ah, there's Mr Collins. Thanks, Mrs Parkinson.'

She waved to Collins who was standing at the top of the stairs.

For a few moments she stood looking around his room. Then she turned to look at him quizzically. 'Not really you, is it?'

'Who knows? Maybe it is.'

'Nonsense,' she said briskly. 'Anyway it's good enough for what we've got to do.'

She gave him a sheaf of typed paper. 'Read that. It's not quite the finished article but it's enough for now. Have you got a Sunday paper?'

'Over there, Patsy. On the bed.'

As he sat at the small table reading he was conscious of her sitting on the bed, humming softly, as she turned the pages of the paper. Then he was engrossed in what she had written. Twenty minutes later he leaned back in the chair and looked at her.

'What's the verdict, oh maestro?'

'They're great, Patsy. I'm proud of you. I wouldn't alter a word.'

'Good. I've got my list here of the rest of the areas we should cover. I thought at first we ought to do it in sections. Heavy industry, light industry, sport, commerce, art and so on but I think that's wrong. We should get it all together and then decide. It's got to hang together emotionally not historically. Like a well-turned sentence. Not even a big bang at the end. Just end so that they wish there was more.'

'Good, good. One more piece of news . . . no, two in fact. Firstly I've got them to agree that the photographs can be bled off all round. No margins. Agreed? It's more compelling. Makes the eye stay on the page.'

'That's your bit, David. I'm sure you're right.'

'Is that promotion?'

'What?'

'You called me David, not Mr Collins.'

She shrugged and smiled. 'It slipped out. Bad discipline. What was the second piece of news?'

'I talked with management . . .' he smiled, 'top, top management and they've agreed that a writer is worthy of his hire. Not very generously, I admit, but you'll get two per cent of the net earnings.'

The pleasure on her face was enough reward but she said very quietly, 'Thanks, David. That pleases me no end.'

'Let's have a celebratory lunch. We can talk as we go.'

'Where shall we go?'

'There's a nice little place called Angel Croft right by the Cathedral in Lichfield. D'you fancy that?'

'Sounds great. Thanks again for speaking up for me. You must have been very persuasive.'

351

'Oh, they weren't too difficult. I think they're beginning to feel the book might actually make them some money.'

'Do you think it will? Really.'

'I'm sure it will now I've seen your pieces. Are you ready?'

'Yes. Let's go.'

Chapter 41

THEY MET only twice in the next three weeks but by then the bulk of the work was done and they knew it was going to be good.

He had driven them out that Saturday to Sutton Park to interview one of the keepers and a boatman. Just before midday they had seen a Sunday school party with several teachers and helpers. They had spent two hours with them, talking, making notes and taking photographs. It was one of those shots that was to make the front cover of the book.

As they drove back to Erdington they knew that the time had come for the toughest part of their work. Discarding both words and pictures that had meant so much hard work.

'Would you like a drink of wine at my place before we call it a day?'

'I'm no good at wine, it makes me dopey. Just one glass is enough to send me off.'

'OK. Coffee? Tea? Coke?'

'You have wine and I'll have tea.'

She sat on the edge of the bed, her notes scattered over the eiderdown.

'By the way. I've got a bone to pick with you, David.'

'Go on then, don't spin it out. I'm listening.'

'I spoke to Alastair Forsyth on Thursday. He told me about your tough deal with top, top management on my behalf.'

'He wasn't there, so he doesn't know.'

'Maybe not, but he knows all right. You didn't persuade them to give me two per cent of the net profits, did you?'

'That's how it all worked out, love. It's in writing. On the files.'

'You told them to take it off your earnings, didn't you?'

'They're only getting thirty per cent, Patsy. And our expenses, mine anyway, are already a bit over budget. Everybody's happy. Here's your tea. Sorry about the mug.'

She took the tea and bent down to put it on the floor. When she straightened up she said, 'I told my Mum what you'd done.'

'What did she say?'

'She was trying hard not to cry and she said, "He was a lovely lad, that David." And my Mum's not one for compliments.'

He smiled. 'I had my eye on your Mum, but it didn't ever get to be anything, as you know.'

'Can I ask you something? Something personal.'

'Sounds ominous, but carry on.'

'What went wrong with you and Mary Hawkins?'

And for the first time ever he didn't mind talking about it.

'What did your Mum say went wrong?'

'She said it was like you were marrying your mother.'

He laughed. 'How does she make that out?'

'She thinks your Mum and Mary Hawkins were the dead image of one another. Good neighbours, good women but no imagination and no loving.' She smiled. 'She said you'd have done better marrying her.'

Collins smiled. 'She's probably right.'

'Tell me what you think went wrong.'

'I'm not sure that I know, even now. Mary never wanted to leave Birmingham but I felt I had to get on. And I didn't have the roots here that she had. Relations and friends.' He shrugged. 'And basically she didn't think much of me. In the end . . . well, there was somebody else.'

'Why didn't you marry her? The somebody else.'

'I had a breakdown. Too much guilt and too much . . .' he shrugged, '. . . harassment from all sides. She loved me very much and she walked off into the snow because she thought that she was part of the problem.'

'Was she?'

'In a way. Not because of her, but she was with me. She saw how they were grinding me up. I'd rather not talk about it. Gives me the heebie-jeebies.'

'What happened to the girl?'

'She married somebody else. An Italian. Looks a nice guy.'

'Alastair said you had one of the top studios in London. Making lots of money and you walked out on that.'

'Makes me sound pretty unstable. Somebody pulled a fast one on me. I wanted to get away from situations where other people could pull the rug out from under me. I suppose I'm a natural cutter-off of my nose to spite my face.'

'What are you going to do after the book's finished?'

'I was thinking of buying a boat. Wandering round the Med. Italy and the Greek Islands and all that.'

She shook her head. 'Don't do that. It would be a mistake.'

'Why?'

'I'll tell you when we've finished the book.'

'Why not now?'

She shook her head and sighed. 'It's not the right time now.'

'Tell me about your mother and father.'

'I suppose my mother's much the same as she always was. Warm-hearted, encouraging and a good wife. She made a lot of sacrifices to let me go to university and . . .'

'I didn't know you'd been to university.' He smiled. 'And you don't look old enough.'

'I'm twenty-five and yes, I went to university. I read history. Got an Upper Second. My father is much like old Sam. A bit more ambitious maybe, but from that background he never really had a chance. All he's got is his physical strength. And some skill as a moulder of course. They get on well together. They love one another. That's about it.'

'What do you think your father could have been if he'd had the chance?'

'A farmer or a vet. He's got a fantastic way with anything growing.' She smiled. 'He started teaching himself Latin so that he could understand the Latin names of plants and diseases. Gave it up because he couldn't understand datives and accusatives. He used to play football against your team in Kingsbury Road park.'

'Would your Mum let me take you all out for a meal one night?'

'She'd love it. I don't know about Dad. Let's wait until the book's finished and they can celebrate with us.'

A month later the pages of the text had been typeset and pulled on the paper that was going to be used, and Alastair Forsyth gave them his office to go over the proofs. When they had corrected the few literals Collins leaned back and said quietly, 'You know what's wrong, Patsy. It's this paper. It's too heavy. Too important. It's saying the wrong things.'

'What's all that mean? It's beyond me.'

'This paper says – "This is an important book. A work of art. Expensive paper, beautiful typography and high-quality printing." And that means you don't need to bother with the contents. You needn't read the words. Just riffle through the pictures and then put it on your coffee table so that your friends can admire your taste. And that's not what this damn book is meant to be.'

'So what do we do?'

'We use lighter, cheaper paper and we scrap this beautiful binding and have a laminated soft cover instead.'

'You're still happy with the book itself?'

He smiled up at her as she stood there looking worried.

'Of course I am. More than happy. Let me make some notes for the production people, then let's go and eat. I think . . .' he said slowly, '. . . that tonight is Albany night. That's where we started, that's where it ends.'

'If that's what you want.'

'Would you prefer somewhere else?'

'Not really. Shall I meet you in the lounge just after five?'

'Yes. Let's do that.'

He was surprised that she had asked for a whisky and she sipped at it as if it were hemlock.

'Is anything the matter, Patsy?'

'What made you think there is?'

'I don't think it. I know it. You're unhappy about something. Is it because we came to this place?'

She shook her head. 'No,' she sighed. 'There's something I have to tell you.'

'Something bad?'

'I don't know. Yes, I suppose it is, really. Mum heard that your wife is getting married again. And there's an announcement about it in the small ads in tonight's paper.'

'Ex-wife, Patsy. Not wife.'

'Does it upset you?'

'No. It will probably make it more difficult for me to see my son. But otherwise . . . no, it doesn't upset me at all.'

'It will affect that, David. She's marrying a Canadian and they're going to live in Canada. A place called Hamilton in Ontario. I looked it up in our reference section. It's an industrial city. A bit like Brum.'

For a moment he sat in silence and then he said quietly as he looked at her face, 'It never ends, does it? The ripples on the pond.'

'Is there anything I could do to cheer you up? Anything at all?'

'Anything?'

'Yes.'

'Yes. Don't walk away from me. Don't leave me.'

'Why should I walk away from you?'

'Because I bring bad luck. I'm a . . .' He shook his head and she saw the tears in his eyes as he smiled at her. 'Let's go and eat.'

She tried to make conversation as they ate but it wasn't easy. His mind was so obviously elsewhere. And she knew that the mind that saw the gentleness in other people and the security in a child's hand on its father's leather belt was paying the price for being what it was. And she knew that he was right. For him the ripples on the pond never did stop spreading. Slowly and inexorably.

For once she let him drive her home and as they pulled up at the house she asked him if he'd like to go in and see her parents. He looked at his watch. It was nearly eleven. 'They'll have gone to bed an hour ago. But thanks for asking me.'

'How long will it be before the book is ready?'

'It's not a big run. Only four thousand. A week should do it.'

'Can I see you tomorrow?'

'Sure. Where?'

She smiled. 'My favourite place. The station cafeteria.'

He smiled. 'You know, I've grown to like that place.'

She kissed him on the cheek as she opened the car door.

'Try and sleep, David. I'll be thinking about you.'

'Thanks. See you tomorrow.'

He waited until her key was in the lock and as he started the car she turned and waved and the tears were cold on his cheeks.

She waited until seven o'clock and then, panic-stricken, she took a taxi to his place.

Two or three men smiled at her in the hall as she hurried to the stairs.

There was just enough light from the street to see him lying on the bed.

She searched for the light switch and as it went on she saw that he was still wearing the clothes that he had worn the previous night. He was lying quite still, his eyes open, staring into nothingness, his face pale and drawn.

For a moment she just stood there looking down at him, and he was no longer the big name from London but just a man. She sat down gently on the bed and took his hand in hers.

'David. Look at me . . . please look at me.'

He turned his head slowly and she said softly, 'Tell me how I can help you.'

His voice was just a whisper. 'Don't walk away from me. Please stay.'

'I didn't walk away, Dave. I waited two hours for you in the cafeteria.'

He shook his head slowly. 'You don't understand.'

'I'll understand if you tell me.'

'Take too long . . . a lifetime.'

'Try, Dave. Just try.'

'Will you do something for me?'

'Of course. Anything.'

He pointed, his hand shaking. 'There's an address book on the table.' He paused and sighed. 'Look up Amis. Trevor Amis. Phone him and ask him to come down.'

'OK.'

She sat at the table and scribbled the number on a scrap of paper. As she stood up she said, 'I'll be back in a couple of minutes. Just close your eyes and rest.'

'You can use my telephone.'

'Just close your eyes like I said.'

'Amis.'

'Is that Trevor Amis?'

'Yes.'

'My name's Patsy Thatcher and I'm speaking on behalf of David Collins.'

'How is he? How's the book going?'

'The book's fine, but David's in a bad way. He asked me to phone you and ask you to come and see him.'

'What's the matter with him?'

'I'm not sure. He had some bad news and it's made him very down. Very depressed. I think he needs your help.'

'Where can I contact you?'

'I'll stay with him until you come. He's at the Fentham Hotel, a boarding-house in Erdington. You will come?'

'Yes, of course I'll come.'

'Thanks. I'm very grateful.'

'Are you a friend of his?'

'I'm working with him on the book.'

'OK. Tell him the Fifth Cavalry's on its way. By the way, what was his bad news?'

'His ex-wife is marrying again. Going to live in Canada so he won't be able to see his son.'

There was a pause and then Amis said slowly, 'OK. Leave it to me.'

When she went back to his room she was relieved to see that he was asleep. She looked on the mantelpiece at the row of paperbacks and took down the Palgrave. It fell open at one of the sonnets – 'Love is not love that alters when it alteration finds or bends with the remover to remove . . .'. She sighed and walked over to the table and sat down.

She read for two hours and then went downstairs to phone a neighbour asking her to tell her mother that there was an emergency and she'd be home very late. She felt a slight twinge of guilt when she implied that the emergency was at the *Mail*.

At two o'clock the phone rang and she grabbed for it. It was Trevor Amis, he was outside the hotel and she said she would go down. David Collins had stirred but was still sleeping.

Trevor Amis was lifting a bag out of the boot of his car.

'Hello. I'm Trevor. You must be Patsy. Is there anywhere we can talk?'

'He's asleep now. We can talk up there if we talk quietly.'

'OK. Lead the way.'

Amis walked over to the bed and looked at Collins then turned.

'He'll be OK. Don't worry. Tell me what happened.'

'We were due to meet in town at five. By seven he hadn't come so I came out here. He was just lying there with his eyes open staring at the ceiling.'

'Did he say anything?'

'He said for me not to walk away from him. Not to leave him.'

'And what did you say?'

'I said I wouldn't.'

He looked for long moments at her face. Then said quietly, 'Why did you say you'd stay?'

She shrugged. 'Why shouldn't I? He needs help.'

'But why should you bother?'

'Because I like him,' she said softly. 'He's a very special man.'

'How about your boyfriend?'

She frowned. 'What boyfriend? I haven't got a boyfriend. I'm far too occupied with my job.'

'But not too occupied to care about David Collins.'

'No. What is all this? Why the interrogation?'

Amis smiled. 'Because I've known David Collins for many, many years. I won't say I know all that goes on in that mind of his, but I know most of it. That's the first reason for the questions. The second reason is that I've got a funny feeling about you.' He smiled. 'I've got an idea that you're part of the problem and most of the cure.'

'I don't understand.'

'I'll tell you some other time. How's the book gone? Is that part of the trouble?'

'No, the book's fine. It really is.'

'So why did the news about his ex-wife bowl him over?'

'I don't think it was just that. I think it's an accumulation of things. You know that he's closed his studio?'

'Yes. He dropped me a note. I thought it was a bit extreme closing it down almost overnight. But that's our David all over.'

'He said somebody had pulled the rug out from under him.'

'True enough. The man was his partner for years and the girl was his business manager. She was stupid and I think she made a pass at him and he turned her down. I'm not sure, but my wife thinks that was the real problem.'

'I think he feels he's a Jonah . . . brings bad luck to other people. And they walk out on him to escape.'

'What rubbish. He's just like the rest of us. Sometimes we're lucky, sometimes we're not. He's always taken these things too much to heart. But he survives.'

'He's a very sensitive man. He can't help it. It's part of why he's a good photographer.'

'You know what he needs to put him back on the rails right now, don't you?'

'No. I wish I did.'

'Did he ever tell you about a girl named Sally Major?'

'I asked him. I didn't know her name but I'd heard gossip about a girl . . . but he wouldn't talk about it. Just said she'd walked out into the snow to help him.'

'She was very young and very pretty. And she loved him a lot. I'm pretty sure he loved her too. But the timing was wrong. His wife found out about them. Gave him an hour to decide between them. He chose Sally but it didn't work out because of the pressures on him. She was wrong to walk out on him. She should have stuck it out. But she meant well. She saw it as a sacrifice that would pay off. It didn't.'

'So what will help him now?'

'He asked you not to walk out on him, didn't he?'

'Yes.'

362

'So don't walk out on him now.'

'I don't understand.'

Amis looked at her face and said quietly, 'It isn't just liking, is it? You love him, don't you?'

For a long time she just sat there. Then she nodded and said, 'Yes,' very quietly.

'Have you told him?'

'No, of course not.'

'Why not?'

'It would embarrass him.'

'You're crazy. You don't think he'd be lying there like that if it was just because of the news about his ex-wife.'

'Why is it, then?'

'Because he needs you. And that's why he asked you not to walk away. Not to leave him. He doesn't mean now. He means for ever.'

'You mean you think he cares about me?'

'I'm sure he does. What probably depressed him wasn't just the news about Mary but the fear that it was all going to happen again. The walking out because he was a bringer of bad luck.'

'He said almost those words the other night when I told him about his ex-wife.'

'So. Are you going to walk out? Not today, nor tomorrow, but someday?'

'Not if he wants me to stay. I'd never let him down. But he needs straightening out. He needs help.'

'Tell me.'

'He looks so sure of himself, but he isn't. He's terribly insecure. But I've got a theory about him. I think he belongs here. In Birmingham. He's been happy and re-laxed and really creative doing the book. He should never have been in business of any kind. He shouldn't have taken on responsibility of any kind. The reason why his photographs are so good is because he's got an innocent eye. A child's eye. He's very childlike in many ways. Not childish but childlike. Very easy to please and very easy to put down.'

363

'You're smiling. Why?'

'Because you said he cares about me. I hope you're right.'

Amis laughed softly. 'You're a honey.'

'He sometimes calls me honey without realising.'

'Have you got a driving licence?'

'Yes.'

'OK. Here's the key to the hire car. Buzz off home, get some sleep and I'll hang around here and administer first-aid. Phone me when you can get here. But for Christ's sake come. OK?'

'Are you married, Trevor?'

'You bet.'

'All the same, right this minute I love you. I'm so happy.'

'Get on your way and keep in touch.'

Amis went down and introduced himself to Mrs Parkinson with an explanation that Mr Collins had been overworking and needed a rest. He took a tray back upstairs with breakfast for both of them.

He roused Collins gently and when he opened his eyes he said, 'It's time for breakfast, old pal.'

The sleep had obviously done Collins good and as they finished the last of the coffee Amis said, 'Patsy's called twice to see how you were and she's coming here straight from work. She's got my hire car so there's no problem.'

'You're a real tonic, Trevor, taking charge of the wounded like this.'

'I've phoned Connie. She sends you her love. I've told her I'll be back in a couple of days. Is that OK?'

'I must be a real bloody nuisance to you, Trevor. Taking up so much of your time.'

'You aren't. You never have been. And I've all the time in the world for you. You know that.'

'Patsy Thatcher must be thoroughly ashamed of me.'

'What does it matter what the hell she thinks of you?'

'She's a very nice girl, Trevor. I'd hate to disappoint her. She's done a wonderful job on the book.'

'Speaking of the book, I gather that she's bringing a finished copy with her tonight. Hot from the press.'

'That's great. I'll look forward to seeing it at long last.'

'And now what? What next?'

'God knows. I'd thought about buying a boat and cruising around the Med.'

'That would be crazy.'

Collins half-smiled. 'You know . . . that's what Patsy said when I told her. Said it was all wrong for me.'

'Did she say why?'

'No. Went a bit mysterious about it. I'll have to ask her. Why do *you* think it's crazy?'

'The same reason that she thinks it.'

'How do you know what she thinks?'

'I've talked with her about you. Half the night while you were sleeping.'

'What was the verdict?'

'Tell me about you and Patsy.'

'There's nothing to tell. We've just worked together on the book.'

'Come off it, David. You don't need to pretend with me.'

'What do you want me to say, for heaven's sake? I'm old enough to be her father. Good God. Way back I fancied her mother. And what have I got to offer her? Nothing any sane girl would want. She'd be horrified if she knew I had such thoughts about her.'

'Faint heart never won fair lady and all that.'

'Trevor, it would be baby-snatching to even try.'

'How old is she?'

'Twenty-five. Twenty-six in three months' time.'

Amis smiled. 'Don't tell me you haven't thought about it if you've worked out how long before she's twenty-six instead of a mere twenty-five.'

'Of course I've thought about it. But I couldn't bear that to happen again.'

'This one wouldn't walk out on you. She'd hang on and dust you off.'

'How the hell do you know what she thinks? You've only just met her.'

'It's my winning ways with the ladies. The big brown eyes and what they tell me is a "safe" face.' He paused. 'She loves you, Dave. Real solid stuff. The stuff that lasts.'

'I don't believe it.'

'Ask her, then.'

'For Christ's sake. I've never even kissed her. Never even held her hand.'

'I take that as a good sign. Full marks to both of you.'

'You think she might consider me as a husband? An old fart like me?'

'Don't overdo the modesty, chum. You don't really believe it yourself. I think she'd be delighted to have you as a husband or anything else. She's got a programme all worked out.'

'You mean you've actually discussed this with her? In so many words. Right out in the open.'

'Yes. If you can call this musty room of yours "out in the open".'

'When?'

'Like I said. While you were asleep. She loves you, Dave. Said it herself. Out loud. Straight from those ruby lips. I'd be happy to be best man.'

'I can't believe it.'

'She'll be here in a few hours. Just get on with it. Talk to her.'

Collins stood up shakily and walked to the window. For several minutes he just stood there and then he turned.

'You know, I never thought I'd say that Birmingham was beautiful. But it is. Today it is.'

He walked back and sat down at the table. 'I've got so much to thank you for, Trevor. Right now I feel I could do anything. Put the whole world to rights.'

'Well don't, my friend. Times are a-changing and small

is beautiful now. You just do whatever that girl tells you to do. She's got you weighed up, I assure you.'

Collins laughed, banging his fist on the table so that the crockery rattled. 'I'm so happy, Trevor. I can't believe it.'

'Fine. One last word of advice from me, old friend. This time, believe that you deserve it. Because you do. If I had a bright daughter of twenty-five I'd be delighted if I could palm her off on to you. You're the nicest guy I know. So relax and enjoy it. Your turn has come.'

He stood for half an hour on the landing outside his room where the window looked out on to the street. Waiting for her to arrive. Tempted to pace up and down to relieve his tension but anxious to see her the moment she got there.

He had rehearsed the words a score of times, altering a word here and there to make clear that she had a choice. Apprehensive that perhaps she had changed her mind or that Trevor Amis had misunderstood. Or translated some expression of mild affection into something more positive. His mouth was dry and his hand shook as he reached out to steady himself against the frame of the alcove.

Then the car drew up. A large black limousine, and a chauffeur opened the rear door. She stepped out, a parcel in her hand. It must be the book. And then a man got out from the other door. A man in his fifties. Stocky, with black hair and a black moustache and he took the girl's arm as they walked towards the hotel entrance. Collins walked hurriedly back to his room as he heard their voices in the hall.

His voice was harsh as he shouted, 'Come in,' to the knock on the door. She came in smiling.

'David, this is Mr Stone. He's from the publishers who are going to market the book. Mr Stone, Mr Collins. David Collins.'

The man came forward, his hand outstretched. 'I couldn't go back to London without meeting you, Mr Collins. I've seen the book and I'm overwhelmed. We shared the production costs with the newspaper with a feeling that we might be making a small contribution to something worthwhile.' He paused. 'Enough to say that I phoned the printers this afternoon and asked for a further run of twenty thousand. I suspect it won't be enough.'

Collins nodded. 'I'm glad you were satisfied.'

'Not satisfied, Mr Collins. Absolutely delighted. We shall claim all the credit we dare.' He smiled. 'I'm not a Birmingham man but we shall be getting in touch with you to persuade you to contract similar books on other cities. Manchester and Glasgow would be prime examples. Now I must go. You two must have a lot to talk about.'

Patsy took Mr Stone down to the hotel entrance and when she came back she was laughing.

'Straight out of Dickens, but what a charmer.' She paused and looked at him. 'I've rehearsed a piece a dozen times, David. And I can't remember a word of it.'

Then his arms were round her, her face upturned to his. 'Don't let's jump through the hoops. Trevor told me what you'd said. I love you, Davie. Please marry me.'

'I love you too, Patsy. I can't really believe it, but I'm terribly happy. Thanks for having me. What about your parents?'

'I'll talk to them. Don't worry. It'll be fine. Look at the book. You'll love it. Look at the cover.'

As they sat at the small table he looked at the cover of the book. Like all the photographs it was black and white. A close-up of the child's face in Sutton Park. Solemn and big-eyed, a broad freckled nose. One side of the shirt collar turned up where the man's hand was resting on the small shoulder, one finger touching the boy's slender vulnerable neck. The broad fingers of the man's hand were covered with bushy black hair, the big nails heavily striated, their edges rough and marked with the irremovable grime of a lifetime's factory work. Even those who didn't notice its intended counterpoint would like the picture.

Collins leafed carefully through the book, reading text as well as glancing at the photographs. It had done all that he had intended and there was no doubt that the text added an extra dimension that he could not have provided himself.

Eventually he looked up and across at her face. 'You know, in a way, I think your text is going to be more important than the photography in the end.'

She smiled. 'Why? You're just being nice, aren't you?'

'Not at all. The photographs will stop people just turning the pages. But, in fact, they are just signposts to the text. They can only make one single point. The text can make far more. You wait and see.'

She reached out and touched his hand. 'Trevor said that creative people loved working for you because you could see the good they did and make it better. You're terribly honest. You don't try to hog the kudos.'

He smiled. 'You ever tried hogging a kudos, kid?'

'Are you well enough to go out and eat?'

'Our place?'

She laughed. 'Where else?'

The cafeteria was almost empty. The pork pies had been terrible but the coffee, as always, was good. And they were too happy to notice either.

'You know, I think this place is a lucky place for us, Dave. Maybe it's just the lights are so bright. Or something.'

'You're going to say something aren't you? Something important.'

'How on earth did you know?'

'You always lick the side of your mouth when you're going to do that, and a little pulse starts up at the side of your forehead.'

'Will you listen carefully? Promise?'

'Promise.'

'I've thought so much about you these last weeks and I think I know what we should do to make life right for you. Can I say it?'

'Go on.'

'Well, oddly enough, I think Mary Hawkins was right. You belong to this town, city, whatever. And you were never cut out for business. You did fine, I admit, but you did it because you had to. You had no qualifications so you had to make the best of what was offered to you. If you'd only been concerned with creative work you'd have been far happier.

'I don't like saying the next bit but it has to be said. It's not said as a criticism but as a fact of life. Responsibility doesn't suit you. You respond badly. You panic. You're easily tempted into having a go at doing things, but when the chips are on the table and there are decisions to be made you back out mentally. So. I want to make a positive suggestion. It will horrify you, but I'm sure it's right.' She paused and took a deep breath. 'You know Inkerman Road at the back of Alma Road? The houses are exactly the same as ours. Two up, two down. An outside loo. And a garden like a slag heap. There's one of those for sale. Number forty-five. Backs on to our house. It's going for £4,250. I want us to buy it and live there. I worked out a budget this afternoon. We could get by on my salary alone. With you contributing we'd not have a financial care in the world. We'd need £4,000 a year at the outside. I earn nearly that much. You'd earn more but you won't get involved in any business. No advertising work, no fashion stuff. Just people, and preferably books like this one.' She sighed. 'And that's it. Tell me how wrong I am.'

He sat looking at her for a long time and then he said quietly, 'You're not wrong, my love. You've hit all the nails on the head. Let's look at the house tomorrow. Tell me something. You've put your finger on what's wrong. Why am I like this? Do you know?'

'I think I do. From what I've heard from my mother and from grandad you not only had no qualifications but you had an even worse handicap. You didn't come from a loving family. You weren't loved and you weren't encouraged. You took it for granted that nobody cared about you or liked you in even the most ordinary way. So when

370

anybody said something nice about you, you either married them, fell in love with them, or worked for them. That's all that was the matter. And it won't ever happen again.'

'Why didn't I meet you a long time ago?'

'It didn't have to be me. Lots of girls would have been OK for you. You picked one who was too much like your mother. Lots of men do that and it works because their mothers thought they were wonderful. Yours didn't. Mary Hawkins carried on the tradition. She wasn't always wrong but she didn't love you, so she didn't put her case over in a way that would appeal to you.'

Chapter 42

JOAN THATCHER, née Latham, reached out to put the last of the cups on the draining board. And as she wiped her hands instinctively on her apron she turned to look at her daughter.

'Well, little girl, out with it.'

'Out with what?'

'Whatever it is you're dying to say.'

'How did you know?'

'For heaven's sake, you've been walking around like a cat on hot bricks ever since you came in. If it helps, I'm pretty sure I know what it's all about.'

'What is it? Tell me.'

'It's Davie Collins. Genius, knight in shining armour, hero and breaker of girls' hearts. And you're going to run away with him and live happily ever after in a lovely apartment in Mayfair.'

Patsy burst out laughing. 'So that's why you were looking at "What the Stars Foretell" in the Sunday paper. You're half right. But I'm not running off with him. We're going to get married and we're buying the house at the bottom of the garden. The one in Inkerman Road. And we're going to live happily ever after.'

Joan Thatcher sat down slowly at the kitchen table. She shook her head slowly as she looked at the flushed face of her daughter. 'You know, you never cease to amaze me. Sometimes I think you're more grown-up than I am.' She pointed at one of the chairs. 'Sit down and tell me all about it.'

As Patsy sat down she said, 'Have you told Dad what you were thinking?'

'No. Don't worry about him. Tell me about the house. The price I heard sounds outrageous. Over £4,000.'

'You really are the limit. Here am I going to marry a special man and you start talking about the price of the house.'

'I know about the man, duckie. He'll be fine. So will you. But why that house? I'd have thought you wanted something better than that. Something a bit modern, in a better district.'

'In a way I would, Mum. But he's had a rough time and I want him to know that he hasn't any money worries and no great responsibilities.' She smiled. 'He's like you, love, he's never really grown-up. I want him to have a fresh start. He's been earning more in a week than I earn in a year with worries to match. You know, that fellow's never been a kid. But he'll be fine when I've got him trained.'

'You'd better bring him round to tea on Sunday.'

'And you'll tell Dad and smooth him down?'

'He'll be all right, girl, don't worry.'

'If you touch a piece you have to move it.'

'That's crazy.'

'Maybe. But that's the rules. If you just want to tidy it up you can say *j'adoube* and then it's OK.'

'Shall I take your knight?'

'You can, but if you do my pawn takes your castle and a castle's worth more than a knight.'

She looked towards the window. 'It's snowing, David. We might have a white Christmas.'

They were sitting on planks supported by paint tins in 57 Inkerman Road. They had bought it outright two months earlier, and apart from the floors and stairs, all the work and decoration they had done themselves. Her father and Sam Thatcher had lent a hand with the heavy work and with the garden, and there was little left to be done once the carpets were laid. She was surprised at how nice it all looked. They had chosen the furniture together and it was mainly plain Scandinavian teak. She had been pleased that he cared so much about every detail of their house.

She knew that the rave reviews of the book had both pleased him and given him confidence, but the signing of the three-book contract that assured them of £10,000 a year for the next three years had justified her thinking. He was relaxed and happy, and when small things went wrong he took them in his stride, doing whatever was necessary to put them right. They already had a circle of friends whose houses and families were open to them without ceremony. People they had met while doing the book or people he had known in his youth. Sometimes she felt a stab of sadness when she saw other people's babies and children, but she had no intention of loading the responsibility of a child on to their marriage.

Patsy and David Collins never moved from the house in Inkerman Road. In the early days Collins declined many offers of work from London agencies and fashion magazines. The book had made him a name once again but he stuck firmly to his wife's advice to turn down all commercial work.

Over the years the book series expanded and became known as *The Cities of Man*, and covered Delhi and Bombay, San Francisco, Paris, Rome, Dublin and Singapore as well as several British cities. Their income from the books was far beyond what they needed, and their savings were unadventurously invested in several building societies. Most years they were overseas for a couple of months for their work.

Several magazines asked if they could do features on their house to show what could be done with low-standard housing. And Patsy had vehemently refused. David saw Jimmy, his son, once a year when he came over from Canada to visit his grandparents.

Trevor Amis finally had enough of the agency and went freelance. Harry Parsons is the chairman of a group of several amalgamated agencies and Mary Hawkins, now Mary Loftus, still lives in Hamilton with her husband.

There is no doubt that they were the happiest years of David Collins' life. Patsy had had her thirty-sixth birthday two weeks before she got the call that night to go to the General Hospital. Instinct made her take her mother with her. He was already dead when they arrived, and the tubes and instruments that had supported the last half-hour of his life had already been removed. He had been killed by a drunken driver as he walked across a pedestrian crossing in Corporation Street. Another man had been seriously injured in the same incident. David Collins was buried in the churchyard of the parish church in Erdington.

Patsy Collins has often tried to remember what were the very last words she had said to her husband and he to her. No matter how banal they might have been they would have given her comfort if she had been able to remember them. It would be consoling to say that she gradually settled down to her new life but it wouldn't be true. She had no financial worries and no need to work, but she eventually took on a job as a social worker, a job she did satisfactorily, but not happily, for almost five years. She often regrets that they hadn't had a child she could love because it was his child.

Despite having given David Collins, and herself, ten years of great happiness, it seemed to her both sad and unreal that you could say goodbye one morning, without there being any warning that they would be the very last words you would ever say to the man you loved.